A Love Like This

MARIA DUFFY

HACHETTE
BOOKS
IRELAND

First published in 2015 by Hachette Books Ireland
A division of Hachette UK Ltd.
First published in paperback in 2016

A CIP catalogue record for this title is available from the British Library.

ISBN 978 1473614680

Typeset in Caslon by redrattledesign.com

Printed and bound by Clays Ltd, St Ives plc

Hachette Books Ireland policy is to use papers that are natural, renewable and
recyclable products and made from wood grown in sustainable forests. The logging and
manufacturing processes are expected to conform to the environmental
regulations of the country of origin.

Hachette Books Ireland
8 Castlecourt Centre
Castleknock
Dublin 15, Ireland

A division of Hachette UK Ltd
Carmelite House
50 Victoria Embankment
London EC4Y 0DZ

www.hachette.ie

For Mam and Dad, with love on your
sixtieth wedding anniversary

'The future belongs to those who believe in the beauty of their dreams.'

Eleanor Roosevelt

Part One

Chapter 1

Dublin Maternity Hospital
13 August 1985

He was going to be a doctor, a lawyer, a scientist. He was going to find a cure for cancer, a solution to poverty; he was going to rule the world. Vivienne Cooper-Smith looked at her little five-hour-old bundle sleeping soundly in his cot and her head filled with ambition for him. Her own experience had proven that it was never too early to strive for your dreams and she was going to make sure William Cooper-Smith had every opportunity in life.

She lay back on her pillow and winced as the pain down below took her breath away. At thirty-four years old, Vivienne wasn't a typical Irish mammy. She wasn't a clucky, doting mother like most of the others in the ward. She didn't embrace the notion of 'You forget the pain as soon as you hold your baby in your arms'. In fact, the whole mammy thing didn't come naturally to her and she'd balked at the idea of allowing the child near her breast. It's best for baby, one nurse had told her. It's totally natural, another had said, in a patronising tone that made Vivienne want to slap her. Who cared about natural? She couldn't understand these women who wanted to be everything to their babies and have them stuck to their nipple twenty-four hours a day. It definitely wasn't for her. She had a life.

Her eyes grew heavy and she began to doze until a hand on her arm jolted her awake.

'How's the pain, Mum? Would you like me to give you something for it?'

Vivienne resisted the urge to scream at the nurse that if she hadn't woken her up, she wouldn't need anything. And this 'Mum' business was driving her mad. Had she suddenly lost her identity? Was she going to be forever more known as 'Mum'?

'So what do you think? Will you take something?'

'Yes, please. I'll take whatever you have.'

'Good girl. No need to suffer.' The nurse, who looked like a child playing dress-up, peered into the cot as she handed over the drugs. 'Ah, he's a little dote. And looks like he's a sleeper too.'

'Let's hope it stays that way,' said Vivienne, popping the two pills into her mouth. 'And what time can I expect to get into the private wing? The nurse who brought me back here said it could take a while.'

The young nurse shifted uncomfortably and busied herself writing on a chart.

Vivienne's heart sank. 'I *will* get into a private ward, won't I? I mean, I have ridiculously expensive health cover and there's no way I can put up with the screaming babies in here.'

'I'm afraid I can't guarantee anything at the moment. The babies just keep coming and we're full to the rafters.'

'But I've paid to go private. I … I don't understand.' Vivienne felt a lump form in her throat and tears prick her eyes. The baby was starting to stir and all she really wanted to do was sleep.

The nurse did the head tilt – the one that said 'I feel your pain but there's nothing I can do about it' – before patting her patronisingly on the arm and leaving the room as fast as her feet could take her.

Being her own boss, Vivienne was used to getting her own way, and the injustice of being left in a common public ward when she'd paid for private was almost too much to bear. But William was squirming in his cot now and, judging by the squelching sounds and accompanying aroma, she was going to have to face the inevitable nappy change. Pulling herself out to the side of the bed, she bent to check she had everything she needed before heading to the changing area.

Despite her mood, Vivienne's heart melted when she lifted her tiny baby onto a changing mat. He was beautiful. They'd said he was a long baby but he was still the tiniest human being she'd ever seen. His whimpering stopped as soon as she opened his nappy and he managed to fill it a little more just as she was about to whip it away. She almost gagged at the sight of the thick black stuff and wondered, not for the first time, if she was cut out for all this. But it was just first-time mother nerves. She was sure of it. As soon as they were home, she'd manage William just as she managed everything else in her life – with confidence, skill and military precision.

Vivienne and her husband, George, had planned well for this baby. With George an underwriter for a large insurance group and Vivienne a solicitor with her own business, neither was prepared to take any more time off than necessary. Luckily it had been a relatively easy pregnancy and Vivienne had been able to work right up until a week before the birth. The decision to have a child at all had been a difficult one. Vivienne had never really seen herself as a mother and it was only with a gentle nudge from George that she'd even considered the possibility. George had become estranged from his family a long time ago and had felt strongly about having a child of his own. But they'd agreed just one child and then they were done. They knew it wouldn't be easy but they were confident that they could slot one child into their busy lives without too much disruption. And besides, it would stop the questions and pitying looks from people who assumed that they were having trouble conceiving.

William began to cry so she lifted him into his cot and headed back to the ward. There was no chance of her getting any sleep now. He'd have to be fed and then changed again. She wondered idly if the nurses took a more active role in the private wards. Maybe if she could get herself in there, they might take the baby to let her sleep for a while. It was only hours since he was born and she was already becoming obsessed with sleep. Her friends with children had warned her about that but she'd shook her head, saying that sleep was never a priority for her. But after a twelve-hour labour and a tough delivery, she was bound to be exhausted.

As she walked back into the room she noticed a group of the women sitting on one of the beds chatting. Some had left their sleeping babies in their cots, others had them clamped onto their boobs. Vivienne shuddered. From what she'd heard so far, most of these women were housewives – some with two or three children at home already. They obviously had no ambition – no drive. They probably wore their motherly role as a badge and stated it as their full-time job. She had no time for people like that. She kept her head down for fear of being asked to go and join them and busied herself getting a bottle ready for William.

Half an hour later, William was snoring softly in his cot and Vivienne was ready to take a well-earned nap. She felt smug as she listened to others trying to pacify their screaming babies. Hers had barely cried since he was born and hopefully it would stay that way. She didn't have time for a difficult baby – it wasn't in the plan.

'Here, mind her while I slip outside for a ciggie.'

Vivienne looked up with a start to see a young girl wheeling her baby's cot over beside William's. 'I … what do you mean?'

'I'll be back in a jiffy – a few minutes, max. She's a bit unsettled but if she starts crying, just rock the cot a bit.'

Vivienne was speechless as she watched the back of the young girl disappear out the door. The bloody cheek! They weren't in some sort of commune where responsibilities were shared. How dare that woman assume she was going to look after her baby. Well, she wasn't having it. She swung her legs out of the bed. She was going to go and find a nurse and demand she be put into a private ward. She'd tell them she was a solicitor. Threaten them with legal action. That worked in most situations. But just as she stuck her feet into her slippers, a wail came from the baby girl's cot. God, she had a pair of lungs on her. And now William was waking too. Tears pricked her eyes again and this time she let them flow. Jesus!

* * *

Catherine O'Neill wrapped her dressing gown tighter around herself as she took a long drag of a cigarette. God, she needed that. She could feel herself relaxing straight away and smiled as she thought of the face of the posh woman she'd left her baby with. She'd looked at her as though she was entirely mad. But Catherine didn't care. In her world, you did what you had to do to survive, and having a cigarette seemed like the most important thing in the world at that moment.

She tapped her ash onto the ground and shifted on the wooden bench. Her nether region felt like it had been put through a cement mixer. It had been an awful birth – nothing like when her other daughter was born two years ago. This time they'd used a forceps and had to make a cut. Jesus, it was no wonder. The bloody baby was the size of a small elephant. Almost ten pounds. She shook her head at the memory of the distorted, cone-shaped head and fat red face they'd thrust upon her that morning. She knew that mothers usually thought their babies were beautiful no matter what, but she just thought that her daughter was the ugliest thing she'd ever seen. But the nurse had said the head would go back to a normal size soon so that was something at least.

She sighed and stubbed out her cigarette. She probably should be getting back, but she wished she didn't have to. It wasn't that she found motherhood difficult. In fact she was quite good at it. But at twenty-one with a two-year-old, a newborn and a partner in prison, her life wasn't turning out exactly the way she'd wanted it to. The first baby had been planned. She'd been in love with Del and they were going to be a happy family. And it had seemed to work out that way at first. But then she'd gotten pregnant a second time and everything had changed. It had been a mistake. With neither of them working and just living off social welfare payments, Del had decided that armed robbery was a good idea. So now he was gone down for a ten-year stretch and she wasn't looking forward to bringing up two babies on her own. But life was shit sometimes so she'd just have to find a way to cope.

The sound of babies crying filled the air as she walked slowly back towards the ward. As she passed the nurses' station, a middle-aged nurse was humming the tune to Madonna's 'Papa Don't Preach'. That was it! Madonna. She'd call her baby Madonna – Donna for short. Donna O'Neill. It was perfect. She'd struggled with a name for the baby and her mother had said that maybe it was because, in the back of her mind, she didn't want her. She was probably right. But now that her little girl had a name, maybe she could start to bond with her. She walked back into the ward with a little more spring in her step but stopped dead at the scene that met her.

Chapter 2

'I just didn't know what else to do,' said a frazzled Vivienne. 'They were both crying and I couldn't pick them both up and I just thought … and anyway, you shouldn't have left me with the two of them like that.'

Catherine grinned. 'Relax, will you? How do you think people with twins do it? And I think they look really cute.'

Vivienne had to bite her tongue. She couldn't get over the cheek of the other woman, leaving her baby like that. Within minutes the two babies had been screaming the place down so she'd resorted to sticking them both in the same cot. She had to admit, it did look pretty cute and it had miraculously quietened them down, but that wasn't the point.

Catherine was still talking. 'So they look pretty settled there. Maybe I'll go and have a quick shower while all is quiet.'

'No. You. Will. *Not.*' Vivienne was incensed. She was aware of the stares of other mothers on the ward, but she didn't care. 'You can take your baby away with you. It's hard enough to get used to one baby, let alone look after someone else's.'

'Ah, so you're a newbie, are you? First baby?'

'Well, yes. But I don't see how that makes any—'

'What's his name?'

Vivienne sighed. She obviously wasn't going to get through to this woman. 'It's William. After my husband's father who died last year.'

'Lovely. My girl is Donna – after the pop star, Madonna. And my two-year-old is Tina.'

'Don't tell me,' Vivienne sneered. 'After Tina Turner.'

'How did you know?' She looked impressed. 'I'm a big fan of pop music so it seemed like a good idea. I toyed with "Whitney" but, to be honest, I thought it sounded a bit common.'

Vivienne was about to respond when the other woman stuck out her hand.

'We haven't properly met yet. I'm Catherine O'Neill.'

'Vivienne Cooper-Smith.' She thought briefly about saying 'nice to meet you' but the truth was, it wasn't. 'Now would you mind taking your baby away – I need to feed my son.'

'No problem, Vivienne Cooper-Smith. I'll leave you to it.' She picked up her daughter with the deftness of someone who knew what she was doing and returned to her bed.

Thank God it was almost visiting time. She'd get George to have a word with the nurses about a private room because if she had to put up with this for the next few days, she'd go insane. At least William was sleeping now. But in fairness, when she'd put the little baby girl down beside him earlier, he'd stopped crying straight away. She wasn't saying she'd be repeating it, but it was worth bearing in mind.

* * *

'Come on, William. Please just take the bottle.' Vivienne was at her wits' end. It was the middle of the night and she'd been trying to get her son to feed for the last half hour but he didn't seem to want to latch on to the bottle. And yet, when she took it away he screamed the place down. She didn't know what to do.

She looked around the ward at the other mothers all conked out, their exemplary babies fast asleep in their cots beside them. What on earth was she doing wrong? It wasn't supposed to be this hard.

Suddenly there was a whimper from another baby and Vivienne felt relieved. Someone else was going to have to get up and do a feed too. Catherine stirred in the bed beside her and she realised the noise had been coming from Donna's cot. She hoped the woman wouldn't be looking for a chat. It was the last thing she needed at the moment. But it seemed a chat was the last thing on Catherine's mind too. She rolled over and deftly lifted Donna from her cot. Without any fuss, she opened her nightshirt and the baby latched on straight away. Vivienne watched in envy as Catherine closed her eyes and relaxed completely as her baby fed. It seemed like a much easier option but Vivienne just couldn't do it. It wasn't for her. No, she'd keep persevering with the bottles because once she was home, George would be taking the night feeds to allow her some well-earned sleep.

* * *

'It's great to get a bit of quiet time, isn't it?' said Catherine, dipping a biscuit into her tea. It was mid-morning and, miraculously, all the babies on the ward seemed to be sleeping. 'I'd forgotten how hard it can be with no sleep.'

Vivienne nodded. 'I know. I can't survive on such little sleep. I just hope he gets the hang of those bottles soon.'

Catherine decided not to say anything. There were enough nurses telling Vivienne how much better off she'd be if she gave the breastfeeding a try. But it was true. No washing and sterilising bottles. No making up feeds and checking temperature. Just straight out of the cot and onto the breast. But some people just wouldn't be told. It struck Catherine that Vivienne thought she was too posh for breastfeeding – as though it was something for the common folk who couldn't afford the milk.

'So where are you from?' Vivienne broke into her thoughts.

'I'm from Finglas but we're renting a little house just off the Navan Road. I suppose you're from Foxrock or somewhere posh like that.'

Vivienne glared at her. 'Actually, we're not too far from each other. We live in Castleknock. Both myself and my husband grew up not too far away and we decided to stay around when we got married.'

'Lucky you,' said Catherine, gulping down the last of her tea. 'Having a husband, I mean. My fella is inside so we won't be seeing him for a while.'

'Inside? Inside where?'

Catherine wondered if she was actually that stupid. 'Inside – as in jail!'

'Oh, I see. I'm sorry. I mean, that must be hard.'

'It's his own bloody fault. He's a loser, to be honest. We're probably better off without him.'

Vivienne paled. 'And what do you work at? Will you be able to manage on one salary?'

That made Catherine laugh. 'On one salary? Chance would be a fine thing. I'm living on benefits at the moment. We get by – just about. But this baby is going to put a real strain on the finances. She was a mistake, to be honest. I even drank a whole bottle of vodka when I found out, hoping I'd have a miscarriage.'

'Oh my God. You did not!'

'I did. And don't judge me. You should try walking in my shoes for a bit and see if you wouldn't have done the same. Actually, a vodka or two wouldn't go amiss now.'

'I … I think I'll try and squeeze in a little nap while William is asleep,' said Vivienne, sinking further down under the covers. 'God only knows when I'll next get the chance.'

Catherine watched as the other woman buried herself under the covers. Posh bitch. It was clear she was looking down her nose at her. Just who did she think she was? She might have a big house and fancy cars, but she was certainly clueless when it came to baby stuff. To be fair, everyone was with their first. But Catherine had watched her the previous night as she tried to get the bottle into the child's mouth and it was obvious she hadn't a clue what she was doing. But someone like her would probably have a nanny to do it all for them.

She glanced down at the little girl in the cot. *Her* little girl. Her friend was minding Tina and had brought her up to the hospital earlier. God, it had been stressful. They'd brought a little brown teddy bear for Donna but Tina had got very jealous and had insisted on holding on to it herself. She'd get used to the new arrival in time. She was only two years old after all. But Catherine had no such excuse. She was twenty-one years old and right now, she couldn't imagine herself ever getting used to having two babies and bringing them up on her own.

* * *

'So much for bloody private health care,' moaned Vivienne, as she packed up her bags to go home. 'I mean, three days in this public ward, treated just the same as everyone else, and you can be damn sure none of them have paid the amount of money I have.'

George nodded and pushed his black-framed glasses back up on his nose. 'I know, love, but we always knew that a private room wasn't guaranteed. We were just unfortunate that our William was born in the middle of a baby boom.'

'Well, it's not good enough and I'll be writing a letter of complaint to the hospital.' Vivienne thought she'd never get home. The combination of lack of sleep and hospital food had her in rotten form and, on top of everything else, her milk had started to come in. It had given the nurses another opportunity to tell her that breastfeeding would relieve the pain, but it had fallen on deaf ears. She'd prefer to get some cabbage leaves and stick them in her bra – a tip she'd picked up from her mother.

'So have we everything?' George asked, picking the baby up and securing him in his carry-cot for the car.

Vivienne nodded. 'Let's get off as quick as we can. Catherine is gone down to change the baby and she'd been saying something about swapping phone numbers and addresses. There's no way I want that woman in our lives.'

George looked over his glasses. 'That's a bit harsh, isn't it? I thought she gave you some good advice about settling William.'

'She did, but that doesn't mean I want her to be my new best friend. Our lives are very different – we've nothing in common.'

'Except the babies.'

'Well, yes, but millions of people have babies. Now, are we going to get out of here?'

'You weren't going to head off without saying goodbye, were you?' Catherine appeared at the door, pushing the cot. 'Donna here would have been very upset. She's taken quite a shine to your William.'

'Of course we weren't,' said Vivienne, lying through her teeth. 'It was nice to meet you. I hope everything goes okay for you.'

Catherine smiled. 'And you too. Maybe I'll see you around sometime.'

Not if I can help it, thought Vivienne. She couldn't get out to the car quick enough, terrified Catherine would run after her looking for her contact details.

Five minutes later they were on the road and Vivienne sighed with relief. Once she was home, she'd get herself into a better pattern and it would be easier to mould William into a routine. She hadn't liked the feeling of not being in control in the hospital. She needed to take charge again and not be feeble. She glanced around at William, who was starting to cry.

'The bag with his stuff is behind your seat there, love,' said George. 'I stuck that teddy he likes on the top.'

Vivienne smiled at her husband. 'He's a bit young to have preferences, George. I'm not sure he can even see it.'

'But he can smell and feel it. Go on, humour me. I bet it quietens him down.'

She reached behind for the bag and immediately put her hands on the teddy at the top. But when she looked at it, her heart sank.

'This is not William's teddy – it's Donna's.'

'How do you know that, love? It looks like the one I bought.'

'Donna got the same one. But I saw her sister with it at the hospital yesterday and she pulled the eye right out of its head. I can't believe we've ended up with their scabby one-eyed one.'

William's screams got louder and louder until Vivienne just thrust the one-eyed teddy at him. Miraculously, the screams stopped. It seemed a one-eyed teddy was better than no teddy at all. Vivienne made a note to wash it thoroughly when they got home.

Chapter 3

13 August 1995

'Come on and help me with these lights, William. We only have another few hours before your guests arrive.'

William Cooper-Smith sighed as he followed his mother out to the marquee in the back garden. He was fed up. It was his tenth birthday but, as usual, his parents had taken control and were having a party to suit *them*. A giant marquee, caterers and a whole load of kids he barely knew. He'd begged them for a football party. Some of the boys in his class had rented pitches in the local sports club for their birthdays and it had been the best fun he'd ever had.

Football was brilliant. He played it every day in the school yard but his mother said he couldn't play for the local team. Some of his friends were on the under-ten team and were always asking him to join but his mother said there wasn't time. His nan minded him during the day when his parents were at work and it was enough for her to have to get him to piano lessons and tennis. He hated tennis. It was a poncy game. And he wasn't even any good at it. Not like football. In football he could juggle with both feet and dribble past every opponent on the pitch before sticking the ball in the corner of the net. Gooooooooaaaaaallll! He kicked his foot in the air, catching it on one of the catering tables, which promptly fell over.

'William! For God's sake. Can you help me out here rather than making more work for me.'

'Sorry, Mum.'

'You know your daddy and I have given up our Sunday to do this party for you. The least you could do is show some gratitude.'

'But I—'

'Seriously, William. You should be grateful that we're going to so much trouble for you instead of what some of the other parents do. They think an hour in a grotty sports hall and a McDonald's is a decent party.'

William couldn't think of anything nicer. But he said nothing and held the fairy lights up for his mother to nail them to the wall of the marquee. There was no point in arguing with his parents. It never got him anywhere – except a grounding to his room and an extra couple of hours of study. Sometimes he hated them. They worked all the time and he saw way more of his nan than he did of them. And now, because they were throwing this stupid party for him, he was supposed to think they were great.

Forty-two kids. That's how many were coming today. He knew about fifteen of them and, even at that, none were his best friends. They were the kids of his parents' friends mostly, a few who lived on his street and just a couple from school. Jack Fitzpatrick was his best friend in school but there was no hope he'd be allowed invite him since he was heard shouting 'fuck' at the school sports day when he lost the two-hundred-metre sprint. William's mother hated bad language and had told him in no uncertain terms that he wasn't to associate with riff-raff who expressed themselves in such a vile way.

'Fuck, fuck, fuck, fuck!'

'What was that, William?'

He almost jumped out of his skin. He hadn't meant to say it out loud. 'Nothing, Mum. I'm just singing.'

His mother stared for a moment before turning her attention back to the lights. Thank God for that! He would have been grounded for the rest of his life if she'd heard what he'd said. He smiled to himself. Maybe the day wouldn't be so bad after all. Wait until Jack heard about the 'fucks'. He'd crack up laughing.

'I've organised for Nan to take you down to the party shop for some balloons when the caterers come. She'll be here any minute.'

'But I want to stay here,' said William, glaring at his mother. 'Can't Nan go on her own for the balloons?'

'No, she cannot! The caterers need space to set everything up and you'll only be in the way. Besides, I want you to help her pick out some nice metallic colours – not those tacky multicoloured ones.'

'But why can't we get the colourful ones? They're the best. John Delaney had fifteen different colour balloons at his party and they looked really cool.'

Vivienne Cooper-Smith stood back to survey her work. 'Well, John Delaney's mother obviously has no taste. Now go and wash your hands and tidy yourself up. I've left a nice pair of chinos and a shirt on your bed for the party but it's probably best to wait until then before you change.'

William sighed as he headed up the stairs to wash his hands and face. But despite his mood, he couldn't help feeling a little bit excited. Forty-two children. They may not be the kids he wanted there but it still meant forty-two presents. He prayed he'd get some Power Rangers and footballs but he was doubtful about it. The previous year, his mother had told parents that he'd prefer cash and they'd made him put it all into a savings account.

Ten years old. He was in double figures at last. Almost grown up. It made him feel excited. He'd made up his mind what he wanted to do when he left school – and it wasn't going to be anything like his parents. He couldn't understand why they stayed in such boring jobs when they were rich. If he had all their money, he wouldn't work – he'd just travel around the world. And that's what he was going to do. He was going to be an adventurer – unless, of course, he got called up for a Premier League football team. But there wasn't much chance of that when he wasn't even allowed play the sport.

He took a facecloth from the pile on the bathroom shelf and squeezed it under the flow of hot water. He quickly wiped his face and dried it with the hand towel on the rail. He looked at his face in the mirror and allowed himself to enter his imaginary world.

William Cooper-Smith, the world famous adventurer, climbs Ayers Rock in his bare feet.

The world's most loved explorer, William Cooper-Smith, jumps out of a plane blindfolded.

William Cooper-Smith breaks another world record.

William loved having his dreams. They were sometimes the only things that got him through the humdrum of the day. When his parents would send him to his room to do some extra study, he'd lie on the bed with his books in front of him but his mind would go to an entirely different place. He placed the towel back on the rail and headed into his bedroom.

The room was far bigger than he needed, with a double bed for himself and a spare single one. He could never understand why they had a need for a spare bed when they never let any of his friends stay over. He lay down on top of the covers and felt under the pillow for Cookie. Cookie was his beloved teddy that he'd had all his life. He was a filthy one-eyed creature but William adored him and, despite all the new teddies he'd collected over the years, Cookie was his firm favourite.

'One day, Cookie, I'm gonna travel the world, and you're gonna be right there with me.'

* * *

Donna O'Neill opened her eyes and it took her only a moment to remember what day it was. Ten years old today. It was the most exciting day of her life. She'd spent her seventh, eighth and ninth birthdays craving the day she'd be into double figures – all grown up at last.

She pushed the duvet off her body and swung her legs out the side of the bed. The sun was streaming through the cheap, yellow curtains, highlighting the little dancing bits of dust in the air. Her mam hadn't mentioned her birthday yet and Donna was hoping it was because she was planning a surprise and not that she'd forgotten. Her mam was forgetting a lot of things these days. She seemed to spend more time drunk than sober, and even when she was sober, she seemed to be confused and forgetful. Still, she'd never forgotten a birthday yet and Donna couldn't wait to see what was in store for the day.

She glanced at her bedside clock. Nine o'clock. Her sister, Tina, was staying in her friend's house but said she'd be back with her present at lunch time. Tina was almost a teenager and often more like an adult than their mother. Sometimes when their mother was drunk or out with her friends, Tina would make lunches for school, put some sort of dinner together from whatever she could find in the fridge and make sure their clothes were washed. She was a bit serious at times, but Donna loved her to bits.

Slipping into her well-worn dressing gown, she skipped down the stairs, excited to see what would be waiting for her. But her face fell as soon as she walked into the little kitchen. There were dirty dishes piled high in the sink, the remains of a Chinese takeaway on the table and a half-empty bottle of vodka on the floor. Her mother had seemed okay when Donna had gone to bed last night so she must have decided on a party of her own later on. There wasn't a sign that it was her birthday today – no balloons, no cards or presents – not even someone to give her a birthday hug. She felt tears in the corners of her eyes and, not for the first time, wished she belonged to a different family.

But not one to dwell on the negative, she filled the sink with hot water and added a squirt of washing-up liquid. Maybe if she got the place cleaned up a bit, her mother would get up in a good mood and they'd have a decent day after all. Maybe things weren't so bad, she thought, as she piled the sudsy plates high on the draining rack. It was still early so there was plenty of time to celebrate.

When she'd finished her cleaning, she emptied the end of a box of cornflakes into a bowl and took them into the sitting room to watch telly. It was a small but cosy room with a two-seater red corduroy sofa and a matching armchair. The walls were a scruffy cream but Tina had made them hang their artwork from school on the walls to hide the dirt.

Her mam would be up soon and they could discuss what they were going to do for the day. She knew there wouldn't be a party – there just wasn't enough money. She'd learned to accept that over the years, and once there were a few presents and a birthday cake, she was happy enough with that. Sometimes they'd go to the cinema – just the three of them – and maybe even McDonald's after, if the money would stretch that far. Her mother wouldn't win any awards for mother of the year but, in fairness to her, she always tried to make birthdays special for both her girls.

Two hours later there was still no sign of her making an appearance so Donna thought she'd go and give her a gentle nudge. Dashing up the stairs, she paused outside the bedroom door, where she could hear her mother's snores. Her heart sank a little. Snoring usually meant drunk. Donna said a silent prayer that she wouldn't be in a state today of all days. She shoved open the door and almost immediately gagged. The stench in the room was unbearable. Her mother was sprawled on the bed, still fully dressed and her head pointed in the direction of a bucket on the floor. Donna held her breath and walked a little closer. There was sticky drool coming out of the side of her mother's open mouth and the bucket contained a substantial amount of vomit.

'I hate you, I hate you, I hate you!' Donna picked up a shoe from the floor and threw it at her mother. It hit her arm but she barely stirred. It was obvious there'd be no celebrations today. Big fat tears poured down Donna's face as she ran out of the room and slammed the door. She was the unluckiest girl in the world. She had a drunken mother, a father who didn't want to know her and a sister who couldn't even be here for her important day. Well, she didn't need them. None of them.

She went back into her own room and pulled a tracksuit out of the wardrobe. She was going to go and have a celebration of her own. Lexie would know what they should do. Lexie was her next-door neighbour and her best friend in the world. The two girls had been friends all their lives, having a common bond of a dysfunctional family. Lexie's parents had handed her over to her grandmother when she was born because they were both hippies and wanted to go and live in a commune in Spain. Apparently they'd always planned to come and get Lexie as soon as they were settled but that had never happened and, last she'd heard, they were busking on the streets of Greece. Donna always hoped that they'd never come back. She couldn't imagine a life without her best friend.

She heard a cough and a splash from her mother's room as she passed and wrinkled her nose in disgust. She couldn't wait to get out of there. Lexie's granny was nice and might even let them bake a cake. Donna loved baking but it wasn't very often they could afford ingredients. Back downstairs, she slid her hand down the back of the old sofa and found eighty pence. At least it would get her and Lexie a packet of crisps and a lolly.

'Happy birthday to me.'

* * *

'So what do you want to do, then?' asked Lexie, as the two girls sat on a wall close to the shops on the main road. 'We could always ask Granny to bring us to the Phoenix Park and go in the playground for a while.'

Donna shook her head. 'Nah. I probably shouldn't stay out for too long. Tina said she'd be home at lunch time and she'll be worried if I'm not there.'

'But it's your birthday. We have to do something.'

'It's a load of shite, isn't it?' Donna sighed. 'One day of the year that's supposed to be special and my stupid mother goes and gets herself drunk.'

Lexie put an arm around her and pulled her close. 'Don't worry about her, Donna. I know exactly what will add a bit of excitement to your day.'

'What's that?'

Lexie's eyes twinkled. 'Let's go down to O'Malley's and pick up some sweets. Granny said we can bake but she only has the flour and eggs and stuff. We could make a cake and decorate it with the sweets we get.'

'But eighty pence isn't going to get us much. Unless you mean …'

'Well, there'll be a crowd in there after mass and if we just happen to *accidentally* bump into the sweet display and some stuff *accidentally* falls into our pockets, what can we do about it?'

Donna's eyes lit up and she hopped down from the wall. 'Well, what are we waiting for? You're a bad influence on me, Lexie Byrne. But thank God I have you!'

Twenty minutes later they were back on the wall, giggling at the memory of the clueless shopkeeper who was so addled by the queue of customers that he didn't notice the two girls filling their pockets.

'We'll make a brilliant cake with this lot,' said Lexie, emptying half a carton of Smarties into her mouth. 'You can get Tina to come in to ours and we'll have a little party.'

Donna felt sad all of a sudden. She should be having a celebration in her own house, not in the next-door neighbour's. How could her mother have forgotten something as important as her tenth birthday? It just wasn't fair.

Lexie must have noticed her change in mood. 'What's wrong, Donna? Are you not having a good time?'

'Of course I am. I was just thinking about Mam. She never forgets my birthdays. Maybe she's up by now and getting something organised.'

'I doubt it. Judging by the state you said she was in, she probably doesn't even remember her own name. Stupid bitch.'

'Don't talk about her like that!' Donna jumped down from the wall and glared at her friend. 'She's not always like that. In fact, she usually makes sure I have a really good time on my birthday. Maybe she had some bad news … or she felt sad … or—'

'Stop making excuses for her, Donna. Now, are you going to let her ruin your birthday or are you coming to mine?'

Donna paused for a minute before nodding. 'You're right. Why should I worry about her when she obviously doesn't care about me? Let's go and make that cake.'

'And it looks like we might even be able to get ourselves some party decorations,' said Lexie, nodding her head in the direction of the shops.

An old lady was walking towards them with a boy who was holding a bunch of helium balloons. They were those expensive metallic ones. Donna felt a pang of jealousy at the look of excitement on his face. She could tell by the look of him that he was a rich kid, probably used to getting whatever he wanted.

'What are you suggesting, Lexie?'

Lexie produced a penknife from her pocket. 'One snip of this and they can be ours!'

'Jesus, where did you get that?'

'John O'Reilly nicked it out of his da's toolbox and I said I'd be his girlfriend if he gave it to me. Right, here they come. Let's walk behind them and when I say go, you grab a handful of the balloons and I'll cut the strings.'

Donna's heart was beating like crazy. The boy looked to be around her own age. He was lovely-looking, with black hair and a tanned face. She met his eye as they passed by and felt slightly guilty for what they were about to do. Amazingly, the balloons even had '10' printed on them, which probably meant it was his birthday too. Ah well, chances were they'd just go back to the shop and buy another bunch afterwards.

'Go!' said Lexie, and the two girls ran up behind the woman and boy. It all happened in a flash. Donna managed to grab a handful of the balloons, which were wrapped tightly around the boy's hand. Lexie cut the strings, sending some of them up in the air but some stayed firmly in Donna's hands. Both girls ran like crazy around the corner and towards home. The balloons tangled up as they flew in the wind behind them and the screams of the old lady could be heard echoing down the street. As they approached their houses, they looked behind but there was nobody in sight. They'd gotten away with it.

'That was so much fun,' Lexie puffed, holding her sides. 'Come on. Let's go in and get started on making that cake.'

Donna hesitated. 'I'd better just check to see if Tina is home first. And if she's not, I'll leave her a note to follow us in.'

They walked into the house but it was still quiet. Donna felt a lump in her throat. It looked like Lexie was right. It seemed like her mother wouldn't be making an appearance after all.

'I'll just grab a pen and let Tina know we're next door.' She opened the kitchen cupboard that was home to all manner of stuff and that's when she saw it. It was small and no doubt cheap, but Donna's eyes opened wide when she saw the boxed cake together with a packet of candles and a bag of six balloons. She knew it! Her mother *hadn't* forgotten. She must have planned for them to have a little celebration.

'What is it?' asked Lexie, straining to see what Donna was looking at.

'Hold on just a sec.' Donna bounded up the stairs, half expecting to see her mother up and dressed and ready to come down, but her heart sank when she heard the snores again. She was still out for the count. Shit! It wasn't meant to be like this. She turned and headed back downstairs. Part of her hated her mother at that moment but she felt a little glimmer of hope. At least she'd remembered.

'What do you say we have a go at this?' said Lexie, as Donna walked back into the kitchen. Lexie had found the half-empty bottle of vodka and was holding it up, her eyebrows raised. Donna hesitated for a moment and then nodded. It was her birthday, after all. Double figures. Almost a proper grown-up!

Chapter 4

November 1998

'You're walking home with me today, Donna,' said Tina in her best mammy voice. 'There's something I want to talk to you about.'

Donna slung her bag over her shoulder and shook her head. 'We can talk later. Lexie is waiting. We're going into town.'

'Not today, you're not.'

Donna glared at her sister. 'Who do you think you are, telling me what to do? You know I always go to town on Thursdays after school.'

'I know you do. And that's what worries me.'

'Oh for God's sake,' said Donna, moving aside as the hordes of school kids flocked past, buoyed up with the freedom of their half day. 'I'm hardly a kid any more and what else would I be doing anyway?'

'Come on, Donna. Are you coming or what?' Lexie looked impatient as she and another two girls stood waiting.

'I'll be there in a sec.' She turned to her sister. 'Look, I haven't time for a chat now but let's catch up later.'

'Sorry, girls,' said Tina, turning to the group of waiting friends. 'Donna has something else on today. She's coming home with me.'

'What the fuck?' Donna was fuming. How dare her sister butt into her business like that. 'This better be a life or death situation because otherwise you and me are going to fall out big time!'

Tina sighed. 'I'm sorry, Donna. But since Mam isn't much use these days, I feel sort of responsible for you. And I can see where things are heading if I don't intervene now. Come on, let's walk.'

Donna walked alongside her sister but she was getting nervous. Surely Tina didn't know what she'd been up to. She'd always been so careful to hide it from her. She didn't have to bother hiding stuff from her mother any more because she was drunk most of the time, but Tina was a different story. Although only fifteen, Tina was the real adult in the house. She controlled the money, when she managed to get it from their mother, and she did most of the cooking, washing and other housework. She even had a part-time cleaning job so she could contribute to the money coming into the house. Donna adored her, but she sometimes wished she'd be more of a sister and less of a goody two-shoes parent.

'So, do you want to tell me what's been going on?' said Tina, as they walked towards home. 'And don't even think of lying to me.'

'Wh– what do you mean?' Shit. She definitely knew something.

'You know damn well what I mean, Donna. I saw the wallets in the bedroom. And don't think I haven't noticed that you come home from town every week with a new top or pair of trousers.'

'It's not *every* week and, besides, most of that stuff comes from charity shops.' She knew Tina wasn't buying it so she thought the angry approach might deflect things. 'And what were you doing snooping in my stuff anyway? Am I not entitled to any privacy?'

'Donna, you're thirteen years old. It shouldn't be my job to keep you in line but that's the way it is, unfortunately.'

'I know you mean well but –'

'No buts, Donna. I can see the road you're going down and I don't like it one bit. It's going to stop *now*.'

They'd reached the house and Tina let them in with her key. As usual, there was no sign of their mother and the dirty dishes from that morning still lay on the table.

'Right,' Tina continued. 'Get yourself a snack and change out of that uniform. Then you're coming with me.'

'But aren't you going to work?' Donna didn't like where this was going.

'Yes, I am. And you're going to learn what it's like to earn an honest crust.'

Tina was gone upstairs before Donna had a chance to argue. She found a few slices of bread left from a sliced pan and took two to make a sandwich. There was nothing much in the fridge so she made do with some strawberry jam and plonked herself down on a kitchen chair to eat it.

Tears stung her eyes as she looked around the filthy kitchen. Everything was going wrong. Why was her life so shit? She envied those girls in school who went home to a family who loved them. She'd gone home with Christine McEvoy a few times and she hadn't wanted to leave. Christine's mam had made a lovely roast dinner and they'd even had dessert after. But it wasn't just the food. Mrs McEvoy had asked them about their day – about insignificant stuff – but at least she'd been interested. Her own mam didn't know what day of the week it was, let alone what happened in school. When Donna had got her first period a few months back, it wasn't her mother she'd gone to – it was Tina. Tina had provided her with pads and explained the whole process.

Tina. She was the most wonderful sister in the world. Donna honestly didn't know what she'd do without her. Suddenly she felt guilty. She'd let her down. If Tina had sussed out what she was doing, she must be really disappointed in her. She was disappointed in herself, to be honest. She'd never set out to do what she did, but it had just seemed so easy and it had become a habit.

'So, do you want to explain to me what's been going on, then?'

Tina appeared in the kitchen, interrupting Donna's thoughts. 'I know you've been stealing wallets so don't even think of lying to me.'

Donna looked at the table and played with the crumbs of her sandwich.

'Come on, Donna. I want to help you. Talk to me.'

'It's not as bad as it seems. I only did it a few times.' It was true. She and Lexie had just started in first year in secondary school this year and had been desperate to get in with the popular girls. A few of the second years had taken a shine to them and had allowed them to be part of their gang. She honestly hadn't realised what being in their gang had entailed at first, and when it had become obvious, she was in too deep to get out.

It all poured out now and Tina listened quietly. The older girls had brought her and Lexie into town one Thursday after school and told them that if they wanted to be part of the gang, they'd have to prove themselves. They were instructed to rob a wallet out of someone's pocket or bag and bring it back to the waiting girls. Donna had balked at the idea at first but, in the end, she'd done it and it had been easier than she'd expected.

Tina inhaled deeply. 'So while I'm down on my hands and knees cleaning houses on a Thursday afternoon, you're out in town robbing people's hard-earned money.'

Donna bowed her head and felt mortified but Tina continued. 'And did it never occur to you that the people you're taking from are most likely people like me – people who work hard and can little afford to have their money taken away from them.'

'But I try to target people who look like they can afford it – people with bags from expensive shops and dressed in designer gear.'

'And that makes it okay?' Tina was shouting now. 'Robbing money off *anyone* is wrong, no matter what way you try to justify it. And where have you been putting all this money? Have you just spent it on clothes and stuff?'

'We rob the wallets and give them to the older girls. They take most of the cash out and leave us with a fiver or tenner – depending on what's in there.'

Tina shook her head. 'You're going to have to give me the names of these girls. They need to be stopped.'

'NO!'

'But, Donna, if they're making you do these things, they should be reported.'

'Please, Tina, please.' Donna started to cry. Big fat tears plopped from her cheeks onto the kitchen table as she held her head in her hands. 'I won't do it any more. I promise. Me and Lexie never really wanted to. It was one thing robbing sweets or a few magazines but people's money is totally different.'

'I'll pretend I didn't hear that bit about you robbing sweets and magazines.'

'I didn't mean …' Donna looked up and saw that Tina was smiling and she couldn't help laughing. 'I swear, I'm not going to do it any more. And I bet if I won't, Lexie won't. Just please don't make me rat on the other girls.'

'Right,' said Tina, standing up. 'If I have your word that you'll stop, I'll leave it at that for now. There's enough shit going on in this house without me having to worry about what other kids are getting up to.'

Donna stood up and hugged her sister. 'You have my word. Now shouldn't you be heading off to work? I'll clean up a bit here and maybe make some bread to go with the leftover soup from yesterday.'

'Nice try, Donna. But I've already told you – you're coming with me.'

'But I'll be fine here. You know I'm not going into town so you don't have to worry.'

'It's not negotiable. You're going to come to work with me to learn a few things. It may not be glamorous but it's an honest job and it's good to feel you've earned the money in the end.'

Donna sighed and went upstairs to change out of her uniform. Her sister didn't often put her foot down but when she did, Donna knew not to go against her. Tina was her lifeline. Only for her, Donna would have been sent into state care long ago. Tina always ensured that she turned up for school every day with a clean uniform, a breakfast inside her and made sure that, despite the fact they had no parental supervision, they managed to lead a relatively normal life. So if Tina wanted her to roll her sleeves up and scrub some rich family's dirt, then that's what she'd do. There was nothing she wouldn't do for her sister.

* * *

'Goooooaaaallll!' William pulled up the front of his school shirt and stuck it over his head as he ran around doing a victory dance. God, he loved football. He'd never really had a chance to participate in the sport when he was younger but now that he was in secondary school, he had a lot more freedom. Both his parents worked until at least seven every evening and his nan looked after him. She used to drive him home from primary school every day but he'd pleaded his case and was now allowed to walk home with his friends. And his nan was gullible. He'd tell her most days that he had a project to finish or some extra study to do and she'd never raise an eyebrow when he'd arrive home late. The truth was he could be found most days playing football with his friends in the school yard. It was ace.

'I'd better head off home, lads,' said William, tucking his shirt back into his trousers and picking up his bag. 'It's already a quarter to five. Anyone want to come to mine for a game of Playstation?'

'Yes!' said all three in unison, and William smiled to himself. His dad had organised for a guy in work to bring a game called *Crash Bandicoot* back from America a couple of weeks ago and, as it hadn't even been released in Ireland yet, everyone wanted to be his friend.

'I bagsy first go.' Terry Dillon was in second year and fancied himself as the leader of the little group. William was happy to let him take on the role because he was a brilliant football player and was teaching him everything he knew.

'Me second,' said Ryan, a quiet boy who'd latched on to William from the first day of secondary school.

'I'm just happy not to have to go home yet,' said Jack, William's best friend.

They chatted animatedly about the Irish football team during the ten-minute walk home and debated who was the better player, Roy Keane or Robbie Keane.

'I wonder if any of us will ever play for Ireland,' said William, imagining the glory of stepping out onto the pitch in Lansdowne Road to thousands of fans screaming his name.

'I think you're in with a shot, William.'

William's head shot around to look at Terry. 'You really think so?'

'Yeah. The Irish tennis team!'

Everyone laughed and William joined in but he wasn't laughing on the inside. He hated his parents for making him play tennis. They loved mingling with the elite in their posh tennis club, and being able to say their son was a star player in the club earned them lots of respect. And why wouldn't he be a star player? If they allowed him the same amount of time for football lessons as they did tennis lessons, they'd be chasing him for the Irish football team as soon as he was the right age.

'Right, if Nan asks, we're going up to my room to do a project, okay? We can grab something to eat first and bring it up with us.' He turned the key in the door and the four of them walked inside. Shit! He almost broke his neck as he stepped onto the wet floor. He'd forgotten it was Thursday – cleaning day.

'Take off your shoes at the door, lads,' he said, stepping out of his. 'The floor's just been washed.'

The cleaning girl stepped out of the downstairs bathroom with a bucket of water and nodded her thanks to him. She was a nice girl. William hadn't spoken to her much but he knew her name was Tina. He always felt awkward about somebody else coming to clean his house. He felt they should be doing it themselves. But when he'd brought up the subject with his mother, she'd convinced him that those cleaning girls were quite happy to clean to earn money. That's the way the world goes around, she'd said. And so he'd learned to accept it but it didn't stop him feeling embarrassed to see her cleaning and he had to fight the urge to ask her if she needed help.

'Well, I'm not getting my socks wet for nobody,' said Jack, starting to walk across the floor in his mucky shoes. 'Isn't that what cleaners are for?'

William grabbed a hold of his shirt and pulled him back. 'Don't be an idiot, Jack. She's already washed it once.'

'Well, then she won't mind doing it again, will she?'

William noticed the look of despair on the cleaner's face and felt mortified. 'Get out, Jack!'

'Wh– what?' Jack stopped in the middle of the hallway and stared at his friend.

'I said get out! Look at the dirty marks you've made on the floor.'

'You can't be serious …?'

William was shaking. He liked Tina and hated how Jack was treating her.

'It's okay, William,' said Tina. 'I'll just wipe over it. It won't take me a minute.'

'Come on! Are you going to feed us before this Playstation tournament?' Jack headed into the kitchen with the other boys, ignoring William's request for him to leave.

William was too embarrassed to say any more so he nodded at Tina and followed. He suddenly didn't feel like playing video games. He was in a bad mood. Jack was great fun and a brilliant friend but sometimes William hated him. He was cocky and self-assured and never let anybody get in the way of what he wanted. He was always telling William how he envied him being rich but William would swap with him in a heartbeat. Material things didn't mean anything to him and one day he'd leave it all behind and head off into the world. But for now, he'd have to accept how things were.

'Right,' he said, fixing a smile onto his face. 'Let's get this game underway.'

* * *

Donna sat on the bus, relieved Tina had let her go home early. She closed her eyes and thought about the events of the last few hours. It had been an eye-opener for her. She'd wanted to make it up to Tina so she hadn't balked at wearing the horrible yellow rubber gloves or refused when Tina had asked her to unblock the toilet. But what a disgusting, rotten job! And to make it worse, the old lady in the house had spoken to them as though they were the lowest form of humanity.

'You can start by cleaning that kitchen,' she'd said, standing with her hands on her hips. 'And then all the bathrooms need a good scrubbing. Snap, snap. Time is ticking.'

Donna had wanted to say something to her but the look on Tina's face had warned her against it.

'We just have to suck it up and do it,' Tina whispered. 'It pays the bills.'

Donna couldn't believe the amount of work they'd had to do for a measly four pounds an hour. She could have a wallet whipped out of someone's pocket in a matter of seconds and get twenty or thirty pounds out of it. She understood that Tina needed to work to earn some money but it was a damn hard way to earn it.

But at least the day hadn't been a waste of time. It had made her rethink a lot of things. She was going to really try hard at school and make Tina proud. She was going to make something of herself and get them out of the horrible situation they were in. She wouldn't resort to pickpocketing again but she certainly wouldn't be cleaning for a living.

The steady drone of the engine was making her sleepy and she began to relax. She felt sorry that Tina still had another hour or so left to clean but she was glad she was out of it. She had a few pounds on her so maybe she'd stop off at the shop and buy the makings of a cake. Donna loved to bake and Tina loved testing her various recipes. Tonight was definitely a chocolate night. She had a recipe that Lexie's granny had given her for a chocolate sponge so she'd give that a try. Suddenly things began to look better. There was nothing like a bit of baking to cheer a girl up!

Chapter 5

October 2004

Donna grabbed the jeans that she'd thrown on her bed the night before and stepped into them. She wrinkled her nose as she sniffed last night's T-shirt and discarded it on the floor before managing to lay her hands on a clean one. She was due in work early this morning because she had a birthday cake to have ready for ten but there was something she had to do first. And she was dreading it.

She stuck a piece of bread in the toaster and went in search of a bobbin to tie up her unruly red hair. At least she never bothered with make-up. She couldn't imagine anything worse than having to spend hours in front of a mirror every morning as most of her friends did. They went to great lengths to conceal every spot and blemish whereas she had a full face of freckles but didn't give a toss.

She quickly buttered the toast and poured herself a glass of milk. Six o'clock. It was funny how she used to hate early mornings when she was in school. She used to always roll out of bed at the very last minute to get herself to school and at weekends she'd sleep until lunch time. But now that she was doing a job she loved, this was her favourite part of the day.

Wiping the crumbs from her top, she ran upstairs to brush her teeth. There wasn't a sound from her mother's room, which wasn't surprising, but she could hear Tina stirring. Her sister was working full-time now for a company of corporate cleaners and worked tirelessly to bring in much-needed money to the household. She usually started her shifts around eight so would often be just getting up as Donna was leaving. Donna tiptoed back downstairs and, grabbing her denim jacket from the banister, was out the door in a flash.

She hopped over the railings separating her house from Lexie's and tapped on the door. She didn't have much time to spare, which was just as well, because she didn't want to go to work looking like a blubbering mess. Within seconds the door was swung open and Lexie stood there with a huge smile on her face.

'Donna! I wondered if you'd come. Come in, come in. I'm just trying to fit Granny's sandwiches into my hand luggage. Along with the crisps and crackers and the brownies she made. I think someone forgot to tell her that they've invented shops in airports now!'

Donna giggled as she stepped inside and followed her friend into the living room. 'Is that it? Is that all you're taking?'

'Yep,' said Lexie, nodding towards the large, bulging rucksack and smaller one beside it. 'There's no point in taking suitcases of stuff when I'll be travelling around.'

Tears sprung to Donna's eyes and she fought hard to conceal them.

'Ah come on, Donna. Don't be upset. We'll keep in touch and I'm still going to keep nagging you to join me.'

'You know I can't, Lexie.'

'You can't or you won't?'

Donna wiped her eyes. 'I can't. It wouldn't be fair to leave Tina here with Mam. And you know that *she's* the one who wants to travel. I'm more of a home bird.'

'Well, maybe the two of you should come over. Come for a month or two and see if you like it. Go on – live a little.'

'Maybe if things were different. Oh, Lexie, I'm going to miss you so much.' She didn't hold back the tears this time. She flung her arms around her friend and clung onto her, her shoulders rising and falling from the sobs.

It wouldn't have been so bad if Lexie was just going to London or even Europe. Somewhere that wouldn't take more than a few hours to get to. But the fact that she was going to Perth in Australia – the other side of the world – was almost too much for Donna to bear. But Lexie deserved some happiness and Donna wasn't going to spoil it for her.

'Right,' said Donna, pulling away from the embrace and wiping her tears with her sleeve. 'I'm just a stupid softie. You know me – I'd cry at the drop of a hat.'

Lexie watched her carefully. 'You'll get used to not having me around. And you still have Tina. Do you know what I'd do to have a sister like that?'

Donna smiled. 'I know. She's great, isn't she? Now go on. Go and finish your packing. I'll be late for work if I don't get a move on.'

'That's more like it,' beamed Lexie. 'And I'll try and get my hands on some fabulous Aussie recipes for your collection – once you promise to make them for me when I see you again.'

'Deal!'

Lexie walked her to the door and they hugged again – but more briefly this time. Donna was just going to have to get used to not having her best friend around. To not being able to run next door and cry when her mother came home senseless drunk or not being able to lie on Lexie's bed beside her, discussing which pop stars were the sexiest and who they planned to marry.

She tried to fight the tears as she headed to the bus stop. She always knew Lexie would spread her wings and fly as soon as she could. She'd obviously inherited the appetite for travel from her parents. Donna just hoped she hadn't inherited their nonchalance because she couldn't bear the thought of not having her friend in her life.

Half an hour later she arrived at the city-centre bakery where she worked. As soon as she walked in the door and the waft of freshly made pastries hit her nose, she felt relaxed. This was where she felt happiest. In fact, Tina often said that the shop had saved her. Donna had been a restless teenager, always in some sort of trouble, whether it was fighting with her teachers or failing her exams. But a gentle push from Tina a couple of years ago to find a job had led her to the shop and she'd been working part time there ever since.

'Morning, Donna, love,' came the chirpy voice of the owner, Jan, who appeared from the kitchen in a puff of flour. 'I've got the sponges ready for that birthday cake so you can fire ahead with the decorating once they cool.'

Donna followed her back into the kitchen. 'Thanks, Jan. It's exactly what I need to take my mind off things today. I love getting stuck into a good cake.'

'Lexie?' The older woman raised her eyebrows.

Donna nodded. 'I know I should be happy for her but I can't help just feeling sorry for myself. It seems I can't hold onto people in my life I care about.'

'Ah, don't say that, love,' said Jan, putting a chubby arm around her. 'I know you have it tough sometimes but haven't you got Tina? And you know you have me too, right?'

'I know, Jan. You're very good to me. It's just that … well, you know how it was with Lexie. She was my best friend in the world. She's been next door my whole life.' To Donna's dismay, big tears began to form at the corners of her eyes and fall down her cheeks.

'Ah, poor love.' Jan pulled her even closer and Donna gladly laid her head on the woman's broad shoulders. 'You let it all out. And then when you're done, you take all that emotion out on the cake and see if you can produce the best one yet.'

Donna laughed at that. Jan Adams was such a passionate baker. She believed in channelling emotions into the cakes she made. She swore that she could bake a much better cake if she was either really sad or really happy. If she wasn't feeling anything, her cakes would flop. Or so she said. But the truth was, Donna had never seen her produce anything that was a flop. She was brilliant at what she did and, because she'd taken Donna under her wing to teach her everything she knew, Donna was becoming a pretty good baker too.

After sticking her hair into a net and donning her white baker's coat, Donna began to work her magic on the cake. It was for a sixteenth birthday and the mother had asked for something pretty and girly, leaving the detail completely up to her. Donna loved being creative and had decided to do a two-tier cake covered in party pink icing and piped with various shades of purple. She was going to make some bags and shoes with icing and top the cake with them. It was a big task but Donna was pretty sure she could make it work.

A loud bellowing laugh came from the other side of the kitchen and she looked over to see Jan chatting to one of the other bakers, a guy in his thirties who'd worked for her for the last ten years. Jan treated and paid all her workers fairly but she was much more than just an employer. They all confided in her and she looked out for them. Donna had known her almost three years now and, in that time, the woman had been more of a mother to her than her own mother had ever been.

When she'd left school just a few months ago, there'd been no doubt in Jan's mind that Donna would come and work for her full-time. 'You're my star baker, so you are,' she'd said. 'And more than that – you're the daughter I never had.'

Those words had warmed Donna's heart like nothing before ever had and, for the first time in her life, she felt like she really belonged. She didn't hate her own mother – in fact there were times when she really loved her. Times when she was sober and would make an effort to cook something for them or times when she'd show an interest in what her two girls were up to. But sadly, those times had become few and far between and Donna had learned to live with that. Donna had never even realised that there was a void there but when Jan had stepped in as a sort of surrogate mother to her, she'd finally felt that the missing piece of the puzzle of her life was in place.

She stood back and surveyed her work. It was getting there. Ideally she'd like more time to perfect it but she knew that Jan relied on custom cakes to bring in the cash and time was money.

'Looking good,' said Jan, peering over her shoulder. 'What did I tell you? You can never go wrong when you use emotion.'

Donna nodded, a lump forming in her throat. Lexie would be at the airport by now, saying her goodbyes to her granny and granddad.

As if reading her thoughts, Jan continued. 'And I think that level of work needs to be rewarded with a nice cup of tea and a cake. What do you say?'

'I've only been here an hour, Jan. I shouldn't really.'

'Listen to Jan, love. I can tell when you need a break. I'll stick the kettle on and you go and grab a couple of cupcakes from the display outside. I made some fresh this morning with that lemon icing you love.'

Donna wasn't about to argue and, besides, she'd barely eaten a bite of her toast earlier because she'd been dreading saying goodbye to Lexie. A cup of tea and a cake sounded perfect. The doors of the bakery had just been opened and there was already a customer in the shop. Donna opened one of the glass displays to take two of the cakes and couldn't help smiling to herself when she heard Talia flirting with the customer. Talia was just seventeen but was desperate to find herself a nice man. Donna couldn't help delaying a little to watch the scene unfold.

The guy looked awkward as Talia threw a load of questions at him. Where did he work? Oh, he was in college. Which one? Trinity, that's fabulous. What was he studying? Law! He must be very brainy. And so the questions continued until he made his excuses, saying he was late for a lecture, and grabbed his doughnut before dashing out the door.

'Talia, that poor guy!' Donna laughed as the young girl strained her neck to catch a last glimpse of the object of her affections. 'He'll never come in here again.'

'But he was gorgeous, and sexy and polite. Did you see him?'

Donna noticed how the other girl's eyes had glazed over and she felt a little pang as she walked back inside with the cakes. She wanted a man to make her feel like that. She'd had a couple of boyfriends over the last few years but none of them had been special. She often wondered what it would be like to be in love with somebody and to have them feel the same about her. She'd become obsessed with the movie *Love Actually* since it had been released the previous year and had watched the DVD again and again. She loved how it made her feel and cheered every time that Hugh Grant and Martine McCutcheon's characters got together in the end. Maybe some day she'd find her own little piece of forbidden love because, according to the movies, that was the best love of all.

* * *

Will thought he'd never get out of that shop. The girl serving him was mad. He'd thought for a minute she was going to jump right over the counter and kiss him. He laughed to himself at that. He'd been watching too many romantic comedies of late instead of studying.

It was a gorgeous day, considering it was coming into the winter months, and he was happy to take his time walking towards Trinity. He couldn't believe he was actually in college studying law. The one thing he'd always promised himself he wouldn't do. But he'd done a good Leaving Cert, got the points and had just been carried along by his mother's wishes. It wasn't so bad, really. He'd no intention of ever working as a solicitor like his mother, but college was proving to be fun so he'd just bide his time there for the moment.

He stared up at the Spire in the centre of O'Connell Street as he headed towards O'Connell Bridge and immediately spots floated in front of his eyes from the glare of the sun. He hated that the summer was over again for another year and thought about his childhood plans. He still hadn't given up on his dreams to travel and some day, whenever he felt the time was right, he'd say goodbye to his parents and step out on his own for the first time in his life.

He'd mentioned it once to them and they'd balked at the idea. 'Don't think for a minute we'll be supporting any such foolishness,' his mother had said. 'You have a perfectly good home here and a ready-made job when you finish college.' Although he wanted independence, it wasn't easy to turn his back on the allowance that was lodged to his account every month and suffer the wrath of his parents at the same time. He'd do it some day but for now he'd have to live their dreams rather than his own.

'Hiya, mate.' Will looked up to see his friend Jack falling in step with him as they walked in the entrance of Trinity College. 'What time have you a break at? Want to meet for lunch?'

'Yeah, sure,' said Will, pulling out his timetable to check his schedule. 'Canteen at 12.30?'

'Fine by me. See you later so.' He veered off and headed in the opposite direction across the campus.

Jack Fitzpatrick was a great example of a kid who hadn't turned out anything like everyone thought he would. He'd been Will's best friend in school but had always been in trouble. Will's parents had often said: 'That child will end up in prison, you mark my words' or 'He's a wrong one, that one.' How wrong they'd been. Jack had met a girl in fourth year and she'd turned everything around for him. She was a science geek – the sort of girl Jack would have laughed at in the past – but he'd fallen head over heels in love with her. He'd turned his attention to his books and discovered a love of learning that he'd never known he had. He was now studying science along with Tessa and it often made Will a little jealous to see them together. They were like soulmates – 'Cut from the same cloth,' his nan would have said. He'd been through his fair share of girls himself but none of them had felt like the one for him. Maybe one day he'd meet his soulmate but not before he became that adventurer that his ten-year-old self always dreamed of.

Chapter 6

February 2008

Will downed his vodka in one and winced as the liquid burned the back of his throat.

'Jesus!' said Jack, taking a sip of his own pint. 'Take it easy with that.'

'I know. I just needed that first one. Honestly, if you'd had the day I had, you'd be doing the same.'

'Mummy on your back again, was she?' Jack wagged his finger at Will in a teacher-like manner and Will made a friendly swipe at him.

'I'm so fuckin' fed up, Jack. What the hell is wrong with me? I've been saying since the day I left school that I was going to go off and see the world and here I am, five years later, still stuck in a rut and doing the one thing I swore I'd never do.'

Jack didn't respond so Will continued.

'I mean, working as a solicitor is bad enough but working with my mother is hell on earth. I can't move sideways without her breathing down my neck. She wants us to have lunches together, go to and from work together ... honestly, it's a nightmare.'

'Do something about it, then. Nobody is holding a gun to your head.'

Will glared at his friend. 'It's not that easy.'

'It's as easy or as difficult as you make it. Look, you're a young guy, you've got qualifications now and you've no ties. Your mother will always be your mother but you've got to learn to be yourself. Get yourself out into the world and do what you've always wanted to do.'

'That's okay for you to say, with your perfect job and your perfect woman. Your life is pretty much sorted.'

Jack slammed his pint down on the table. 'Get a fucking grip, Will. Nothing is ever perfect. Things aren't always what they look like from the outside.'

The outburst took Will by surprise. 'Is there something wrong, Jack? Are you and Tessa okay?'

Jack fiddled with a beer mat.

'Jack? Talk to me.'

'It's just that … ah, it's nothing. Don't mind me.'

'Tell me,' said Will, beginning to worry. 'You know you can talk to me about anything.'

Suddenly a smile spread across Jack's face. 'Me and Tessa are talking about taking things to the next level – marriage, kids, a mortgage.'

Will looked at him in surprise. 'Seriously? Wow! That's brilliant news. I wasn't expecting to hear *that*.'

'And why not?' Jack raised an eyebrow. 'Did you not think Tessa and I would last the distance?'

'I *knew* you two would last. I just didn't expect you to be talking about the pitter-patter of little feet just yet. I'm a bit jealous, if I'm honest. Here's you with your life mapped out and I haven't even decided what I want to do with mine.'

'Well, the first thing you need to do is move out of that house. You're twenty-two, for God's sake. Who still lives with their parents at that age?'

Will sighed. 'I know. It's just the effort of looking for somewhere and, besides, I'm not sure I could take the hysterics from my mother when I'd tell her I'm moving out.'

Jack shook his head. 'Grow a pair, man, will you? And what about Laura? I thought you two were getting close. Would you not think of moving in with her?'

'God no,' said Will, a little too quickly. 'Laura is great but definitely not live-in material. It's just a bit of fun.'

'Well, you'd want to tell *her* that. Tessa was talking to her the other day and she was saying how she felt things were moving in the right direction.'

'Shit. I think I'll be having a chat with her this weekend. She's a lovely girl, but there's just nothing there. Nothing like what you have with Tessa.'

Jack smiled. 'When you've found the right one, you'll know.'

'As I said before, you're a lucky man.' Will saw how Jack's eyes lit up at the mention of Tessa. They'd been together six years now and they were more in love than any couple he'd ever seen. Part of him wanted a relationship like that but the other part of him knew that he needed to go travelling. If he met someone and settled down now, he'd always regret not going out and seeing the world. But Jack was right; he needed to grow a pair and start to live his own life. He'd spent twenty-two years doing exactly what his parents wanted him to do and now it was time he did something for himself. But he'd just have to find the right moment to broach the subject with them.

'Another one for the road?' said Jack, breaking into his thoughts.

'Go on, then. Maybe just one more.' He watched his friend go to the bar and wished he could swap places with him. His own life was an embarrassment. He even drank vodka instead of beer so his parents wouldn't smell alcohol off his breath. They knew he'd have a glass of champagne at a function or a glass of wine over dinner, but other than that, they thought he didn't indulge at all. How ridiculous was that? But he'd spent a lifetime with them, living the life they wanted him to live and trying to be who they wanted him to be. Old habits die hard.

'So tell me more about your plans with Tessa.' Jack was back from the bar with the drinks and Will was aware that he'd monopolised most of the conversation with moans about his situation. He wasn't usually so fed up but seeing Jack so happy always made him feel he was missing out on something.

'Nothing much to tell really,' said Jack, taking a slug of his pint and sitting back on the seat. 'She thinks we're throwing money away by renting when we both have good jobs and could afford a mortgage. She feels that after six years together, we should be thinking about where our future is going.'

'But what do *you* think? Are you ready for all that responsibility?'

'I was born ready, mate.' Jack beamed but Will noticed the smile didn't reach his eyes.

'Are you sure everything is okay?' Will asked, searching his friend's face. 'It's really great that you're settling down but I sense you're not completely sure about it.'

Jack was about to say something then took a sip of his pint instead.

'Come on, Jack. What is it? If you're having doubts about Tessa, don't let yourself get carried away in a fairy tale. You have to say something.'

Jack's head shot up. 'I'm not having doubts, Will. I adore Tessa. You know that. I suppose it's just scary to think of a mortgage, a wife, kids. I'll have to grow up once and for all.'

Will laughed at that. 'Well, it's understandable you'd feel like that. It's a big step but I've no doubt it's the right one for you. You two were made for each other.'

'Right, enough about me,' said Jack. 'We came out tonight to sort you out. Remember? Now what are we going to do about getting you a life of your own?'

Another hour and two more drinks later, they were ready to leave the pub. Will felt more positive than he'd done in a while. Jack was a tonic. He'd phoned him earlier to ask him to go for a pint in town but Will had refused at first because of it being a Monday. Jack had pushed him, saying that he was fed up of him moaning about things and he wanted to talk to him about getting his act together. Who would have thought it – Jack Fitzpatrick giving advice? It was probably because of him getting his own life sorted that he wanted to see Will do the same.

'Burger and chips?' Jack asked, as they stumbled down the street.

'Definitely. I'll need a good feed inside me to sober me up before I go home.'

Jack punched him playfully on the shoulder. 'Have you not listened to a word I said tonight? *Be* drunk! Go home and wear your drunkenness like a badge of honour. Be happy.'

Will laughed and threw an arm around his friend as they walked. Maybe it was the alcohol giving him Dutch courage but he suddenly felt ready to face his parents and tell them he was moving on. The future was looking bright and it was thanks to a friendly nudge from Jack. It was good of him to want to spread the happiness. Will hoped that one day, when he was ready, he'd fall in love and be as happy and settled as Jack was.

* * *

Will looked at his bedside clock for about the tenth time in the last hour: 4.10 a.m. He shut his eyes tight and willed sleep to come but he got nothing but a head full of jumbled thoughts. The alcohol was making him feel woozy but he was sober enough to feel worried about his conversation with Jack earlier. Something didn't feel right.

Jack was always so self-assured. So confident in knowing what he wanted and not afraid of going for it. But there was something about how he was acting tonight. Not cagey exactly, but unsure. Manic, even. He'd been serious one minute and it had seemed as though he was going to tell Will something. Then he'd changed his mind and was full of chat about his and Tessa's plans for the future. It just didn't ring true.

Will turned onto his other side and his legs became tangled in the duvet. He kicked in frustration until he'd knocked it right onto the floor. God, he wished he could think straight. That he could figure out what was up with Jack. Because the more he thought about it, the more he was sure that his friend had other things on his mind than talk of marriage and kids.

He wished he hadn't monopolised the conversation so much. Maybe if he'd given Jack a better chance to speak, he'd have told him what was worrying him. Suddenly his eyes became heavy and it seemed sleep was going to come at last. Thank God for that. He'd make sure to ring Jack tomorrow and arrange to meet up again. And this time he'd be insisting that *Jack* was the centre of attention. If Will had been guilty of not listening enough lately, he was damn well going to make up for it from now on. Jack was the best friend he'd ever had and there was nothing he wouldn't do for him.

Chapter 7

Will was in a daze. It didn't feel real. How could this have happened? He was suddenly gripped with a pain in his stomach and had to run to the bathroom. He vomited again and again into the hand basin and when he was done he sat down on the tiled floor and let the tears flow. It was as though someone had reached right inside him and ripped his guts out.

'Are you okay in there, William?' came a voice from outside the door. 'Your daddy and I are worried about you. You've had such a shock.'

'I'm okay, Mum. I'll be out in a minute.' He honestly didn't know if he'd ever be okay again.

Jack. Funny, happy, clever Jack. His best friend, Jack, was dead.

He'd got a frantic phone call from Tessa earlier. She was crying and screaming for him to get over there. She'd come home from work to find Jack hanging from a noose in the bedroom. Will's immediate reaction was to ask if she was joking. How stupid was that? And then if she was sure. That's how ridiculous it seemed. It had only been two days since their night in the pub when Will had envied him for having such a perfect life.

He formed a fist with his right hand and, closing his eyes, he punched himself in the head. Surely he'd wake up in a minute. He'd open his eyes and be curled up in his bed and would breathe a sigh of relief that it had all been an awful nightmare. He took a few deep breaths and opened his eyes slowly. There was no nightmare. Only the cold, hard reality that his best friend was dead.

He'd taken his mother's car and had driven like a maniac to the house Jack had been renting with Tessa on the Navan Road. By then, the house had been filled with people in uniforms, who were going through the motions of filling out reports and doing their jobs. He'd followed the ambulance to the hospital where he'd met Jack's parents. It was then he'd learned about Jack's depression. He'd been close to him for most of his life but he'd never known.

Apparently Jack had suffered from depression from the time he was twelve. His parents had hidden it from everyone. To protect *him*, they'd said. But Will knew enough about people like them to know that they'd been looking out for themselves. They probably thought that having a son with depression would reflect badly on them. They didn't want the finger pointed at them when they were hobnobbing at the golf club or dining with their middle-class friends.

And poor Tessa. She'd been living with the guy for the last two years, going out with him for six, and she'd never known. The poor girl had been inconsolable. She'd said over and over again that if she'd known about the depression, she wouldn't have put so much pressure on him to get a mortgage or settle down. But it wasn't her fault. And none of that really mattered now anyway. Jack was dead and no amount of pointing the finger was going to bring him back.

A gentle tap on the door startled him. He had no clue how long he'd been sitting there.

'Come on, pet,' said his mother, in an uncharacteristic show of emotion. 'Please come out and talk to us.'

Talk to them. That's what Jack had wanted him to do. And now that he thought of it, Jack had asked him out that night to try and push him into following his dreams. He must have planned his death. And one of his priorities had been to make sure his best friend was going to be okay. But Will still couldn't understand how he could have done something so horrendous.

He reached out to grab the edge of the sink and pulled himself onto his feet. Wincing at his face in the mirror, he splashed some cold water on it and ran his fingers through his hair. The coming days were going to be tough but he was going to get through them. And then he was going to quit his job and go and do what he should have done years ago.

As he opened the bathroom door, memories of their childhood flooded his mind. He could hear Jack shouting: 'Run like fuck!' when their football hopped off Mr Lenihan's car as he was driving out of the school yard. He pictured the two of them trying to hold in their giggles as Jack let a loud fart escape in history class. Or the time Jack broke his Bunsen burner in science and swapped his for Tracey Dillon's so she'd get the blame.

'Why did you do it, Jack? Why, why, *why*?' He felt his mother's arms around him then and he wept on her shoulder. Things would never be the same again.

Chapter 8

Donna and Tina blessed themselves as the funeral cars passed. They were sitting outside on the railings where Tina was having a smoke. Donna liked the idea that her sister was a smoker. She was so perfect in everything else she did that somehow the smoking thing made her seem more human.

'Looks like a big funeral,' said Tina, indicating the endless stream of cars that were following the hearse. 'Seeing a coffin always gives me the shivers. God love them, whoever they are.'

'It could be that guy from down the road. The suicide one. Apparently he was only my age.'

Tina shook her head. 'Awful, isn't it? So young with a whole life ahead of him. I wonder what makes people do it.'

'I honestly don't know. I can't imagine contemplating it, no matter how bad things got.'

'Come on, let's go inside.' Tina took a long drag of her cigarette and stubbed it out on the ground. 'I'll make us a nice cup of tea.'

Ten minutes later they were drinking tea and eating some of the cakes Donna had brought home from the bakery the previous day. The passing funeral had brought a sombre air to the house and both were lost in thought.

'Do you think we'll ever get out of here?'

Donna looked at her sister, startled by the question. 'What do you mean?'

'I mean, this situation. Do you think we'll ever get out of this goddamn awful situation?'

'I often wonder that myself,' said Donna, breaking a piece off a lemon slice and popping it into her mouth. 'But unless either of us meets the man of our dreams who'll whisk us off to a castle, I'm guessing that this is it for the foreseeable future.'

Tina continued. 'But don't you want more? Look at Lexie and how she's spread her wings. Her life sounds wonderful compared to the drudgery we live every day.'

Donna was alarmed at Tina's words. 'That's not like you, Tina. I thought you were happy enough with how things are.'

'Happy enough. That's exactly it. It's just sometimes I feel life is passing me by. Do you think I aspire to being a cleaner? I'd rather cut my hands off than do that for the rest of my life.'

'Tina! What's got into you?'

'Sorry, Donna. I think it was that last postcard from Lexie that did it. It really unsettled me.'

Donna glanced at the postcard of Monkey Mia on the fridge. It was a beach in Western Australia where Lexie had just spent a couple of weeks.

'I'd just love to be brave enough to do what she did,' continued Tina. 'But it's not really an option with … you know …'

'Mam, you mean?'

'Well, yes. Mam *and* you. I know she's not much good, but I don't think I'd feel right heading over to the other side of the world and leaving her. You know how much like a child she is most of the time. And it certainly wouldn't be fair to leave you to look after her.'

Donna began to panic a little. Was Tina hinting? Looking for her approval to go off and see the world? Donna didn't really want to travel but the thought of staying here on her own and looking after her mother was the scariest thing she could imagine. Tina obviously noticed her face and was quick to reassure her.

'Don't worry, Donna. I'm not going to leave. Maybe some day I will, but not as things are. I'll just keep planning and some day, even if it's when I'm old and grey, I'll do it.'

'Where would you go?' Donna was relieved that it was nothing but a dream for Tina.

'Oh, I'd go everywhere. Do you want to see my route?'

'Your route?'

Tina jumped up from the table and opened a drawer. 'Yes. It's my dream travel itinerary. I'd go to Perth, where Lexie is, and then move on to see the rest of Australia, then New Zealand and a few more stops before the US.'

'Wow! You really *did* plan it all, didn't you?' Donna looked in amazement at the well-thought-out pages that her sister put in front of her. 'It looks fantastic.'

'It's just a dream at the moment,' Tina said, sadly. 'But one day I might make it happen.'

'What's that you have there?'

The voice startled them both and they looked up to see their mother standing at the bottom of the stairs.

'I thought you were still in bed, Ma,' said Donna, hopping up to stick the kettle on. 'Do you want a cup of tea? Something to eat?'

'Why don't I make us some sandwiches and you make the tea? I see you've made some bread, Donna. There's a bit of cheese in the fridge that'll go nicely with it.'

Both girls stared at their mother. It felt strange for her to be sober – to be looking after them for a change. Strange but nice.

Donna was first to speak. 'I'll look after the bread. It's still a bit warm so might be tricky to cut.'

'Grand. And don't bother with tea for me, love. I'll have the end of that white wine. You can't have cheese without wine.'

Donna's heart sank. It was lovely to see glimpses of their 'nice' mother but sadly they were just that – glimpses. Tina had been quiet during the exchange and Donna noticed tears in her eyes.

'So go on,' said Catherine, filling her glass to the brim. 'What's all that, then?'

Tina quickly folded her precious list and stuffed it in her pocket. 'Just dreams, Ma. Nothing but my dreams.'

* * *

'I'm going to quit the job, Mum. I'm leaving to go and do some travelling.'

Will fell silent to let his parents digest the words. It was the day after Jack's funeral and they were sitting in the dining room having dinner. He'd been rehearsing what he was going to say all day but his mind was made up, no matter what his parents said.

'Don't be silly, William.' His mum was as dismissive as ever. 'You've had an emotional few days. You're not thinking straight.'

'Your mum is right,' said his dad, never one to have his own opinion. 'This is not a time to be making important decisions.'

Will wasn't going to be fobbed off. 'But that's where you're both wrong. I've never felt so sure about anything in all my life. You know I've always wanted to travel but I've been putting it off for … well, you know …'

'Well, I hope you don't mean you've been putting it off for *us*, William,' his mother sniffed. 'All we've ever done is offer you the best opportunities in life.'

Will clenched his fist under the table. *Offer* him, she said. They may have offered him the opportunities, but they pushed, coerced and pressurised him into taking them.

She continued. 'And we've always wanted what's best for you – sometimes I think we know you better than you know yourself. And right now, the best thing for you is to stay in a routine and work hard. Jack would have wanted you to be successful in your career.'

'You see, that's where you're wrong!' Will was aware his voice was raised but he needed them to understand. 'He wanted me to be successful, but not necessarily in my career. In life.'

'Isn't that the same thing?'

Will looked at his mother and felt a glimmer of pity for her. 'No, Mum. It's not. Success can be interpreted in a whole lot of ways. Success to me means happiness. I want to be happy. Jack wanted me to be happy.'

'Don't you be getting all philosophical on me, William Cooper-Smith.' His mother sniffed, pushing her half-empty plate away. 'And are you telling us now that you're not happy?'

Will nodded his head but couldn't look his mother in the eye.

'Well? Are you happy or not?'

'No, Mum. I'm not happy. I've always felt … I don't know … incomplete, I suppose. I need to get out and see some of the world. I need to find out what makes me happy.'

'And what about Laura?' It was his father's turn to try and make him see sense. 'Is she going with you on this little trip of yours?'

'I had a chat with Laura last night after the funeral. We've agreed to go our separate ways.'

'You see!' Vivienne stood up suddenly, startling both Will and his father. 'It's the grief. You can't go making rash decisions while you're mourning.'

'Sit down, Mum. I'm not mourning. Well, I am, but it's got nothing to do with the decisions I'm making. If anything, I'm seeing things more clearly now. I don't love Laura and it was never going to work.'

His mother sat down and sighed. 'But you've been going out with her for the last year. And she's from such a good family.'

There it was – the class thing rearing its head again. He had to bite his tongue for fear he'd say something he'd regret. But to his surprise, his father jumped in.

'Vivienne, love, leave the lad alone. If Will says he didn't love the girl, well then he's doing the right thing by leaving her.'

'But at least he should wait until the grief goes away – not make all these rash decisions.'

His father spoke again. 'We've got to let him live his life, love. He's twenty-two years old. We can't hold on to him forever if he wants to spread his wings.'

Both Will and his mother stared at his father and Will felt a lump in his throat. He'd never heard his father stick up for him. He usually went along with whatever his mother said to keep the peace. But Will could see his mother was about to object again so he decided to jump in.

'Dad's right, Mum.' He reached over and patted her hand. 'I need to spread my wings. I'm not going to go away forever and I won't be going for a while yet but I know I definitely need to go.'

Tears formed at the corners of Vivienne Cooper-Smith's eyes and Will realised that he'd barely ever seen his mother cry, except tears of rage when something didn't go her way.

'I'm sorry, son, if we haven't made you happy. Where will you go?'

'It's nothing you've done, Mum.' There was no point in making her feel worse. 'There's just something inside me that wants to travel and see the world before I settle down. And I'm thinking Australia. I'm not sure exactly where yet but I'm going to look into it.'

'Don't you need visas and the likes for over there?' said his father, who looked relieved that the conversation had calmed down.

'Yes, and that's why I won't be going for a while. I'd also like to continue working for the next few months and get together as much cash as I can. I'll probably do some work while I'm away but I don't want to feel under pressure to work all the time.'

His father nodded. 'That sounds like a sensible plan. Don't you think, Vivienne?'

The stony look had returned to her face, all traces of vulnerability gone. 'I suppose so. I'll have to start looking for a replacement so you'll have to give me proper dates. It's all a bit inconvenient.'

'Don't worry, Mum. I'll keep you informed every step of the way.' He got up from the table and kissed his mother on the cheek. 'And don't think I'm not grateful for everything you've given me. Because I am. It's just time for me to stand on my own two feet.'

He didn't wait for an answer but headed up the stairs to his room. When he had the door closed behind him, he flopped down on the bed and breathed a sigh of relief.

'I did it, Jack, I did it,' he whispered. 'I'm finally free and it's the best feeling in the world!'

Chapter 9

February 2009

'I swear, I'm going to kill that woman.' Donna stomped into the bedroom and slammed the door so hard, the room shook.

'What's happened?' asked Tina, turning from the mirror where she was applying her eye-shadow. 'And take it easy on the door, will you. We can't afford repairs on top of the rest of the bills.'

Donna lay down on her bed and began to cry. 'What do you think happened? Mam happened!'

'What has she done now?' Tina came over and sat beside her and stroked her hair. 'You've got to stop letting her get to you like this.'

'I can't help it.' Donna sniffed. 'She's getting worse. She's just spilt half a bottle of red wine over my recipes. She was so drunk when she was pouring it that she completely missed the glass.'

'Oh no. Not the ones you've been collecting? Are they ruined?'

'Well of course they're ruined. It was bloody red wine! All the ones Lexie sent me and everything.' She started crying again. Living with her mother was just like living with a bad flatmate – most of the time she could ignore her but now and again she'd do something to make her want to scream.

Catherine O'Neill was a full-blown alcoholic. The two girls had tried over the years to help her to get sober. They'd tried to get her to see sense and when that hadn't worked, they'd tried to force her into a detox programme at home. But nothing had worked and for the last number of years they'd just accepted the status quo. She'd drink most days – usually whatever cheap wine or spirits she could get her hands on – and then sleep it off for twelve or more hours at night. Tina was now the adult in the house.

'Look, I won't go out tonight,' said Tina, breaking into Donna's thoughts. 'I can't leave you here like this. Not when she's home.'

Donna sat up and wiped her eyes. 'Don't be silly. Your night is all planned. You deserve some time out.'

'But look at the state of you. No, I'm not going anywhere. And in fact, I think you should get out yourself. Go and stay with one of your friends for the night. I'll stay here and keep an eye on her.'

'That's not fair on you, Tina. I couldn't …' But Donna already knew she would. She needed to get out of there. She felt a bit mean about it, since Tina had planned to go out, but she reckoned *she* needed the escape more than Tina tonight.

'Go on,' said Tina. 'Pack yourself an overnight bag.'

'Are you sure?'

'Of course I'm sure. Now go! I wasn't in much form for going out really. I fancy an early night with a good book.'

Donna threw her arms around her sister. 'You're a star, do you know that? What would I do without you?'

'Well, hopefully you'll never have to find out.'

Donna couldn't get out of there quick enough. She knew she'd be fine again tomorrow but sometimes she just got overwhelmed with everything and needed some time out. She had a number of friends she could go to but the one she really wanted to see tonight was Jan. Jan lived just a few short bus stops away in Cabra West and Donna had stayed there a few times in the past when she'd felt the need to get away. It was different for Tina. She had a better tolerance for their mother than Donna had. Or maybe she just bottled it all up. But either way, she seemed okay about staying home so Donna wouldn't let herself feel too guilty.

She peeped into the sitting room as she headed for the front door and saw her mother had dozed off, her glass of wine tilted in such a way it was dripping slowly on the wooden floor. Stupid woman. Not for the first time, Donna imagined what life would be like for her and Tina if her mother wasn't around. It was like having a baby to look after. But the strange thing was, she didn't hate her. She hated what she'd become and she hated the fact that she didn't really care about either girl, but Donna also knew that some part of her still loved her mother. But not tonight. She made sure she slammed the front door on the way out.

* * *

Will sat back on his sun lounger and raised his face up to the sun. God, he loved it here. Coming to Perth was the best thing he'd ever done. For a while, he hadn't thought he'd go through with it because his mother had thought of a million reasons why he shouldn't go. But he had just kept thinking of Jack and his last piece of advice to him and he'd overruled all his mother's concerns.

He'd been there for the last two months. After an initial few nights in a hostel in Perth city centre while he was getting his bearings, he'd rented a mobile home on a site just off the beach. It was glorious. He couldn't get over the blue skies and sea and the warm, golden sand. It was like a paradise.

He'd found himself a job very quickly, picking fruit at a farm a few miles outside Perth. He'd needed a car for that so he'd bought himself an ancient Toyota. It was rusty and chugged a lot but it did what he needed it to do. The job paid okay but he earned his money.

He'd start at five some mornings and spend eight hours picking fruit with very few breaks. It was a tough job, done in forty-degree heat with the smell of chicken manure filling the air and flies buzzing incessantly in his face. He'd no intention of doing that for long – just long enough to build up some more cash for his travelling fund.

He was also doing a few shifts in an Irish bar in the city and, although it didn't pay as well as the farm job, he really enjoyed it. He loved meeting new people and the bar job allowed him to do just that. The staff were a mixture of Irish and Aussies and all equally as friendly. He'd also reinvented himself by dropping the 'Cooper' from his name. He was just plain old Will Smith now, which always elicited a giggle from both punters and staff. There was just something about Perth. It felt like Ireland in a way, in that it was fairly laid back and the people were friendly, but it also had a buzz about it – a sense of excitement in the air. Or maybe that was just him. He was excited to be fulfilling his dream at last. He knew he wanted to move on at some stage but, at the moment, there was nowhere else on earth he'd rather be.

He felt a slight chill from a breeze coming in from the sea and realised it was getting late. He had a shift starting at eight in the bar so he'd need to get himself organised. But he had time for a quick walk on the beach so he locked the door of his little mobile home and headed down towards the sand.

He looked out at the clear blue sea as he walked and thought how Jack would have loved it here. A group of them used to go out to Dollymount Strand when they were teenagers and Jack would make them go into the freezing water and tell them to close their eyes and imagine they were on a tropical island. It had never worked – and they used to go almost blue with the cold – but Jack would laugh and say that they were all wimps. Will felt tears well up in his eyes as he thought of his friend.

The first anniversary of his death had just passed and Will had felt very lonely that day. He'd rung home and chatted to both his mum and dad and then spoke to Tessa, who'd been very down in the dumps. The poor girl hadn't picked herself up at all since her boyfriend's death and Will had felt slightly guilty for getting on with his life. But he also knew Jack would be happy if he saw him now. Maybe he did see him. Maybe he was looking at him now and saying: 'Good on ya, Will. You grew yourself a pair!' Will smiled at the thought and his good mood returned. He checked his watch and saw he just had half an hour to shower and be in work.

As he walked back towards his new home, he thought about his job back in Ireland. He remembered getting up to grey skies and going in every morning to a busy office with no windows. It was no wonder he hated that life. There was definitely something in the theory that sunlight improved the mood. The bar he worked in was bright and airy and had a whole section of tables outside. His boss, Brendan, was an easy-going sort and Will had clicked with him straight away. He'd often say to him: 'Hey, Will. You can work on the tables outside. You Irish need to get a bit of sun on your bones.' Brendan was a full-blown Aussie but married to an Irish girl. Will had yet to meet her but she sounded like a good laugh and Brendan was completely besotted with her.

He let himself in to his mobile home and threw his keys on the table. He quickly undressed and hopped into the tiny shower. As the water sluiced over his body, he thought about Laura and wondered how she was. He hoped she was okay. She'd been very upset at their break-up and he'd felt awful letting her down like that. But he knew she wasn't the right woman for him. He was a bit of a romantic really and felt that there was someone for everyone in the world. He knew that his soulmate was out there somewhere and he looked forward to meeting her one day. He still had some things he wanted to do with his life but one thing was for sure – his ultimate dream was to find love.

* * *

'Come on in, love,' said Jan, opening the door wide. 'I've put the kettle on and I have a batch of scones just out of the oven.'

Donna hugged the other woman tightly. 'Thanks, Jan. You're a life-saver. I just needed to get out of that house.'

Jan led the way into the kitchen where the heat from the stove and the waft of baking made it the most inviting place you could imagine. Not for the first time, Donna imagined what it would have been like to grow up in a house like this, with a mother like Jan. Her life would have been so much different to the one she lived now.

'Right, here we go.' Jan placed a teapot on the table, followed by a large plate of warm scones. 'Dig in and, when you're ready, you can tell me what happened.'

'Any of those spare for me?' Jan's son, Bob, appeared at the door, bringing a waft of pungent aftershave with him.

Jan smiled and Donna noticed how her face lit up at the sight of her son. 'When have you ever known me not to have enough cake? Come on, sit yourself down. There's plenty to go around.'

'Sorry, Ma. I've got to fly. I'm meeting the lads in town and I'm already late. I'll just take one of those on the run.' He reached over and grabbed one and flashed Donna a huge white smile. 'Hiya, Donna. I'm glad you're here. You might be able to stop Ma from baking any more. My stomach is expanding by the minute.'

Donna glanced at his washboard stomach that could be seen through his thin white T-shirt and involuntarily sucked her own in. 'You could never be fat, Bob. Just like your ma could never stop baking. Have a good night.'

'He's a pet, isn't he?' said Jan, when the front door had slammed behind her son. 'And he's so good to me and his dad.'

'You're very lucky with him alright,' Donna agreed. 'And I'm surprised he doesn't have a girlfriend, he's so handsome.'

Jan stared at Donna for a moment. 'Handsome? Do you think so? It's funny, I've never really thought about it before because of the age gap but four years isn't much really, when you think about it.'

'Four years for what?' Donna was confused.

'Between you two. There's a four-year age gap. Bob is twenty-seven.'

Realisation suddenly dawned on Donna. 'No way! You can get that out of your head once and for all.'

Jan's face dropped. 'What? What's wrong with him?'

'There's nothing wrong with him, Jan, but it's just … it's just …' She couldn't really think of an answer. Bob *was* gorgeous. He was polite, kind and he loved his mammy, which was always a good thing. But she'd honestly never thought of him in that way.

'Well?' Jan was still waiting for an answer.

'It's just he's more like a brother to me. And I'm sure he doesn't think of me in that way either.'

Jan sighed. 'It was just a thought. I'd love to see him settled and happy.'

'But he *is* settled and happy. He'll find someone one day but for now, it looks like he's perfectly happy to be here with you and Chris.'

'Thanks for saying that, love. You know he's the apple of my eye, that one. I'd do anything for him. Now enough about me and my family. Tell me what's been happening at home that made you want to get out.'

They chatted for a while in the kitchen before bringing a fresh pot of tea into the sitting room where Jan's husband, Chris, had lit a blazing fire. Chris was a lovely, quiet man and adored Jan. When he'd realised the two women were deep in conversation, he'd told them he was having an early night and they could have the sitting room to themselves. Bob was very lucky to have two such wonderful parents.

The time passed quickly as Donna poured her heart out to Jan. Jan was a brilliant listener and seemed to know when the time was right to give her opinion and when to just nod in agreement.

'No family is perfect, love. And I can tell you *that* from experience.'

Jan never spoke about her own family and Donna never asked, but now seemed like the right time. 'Whatever happened between you and your brother, Jan? I mean, tell me to mind my own business if you like, but you said you had just one brother, is that right?'

Jan nodded slowly. 'That's right, Donna love. We fell out years ago but it's a long story. I'll tell you about it some day but have you seen the time?'

Donna glanced at the clock on the mantelpiece and couldn't believe it was already after midnight. She felt bad for having monopolised the conversation all night but it was obvious that Jan didn't really want to talk about her own situation. She made a mental note to ask her about it again. Donna hoped she could be as good a listener as Jan was.

'You head off to bed, Jan. I'm sure your head is bursting from everything I've told you tonight.'

'Not at all, Donna love. I always enjoy our little chats. But you could probably do with a good sleep yourself. At least tomorrow is Sunday and neither of us has to work.'

'Thank God for that,' said Donna, yawning herself and realising that she was exhausted. 'And thanks so much for everything. You're a star.'

'The feeling is mutual.' Jan stretched and stood up from the deep armchair.

Just then, Donna's phone began to ring, startling both of them. She jumped up to grab it off the mantelpiece and looked at the display.

'It's Tina. That's strange for her to be ringing at this time.' She pressed the green button. 'Hi, Tina. What's up?'

It wasn't Tina. It was Detective Joseph Simpson ringing from Tina's phone. The words were all a blur. A house fire … her mother asleep with a cigarette … whole place filled with smoke … firefighters did all they could … no hope … dead … dead … dead …

The last thing Donna remembered was screaming, 'Noooooooooo,' as the world began to spin and she felt herself sliding downwards into oblivion. She needed to remove herself from the grim reality that was going to change the rest of her life.

Chapter 10

April 2010

Will hopped out of the shower and walked out into his little kitchen, allowing the heat in the air to dry his naked body. There was no need for modesty because there was nobody there to see him. He loved the freedom of living on his own – being the king of his castle, the master of his own destiny.

Things were going well for him in Perth. He'd given up the fruit picking and was now working full-time in the bar, which he loved. He still rented the little mobile home on the beach and had grown to think of it as home. Sometimes he couldn't believe he was still there, sixteen months after leaving Ireland. He'd been so sure he wouldn't settle anywhere for more than a couple of months but there was something about the city that made him want to stay.

He flicked the switch on the kettle to make a cup of tea. There were still two hours before he had to be at Brendan's for dinner so he might just sit outside and read for a bit. April was a lovely time of year because the stifling heat of the summer had passed and, although there was still heat in the air, there was a cooling breeze that came with it. It was funny to see the locals beginning to wrap up warmer in their long sleeves and ditching the shorts in favour of jeans. To Will, it was still warmer than any summer months in Ireland.

Stepping into his little bedroom, he caught sight of himself in the full-length mirror attached to his wardrobe. Not bad. He'd been working out on the beach every morning before going for a run and it was really beginning to show. He ran his hand over his tanned stomach and could definitely feel the beginnings of a six pack. He'd always been relatively fit but had never cared much about how toned his body was. But spending time on the beach and seeing tanned muscular surfers with their white blond hair blowing in the breeze had made him feel completely invisible and he'd vowed to do something about it.

He stepped into a pair of tight jersey Calvin Klein boxers and checked himself out again. Nice! He pulled a Diesel T-shirt over his head and slipped on a pair of cargo shorts and he was good to go. He'd enjoy an hour of the evening sun before heading out. Part of him was tempted to have a beer and just get a taxi tonight but he fancied taking the car so he made do with his cup of tea.

He and Brendan had become firm friends this last year and Will was really grateful to him for his friendship. Brendan had taken him out on a number of occasions to meet the lads and they'd enjoyed many good nights on the town. He'd met Brendan's wife a couple of times too but had never really got to have a proper chat with her. It was usually just a quick hello when he'd call to the house to pick Brendan up to go somewhere or in a noisy bar when Brendan would bring her out with them. Since she was Irish too, Will was looking forward to having a good chat with her over dinner. From what he'd seen of her so far, she was bubbly, sweet and a lot of fun.

He adjusted his chair outside to face the hazy sun and balanced his mug of tea on the arm. His mother had sent him over a supply of Barry's teabags and, he had to admit, he was really grateful for them. The tea over here wasn't a patch on the Irish tea and, once he'd had his first sip of Barry's, thoughts of home had filled his head.

His dad would be sixty soon but he wouldn't be home for it. He remembered that phone call back in November, when his mother asked what date he'd be home and he'd had to tell her that he was extending his visa for another year. 'But what about your job?' she'd cried. 'I was keeping it open for you for a year. And what will you do for money? That bar job couldn't be paying you much. And what about your daddy's birthday? How am I going to tell him his only son is going to miss his big sixtieth birthday?' Will knew his father wouldn't care whether he was there for his birthday or not. He didn't go much for the ceremony of birthdays. He said that it just reminded him he was getting old. But of course his mother would use every trick in the book to get Will to change his mind and come home.

But he'd remained firm in his resolve to stay away for two years. He knew he'd go home eventually but the time just wasn't right yet. Will was living with a constant belief that there was something missing from his life. He didn't know what it was, but he always believed that he'd know when he found it. Maybe it was a job, maybe it was a place or maybe it was the love of his life. It was just a feeling that his life was a puzzle and there was a piece missing. When his one year had been almost up, he'd known that it just wasn't enough. But he also knew now that he'd have to think out his next few months very carefully. Much as he loved Perth, he was going to have to see more of Australia before his second year ran out, because he'd always regret it if he didn't.

He checked his watch. Six o'clock. Maybe he'd just close his eyes for a bit. It wouldn't take him long to drive to Will's home in Joondalup, a lovely, vibrant cosmopolitan area twenty minutes from Perth city centre. If Will was ever going to settle in Perth, Joondalup would be one of the places he'd consider and he often felt a pang of envy when he'd drive up the street towards Brendan's lovely four-bed detached house. But then he'd tell himself off for thinking like that when settling down really wasn't an option for him at the moment.

Maybe some day, he mused, as he closed his eyes. Whenever all the pieces fit together.

* * *

'I've done it, Jan. I've booked the tickets. Can you believe it?'

'Ah, love, that's brilliant. I'm delighted for you. Really I am.' Jan wrapped her chubby arms around Donna and hugged her tightly. 'And you're doing the right thing, you know.'

'I know,' said Donna, hanging her coat up on a hook and walking with Jan into the bakery out back. 'It's taken me a while to realise that but it's what she'd want me to do.'

'Come on. This calls for a celebration. You go and stick the kettle on and I'll bring us in a couple of jam tarts. I'm just about to take them out of the oven.'

Donna headed into the little staff kitchen and filled the kettle with water. Yesterday had been full of mixed emotions. She'd been filled with trepidation about what she was about to do but once she'd bought the tickets she'd begun to get excited.

The last fourteen months had been hell for Donna. After the fire, she'd found it very hard to pick herself up. She'd spent most of her life trying not to hate her mother for the way she was, telling herself that it really wasn't her fault and that alcoholism was a disease. But in one night, one fateful night, her years of compassion had been thrown out the window when her mother had managed to destroy everything Donna loved. It was ironic. Usually people let go of hate after someone dies but, for Donna, it was really only after her mother's death that she felt she truly hated her.

Most of the house had escaped the flames but the smoke had seeped right through every air vent, every pipe and even the insulation in the walls. Every room had been filled with a disgusting black, sticky substance and the stench had been unbearable. Apparently they could make it as good as new again. Nothing had been structurally damaged so it was a case of months of intense cleaning. But Donna never wanted to set foot in the place again, other than to salvage as much of their personal stuff as she could. After staying with Jan for a few weeks, she'd decided to rent herself a little flat on Dorset Street. It was perfect. It was within walking distance of the city centre – and, more importantly, the bakery.

The switch of the kettle clicked and Donna jumped with fright. A shiver ran down her spine and she had to give herself a mental shake to try and focus on the future and not the past. She'd spent too long being angry and bitter but now she was going to do something productive.

She stood up and popped two teabags in the little yellow teapot. She slowly poured the boiling water in and gave it a little stir. As she carried it over to the table, she smiled to herself. The next year was going to be an adventure – not something she would have planned if circumstances were different, but she was going to embrace it, nonetheless.

When she'd collected their things from the smoke-damaged house, she'd spent all night sitting on Jan's little sofa going through boxes of stuff. Most of it had been junk but then she'd found it. It was a piece of paper covered in Tina's handwriting. It was the one she'd shown her that day at the kitchen table when she'd revealed her dream itinerary for the places she'd love to travel to. 'It's just a dream at the moment,' Tina had said that night. 'But one day I might make it happen.' So from that moment on, Donna had vowed to do it for her. It had taken her fourteen months to save the money and to pluck up the courage to do it, but she'd finally bought the tickets the previous evening.

'Here we go,' said Jan, placing a plate of steaming hot jam pies on the table. 'It's a new recipe so let me know what you think. My Bob made the jam, would you believe? A dab hand at it, he is.'

'Wow. He's a man of hidden talents. He'll make some woman very happy some day.'

Jan shook her head. 'I'm beginning to think I'm spoiling him too much at home. He might just stay with me forever. But anyway, enough about him. Tell me what your plans are.'

'Well, I'm not heading over until the end of August so I still have a few months left. I have bits and pieces to sort out but I'd still like to keep the job for as long as I can, if that's okay.'

'Of course it is, love. You hardly thought I was going to turf you out now, did you? So are you stopping off anywhere or heading straight over to Lexie?'

Donna took a sip of her tea. 'Straight to Lexie. I want to spend a bit of time with her first before I go travelling. I can't believe it's been three years since she's been home.'

'You must really miss her. Especially since … well, you know …'

'I really do. And I can't think of a better tonic than spending a few weeks with her.'

'It'll do you the world of good, Donna. Your life hasn't been much fun these last few years,' Jan said.

Donna nodded and all of a sudden, she felt tears well up in her eyes. 'You'll look after things here for me, Jan, won't you? I mean, you know, the visits and everything. I know it's a lot to ask of you but …'

'Of course I will, love.' Jan reached over and took her hand. 'You know you can rely on me.'

'I know I can, Jan. But I keep having doubts about whether or not I'm doing the right thing.'

'Listen, love, I want this to be the last time you doubt yourself. You're doing this for Tina. You love her and miss her and you can think of her fondly as you travel to all the places she wanted to see. It will be hard at times but it's the right thing to do.'

'You're right, Jan. I'm looking ahead to the future now. No more lingering on the past.' She wiped her tears and smiled at the other woman. But Donna knew that she could never really be rid of the past as pictures of her mother kept flooding her brain. Her mother. Catherine O'Neill. Catherine had never given her much when she was alive and even as she died she'd managed to take away the thing that Donna had loved more than anything else in the world. It was hard to forget that.

* * *

'Hiya, Will.' Brendan opened the door, looking relaxed and casual in swimming shorts and a tank top. 'We've decided to stick on the barbie rather than cooking inside. I hope that's okay with you?'

Will stepped inside and handed Brendan a bottle of red wine and a six pack of beer. 'That's perfect for me, thanks. It smells divine.'

'Well, it appears the wife is better at handling the snags than I am. Apparently I don't understand how to get them brown all over.'

Will grinned. 'Well, if she's willing to look after the cooking, you should take full advantage and crack open a beer.'

'Are you joking me?' Brendan laughed, shaking his head. 'She's given me the role as commis chef so I guess I'll actually be doing most of the work.'

Will felt relaxed and happy as he followed his friend out to the back garden. More than two years on from Jack's suicide, he was finally able to live his life again without feeling guilty. Jack had made his own choices and it wasn't Will's fault. He smiled as he stepped out into the sunshine and saw Brendan's wife looking flustered as she tried to juggle the numerous things on the barbeque.

'Maybe I should take over, love,' said Brendan, a victorious smile on his face. 'Why don't you sit down with Will and have a chat.'

'Hi, Will. Lovely to see you again.' She abandoned the barbeque to go and kiss Will on the cheek.

'Lovely to see you too, Lexie. I can't wait to have a proper chat with you at last.'

Chapter 11

'So tell me, Will.' Lexie leaned across the wooden patio table. 'How come a great catch like you is still single?'

Will laughed. 'It's not for the want of trying, Lexie. I've had a few dates with women over here but, for some reason, none of them seem to want to stick around.'

'Don't believe a bit of it,' said Brendan, refilling a plate with chicken wings from the barbie. 'He's the most eligible bachelor in town – they're queuing up for a piece of him.'

'I can imagine.' Lexie looked at him admiringly. 'The George Clooney of Perth!'

'I wish,' said Will, blushing. 'I can assure you, if the right girl came along, I'd be more than happy to have a relationship.'

Lexie's eyes twinkled. 'Well, maybe I can help you with that.'

'Lexie!' said Brendan, looking embarrassed. 'Don't throw yourself at our guest.'

'Don't be ridiculous, Brendan. I don't mean *me*. I'm talking about Donna.'

'Well, that's a relief.'

Lexie rolled her eyes and turned her attention to Will. 'I can't wait for you two to meet. You're going to love her.'

'So who's this, then?' Will didn't want anyone matchmaking for him but was curious all the same.

'She's my friend from back home. I haven't seen her since I went over for a visit three years ago and she's coming here to stay for a while in August.'

'I haven't met her myself,' said Brendan, chomping on a chicken wing. 'But she and Lexie grew up together and she sounds like a lovely girl. Cute too, if the pictures are anything to go by.'

Lexie was quick to agree. 'She's gorgeous and great fun. You two will get on brilliantly.'

'The thing is,' said Will, reluctant to disappoint Lexie but not wanting to string her along, 'I may not be around in August.'

Brendan was just about to take a bite out of a sausage but stopped to stare at Will. 'That's news to me. I thought your visa wasn't up until the end of the year.'

'It's not. But I never intended to stay in one place all this time. There are other places I want to see before my time is up.'

Lexie looked disappointed. 'But you've got a job and a home here. Why don't you at least wait until closer to the end of the year?'

'Lexie! Will isn't going to stay around just so you can matchmake.' Brendan turned to Will. 'When are you thinking of heading off, mate? We'll miss you but it really would be a shame if you spent all of your two years here in Perth and didn't get to experience anywhere else.'

'I know. But Lexie is right. I'm pretty settled here at the moment so I may not head off for another few months. There might be time to meet this friend of yours yet.'

Lexie beamed. 'Fantastic. She's ringing me later so I'll tell her about you. She's desperate to find a man so she'll be thrilled.'

'Oh, thanks for that,' said Will, feigning a look of disgust. 'So I'm only fit for someone who's desperate?'

'Oh, God, I didn't mean … I wasn't saying …'

Will laughed. 'I'm only having you on. I'd love to meet your friend.

She sounds like a lovely girl. But I hope we don't get on too well because I'll definitely be moving on before the end of the year.'

'Well, we'll cross that bridge when we come to it.' Lexie winked at Will. 'Now come on, let's go inside. I've got goose bumps all over my legs.'

'Actually, I might call it a night,' said Will, seizing the opportunity to leave. 'I've been getting up early all week to run on the beach and, as a result, I can't seem to stay awake past ten at night.'

'I thought you Irish were party animals,' said Brendan, looking from his wife to Will. 'Lexie here is the same – come ten o'clock and I'm trying to peel her off the sofa!'

Lexie gave him a friendly slap. 'It's okay for you. Your job means you're usually on late shifts so don't have to be up early. I'm up at five most mornings.'

Will nodded. 'The early mornings are definitely a killer. You work at the hospital, don't you?'

'Yep.' Lexie's face lit up. 'I'm just the breakfast lady – but I adore my job.'

'Don't say you're "just" anything,' Will chastised. 'Your job is as important as anyone else's.'

'Ah, you're very good for saying that but I have no illusions about it. I never bothered going to college so I'm trained to do nothing.'

Brendan joined in. 'Will is right, love. Those patients would go hungry if it wasn't for you. So in a way, just like the doctors, you keep them alive.'

Lexie roared laughing. 'I'll tell the bosses that in the morning so. I wonder if they'd consider paying me as much as they pay those doctors. Wouldn't that be lovely?'

'But seriously,' continued Will, 'don't you hate the whole class thing? How people are judged on what job they do? When I'm out and I tell women I'm a lawyer, their eyes often light up and they ask me loads of questions. When I say I'm a barman, they often lose interest very quickly.'

'I'm doomed so,' said Brendan, shaking his head. 'I can't imagine I'll ever be any more than a lowly barman.'

'Hey!' Lexie reached across and flung her arm around him. 'You're taken, so what does it matter? And you're no lowly barman anyway. You're the sexiest, most intelligent, kindest barman I know.'

'Thanks, love.' Brendan leaned in for a kiss and Will took that as his opportunity to leave.

'Right, on that note, I'll love you and leave you. Thanks for a fantastic evening. I'll have to return the favour soon, although it will be a bit of a squeeze at my place.'

Brendan stood up. 'No problem, mate. Glad you had a good night. See you tomorrow night?'

'Yep. I'm in at seven so I'll see you then.'

The three of them walked through the house to the front driveway where Will had parked his car. The breeze had picked up and it had become quite chilly, despite the lovely sunny weather earlier.

'It was lovely to see you again, Lexie,' said Will, leaning across to plant a kiss on her cheek.

'You too, Will. We'll have to do it more often.'

Will jumped into his car and reversed out the driveway, waving them back inside as he did so. He'd really enjoyed the night but being with Brendan and Lexie tonight had made him feel lonely. They were the perfect couple. They had a laugh at each other's expense and yet it was clear that they adored each other. It must be brilliant to feel settled in the world – to know you were where you were supposed to be.

He pulled the car up beside his mobile home and stepped out onto the dewy grass. He could feel frogs jump at his feet and he smiled to himself. Frogs were just part of everyday life here and hundreds of them could be found jumping around after dark on the campsite.

He imagined his mother's face if she even saw one anywhere near her house. Life was so different here.

He let himself inside and locked the door behind him. Now that he was home, he might just have one beer before hitting the sack. He grabbed one out of the fridge, sank into the little sofa and flicked on the telly. He didn't watch it much but it was company sometimes. His mind wandered to his conversation with Lexie earlier and this friend who was coming over. It might be a bit of fun to go out on a few double dates and get to know her. He was sick of meeting girls in the bar or on the beach and having no connection with them. Maybe this girl would be more interesting – especially since she was Irish. Well, he'd just have to wait and see. And anyway, August was four months away and anything could happen between now and then. If there was one thing he'd learned over the last few years, it was that life could be very unpredictable.

* * *

'Hiya, Lexie. It's not too late, is it?' Donna had just got home from work. It was only 5 p.m. in Ireland but she was aware it was midnight in Perth. She wouldn't normally ring so late because she knew Lexie went to bed early but she'd promised her she'd ring tonight.

'It's fine,' said Lexie, in a sleepy voice. 'Brendan has gone to bed but I was waiting up for your call.'

'God, I'm sorry. We can chat tomorrow if you'd prefer.'

'Don't be daft. I'm dying for a chat. So, did you get the tickets sorted?'

'Yep! All booked. Can you believe it?'

'Oh my God! After all these years. I can't believe you're finally coming over to see me. I actually cannot wait!'

'Me neither.' And Donna meant it. The thought of seeing her

friend again and being able to spend precious time with her was the only thing she could think of at the moment.

'Right, you'll have to email me all the travel details and I'll make sure I'm at the airport to collect you. We're going to have a ball. And I might even have a man for you.'

Donna felt alarm bells ringing. 'What do you mean? You'd better not be matchmaking or I'll cancel those tickets tomorrow.'

'Relax, will you, Donna? There's just this guy …'

'Lexie!'

'Let me finish before you start jumping to conclusions. He's a friend of Brendan's and a really nice guy. I just thought it might be nice if the four of us went out some time. I mentioned you to him and he was all on for it.'

Donna sighed. 'I'm happy to meet your friends, Lexie. But I'm not going over there for romance.'

'Okay, okay. But maybe you'll change your mind when you meet him.'

Donna couldn't help laughing at her friend's determination. They chatted amicably for the next half hour about everything. Donna felt as though Lexie was sitting there beside her on the sofa. Even the distance hadn't made things awkward between them. They'd been friends all their lives and had remained in constant touch from the day Lexie had got on that plane to a new life.

Donna suddenly felt light-headed and realised she hadn't eaten since breakfast. It had been so busy in the bakery today that she'd barely taken a break at all. 'Sorry, Lexie, I'm going to have to go. My stomach thinks my throat's been cut. I'll email my itinerary over to you later so you can have a look at it tomorrow.'

'Great,' said Lexie, and Donna could almost picture her smile. 'I'm ready to fall into bed so I'll say goodbye and I'll give you a buzz in a few days.'

'Night Lexie. And for once I can actually say, "See you soon!"'

Donna pottered into her little kitchen to see what was in the fridge. Thankfully there was a bit of roast beef left from yesterday's dinner so she'd make a sandwich with that. She was due back out in an hour so she'd just about have time to eat and shower before she left. It was the story of her life – work, home for a quick wash and bite to eat, and then back out again. She'd fall into bed exhausted most nights. Her evening visits were really taking a toll and she knew she'd have to cut back. What was the point in her going every night anyway when nothing changed? She felt tears prick her eyes and she blinked them away quickly. Feeling sorry for herself wasn't going to get her anywhere so she'd just have to get on with it. And, really, she had a lot to be grateful for.

As she poured boiling water into her mug, the negative thoughts disappeared and she began to feel almost happy. Bubbles of excitement rose in her stomach. She was going to Australia. She was actually going to do it. It had never been in her life plan but it had been in Tina's, so she was going to make sure she did it for her.

Chapter 12

13 August 2010

'Happy birthday to you, happy birthday to you, happy birthday, dear Donna, happy birthday to you.'

Donna flushed as a magnificent cake was put in front of her. She hadn't expected *that!* It was Friday and her last day in the bakery because she was flying out to Perth the very next day. She hadn't planned on celebrating her twenty-fifth birthday but Jan wasn't one for letting a day like that pass.

'Go on, love,' said Jan, a huge smile on her face. 'Make a wish – and make it a good one.'

Donna closed her eyes tightly. There was only one wish she wanted to come true and she said it again and again in her head as she blew out the candles. There were cheers and then shouts for her to cut the cake and pass it around.

'You're so good to organise this, Jan,' she said, when everyone had gone back to their stations and she was left with the older woman in the little kitchen. 'I haven't been much of a fan of birthday celebrations these last few years.'

Jan patted her hand gently. 'I know, love. You've had it tough. But

I couldn't let you head off to the other side of the world without at least a little fuss. If it hadn't been a birthday cake, it would have been a farewell cake.'

Donna stuffed another mouthful of the chocolatey sponge into her mouth and closed her eyes as she allowed her tongue to have the full chocolate experience. It was one of the first things Jan had taught her. If you shut off some of your senses, the remaining ones are more powerful. She'd learned that taste is a lot more intense if you close your eyes.

'Well, is it okay?'

'Okay?' said Donna, wiping her mouth. 'It's absolutely divine. You're such an amazing baker, Jan. I wish I could bake as well as this.'

'Ah, thanks, Donna love. But you're a far better baker now than I was at your age. I just hope and pray that you'll come back to it after your travels and let us develop that talent of yours further.'

'Of course I will. You know I won't stay away for too long. This is where I belong.'

Jan nodded and picked at her piece of cake and Donna realised with a start that the older woman was crying.

'God, Jan, what's up? It's not like you to get upset.'

'Don't mind me, love,' she said, grabbing a piece of kitchen roll from the table and blowing her nose. 'It's just the thought of not seeing you for so long. You're like …' Her words trailed off and she bowed her head.

'I'm like what?'

'I was going to say you're like a daughter to me but I didn't want you to think it was any disrespect to your own mother.'

Donna bristled. 'How could you be disrespecting her? She was never a real mother to me and, if I'm honest, I've spent the last number of years wishing I'd grown up with *you* as my mother.'

The words hung in the air for a moment until Jan broke the silence by sobbing. Great big heaving sobs. Donna was startled and jumped up and knelt down beside her. They hugged for what seemed like ages until Donna pulled away and looked at the other woman.

'What is it, Jan? This feels like more than me just going away. Is there something else? It's not you and Chris, is it?'

Jan took a deep breath and dried her tears. 'No, of course not. Sure don't you know that me and that fella were made for each other. Barely a cross word in thirty-eight years.'

'That's a long time alright,' Donna mused. 'But what has you so upset, then?'

'I had a little girl once. Abigail.' Her eyes glazed over again and Donna was almost afraid to breathe. 'Never took a breath in this world. But she was perfect. Ten little fingers and toes and the most beautiful little rosebud mouth you've ever seen.'

'Oh, Jan.' Tears pricked Donna's eyes. 'You had a stillborn baby? I never knew. That must have been horrific.'

'It was, love. She would have been thirty next month. Can you believe it? Thirty years old and not one of her birthdays has gone past without me making a cake and sticking the relevant number of candles on it.'

'So she would have been your firstborn?' Donna sat back down but kept a firm hold of Jan's hand.

'She was. I had Bob two years later and I'd somehow thought that having him might dull the pain but it didn't. The only thing that helps is time – the pain never goes away but it becomes more manageable in time.'

Donna nodded, thinking of her own situation. She'd definitely agree with the time thing. She still felt devastated and cheated about the fire but, bit by bit, she was managing to piece her life back together and each day was becoming a little easier.

Jan's hand flew to her mouth suddenly. 'Jesus, Donna. I'm so sorry. I wasn't thinking. Here's me going on about something that happened thirty years ago and you're still in the early days of loss.'

'Don't worry, Jan. I think losing a child must be one of the worst things a person can experience. I'm so sorry you went through that.'

'Thanks, love. As I said, it was a long time ago but sometimes I can't help looking at you and wondering if she'd have turned out just as wonderful.'

'Stop, Jan, will you? I'll be a blubbering mess in a minute.'

'Look, Donna. I just want you to know that I'm here for you. You know I'm going to take care of things while you're gone away, but if you ever want to talk or cry or just hear a voice from home, I'll be on the other end of the phone.'

Donna nodded. Sometimes there just weren't words. It was good to know there was somebody who cared so much about her. God only knows how lonely she'd felt for most of her life and especially in the last few years. But Jan, as she said herself, was like a mother to her and having a mother was something she had very little experience of.

'Come on,' said Jan, standing up. 'It's your last day so you'd better make it count. There's a vanilla sponge there ready to be iced for a birthday. All the details are in the notebook.'

Donna stood up too. 'Yes, boss. I'll get right to it.' She felt a little sad to be finishing the job she loved today but as soon as she started mixing the icing to decorate the cake, her heart soared. This was where she felt happiest. This was what made her feel alive. She was looking forward to her trip but she had no doubts that, when it was over, she was going to be right back here doing what she loved. For the first time in her life, she felt like she belonged.

* * *

Will looked around at the half-empty bar and, for the first time in a long time, he felt a little pang of loneliness. There wasn't a lot he missed about his life in Ireland, but one thing he did miss was the nightlife. Dublin city centre would be heaving at this time on a

Friday night and it would be impossible to get a seat in any pub in the capital. There were a lot of things he loved about Perth but it just didn't compare to his hometown when it came to partying.

'Here we go,' said Brendan, placing a tray of drinks on the table. 'Drink up, birthday boy. It's not every day you reach a quarter of a century.'

'Thanks for reminding me.' Will smiled and took a slug from his bottle of beer. 'Twenty-five years old and still aimlessly wandering.'

'It's not a bad thing, mate. Look at me – I'm not much older than you and I've never really had a chance to wander. Take it while you can.'

Will stared at Brendan. 'What are you talking about? I thought you and Lexie were rock solid. I thought wandering would be the last thing on your mind.'

Brendan lowered his voice so as the other friends around the table wouldn't hear. 'I do love her, Will. She's gorgeous and funny and, well, she's pretty much perfect.'

'But …?'

'But I just wish I'd done a bit more before I settled down. It feels like we've been married for a lifetime and now she's talking about having kids.'

'And is that not what you want?' Will was shocked by his friend's revelations. He'd envied Brendan and Lexie's relationship. They always seemed so together and in love and it was something Will aspired to.

'I've never wanted kids, to be honest. I made that clear to Lexie right from the start and she told me back then that she felt the same. But now she's going on about biological clocks and how women have inbuilt clucky genes.'

'You'll sort it out, though, won't you? I mean, maybe in a few years' time you'll feel differently about kids.'

Brendan took a few long gulps of his beer and shook his head. 'I honestly don't think so. I've never felt a want or need to have kids in my life. In fact, I can't think of anything worse. Does that make me a monster?'

'Of course not.'

'Well, that's what she says. She says it's unnatural to feel that way.'

'But you love her still, right?'

'I really do,' said Brendan, his eyes misting up a little. Will wasn't sure whether it was from genuine emotion or the five beers he'd downed.

'Well, then you'll get over it. You'll work it out.'

Brendan bristled suddenly. 'Shush. Don't say a thing. Here she comes.'

Will looked up and saw Lexie appearing from a door. She'd said she was going to powder her nose but that had obviously been a lie. She was holding a birthday cake with sparkling candles on the top and suddenly all Will's friends broke into a chorus of 'Happy Birthday'.

'Thanks, everyone,' said Will, after he'd blown out the candles and was busy cutting up the cake. 'I really didn't expect that.'

'It was all Lexie's idea.' Brendan nodded towards his wife and Will noted the admiration in his eyes. All wasn't lost yet.

'Well, thank you, Lexie. You're very good. And this cake looks delicious.'

'No problem, Will. Mine is next month so I'll be expecting the same.'

Will raised his eyebrows. 'I think you know full well I'll have moved on by then. In fact I'd be gone by now if it wasn't for you bullying me into meeting this friend of yours.'

'How very dare you, Will.' Lexie pretended to slap him across the face. 'I didn't bully you – I just suggested, enticed, encouraged. I'm telling you, when she arrives on Sunday, you'll be thanking me.'

'Hmm! We'll just have to wait and see.' But Will was feeling excited about it. Something was telling him that he and this girl were going to hit it off and he was really looking forward to meeting her.

'A penny for them.'

'What?' Will looked blankly at Lexie.

'Your thoughts. A penny for them. You were miles away.'

'Sorry about that,' laughed Will. 'I was actually thinking about your friend.'

'Were you now?' Lexie's eyes twinkled. 'And fancy you two having birthdays on the same day. I'm telling you – it's written in the stars.'

Will laughed. 'You don't believe all of that mumbo jumbo stuff, do you? About signs and destiny and—'

Will's phone rang suddenly in his pocket, startling them both. He whipped it out and was surprised to see his mother's mobile number showing on the screen. He'd already spoken to both his parents earlier so it was strange she was ringing again. He headed for the door so he could talk outside with no noise disturbing him.

'Hello, Mum. I didn't expect to hear from you again so s—. What?' Will listened in silence as the happiness he'd felt all night crumbled down around him.

Chapter 13

'Oh my God, you look amazing, Lexie.' Donna hugged her friend tightly, baggage abandoned at their feet. 'I can't believe I'm here. I honestly can't take it in.'

'It's brilliant to see you,' said Lexie, wiping a tear from her eye. 'It's about bloody time you came over to us.'

'And you must be Brendan.' Donna extended a hand to the man standing beside her friend but he wasn't having any of it.

'Come here. You don't think you're getting away with shaking my hand when my wife got a hug like that.'

Donna grinned and happily accepted a hug. She was so relieved. It had been her one dread that she wouldn't like Lexie's husband but from what she saw already, he was a lovely guy. She let herself relax as they walked out to the car park and blinked as the afternoon sun hit her face.

'Gosh, the heat is unreal,' she said, rooting in her bag for her sunglasses. 'I've never felt anything like it.'

Brendan shook his head. 'Well, then you haven't lived. This is actually chilly, to be honest. You'd want to feel the heat in the summer.'

'Oh, I'd forgotten this is your winter. It just shows how bad our weather is over in Ireland.'

'Right, here we are.' Brendan stopped the trolley beside his car and lifted the large rucksack and smaller wheelie case into the boot. 'You travel light.'

Donna nodded as they got into the car. 'I didn't think there was much point taking a lot of stuff since I'll be doing some travelling and I'll be back home in a few months anyway.'

'But I thought all you women needed at least ten pairs of heels to survive.'

'Not Donna,' said Lexie, grinning. 'I don't think I've ever seen her in a pair of high shoes in her life.'

Donna laughed. 'That's true. I'm more of a Converse sort of girl.'

'What?' Brendan's mouth gaped open and glanced around at Donna as they moved off. 'A woman who doesn't wear heels? Now that's a first.'

Donna sat back and looked out the window as they drove out of the airport. Lexie had said it was only a thirty-minute drive so she was already looking forward to seeing where her friend lived and to having a proper cup of tea with real milk instead of those little artificial milk things they gave you on the plane.

The whole experience of flying had been completely new to her. She hadn't been scared like she'd expected but had found the flight long and boring. She'd spent a lot of the time just thinking about things and it had made her realise that she never afforded herself time to reflect. But the eleven-hour flight to Singapore and the further five hour one to Perth had given her time to think about the last few years and about what she wanted for the future.

'Here we are,' said Brendan, pulling up into a driveway. 'Did you enjoy your little sleep?'

'I didn't … I wasn't …'

Lexie laughed. 'You were fast asleep, Donna. There was even a bit of snoring and a grunt or two.'

'Oh God, I'm sorry. I must have dropped off.'

Brendan hopped out of the car and opened the door for her. 'Don't worry. You've had a long day and jetlag is a terrible thing. It will take you a few days to adjust.'

'Come on,' said Lexie, rushing up to the front door. 'Brendan will get the luggage. Let's go inside and put the kettle on.'

Ten minutes later they were sitting outside on the patio, drinking tea and eating cake. Lexie had offered to make Donna a sandwich but she wasn't really feeling hungry.

'Sorry it's not up to your standards.' Lexie nodded towards the shop-bought sponge cake. 'I thought about trying to make one but I'd only show myself up. Baking isn't my thing.'

'Don't be silly. This is delicious.' But Lexie was right. Donna couldn't help comparing every cake she ate to her own efforts. This one was too dry – probably overcooked – and the orange flavour was artificial, as though they'd used essence rather than natural flavours. 'And to be honest, all I really want to do now is sleep. I was going to try and not go to bed until later tonight because I read that it was the best way to combat jetlag, but if I don't close my eyes for even an hour, I'll be fit for nothing later.'

'Lexie will bring you up,' said Brendan, swallowing a mouthful of tea. 'I've left your stuff in the spare room and the bed is all made up and ready for you.'

Donna was grateful. 'Thanks. I really appreciate that. I'll set my alarm to wake me up in a couple of hours.'

'Take whatever time you need.' Lexie smiled warmly at her. 'We might just stick the barbeque on later and have a quiet one. There'll be plenty of time for you to meet everyone over the coming weeks.'

'That sounds great.' Donna didn't even bother undressing when Lexie left the room but instead slipped between the crisp white sheets. As she drifted off to sleep, she thought about Tina and imagined how she'd have felt earlier stepping off that plane. It had been her dream. Donna felt a pang of sadness but she wasn't going to let it take over.

She was going to do all the things her sister had dreamed of and just hope it would make a difference.

'This is for you, Tina O'Neill,' she whispered to herself before she fell into a deep, relaxed sleep.

* * *

'Mum! I got here as quick as I could. How is he?' It had been a fraught couple of days since Will had got his mum's phone call to say his dad had been taken to hospital after suffering a massive heart attack. He'd packed his stuff and gone straight to the airport to catch the first flight home.

'Hello, William.' His mum stood up and kissed him on the cheek before falling back into the plastic hospital chair. 'He's comfortable at the moment.'

'You look awful, Mum. Have you been here since he was brought in? Have you not had any rest?'

Vivienne Cooper-Smith paused and then cleared her throat before speaking. Will couldn't help feeling slightly irritated. Even when she was with her family, she acted as though she was about to talk to a client.

'I've been back and forth,' she said, not looking at him. 'I went home to get some bits and pieces for your daddy and I managed to grab a few hours' sleep too.'

Will sat down on the seat beside her in the family room. 'And is he conscious? I mean, what sort of a state is he in? Can I see him? Are they telling you anything?'

Vivienne clicked her tongue as if agitated. 'Get a hold of yourself, William. One question at a time.'

'Sorry, Mum. I'm just anxious. It's been a long flight and I'm out of my mind with exhaustion and with worry.'

She looked at him then and patted his hand awkwardly. 'I'm sure you must be, love. Come on. I'll take you in to him.'

'But don't we have to ask? Is he in intensive care?'

'No, he's in a ward. Come on and see for yourself.'

Will was dreading seeing his father looking helpless. He'd been talking to a girl in the seat beside him on the flight and she'd warned him about a few things. She was a nurse and said that when people had that sort of trauma, it could put years on them and the families often got upset when they saw how frail and vulnerable their loved ones looked.

'William! How lovely to see you. I couldn't believe it when your mum said you were coming.'

Will's eyes almost popped out of his head when he saw his father sitting up in the bed, reading *The Irish Times*. 'Dad! I thought you were at death's door. I'm delighted you're looking so well but Mum told me you were on your death bed.'

His mother reddened as they both looked at her. 'Well, I hardly said he was on his death bed. Don't exaggerate, dear.'

'But you said it was really serious – that he could die any minute.'

'Vivienne!' Will's dad looked shocked. 'How could you tell the lad that? Why would you say such a thing?'

'Well, it could have been true. I … I was upset when they brought you in. And when they said it was a heart attack, I panicked.'

'Mum, you could have rung me back. You could have put my mind at ease. Do you realise the hell I went through travelling for twenty hours and not knowing if Dad was alive or dead?'

'I'm really sorry, son,' said George, glaring at his wife. 'If I'd known, I never would have let her tell you that. You've had a wasted journey, I'm afraid. I'm not going to pop my clogs just yet.'

'Well, you might, you don't know that.' Vivienne was grasping at straws and Will felt disgusted.

'It's not a wasted journey, Dad,' said Will generously. 'I get to see you, don't I? And I'm really glad you're not on your death bed.'

George grinned. 'Me too. Now why don't you go off home and get some rest. They're saying they might let me home tomorrow so we'll be able to have a proper catch-up then.'

'Tomorrow?' Will was amazed. He'd braced himself for the worst and there was his dad, looking healthier than he'd seen him in a long time.

'Yes. It was just a mild heart attack – more a warning than anything.'

'Come on, William,' said his mother, standing up. 'We'll get you home and settled and we can check in on your dad after you get some rest.'

Will couldn't argue with that because he was exhausted. He said goodbye to his dad and let his mother lead the way to her car. He didn't want to argue with her but he was finding it hard to bite his tongue. How could she have deceived him like that? Did she not consider his feelings and how he'd be fretting for the whole journey home? Sometimes he really wondered if his mother loved him at all.

'So why did you do it, Mum?' They were on the M50 heading home. 'Why did you tell me things were so serious when you knew Dad was going to be fine?'

'Well, I didn't know that at the time, love. And I just felt so alone. Your daddy was gone for tests and all I could think about was having you here with me.'

Will glanced at her and, for the first time ever, he saw vulnerability. His tone softened. 'It's nice you wanted me here, Mum, but to get me home under false pretences …'

'I know, love, and I'm sorry. I know I should have rung you back but when I made that call I really was worried about him. I know I don't always show it, but I really love him, you know.'

They were already home and Will reached out and touched his mother's hand as she turned off the ignition. 'I know you do. And

I love him too. That's why what you did was so terrible. I've had a horrible couple of days.'

'I'm sorry,' she said, looking down at her hands. 'It's just that … it's just …'

To Will's alarm, big fat tears began to stream down his mother's cheeks. He'd never seen her cry before.

'What is it, Mum?' He didn't put his arm around her because he was still upset but he spoke to her in kinder tones.

Vivienne sniffed. 'Oh, William. I missed you so much when you were over in Australia. I couldn't bear not having you around. I know I went about it the wrong way, but I just wanted you home.'

'Well, I'm home now but it won't be for long, so let's make the best of the time we have.'

Part of Will understood why his mother had done it and he even felt a bit sorry for her, but as he stepped inside the house, he didn't feel all warm and fuzzy, remembering happy times. He didn't let the scents of home waft over him and make him feel like he belonged. Instead, he just felt sad. His mother had manipulated him – just like she'd done all his life. Maybe if he'd come home under his own steam, things would be different but, right now, the house just felt like a symbol of everything that made him want to leave in the first place.

'Now, I've freshened up your bedclothes and left some clean pyjamas on the bed.' There was no sign of his mother's earlier vulnerability. 'You go on up and unpack your stuff and I'll make us something to eat.'

'I won't be unpacking, Mum.' Will knew that if he didn't stand up to her now, he was running the risk of falling into old habits.

'Well, if you're tired, you can leave it until later. There's no hurry.' Vivienne led the way into the kitchen, where she filled the kettle with water.

'No, Mum,' said Will, following her in and sitting down on one of the kitchen chairs. 'I won't be unpacking because I'm not staying.'

Her face fell and she looked close to tears again. This time Will went to her and wrapped her in a hug. 'I'll stay around until I know for sure that Dad is okay but then I'll be heading back to Australia.'

'Do you really have to?'

'Yes, Mum. I do. It's what I want, what I planned. I'm going to travel around Australia for a couple of months and then go to New Zealand and America.'

'But William—'

'Don't, Mum.' He wasn't going to let her manipulate him. 'I just have four months left on my visa so I'll be home again before you know it.'

She nodded in resignation and Will knew it would be a good place to leave the conversation. 'Actually, I am feeling a bit tired. Maybe I'll head up and get some sleep and we can go and see Dad together later.'

He kissed her briefly on the cheek and got out of there before she said any more. He didn't waste any time in stripping and slipping into his childhood bed. He was exhausted. He wondered what everyone was up to in Perth. It had been a whirlwind since his party and he'd barely had a chance to say goodbye to anyone. His mind flicked briefly to the girl Lexie was trying to set him up with. It was funny to think that now he was here in Ireland and she was in Australia. Life was just so full of twists and turns.

Just before he fell asleep, he reached into his rucksack beside the bed and pulled out his childhood teddy, Cookie. He stared at him and realised that his other eye was beginning to fall out too. Twenty-five years Cookie had been his companion. He was looking the worse for wear but Will loved him that way. He knew it wasn't cool for a man his age to have a teddy but somehow it was a comfort to have him there. He was his good luck charm. He'd got him through a lot in his life and hopefully he'd continue to bring him luck in the future.

Chapter 14

November 2010

Will lay back on the golden sand and closed his eyes. It was an absolutely scorching day and he could already feel the sun burning his chest, even after he'd put factor fifty on. He'd driven to this beach a few days ago and, even though he hadn't planned on stopping, the place had literally taken his breath away and he'd pitched his tent on the campsite right beside it.

He'd come back to Australia in September, after spending a few fraught weeks at home. When he'd discovered his mother had lied to lure him back home, he'd felt really bitter and he would have turned right around and gone back, except for the fact that his dad actually *was* sick. Maybe he would have gone home anyway if his mother had told him the truth. Maybe he'd have wanted to see his dad and make sure for himself that he was okay. But he'd never know because his mother had manipulated the situation, as usual.

The weeks at home hadn't been pleasant. His mother had tried every trick to get him to stay, and when none of them worked, she'd turned on the tears. Will wasn't used to seeing his mother cry and it had startled him, but it hadn't taken him long to realise that it was just another ploy for her to get her own way. Part of him felt sorry for her. All she was really guilty of was doing everything she could to get her only son home. But on the other hand, she hadn't been fair on him and he was finding it hard to forget that.

The beach was beginning to get a bit crowded and Will sat up to have a look around. The almost white sand was glistening in the sun and the still water was like a mirror. The whole area was an oasis of calm and, at that moment, Will felt like he could stay there forever. He reapplied suncream to his face and body and lay back down.

When he was going back to Perth after his few weeks in Dublin, he'd initially thought he'd go back to the same place, the same life he'd lived for almost two years. But he realised that if he did that, the chances were he'd never move on and wouldn't get to see any of the rest of Australia. So he didn't tell his friends he was going back but instead he decided to do his own thing. When he'd arrived back in Perth, he'd stayed in a motel for a few days, during which time he bought a twenty-year-old Ford Escort Estate and a one-man tent, before heading off on his travels.

His plan was to drive up along the west coast as far as Darwin and then drive back down the east coast, taking in the rainforest and the Gold Coast, until he reached Sydney. But he'd driven down south first to Margaret River, a wine region a few hundred kilometres from Perth. He'd really enjoyed it there. The temperature had felt a little cooler and there'd been plenty so see, including the fabulous Mammoth Cave, which was one of the most amazing things he'd ever seen.

He was now in Monkey Mia, a beach nine hundred kilometres north of Perth. It was funny how kilometres didn't mean as much here as they did back home. In Ireland, two hundred kilometres is considered to be a huge distance, requiring a number of stops and a packed lunch, whereas here you could drive for five hundred kilometres without seeing a single soul, stop for a rest and drive another five hundred without batting an eyelid.

He suddenly heard a commotion down at the water and sat up to see what was happening. A crowd had gathered at the edge of the shore and Will's first thought was that somebody had gotten into trouble in the sea. But then when he heard the excited chatter, he realised it must be the dolphins coming in to greet the beach-goers. He'd read about it but hadn't really thought he'd be lucky enough to see it. He jumped to his feet and headed down to join the crowd.

He'd never seen anything like it. It was amazing. A school of dolphins were right there in the shallow water and were happily swimming around the legs of the delighted holiday-makers. He was even able to reach down and touch them and it felt like one of the most powerful moments of his life. He'd seen dolphins in captivity, dolphins that had been trained to entertain crowds of people at water parks. But this was different. These dolphins lived in the wild and came to this shore of their own free will. He envied them as he watched their majestic bodies twist and turn in the water. It was almost as though they were smiling. And why wouldn't they be? They could choose whether to come to shore or stay away. They could be alone and yet they had each other. They were free to live the life they wanted.

Just then, as the magnificent animals began to disperse, Will noticed a girl in the crowd. She seemed to be on her own as she just stood and watched the dolphins swim back out to sea. He felt drawn to her somehow. Maybe it was just that they were both alone in a crowd that seemed to be chatting excitedly all around them. It was a long time since he'd been with a woman. Ages since he'd felt the warmth of a woman's touch. She looked at him then and their eyes met. It was as though everyone else melted into the background and there was just the two of them standing at the water's edge. He knew at that moment that their lives were going to be linked in some way. Without further thought, he walked across to where she was standing.

'Hi there. Amazing sight, isn't it?'

'Unbelievable. It's the best thing I've ever seen.'

She was beautiful. 'So are you just passing through?'

'Yes, I'm doing a bit of travelling. You?'

'Same here. Do you fancy grabbing a bite to eat?'

'I'd love to.'

'Great.' They walked up onto the golden sand. 'Will is my name. It's lovely to meet you.'

* * *

Donna felt tears running down her cheeks as she stood in the water, the dolphins lapping around her feet. Ever since Lexie had sent that postcard of Monkey Mia some years ago, Tina had said that it was her number one place to visit. She'd googled the place and had squealed with excitement as she showed Donna the pictures of the dolphins swimming around in the clear sea. And now she was here – without Tina – and it was bittersweet.

There were crowds of people standing knee-deep in the water, the dolphins swimming animatedly around them. Nobody dared make any sudden movements and the silence echoed the respect everybody had for the magnificent creatures. There'd been initial shrieks of delight when they'd been spotted coming to shore but, after that, everyone seemed to know instinctively not to startle them or scare them away.

She moved back to the sand and sat down, her feet just touching the lapping waves. Closing her eyes, she pictured Tina sitting there beside her, her face lit up in awe at everything she was seeing. Her sister would have adored this place. And so would Jan. Donna smiled to herself and made a mental note to buy some postcards later and send them on to Jan. She'd made a promise that she'd send one from every place she visited.

Thinking of Tina made her feel lonely but, in a way, she was happy to be travelling alone. She'd had a lovely few months with Lexie but had begun to feel a little stifled. She'd been dying to move on but Lexie had begged her to stay a bit longer. Donna suspected that if Lexie hadn't been married, she'd have packed her own bags to join Donna on her travels.

It had been lovely to spend time with her old friend again. And she was glad to have gotten to know Brendan. He was a good guy and Lexie seemed really happy with him. Her life had changed completely when she'd left Dublin in 2004. She'd gone from being a troubled teenager, unsettled and unhappy, to marrying a man she loved and doing a job she adored. Lexie had had a troubled upbringing too but she'd always been so determined and headstrong that Donna had never had a doubt that she'd turn her life around as soon as she was old enough. Donna envied her. Her life was sorted whereas Donna still felt lost. She knew she was happy doing her job in the bakery in Dublin, but there was just something missing from her life. She hoped that she'd find out what it was while she was travelling.

She looked out to where the crowd was still enjoying the company of the dolphins and noticed how tanned everyone looked in comparison to her own milky-white skin. The only thing she was able to gain from the sun was more freckles and, no matter how much she tried, her skin just never turned brown. But she'd been surprised at how much attention that pale skin had gotten her. Men in Perth seemed to have been drawn to her freckled face and red hair because she'd been asked out on numerous occasions when she was out with Lexie. She'd gone on one or two dates but none of the men had taken her fancy.

She noticed the crowd seemed to be dispersing so she stood up in salute to the dolphins who were heading back out to sea. She watched them so as to etch the picture in her mind forever. And then they were gone. The water was still again and the crowd were chatting animatedly to each other. She stood alone and suddenly felt sad. It seemed almost everyone had someone. With the exception of one or two, who probably had loved ones waiting for them on the beach, most people were chatting to friends or holding hands with lovers. Sighing to herself, she turned and began to walk back to where she'd left her towel on the warm sand. She'd never forget this place.

* * *

Her name was Silvia and she was perfection. Italian-born but living in Perth since she was ten, she had a face that Will felt needed to be painted. He watched as she chatted on the phone in her native tongue and he was fascinated at how her deep brown eyes changed shape as her voice raised and dipped throughout the conversation. He wondered if she was aware of how much attention she was getting from the men around her as she flicked her long chestnut hair over one shoulder and laughed at something the caller was saying.

'Sorry about that,' she said, replacing her mobile in her bag. 'That was my cousin, Arlo. He's a school teacher and rings me every week to get an update on my travels so he can talk to his class about the places I've been to.'

'So you're on the school curriculum? That's really cool.'

'*His* curriculum. I'm not sure what the principal would say about it though.' She laughed, displaying a mouthful of perfect white teeth.

Will shoved a Coke in her direction. 'Here you go. I got ice in it. I hope that's okay?'

She took a long slug of the drink. 'Perfect, thanks. So, do you come here often?'

Will was about to laugh at that until he realised she was actually being serious. 'I'm just passing through. I was working in Perth for the last couple of years so I'm just going to see some of the country before I head back to Ireland. How about you?'

'Something similar. As I said earlier, I've been living in Perth for the last twelve years but I've never been to any other part of Australia. I've just left college so am taking a year out to spread my wings before entering the workforce.'

Will felt smitten. 'It's a great thing to do. I started a job straight after college and never felt comfortable with it. I've always wanted to travel so I kept feeling I was missing out on something.'

'So you left your job then?'

'Yes. It took a pretty big event in my life to get me to make the decision. Otherwise I'd probably be still in the same job and feeling unhappy with my life.' He took a sip of his Coke and thought about Jack. It was really down to him that he was here, doing what he'd always hoped to do.

'So this big event? Was it a happy or sad one?'

'Sad. Very sad. A friend passed away. It made me think about my own life and living it to the full.'

'Oh God, that's awful. I'm really sorry. But I can understand how it made you rethink things. So are you travelling alone?'

Will nodded. 'Yes. I've just two months left on my visa so I'll be heading up towards Darwin and back down to Sydney. How about yourself?'

'I'm heading up north anyway. I'm not sure after that. I've only been gone a few weeks and I already miss my friends and family. It was something I really wanted to do on my own but, to be honest, I'm not sure I'm cut out for the loneliness.'

'We could stick together for a bit, if you like.' Will cringed. Had he really said that? He'd been thinking about it but it had just come out. She seemed like a lovely girl and it would be nice to have some company along the way.

She didn't say anything at first and Will thought he'd completely ruined his chances with her. Then she looked at him. 'Maybe we could.'

'Really?' Will said, hardly able to believe his luck. 'I mean, we wouldn't have to be together all the time or anything. Just if we're heading in the same direction, we could team up … well, I don't mean … I mean we could just keep each other company …'

Silvia grinned then and her face lit up. 'It's okay, Will. I'd love to spend some time with you. How are you travelling?'

He breathed a sigh of relief. 'I'm driving – it's nothing fancy. A banger actually. But it gets me from A to B.'

'Well, if you didn't mind having a passenger, it would be great. I've been bussing it so driving in any sort of car would be pure luxury in comparison.'

'Right, that's settled. I was planning to leave here tomorrow but if you want to stay on any longer, I don't mind waiting around.'

'Tomorrow suits me fine. How about we meet up later and have a look at a map – decide where we might stop next.'

They exchanged phone numbers before Will headed back to his tent. He felt excited. It had been a while since he'd felt those butterflies in his stomach. Silvia was his ideal woman – intelligent and beautiful, with a fabulous personality and a body to die for. He'd loved his time in Perth but something was telling him that these next few months in Australia would be the most interesting yet.

Chapter 15

'I literally think we've found paradise,' said Will, as they sat on a rock looking at the magnificence of Florence Falls. 'Isn't it amazing?'

Silvia reached for his hand. 'It's beautiful. I could sit here forever.'

It was less than three weeks since they'd met, but Will and Silvia had already sealed their relationship and were very much a couple. It had started tentatively. Will hadn't wanted to appear too forward so, although they'd driven together from place to place, they'd made their own arrangements for sleeping at night. Mostly Will had still pitched his tent whereas Silvia had rented a room in a nearby hostel. But that had lasted just a week.

It had been at a place called Kununurra that things had begun to move in a more romantic direction. They'd been told that one of the highlights of the area was Ivanhoe Crossing, a beautiful picturesque spot where a causeway runs over the Ord River. They'd headed down with a picnic and had planned to have a dip in the water – until they'd seen the sign. 'Beware of the Crocodiles' it had said. And yet there were people knee-deep in the water, as though taunting the creatures to come and get them. They'd both laughed their heads off at the sight and had decided that a swim probably wasn't the best idea after all.

There'd been something about how she'd laughed. Her head thrown back in abandon and her face contorted into happiness. He'd really fallen for her at that moment and she hadn't balked when he'd leaned in for a kiss. She'd shared the tent with him that night. It had been wonderful and it had grown from there. It was still early days but Will was enjoying her company and hoped it would last for at least the rest of his time in Oz.

Silva grabbed his hand suddenly and pulled him off the rock into the crystal water. 'Come on, we need to cool down.'

'Jesus, it's freezing!' Will wrapped his arms around himself and shivered for a few seconds before plunging himself completely into the water. 'Right, your turn.'

'I think I might just stick to the paddling,' said Silvia, wading away from Will's grasp.

But he wasn't letting her off the hook. He grabbed hold of her and pulled her underneath the water with him. They both came up spluttering and laughing and swam closer to where the water was cascading down from the double waterfall.

Silvia stopped and looked up, her eyes open wide, droplets of water glistening on her face. 'Wow. I'm so glad we came here, Will. And I'm so happy I met you.'

Will cupped her face gently in his hands and kissed her. 'And me too – on both counts.' And he meant it. Silvia had come along at just the right time for him. She'd given him a renewed sense of hope. A sense that he'd figure out his purpose in life and having her by his side to do it was a bonus. They were kindred spirits and, as they walked hand in hand back to the car, he wished he could freeze this moment in time and not have to think about the future.

They stopped off at a little convenience store on the way back to their campsite to stock up on provisions. They'd cook a dinner over Will's little stove tonight and then, early in the morning, they'd drive the short distance to Darwin. It filled Will with excitement to think that he'd travelled right up the west coast of Australia and he couldn't wait to start heading south towards Sydney. He just hoped his banger of a car would take them the distance, but for such an old car, it was holding up pretty well.

They set up their cooking area outside the tent and Will placed two turkey breasts on the pan. He smiled to himself as he thought of his mother and what she'd think of his living arrangements. He could just hear her say: 'William, is this any way to live?' And he'd reply that, yes, it was the best way he could ever imagine to live. He was still annoyed at her for the cruel trick she'd played on him when his father was sick but it was true what they said – absence makes the heart grow fonder. If he'd stayed in Ireland at that time, he would have ended up really resenting her but now that he was away from her again she didn't seem so bad.

'Can I leave you to the cooking while I go and take a shower?' Silvia said, appearing from the tent with her wash bag and towel. 'My skin is crawling from those flies around the water earlier.'

Will nodded. 'You go ahead. I'll keep an eye on things here and I have to make that phone call. It's long overdue.'

'Good luck with that.'

Will checked the pan before sitting down on the grass and calling up numbers on his mobile. He hated being at odds with anyone and he felt really bad for abandoning his friend the way he had. He dialled a number and felt his heart beating as it began to ring.

'Well, if it isn't the long-lost Will. So you remembered finally where we were, then?'

'Hi, Brendan. Listen, I'm really sorry about not being in touch. It was just—'

'I know, I know. You needed to see the world and not get too caught up in our boring little lives here in Perth.' There was real venom in his voice.

'Don't be like that, mate. You know what happened. I'd have stayed longer if I hadn't got that call to go home.'

'That's not the point, Will. You could have let us know what was happening. You said you were coming back. I kept your job open – got myself into a bit of bother with the owner over that too.'

'Shit. Sorry about that. I just knew that—'

'And then after ringing you God knows how many times, I get a text to say you're half way up to Darwin. That wasn't cool, mate.'

'Look, Brendan. I only had a few months left on my visa and I knew that if I told you I was back in Perth I'd have ended up going back to the job, the caravan, the life. And I really loved the life. You know that. It was just time to move on.'

'I get that,' said Brendan, his voice a little softer. 'But it was just the way you did it. But look, forget about it. What's done is done. Where are you now?'

Will let out a sigh of relief. 'I'm up in Darwin. It's been an unbelievable few weeks. How are things there? How's Lexie?'

'As annoying as ever.'

Will tried to gauge whether he was serious or not but there was definitely an edge to his voice. 'Are you two okay? We never did get to finish that conversation we had on the night of my birthday.'

There was a moment's silence before Brendan answered. 'We're fine. We muddle through.'

'That doesn't sound great.'

'Look, put it this way – Lexie is great company and I love her and all that …'

'But?'

'But there isn't a lot of excitement there. It's nice to play house with her but when it comes to other stuff – let's just say it's better coming from elsewhere.'

Will gasped. 'Jesus, Brendan. Are you saying what I think you're saying?'

'If you mean other women, then yes. And don't judge me – it works for us.'

'So, does Lexie know about these women?'

'God no. She'd cut my manhood up into shreds! What I mean is that I can get that side of things sorted elsewhere and then I can be the sort of husband she wants me to be at home. Then everyone's happy.'

'I see.' Will didn't see. Poor Lexie. He couldn't believe Brendan was being so cruel. He'd really misjudged him. He'd thought he was a good guy. He'd also envied their relationship and was feeling pretty gutted that it wasn't as idealistic as he'd thought.

Brendan was still talking. '… so I might even think about flying across and joining you for a few weeks. I could do with getting out of this place for a holiday. You've put the thoughts of travel into my head.'

'Em, yes, that would be good. Right, I'd better fly. We'll catch up again soon.'

Will turned his attention to the pieces of meat cooking on the pan and flipped them over to brown the other side. Jesus. He couldn't believe how casual Brendan had been about sleeping with other women. Asshole. If he had a woman like Lexie, who was funny and bright and adorable, he'd never turn his attention elsewhere.

'I'm back. How's dinner coming on?'

'Almost done.' Will watched as Silvia disappeared into the tent and paused for a moment to figure out what he really thought about her. She was funny and bright and adorable – just like Lexie was – but was that enough? Well, it was enough for now. He wasn't going to look too far into the future because it was too difficult to predict. It was enough to think about the next few days. They'd seen an advertisement in a local paper today for a campsite in Darwin called the Coconut Club. It looked magnificent and far superior to the ones they'd stayed in so far. They'd decided to splash out a little and book a hut for three nights, just to give them a break from the camping, and he was really looking forward to it.

In just a few weeks' time he'd be leaving Australia for New Zealand and he'd yet to broach the subject with Silvia. He secretly hoped she'd join him but he was almost afraid to ask the question. He'd gotten used to having company and didn't relish the thought of being on his own again. He gave himself a mental shake as Silvia emerged from the tent looking beautiful in a long, flowing white dress, her wet hair dripping onto her tanned shoulders. He needed to focus on the here and now, and that was him and Silvia and three luxurious nights in the Coconut Club.

* * *

Donna almost fell off the sun lounger in an effort to grab her ringing mobile.

'Hello.' Shit. She'd missed the call. And now she'd got suncream all over the display. She grabbed the corner of the towel she was lying on and wiped it clean. Jan! She'd hoped it would be her. It seemed like ages since they'd spoken and Donna was really beginning to miss her. It was more than three months since she'd left home and although she spoke to Jan almost every week, it just wasn't the same.

The phone rang again but this time she was ready.

'Hi, Jan.'

'Ah, hello, love. I'm glad I caught you. I was just going to leave a message this time if you hadn't answered.'

'It's really good to hear your voice, Jan. How are things?'

'All good here. No change. But more importantly, how are *you*? Where are you now?'

'I'm in a gorgeous place in Darwin called the Coconut Club. It's a hostel but has loads of facilities. I'm actually sitting beside the pool as we speak.'

'Ah, you lucky thing. It's lashing rain and miserable here. What I wouldn't give to trade places with you right now.'

Donna felt a pang of homesickness. 'You could come over – you and Chris. Come over for a holiday for a few weeks. You could even come for Christmas.'

'Chance would be a fine thing.'

'But why not? The hostels are dirt cheap and, to be honest, some of them are more like hotels. Go on – live a little.'

Jan chuckled. 'Donna, there's nothing I'd like more but I can't. You know I can't. Who'd mind the bakery, for starters? You're the only person I'd entrust it to and you're not here.'

'I know.' Donna sighed. 'It was just a thought. And anyway, I'm going to be moving on today to Sydney, before leaving Australia for good.'

'I'll be counting down the weeks until you're back then, love.'

'Me too, Jan. So tell me all the news from home. I want to know *everything*.'

Donna closed her eyes and lay back on her sun lounger as she listened to Jan's voice, imagining she was right there beside her. She could picture the other woman, sleeves rolled up ready to start the day's baking. It was Donna's favourite time of the day in the bakery – the early morning when the world was just waking up and they were making magic happen in the kitchen. If her travelling had taught her one thing, it was that she was a home bird. Despite the tragedies in her life, there was nowhere Donna would rather be than back in Dublin.

'I'd better let you go, love. You have a flight to catch and I have a whole heap of cakes to make.'

Donna checked the time display on her phone and couldn't believe they'd been chatting for almost half an hour. 'Okay, Jan. And thanks … you know … for everything.'

Her taxi was due at two and there was one more thing she wanted to do before she left. She'd been chatting to the chef in the little café on site and he'd promised to give her his recipe for his golden syrup dumplings. She'd never tasted anything like them and wanted to add the recipe to her ever-growing collection. Once she wasn't setting up in competition to him, he'd said, wagging a finger at her, then he was happy to share his baking secrets.

She stood up, smoothing down her flowing mint-green skirt, and hauled her rucksack over her back. It had been a good idea to get organised early and enjoy the sun before she was stuck on a flight for the afternoon. Next stop Sydney. It was one of the places Tina had most wanted to see and Donna was going to make sure she enjoyed it.

Twenty minutes later she was sitting in the back of the taxi, armed with the precious recipe and catching a last glimpse of the place that had been home for the last week. She'd enjoyed her time there but was looking forward to the next part of her adventure.

Chapter 16

25 December 2010

'Come on. I promise you, you'll love it.'

'I'm not sure,' said Donna warily, as her new-found friend tried to pull her up off her deck chair.

'Honestly, it's going to be such a buzz. Bert and Leo have the car packed up already and you know Leo will be devastated if you say no.'

'Go on then. Just give me ten minutes to change and I'll be right down.'

Marlee hugged her excitedly. 'It's going to be the best day ever. Wait till I tell the boys you're coming. They'll be made up.'

Donna watched the other girl zip off to share the apparently great news that she'd be joining them on their outing. She'd been feeling desperately homesick these last few days and really hadn't felt like celebrating Christmas but her friend's excitement was infectious and she found herself almost looking forward to the day ahead.

She headed up the stairs to the room where she'd been staying for the last few weeks. It was small and a bit shabby but the hostel was right in the heart of Sydney and it had proven to be a great base for all the touristy things she'd lined up to do. She quickly stepped out of her sun dress and applied another layer of factor fifty suncream. It would take a few minutes to dry so she sat herself down on the edge of the bed and allowed her thoughts to wander to Ireland.

Christmas Day. Everyone would still be in bed back home because it was just the early hours of the morning, but they'd soon be waking up to presents under the tree and a lovely Christmas dinner to look forward to. It was silly, really. Donna had never really been into Christmas in the past but now all she could seem to think of was sitting around a log fire, singing 'Deck the Halls' and eating toasted marshmallows. It just didn't seem right to be celebrating the festive season in the sun.

Her cream was dry so she pulled a pair of denim shorts and a T-shirt out of her rucksack, gave them a quick sniff and stuck them on. She secured her mop of red hair on the top of her head with the help of an extra-large bobbin and threw a few things into a canvas bag. A quick dollop of protector on her lips and she was ready to go. She smiled to herself as she thought about Jan and what she'd say later when Donna told her she'd spent Christmas Day on Bondi Beach.

She'd met her new friends on the very first day she'd come to the hostel. Marlee and Bert were an English couple in their early twenties. They were planning to get married in a couple of years but had decided to spend a year travelling around the world first. 'There won't be much travelling when the kiddies come along,' Marlee had said, holding firm to Bert's hand. He'd nodded in agreement and Donna had thought how wonderful it was to be so sure. To be clear in your mind about where you were going and what you wanted from life.

Leo was also from England – twenty-eight and gorgeous, with white blond hair and startling blue eyes. Marlee and Bert had met him in a hostel in Cairns and he'd travelled with them to Sydney. Apparently he'd taken a six-month leave of absence from his banking job to escape the humdrum of life in the UK. But reading between the lines, Donna reckoned he was running from a broken heart. Despite his good looks, she didn't fancy him but she knew that if Marlee had anything to do with it, they'd be hooked up together before the end of the day.

It didn't take them long to get to the beach and by the time they walked onto the golden sand, Donna's mood had lifted. What was there not to be happy about at that moment? The sun was shining and she was spending time with friends. And Bondi Beach was on her sister's list of must-see places so it was all part of the plan.

'Right,' said Leo, stopping at a spot that wasn't too overcrowded. 'Will we settle here for now? If we move on, we might not get another spot.'

'Here is perfect.' Marlee plonked her towel down on the sand straight away and whipped her dress over her head. 'So who's coming for a swim?'

'Thought you'd never ask,' said Bert, taking off his T-shirt and lifting Marlee up in the air.

'*Stop!* Let me down.'

Donna grinned as Bert took off with Marlee over his shoulder, heading for the sea. 'They're a great couple, aren't they?'

Leo nodded, spreading his towel out on the sand. 'They're fantastic. I've never seen them argue even once since I met them.'

'I know,' said Donna, putting her towel beside his and sitting down. 'They're real soulmates.'

'Do you believe in all that mumbo jumbo, then?'

Donna stared at him. 'Of course. And it's not mumbo jumbo. Don't you believe that there's someone for everyone in this world?'

'Can't say I do. At least it hasn't been my experience.' His face turned dark and Donna realised she must have touched a nerve.

She continued. 'I truly believe that if something doesn't work out, it just wasn't meant to be and there'll be something better around the corner.'

'I hope so,' said Leo, looking at her with his big blue eyes. 'And how come you're so positive about stuff? I mean, considering all you've been through.'

Donna smiled then. 'I suppose it's *because* of what I've been through that I'm so positive. I've learned that we have to have hope and trust in destiny – otherwise, what's the point?'

'Oh my God, you have to come into the water. It's freezing but fabulous!' Marlee and Bert were back already, spraying droplets of cold water over them and interrupting the conversation.

'Maybe later,' said Donna, standing up. 'But I think I'll go for a little walk first.'

Leo jumped up. 'I'll join you. We'll leave you two lovebirds in peace.'

They walked in silence for a bit, weaving their way through the groups of people sprawled around the beach. Donna couldn't believe how busy it was. There were all sorts of things going on. Some people were having picnics, some playing beach games and there was even one group of guys dressed as Santa Claus. Donna laughed when she saw them and wondered how they could stand the heat of the suits. It was a weird and wonderful experience to be there and she wanted to take in every last moment of it so she could relay it all when she got home.

'You know what you were saying about there being someone for everyone?' Leo broke into her thoughts.

'Yes. I really believe that.'

'And have you ever found your somebody?'

Donna didn't hesitate. 'No. Not even close. But I live in hope. You?'

'I thought I had,' he said, kicking a ball back to a group of kids playing dodgeball. 'A couple of years ago. But turned out she wasn't the one.'

'I'm sorry.' Donna genuinely was. He was a really nice guy and deserved a bit of happiness. 'I'm sure you'll find the right girl some day.'

He stopped then and pulled her to him. 'Maybe I already have.'

He leaned in for a kiss and Donna froze for a moment. But as soon as she felt his lips on hers, she went with the flow and she began to relax. He tasted of toothpaste and coconut and as his mouth became more urgent, his tongue more probing, she wanted to give herself to him completely. She'd only ever slept with one man before and that had been a few years ago but suddenly all she wanted was Leo. Was this what that special moment of serendipity felt like? That moment that she'd always felt would happen to her. They say that it can strike like lightning when you're not expecting it and she certainly hadn't been expecting *that*. Well, she wasn't going to analyse it. She was just going to take it for what it was and see where it would lead. Marlee would be one happy lady!

* * *

Will sat on a grassy area and looked down sadly at a couple kissing passionately on the beach. He envied them. They seemed completely unaware of everything that was going on around them. It was as though they'd paused the world so that they could become lost in their embrace. That had been him and Silvia only yesterday. He'd taken her in his arms while they were sitting looking out over Sydney Harbour and they'd kissed for what seemed like an eternity. That was before everything had changed.

'Here you go, grumpy,' said Silvia, suddenly appearing in front of him holding out a large whipped cone. 'This might cheer you up.'

Will smiled faintly and took the ice-cream. 'Thanks. But it's going to take more than a whipped cone, even if it does have a Flake and sprinkles.'

'Well, it's a start.' Silvia sat down beside him and rested her head on his shoulder.

The couple on the beach were still kissing and Will sensed that Silvia saw them too because he noticed her eyes welling up. But he didn't have the strength to comfort her. After all, it was *her* fault. It was all her doing. He still felt angry about it but now his anger was mixed with sadness and loneliness and it seemed as though his head might burst from it all.

Silvia wasn't coming with him. He was leaving for Auckland in New Zealand next week but she wouldn't be leaving with him. They'd had it all planned. She'd booked a ticket on the same flight as him and they were going to tour around New Zealand together. First the north island and then the south. But that was until Silvia had announced yesterday that she just couldn't do it. She missed her family and friends too much. She wanted to go home to Perth.

Will had felt like she'd punched him in the stomach. Neither of them had mentioned the 'L' word yet but he'd really begun to think he was falling in love with her. He'd always known it wouldn't be an easy love because they came from two different corners of the globe, but he'd felt they'd work it out. True love always finds a way. Isn't that what they said? But right now he couldn't see a way. His visa was almost up which meant he had to leave Australia so even if he'd been willing to go back to Perth with Silvia, he couldn't.

'I'm not going to just forget you, you know,' said Silvia, as if reading his mind. 'And it's not that I don't have strong feelings for you, because I do.'

Will spun around to look at her. 'Well then reconsider. Come with me. Think of it as a holiday and you can go home at the end of it.'

Silvia shook her head. 'But that's just it, Will. I'd still be going home and leaving you. I just don't see how this could work.'

Will was about to say something again but changed his mind. He sighed. She was right. It just wasn't going to work, no matter what way he looked at it.

'Come on, let's go,' he said, standing up and holding out his hand for her. 'Let's just enjoy the few days we have left before we have to say goodbye.'

They drove in silence back to their hotel and Will found it hard to bite back the tears. But once they entered the foyer and heard the Christmas music playing, things seemed a little brighter. They had five more days in this gorgeous hotel. It had been a Christmas present from Will's mum and dad. His mum had rung him a few weeks before and had asked him what she could send him over for Christmas. 'A nice soft bed,' he'd said, jokingly, regaling her with tales of camping on hard ground and sharing the tent with a lovely array of insects. He'd also told her how his car had been giving him trouble from the time he was in Darwin and he'd had to eventually abandon it in Brisbane. He hadn't thought any more about it until she'd rung again a few days later and said they'd booked him into a gorgeous four-star hotel close to Sydney Harbour. He'd been really touched by the gesture, especially since his mother really just wanted him back home.

'Do you think we'll ever see each other again?' Will asked, as they got dressed for dinner in the room. 'I mean, do you really think next week will be goodbye forever?'

Silvia looked at him and this time he saw tears rolling down her face. 'I don't know, Will. I wish I had the answers and I wish I could say we'll definitely see each other again but I honestly don't know.'

He took her hand and led her over to the bed, where he gently pulled her down and wrapped his arms around her. He just wanted to hold her. He'd always thought he was independent. He'd initially enjoyed being a lone traveller and not having anyone else to think about. But since the day he'd met Silvia, he realised what he'd been missing. Companionship. Friendship. And maybe even love.

As he lay there, he could hear Jack's voice in his head saying: 'Don't let anything hold you back, mate. You need to get out there and live your life to the full.' And that's what he was going to do. He'd thought that maybe Silvia was his destiny but life had a habit of playing nasty tricks on him so he was just going to have to wait and see what lay ahead.

He was suddenly aware of soft snores and realised that Silvia had fallen asleep in his arms. He looked at her fondly and smiled. Maybe they wouldn't bother with dinner after all. So what if it was Christmas. It didn't matter what they were doing, once they were doing it together. They had just a precious few days left and Will was going to make sure they didn't waste a single moment.

* * *

Well, it certainly wasn't that special moment of serendipity, despite what she'd thought earlier on the beach. Donna just felt empty as she glanced at the figure beside her in the bed. Leo was conked out, his head tilted at just the right angle to allow drool to run down the side of his face, dandruff from his hair evident on the navy bedclothes. Somehow he just didn't look so handsome any more.

After their kiss on the beach, Donna had been in no doubt where the evening was going. They'd gone straight to Leo's room when they'd arrived back at the hostel and had wasted no time in getting down to business. It had been nice. But there'd been no fanfares or moments of wonderment. It had served a purpose but nothing more. A bitter disappointment.

Donna slipped quietly from the bed and retrieved her clothes from the various corners of the room. She took one last glance at Leo before leaving to head back to the sanctuary of her own room. She felt a little annoyed at herself for letting things go so far today. That moment on the beach had been lovely. If she hadn't let it go any further, they might have even enjoyed more of those moments. But not now. Not since they'd crossed that line.

She lay back on her own bed and checked the time on her phone. Six o'clock. Marlee had suggested they all go for a nice Christmas meal somewhere but Donna wasn't feeling like it. A pang of homesickness hit her suddenly and all she wanted was to be back in Ireland, enjoying a cold, rainy Irish Christmas. She wondered what Jan was up to. It was nine in the morning over there so she was probably getting dinner organised and no doubt baking several gorgeous desserts for after.

Just two more months and she'd be heading home. Two more months before she'd be back in that bakery, chatting to Jan over a plate of freshly made scones, and regaling her with stories of her travels. That was it! She needed to talk to her friend. She needed to hear a comforting voice from home. She sat up and grabbed her phone again, dialling the number from memory.

'Hello, love,' came Jan's motherly voice, as clear as though she was in the room beside her. 'I was just thinking about you.'

And that was all she needed. She hugged her knees to herself as she listened to the other woman's voice and thanked God for one good and stable thing in her life.

Chapter 17

21 February 2011

Donna threw her book down on the bed and stretched. For the first time in a while she was having a lazy day and was loving every minute of it. She'd arrived in Christchurch in New Zealand's south island late yesterday evening and when she reached the guesthouse she'd pre-booked, she suddenly felt exhausted. She hadn't even had the energy to eat anything but instead had collapsed into bed and had been fast asleep by nine o'clock.

She'd been shocked when she'd woken earlier and saw it was eleven o'clock. She'd slept for fourteen hours straight. Her stomach had been rumbling so she'd reluctantly dragged herself out of bed and found a McDonald's practically next door. Ten minutes later she'd been back in bed with an Egg McMuffin and a cup of tea, relishing the comfort of her new surroundings.

She took her phone from the locker beside the bed and checked the display. Almost half past two. She should really get herself up and do something. And besides, she was beginning to get really hungry again and had nothing there to eat except a bar of melted chocolate and a few mint sweets.

Humming to herself, she hopped out of bed and went into the little bathroom to take a shower. Although small, this place was pure luxury in comparison to a lot of the hostels she'd stayed in during her travels. She'd been lucky enough to meet a girl in Auckland who'd just come from Christchurch and had given her the phone number of the place. It was a guesthouse right on the main street, just ten minutes from the city centre. It was run by Mrs Garraway, an elderly lady, who prided herself on her hospitality and yet it was only a few dollars per night more expensive than the hostels. The woman had even presented her with a tray of tea and biscuits when she'd arrived the previous evening and Donna had immediately felt she was going to enjoy her stay here.

She switched off the shower and wrapped herself in one of the big fluffy yellow towels that came with the room. Even *that* was luxury compared to the tatty, threadbare ones that had travelled with her for the last few months. She pulled out her old denim shorts and a top from her rucksack and then suddenly had a change of heart. Today felt like a dress day. She only had a couple of dresses and one pair of kitten heels and these were usually saved for special occasions. But today *did* feel special. She wasn't sure why, but it just did. Maybe it was something to do with the fact she'd had such a good sleep and woke up in a great mood or maybe it was because she knew that in just a few short weeks she'd be back home in Ireland.

She stepped into the daisy-patterned sundress and slipped her feet into the shoes. After spending the last couple of months in flip-flops, it felt strange to wear proper shoes again. She took a brush from the pocket of her bag to try and put some order on her unruly hair. She was really looking forward to getting back home. There'd been times during her travels when she wanted to give in – she'd felt alone and scared and had just wanted to be back home where things were familiar. But she felt proud now that she'd continued and visited all the places Tina had on her list. All that remained was New York and, after her few days in Christchurch, she was heading over there for the remaining ten days of her trip.

The piercing ring of her phone interrupted her thoughts and she grabbed it quickly from the locker.

'Hello.'

'Hi, Donna. It's Lexie.'

'Lexie! It's great to hear from you. How are things?'

'Okay, I suppose.'

Donna flopped down on the bed and lay back on the pillow. 'Right, tell me all.'

'All what?'

'Come on, Lexie. I know you so well. "Okay I suppose" isn't exactly a ringing endorsement of how things are going for you. What's up?'

'It's Brendan.' Lexie sighed. 'I … I'm just not sure whether he still wants to be with me.'

'What?' Donna was genuinely surprised. She thought that they were the perfect couple and that Brendan was head over heels in love with his wife. 'What's made you think that? Surely you're just imagining it.'

'I'm definitely not imagining it, Donna. You know how I want a baby and Brendan said we should wait a while?'

'Yes. Go on.'

'Well, it's been more than a while and he still won't consider it. I'm desperate to have a child and he keeps fobbing me off with a different excuse every time. We don't have the money, we haven't got the time, we wouldn't be able to have the fun we have now … honestly, I'm getting really sick of it.'

'I know it doesn't seem fair, but you have to respect how he feels too. You're still both young and he obviously doesn't feel ready.'

'Don't take his side, Donna!'

Donna rolled her eyes. 'I'm not taking sides. I'm just trying to look at it objectively. I'm sure he'll come around to the idea.'

'Well, I'm fed up waiting. I was even thinking of *accidentally* forgetting to take my pill for a while and see what would happen.'

'Jesus, Lexie. You can't do that.'

'And why not? It's my body.'

Donna felt enraged. 'Listen to yourself, will you. You sound like a mad woman. You can't take things into your own hands like that.'

'But I'm sure that he'd come around to the idea if he had no choice. If I was pregnant, he'd just *have* to accept it.'

'Lexie, you're deluded. He could either end up leaving you or, worse still, you'd bring a baby into the world that wasn't wanted. How is that fair on anyone?'

'But he or she *would* be wanted. *I'd* want it.'

'You can't do that to Brendan, Lexie – to your marriage. It's ludicrous. Talk to him again and tell him how strongly you feel.'

'Hmm. Maybe. But let's not talk about that any more. Tell me about you. How is Christchurch?'

'Actually, I haven't really checked it out yet and I'm already running late for a tour of the city I booked. I'll have to catch you again.'

They said their goodbyes and Donna was glad the conversation was over. She'd lied about the tour but she hadn't felt like talking to Lexie after she told her about her plans to fool her husband. Donna knew from bitter experience that it wasn't good to bring a baby into the world that wasn't wanted and she'd been surprised that her friend would stoop so low. But she wasn't going to let Lexie ruin her good mood. She was going to go and get herself something to eat and then get some maps from the tourist office in the city. The lady who owned the guesthouse had given her a few tips for places to visit over the next few days and she wanted to check out what guided tours were available.

She checked her reflection in the mirror and, as a last-minute thought, she rooted in a pocket of her rucksack and pulled out a lipstick that she rarely used. She never wore make-up at all, actually, but every now and then the lipstick would make an appearance for a special occasion. She smacked her lips together and was finally ready. A few minutes later she was walking along the path to the city centre with a spring in her step. There was something magical about this city. She could feel it in the air.

* * *

Will handed the keys to the guy behind the desk and headed back outside into the sunshine. He'd arrived in Christchurch a couple of weeks back but, instead of staying in the city, he'd hired a car and had driven right around the island. He was back now to stay for a few days and explore the city. The guy in the car hire place had pointed him towards the city centre and he headed off in that direction.

He'd managed to get used to being on his own again, after parting ways with Silvia in Sydney. After he'd discovered she wasn't going to be travelling to New Zealand with him, he'd cancelled his own flight and had stayed on for a few extra weeks. That time together had been bittersweet – he'd savoured every moment they spent talking and laughing and curled up together in bed, but it was stained with the knowledge that they'd have to say goodbye.

But when he'd sat on that plane on the way to New Zealand, one thing had become clear to him. He didn't love Silvia. Well, maybe he did a little – but he certainly wasn't *in* love with her. He'd expected to be devastated – to spend the flight trying to bite back the tears. And, yes, he'd felt empty and lonely and missed her from the time he kissed her goodbye. But he hadn't felt devastated. Silvia had come along at a time when he was at a low ebb. He'd been feeling bitter at his mother and he'd been thinking a lot about Jack after his visit home. Silvia had filled a void and had helped him to forget his problems. He hadn't used her. Far from it. He'd really liked her and had loved spending time with her. But parting from her had just made him realise that she hadn't been *the one*.

Only minutes later he found himself in the centre of the city and checked the directions the guy in the car hire place had given him for the tourist office. He walked out towards Cathedral Square where the beautiful Christchurch Cathedral stood regally in the heart of the city. He was looking forward to exploring the city that boasted both beautiful landscapes and architecture.

He checked his watch and saw it was almost four o'clock. Although he was tempted to go and get something to eat first, he thought he'd better get to the tourist office in case it closed. He checked his map again and headed down a side street, smiling to himself as he heard two women with shopping bags chatting. He'd never been able to distinguish between the Australian and New Zealand accents in the past, thinking they were more or less the same, but now he realised that it would be like saying there was no difference between the Irish and English accents. He found the New Zealand accent uplifting, the way they sang their words, but it was also funny how they pronounced their 'e's like 'i's. 'Look at the size of that dick,' he'd heard a woman shout to her husband during a day cruise he'd taken last week. He'd been shocked to hear the words come out of an elderly woman's mouth until he'd realised she was pointing at the deck!

He found the tourist office and stepped inside, glad to be out of the heat for a while. The place was buzzing with tourists and the queues to speak to the people behind the counter were long so he decided to browse for a bit and maybe pick up a few maps and brochures. He was glad now that he'd chosen to come to New Zealand's south island. He'd initially planned to do both north and south but, what with staying on longer than he intended in Sydney, he'd decided to just do one or the other. So far, he'd adored the island and all it had to offer and it looked like Christchurch wouldn't be any different.

The queues weren't getting any smaller so when he saw that the office was open until six, he decided to go and get a coffee somewhere nearby and come back. He grabbed a handful of leaflets to read and was just about to head out the door when suddenly a woman came flying in, having tripped on the step, and he only just managed to save her from falling on her face on the floor.

'Jesus bloody Christ,' she exclaimed, as he held onto her arms to steady her. 'Why on earth would they put a step there?'

Will barely heard what she said as everything and everyone around him melted away. There was just the two of them. He was aware of his heart beating up into his throat and he felt overwhelmed with a feeling he didn't recognise. It was as though he'd just come face to face with destiny. He didn't know her and yet he felt he'd known her all his life. *I'm going to marry this girl*, he said in his own head, before he realised she was speaking.

'I think it's safe enough to let me go now.'

'Oh … I, em, yes. I'm sorry.' He released her arm that he'd been holding on to and, for once in his life, he was completely lost for words.

'Well, thanks for saving me,' she said, smoothing down her dress. 'It could have been way more embarrassing if you hadn't caught me.'

'No problem. You're Irish?'

'Yep.' She held out her hand to shake his. 'I'm Donna. Nice to meet you.'

Chapter 18

His name was William. Donna glanced at him as he browsed the menu and noted how his dark curls spilled haphazardly over his forehead. He was gorgeous. But it wasn't just that – he had an aura about him. He looked familiar and yet she was pretty sure she'd never met him before. He smelt like home and happiness and she was inexplicably drawn to him.

'I'll have a coffee and a slice of walnut cake,' he said to the waitress who was hovering impatiently. 'Donna?'

'Just tea for me, please.' She couldn't eat a thing. Her stomach was in knots and she was still trying to figure out what had just happened.

William stood up. 'I'm just heading to the loo. Don't run away while I'm gone, will you?'

'You'd better hurry up so.' A waft of aftershave hit her as he left the table and she felt dizzy. After she'd literally fallen into William's arms back at the tourist office, there'd been an awkward moment. And then everything had just clicked into place. As though they were old friends, he'd asked her if she fancied grabbing a coffee and she'd agreed. Just like that. It was unlike her to be so reckless but it had just felt right.

'So have you been here long?' William looked at her as he sat back down and her heart did a flip.

'Just since yesterday,' she said, trying not to stare into his deep brown eyes. 'I was over on the north island for a while first. You?'

'I've been here on the south island for the last couple of weeks but only got to Christchurch this morning. It seems like a lovely place.'

'It's beautiful. I was just going to look for some maps of the city when … well, you know …'

'When you fell into my arms?' He grinned at her cheekily and she couldn't help laughing.

'Well, yes. I suppose you could put it like that.'

'So I take it you're just travelling around, like myself.' His eyes were searching hers and she felt as though he was looking right into her soul.

'I've been in Australia for a few months but I'm homeward bound now. It's been great but it's really not my thing.'

'Why did you do it in the first place, then? I mean, did you just discover it wasn't for you while you were away?'

'It's complicated.' She really wasn't sure she wanted to get into the whole story about Tina with a complete stranger.

'Complicated how?'

Donna sighed. 'Let's just say I did it for my sister. But let's not talk about that now. Where in Dublin are you from?'

Just then, the surly waitress came with the drinks and William's walnut cake and banged them down unnecessarily on the table. 'Just to let you know we'll be closing in ten minutes.'

'Service with a smile,' said William, glaring at the young girl who proceeded to bang things around behind the counter. 'Maybe I should say something.'

Donna shook her head. 'Don't bother. I'll have to go in a few minutes anyway.'

'Oh.' William looked disappointed and Donna could have kicked herself for the lie. Something was telling her that this was something special and it was making her nervous. She didn't want to rush in and make a mess of things, but on the other hand, she really wanted to spend more time with him.

'Or maybe I could reschedule a few things and stay a bit longer?'

William shook his head. 'Please don't change your plans on my account. I should probably get an early night anyway. It's been a long day.'

Donna's heart sank. She sipped her tea and watched William demolish his cake.

'But how about tomorrow?' William continued, washing down the cake with a big mouthful of coffee. 'Since we're both planning on exploring the city, why don't we do it together?'

Donna could have leapt for joy. 'That sounds good to me. What time do you want to meet?'

'Is 12.30 okay?'

'Yep. Fine by me.'

'Let's say outside the cathedral. We can explore that first before heading off for the day.'

'Perfect.'

'Excuse me.' The surly one was back, reaching over them to clear away the half-full cups.

'I take it that's our cue to leave.' Donna giggled. 'I wouldn't want to push our luck with that one!'

'Oh, hang on a sec.' William zipped open a pocket of his rucksack and pulled out a pen and piece of paper. 'What's your phone number, just in case?'

Donna said nothing for a few seconds and again could have kicked herself when William spoke. 'Sorry, sorry. I don't want you to think I'm being too forward. Here, this is mine. But I'll see you at 12.30 anyway.'

The waitress was hovering again and Donna took the piece of paper with his phone number and stuffed it into her pocket. She then reached into her bag and pulled out a ten-dollar note and left it on the table.

'I actually paid already when I slipped out to the toilet. I hope you don't mind.'

'Oh, thanks. Well, Miss Happy there can take this as a tip so.' Donna smiled as she saw the girl's face light up at the sight of the generous tip. She may not have deserved it, but Donna was feeling generous. Her life had just taken a turn for the better and, for the first time in a long time, she was excited about the future.

* * *

Her freckles seemed to dance on her face as she spoke. He could barely take his eyes off her. It was as though someone else had taken over his mind back in the tourist office because he could barely remember asking her out. Before he knew it, he'd been sitting in front of her in the coffee shop and wanting time to stand still.

And now they were going to say goodbye. He wanted to tell her not to go. He wanted to ask her to stay with him for the evening so he could find out more about her. He hated having to wait until the next day. But he didn't want to freak her out. She'd said she had somewhere to go so he needed to respect that. But at least his quick thinking meant that he was going to see her again tomorrow. He smiled at the thought, as they walked back outside into the sunshine.

'Well, it was lovely meeting you, Donna.' He shifted awkwardly from foot to foot.

'And you too. I'll see you tomorrow at half twelve.'

'Great. I'll see you then.'

There were a few moments of silence where neither seemed to know what to do. Surely he couldn't lean in for a kiss. No, that would be way too much. But God, he wanted to taste those lips, their soft pinkness calling out to him, strands of her long red hair sticking to them as the wind blew gently on their faces. He wanted to cup that beautiful face in his hands and kiss every inch of it. He wanted to pull her to him and hold her. He felt almost dizzy at the thought.

'William?'

'Sorry, what?'

'I was just saying I have your number in case anything changes but I don't see why it should.'

'Great. I'm looking forward to it.' He stood and watched as she walked down the street, a vision of loveliness in her daisy-patterned dress and kitten heels. Thank God for those heels. Otherwise she may not have tripped and landed in his arms. It was serendipity. He knew it. All his life he'd been looking for something and, mad and all as it seemed, he felt that he'd just found it.

She reached the end of the street and disappeared around the corner and Will slumped back against the wall. He felt suddenly exhausted. It was still early but all he wanted to do now was sleep. He wanted to dream about Donna and when he woke up it would be time to go and meet her again.

He hauled his rucksack up on his back and, with a spring in his step, he headed towards the hostel he'd booked for the week. He'd learned over the years that life had a habit of throwing curveballs, Jack's suicide being the biggest one. But curveballs could be good too and it seemed to him that he'd just experienced something that would change the course of his life forever.

Chapter 19

Two o'clock. Bloody hell. She knew it had been a mistake to go to bed early. She'd thought that the sooner she got to sleep, the sooner morning would come, but how wrong had she been. She'd already been to sleep and woken up three times and it was still an ungodly hour of the morning.

Donna shoved back the bedclothes and swung her legs out of the bed. Maybe a cup of hot milk would settle her back to sleep once and for all. She padded over to the little kitchen and switched on the light. Two minutes later she was back in bed, sipping on her hot milk and thinking of the man who'd come between her and her sleep.

William. She loved the sound of his name. William, William, William. She'd been surprised at how she'd fallen for him – literally. When his hand had touched her arm to save her from falling, she'd felt bolts of electricity like she'd never felt before. And judging by how he'd reacted, he'd felt it too. God, she couldn't wait to see him again today. She left the cup down on the locker beside the bed and thankfully felt her eyes becoming heavy. Twelve thirty couldn't come quick enough.

Four fifteen. Jesus, that was a weird dream. She'd dreamt she was a teenager again and she and William were running away together. But Lexie wanted to come too and then there was this other guy she didn't know and Tina and her mother. They were all at a funfair then and William got stuck up at the top of a ride and she couldn't reach him. She'd woken up with a start, feeling anxious and scared. God, she really needed to get a grip and try and clear her mind of stuff so that she could get some proper sleep.

She almost cried when she opened her eyes and saw it was only seven o'clock. She could get up and do something since it was bright outside but after tossing and turning most of the night she was exhausted. She needed to get a few hours' sleep or else she'd be falling asleep during her date with William later. Or was it a date? She hoped so. Thoughts of him had filled her head all night and she was already thinking of the possibility of them getting together back in Ireland.

There was something about William that filled her head with thoughts of her childhood. She'd been remembering some happy times with Lexie and Tina and even some early memories of her mother bringing her to the park or buying her a jam doughnut. She wasn't sure why he'd triggered those memories – maybe it was just hearing the Irish accent or maybe it was that he made her feel happy.

She snuggled down further into the bed and pictured his tanned, smiley face. She hoped she'd have a chance to touch it, to feel it close to hers as their lips touched. That moment when they'd said goodbye yesterday had been excruciating. She'd so badly wanted him to kiss her but she'd known he wouldn't. But maybe he would today. She allowed herself to imagine what it would be like and it was with that kiss happening in her mind that she finally drifted off into a delicious sleep.

* * *

It was only a quarter past twelve but Will wanted to make sure he was there in plenty of time. He stood at the front door of Christchurch Cathedral and looked around at the passers-by in anticipation. He hadn't been able to stop thinking of Donna all night and his stomach was doing flips at the thought of seeing her again. He was tempted to go inside to have a look at the cathedral but he was afraid she'd come along and think he wasn't there. And besides, maybe they'd start their day by checking it out together.

The sun was shining again and the square was alive with people buzzing around. It was funny. Out of all the places he'd visited these last couple of years, he felt most at home here. As he stood waiting, he pictured himself in Dublin city centre on a Tuesday afternoon, heading out of the office for a bite to eat. Although, considering it was February, it would definitely be a lot colder and darker in Dublin.

It was twenty past twelve now and his palms were beginning to sweat. What if she didn't turn up? He had no way of contacting her because she hadn't given him her number. He didn't even know her surname so there wouldn't be much chance of finding her back in Ireland either. A chill ran down his spine and he shivered. God, he needed to get a grip. It was still early so there was no need to panic.

But something didn't feel right. He had a sense of foreboding. Much as he was excited about seeing Donna again, there was something telling him things wouldn't run as smoothly as he hoped. But maybe that feeling was due to how he felt about her. It was stupid really. He'd only known her for less than a day. Was it possible that he could have fallen in love so quickly? His head was telling him it was an impossibility but his heart said different. It was screaming at him that Donna was *the one* and he needed to know if she felt the same way too.

* * *

Donna jumped out of bed in a panic. After waking up at various stages of the night and morning, she'd eventually fallen into a deep sleep and had just woken up. It was twenty past twelve – just ten minutes from the time she was due to meet William. Shit. She needed to get her act together fast. She abandoned her pyjamas on the floor and hopped into the shower, careful not to wet her hair. She'd planned on washing it but there just wasn't time. Fifteen minutes later she was heading out the door, dressed in her denim shorts and a cute green top, her unruly hair tied up into a high ponytail. She was already late but she'd ring William along the way to let him know she was coming.

Once she was well on her way, she pulled out her mobile and found the piece of paper William had written his number on. She'd let him know she'd be there in five minutes. It was already almost ten to one and she felt bad for keeping him waiting for so long. Still, they had the whole day ahead of them and Donna was looking forward to seeing how it would unfold.

She stopped walking for a moment to dial the number on her phone when suddenly the earth began to shake violently and her ears were filled with a deafening sound. Within seconds there was smoke everywhere. All of a sudden people spilled out onto the street, running from buildings that were beginning to collapse. Donna stood in shock, gripped by fear, not knowing what to do or where to turn. And then she found herself forced to the ground by some falling rubble and screamed as her head hit the pavement. She lay there for a moment, confused and scared, but something told her she needed to get up and move out of there. Panic-stricken, she managed to pull herself to her feet and began to walk in a daze, shocked by the devastation around her.

Terrified, she realised she was in the middle of an earthquake. She'd read about previous ones in Christchurch. There'd been a serious one last year that they were still recovering from but she'd never, for one minute, thought there'd be another while she was there. Especially not one of this magnitude.

People were screaming and running in all directions and it was difficult to see with the black smoke in the air. Then suddenly Donna remembered. William! She realised she still had her phone clutched tightly in her hand and it seemed to have survived her fall, except for a cracked screen. But the number. It was gone. She had no way of contacting him. She began to run in the direction of the cathedral, aware of blood trickling down her face. But she didn't care. She needed to see that he was okay.

She wasn't sure what she'd been expecting but nothing prepared her for what she saw when she arrived at the square. The spire of the Cathedral had fallen down and there were bricks and debris all around. She rushed to where people had gathered and heard words all around her like 'buried alive' and 'people confirmed dead already'. William was nowhere to be seen.

Dust was thick in the air, making it difficult to see and she felt disoriented as she looked all around her, trying to decide which way to turn. Tears poured down her face as she called William's name, but it was useless. Her voice was muffled by screams and cries of those who realised their loved ones were missing and feared dead. Could she call William her loved one? It didn't matter. He was gone – either injured or dead. And her world felt like it had just ended.

A piercing scream filled her ears all of a sudden and it took her a moment to realise it was coming from her own mouth. She was alone in a foreign country and in the middle of the worst disaster she'd ever seen. She tried to move from where she was standing but her feet wouldn't allow her. Everyone around her was dashing frantically around and it was as though she was invisible. Maybe she was just stuck in a terrible nightmare. Maybe she'd wake up in a minute and thank God for being in the safety of her own bed.

'Miss, Miss, are you okay?'

Donna realised she'd been standing there with her eyes closed and when she opened them, she looked straight into the kindest face she'd ever seen.

'I … yes, I think so …'

'It's just you were screaming but not moving. Did you lose somebody?'

She thought for a moment. 'No, no, I didn't lose anybody. I was alone.'

'You should get that wound seen to,' said the kind old man, as he moved on to another woman who was on her knees crying.

Donna looked around her and wasn't sure where to go next. She felt as though she should do something – but what could she do? She was shaking and there was blood pouring from her head. She was certainly in no fit state to be of any help to anyone. She began to walk in what she thought was the direction she'd come from but she wasn't entirely sure. Everywhere looked different now through the black clouds of dust, and the loud, piercing sound of disaster was making her dizzy.

Her legs felt wobbly as she walked away from the square and down what had previously been a vibrant shopping street. A group of people were frantically digging through rubble outside a shop that had partly collapsed.

'Stephanie,' they screamed. '*Stephanie*, can you hear us?'

Donna paused for a moment and contemplated going to help when suddenly a doorway was cleared and a young woman staggered out. The group descended on her and lifted her up and over the rubble. She seemed to be relatively uninjured. She was one of the lucky ones.

As Donna stumbled further down the street, the extent of the damage was beginning to become obvious. There were cars buried under rubble and buildings completely collapsed. The sound of car horns, alarms and screams combined in the air to form an anthem to the disaster. The smoke and dust was making it difficult to breathe and she prayed that she'd get back to her little room in the guesthouse soon. Then an awful thought struck her. Mrs Garraway! Donna hoped she was okay. The thought of the guesthouse being flattened with the lovely old lady inside was enough to give her strength to push forward to try and get back.

'Help her, help her!' A woman appeared in front of her with a baby in her arms. The child was screaming and her face was covered in grey dust, blood flowing from a gash on her head.

'Jesus,' exclaimed Donna, looking around for help. Luckily a team from the emergency services had appeared on the street and one swooped over and took the child from the woman's arms. The frantic mother followed him as he rushed to the truck they'd parked at the end of the street and Donna stood looking after them, fresh tears rolling down her face.

She began to walk again, slowly and steadily, as though she was walking through some awful nightmare. Thoughts of yesterday flooded her brain and she pictured William, standing outside that coffee shop looking gorgeous and so full of life. The lovely William. Where was he now? Had he survived the disaster? Maybe she'd never know. She was aware of unstable buildings shedding debris out onto the streets, but she didn't care. Life had seemed perfect that morning and now everything was shattered into a million pieces.

After what seemed like hours, she arrived onto the street where she was staying and noted that there was very little damage to the houses there. Thank God for that at least. Just as she was walking up to the guesthouse, the door swung open and there was Mrs Garraway. Donna barely knew the woman and yet she felt her body sag with relief to see her.

'Oh, sweetie, thank God.' The old woman's face was etched with concern. 'Are you okay? Look at the state of you. Come in, come in.'

'I'm fine,' said Donna, but she was far from it.

'Where are you hurt? Come in and let me have a look.' The woman put her arm around Donna and led her inside. 'Now let's get you cleaned up a bit first and we can see what the damage is.'

'Thanks, but I just have to make a phone call. They'll be worried back home.'

The other woman nodded and Donna headed into her room. Thankfully her phone seemed to be still working and she called up a number on the display.

'Hello. Jan?' A sob caught in her throat then and threatened to choke her.

'Hello, love. Are you okay? It's not like you to ring so early.'

'Jan, please get me home. I just need to go back home.' And the tears came then, mingling with the blood from her wound and dripping onto her top. All the loss, tragedy and hopelessness of the last few years overwhelmed her and she cried like she'd never cried before.

How life can change in the blink of an eye. Yesterday she'd thought her time in Christchurch was going to be memorable and today she *knew* it would be. But for entirely different reasons than she ever could have imagined. She was sad for the city and all the loss it was experiencing. She was desperately sorry for those who'd perished or lost loved ones. But she was mostly devastated for the love she'd found and lost. Because she was in no doubt now. She may have only known him for less than a day, but William was – or had been – the love of her life.

Part Two

Chapter 20

October 2011

'So, *Bridget Jones* or *Love Actually*?' Bob waved the two DVDs in the air as he sat cross-legged on Donna's floor. 'Or I could go and rent something more action-packed if you'd prefer?'

'I'm too exhausted for any action tonight so I guess you can stick on *Bridget Jones*.'

'Too exhausted for action, eh?' said Bob, raising an eyebrow. 'And I thought I was on a promise.'

Donna laughed and threw a cushion across the room at him. 'If your mother could hear you talking like that …'

'She'd be well pleased. If she had her way, she'd be organising the wedding.' He clicked the DVD into place and stood up. 'I'll go and make us some microwave popcorn while you fast forward the ads on that. Back in a sec.'

Donna picked up the remote control and tucked her legs underneath her on the sofa. She'd been seeing Jan's son, Bob, these last few months and it was a lovely, easy-going relationship – exactly what she needed. She'd had enough drama over the last few years to last her a lifetime so she was grateful to lead a quiet life for a while.

It was eight months since the earthquake and things were finally beginning to settle down for her. She'd been so traumatised in the aftermath that Jan had organised a ticket home for her, and Donna hadn't argued. The woman had taken her into her home, just as she'd done after the fire, and had mothered her for a few months. She'd been a mess. The earthquake had brought back all the feelings of helplessness she'd experienced after the house fire and she'd had to relive that entire trauma again. It had taken a number of sessions of counselling and a whole lot of love and support but she'd got through those dark months and was feeling human again.

The thing with Bob had happened unexpectedly. She'd known him for years and loved him like a brother but the kindness he'd shown to her when she'd returned from New Zealand had helped push their friendship to another level and they'd fallen into an easy relationship. He was everything she could ever want in a man – kind, considerate, smart – not to mention easy on the eye. His job as a fashion journalist ensured he always dressed on trend and, although she was never really into fashion herself, she loved his style. She'd never gone for the pretty boy look in the past but Bob was exactly that. With his trademark hairband atop messy blond hair and his perfect chiselled jawline, he turned many heads when they walked into a room.

She fixed the cushions behind her back and giggled as she heard Bob belting out One Direction's 'What Makes You Beautiful'. It seemed like the only glitch in his armour was that he hadn't a note in his head. He probably knew the words to every single song in the charts, but unfortunately the musicality eluded him. They'd hired a karaoke machine for his thirtieth birthday party the previous week and his friends had barely got a look in. As birthday boy, he'd claimed the right to the microphone and had had a ball singing his heart out all night.

'Here you go, love.' He handed her an enormous bowl of popcorn and plonked down on the sofa beside her. 'I thought I'd do two separate bowls since you eat so fast.'

'Cheek!' Donna pretended to be cross. 'Are you saying I'm fat?'

'Don't knock the over-sized women,' he said, ducking to avoid the friendly slap she was about to give him. 'Sure look at Bridget there – I'd certainly give her one!'

'So you *are* saying I'm fat?'

'Donna, you're perfect.'

He bent over and kissed her gently on the lips. His lips were moist and tasted of salt and she lay back and enjoyed the sensation. Bob was very affectionate and theirs was a loving relationship. When they made love, it was gentle and tender rather than wild and passionate. They didn't do it very often but that was down to circumstance. Bob still lived at home with his mother and Donna was renting a flat on Dorset Street, close to where she'd rented in the past. She liked it there because she could walk to work and was still close to Bob and Jan. Bob sometimes stayed the night and, on those nights, they'd make love before going to sleep. It was lovely. But it was routine. Sometimes Donna wondered what it would be like to feel such passion that they'd want to rip each other's clothes off there and then in the sitting room and make wild, passionate love on the sofa. But everyone to their own and that just wasn't who they were.

She snuggled into him and they laughed their way through the entire movie. She loved that Bob had similar tastes to her. He loved rom-coms and hated anything with blood and gore. Just a few weeks ago he'd dragged her along to see *Friends with Benefits* and he'd been one of only a few men in the cinema. But unlike her, Bob was really self-assured and confident. He didn't care what others thought and was relaxed and comfortable in his own skin.

The sound of gentle snores startled her out of her reverie and she saw that Bob had fallen asleep beside her, head tilted and mouth open. She smiled at the sight. He and Jan had helped her through so much and she'd be forever grateful to them. He must have sensed her looking at him and opened his eyes a slit.

'I think I'll just crash here tonight, if that's okay with you,' he said, closing his eyes again and snuggling back into her. 'I've an early start so I'll be up and out by six.'

Donna ran her fingers through his tangle of blond hair. 'Me too. I have a pile of cakes to do tomorrow and I told your mam I'd be in at the crack of dawn. Come on. Don't go back to sleep here. You head on into bed and I'll lock up and follow you.'

Bob yawned and stretched before pulling himself up off the sofa. 'Don't be long. I know what you're like as soon as my back is turned. You'll be searching the channels for rubbish programmes.'

Donna laughed. He knew her too well. 'Look, telly's off. Now if you want to use the bathroom, I suggest you do it now before I get in there. I might be a while with all my lotions and potions.'

'Well, let's hope they work this time,' he said, jumping away before Donna could react.

'Oh, you'll pay for that.' Donna smiled as she watched him disappear into the bathroom.

She threw the remote control down beside her on the sofa and leaned back on the soft corduroy material. One of the things she'd learned in therapy was to give thanks for the good things in her life. So every night she took a moment to reflect. She was lucky really. She had wonderful friends, a great job, a home where she felt safe, and the best thing of all was that she had family. Because that was what Jan and Bob were now – her family.

But despite her new-found *joie de vivre*, there was still something missing. Obviously the fire had left a big hole in her life but it wasn't just that. At first she hadn't been able to figure out why she felt that way. Bob was wonderful and she knew she loved him, but he didn't make her feel complete. It hadn't taken her long to realise what the problem was – he wasn't William.

Donna had never told another soul about William. Part of her wanted to savour the thought of him to herself but another part of her knew that nobody would take her seriously. How could she have fallen for a man she'd only known for about an hour? It seemed ridiculous, she knew, but that's what had happened. She'd fallen into his arms that day when she tripped her way into the tourist office and her world had changed. He'd lit up something inside her. He'd made her feel complete.

She rubbed her eyes and forced herself up off the sofa. She needed to stop living in some fantasy world. She needed to concentrate on the here and now and stop pining for the past. She brought the empty bowls into the kitchen and rinsed them.

In the aftermath of the quake Donna had been in shock. But it hadn't stopped her listening intently for news of the dead. She'd dreaded hearing that a young Irish man called William had perished. There'd been news of the death of an Irish man but it wasn't him. Even back in Ireland she'd kept abreast of the death toll, praying for the man she barely knew. News of another Irish death had emerged some time later but, again, it hadn't been him. She'd briefly toyed with the idea of contacting the authorities in Christchurch to check if he'd been registered in one of the hospitals following the quake, but she'd never followed through with it. With only a first name to go on, it just hadn't been enough and she'd feared that she'd look like a fool.

She'd got through those first weeks by telling herself that maybe he hadn't turned up. Or maybe he'd left when she hadn't arrived on time and had been somewhere safer when the quake had hit. Those thoughts had given her some comfort and had helped her to move on with her life.

She filled a glass with water and brought it into the bedroom to leave on her bedside locker. Seeing Bob conked out with one leg inside and one outside the duvet made her heart swell with love. He was her life now. William would probably always hold a special place in her heart and she'd always wonder what happened to him but she was going to stop letting him rule her thoughts.

She padded quietly into the bathroom and closed the door. Looking at herself in the mirror, she realised she'd become thin and pale. Even her freckles looked dull and her usually bright eyes were devoid of life. Right, that was it. Beginning this weekend, she was going to start looking after herself. She'd get a good few inches cut off her hair and bring it back to life and she'd stock up on some decent face creams. Then she'd do a proper grocery shop and fill her fridge and cupboards with healthy food. Thinking about New Zealand always got her down but she wasn't going to let it any more. It was time to move on.

She switched off the lights and slipped into bed beside Bob. He stirred and automatically threw his arm across her. She snuggled into him and despite the fact he'd been fast asleep only minutes before, his body began to respond to her. He pulled her in close until his warm breath was caressing her face. They kissed full on the lips and their bodies began to move in unison. It wasn't long before they were making love – slowly and steadily, softly and lovingly. It was lovely and Donna knew that this was where she needed to be. It was safe. It was routine.

Chapter 21

'A masterpiece, so it is,' said Jan, looking at the retirement cake Donna had just finished making. 'The detail is amazing. They're going to love it.'

'Thanks, Jan.' Donna was becoming a whizz at making custom cakes and she was particularly proud of this one. A very smartly dressed woman had come into the shop a few weeks before, asking for a cake to be made for her husband's retirement. She'd left the design of the cake up to Donna but she'd had specific instructions that it had to reflect her husband. He liked golf and played chess on occasion. He dressed mainly in suits and adored vintage cars. His favourite night out was in a swanky restaurant that served haute cuisine and fine wines. Donna had it all on the cake and, as Jan said, it was a masterpiece. She lifted up her icing bag to put on the final touch: 'Congratulations, George'.

It was only ten o'clock but Donna had been in since six and felt exhausted. She placed the precious cake into a box and stuck the receipt on the top. The woman was coming in for it at lunch time and Donna couldn't wait to see her reaction. She was planning to start making some of the decorations for an eighteenth birthday cake that was being collected at the end of the week, but she'd need a cup of tea first.

'Right, I'm off to the wholesalers,' said Jan, popping her head into the little kitchen just as Donna was filling the kettle. 'Are you okay to get on with things here for a few hours?'

Donna nodded. 'Of course. I'm already ahead of myself and it's only Monday.'

'Great. And it's quiet enough out front so Megan should be able to manage on her own. I'll tell her to give you a shout if it gets busy.'

Donna sat down at the small wooden table and wrapped her hands around the steaming cup. She wasn't very hungry today. She'd allowed William back into her head last night and it had unsettled her.

After returning to Ireland, she'd thought about how she could find him. He was the great love of her life, after all. There had to be a way. But as the days and weeks had passed, she'd realised that her search was futile. She'd gone through every option – Google, Twitter, Facebook – but it had been hopeless. If only she'd quizzed him more when they were in that little coffee shop. She remembered how they'd started to talk about where they lived when that surly waitress has interrupted them and they never got to continue the conversation. The fact that she'd never even asked his surname would haunt her for the rest of her life. If only she'd known. If only she could rewind time.

She took a sip of her tea and gave herself a mental shake. She'd promised herself last night that she'd be more positive from now on. After all, she had a lot to be grateful for. Her stomach began to rumble and she realised that she hadn't eaten since the popcorn she'd shared with Bob the previous night. Right, the healthy eating could start tomorrow. She was going to sample one of those rosewater cupcakes that Jan had made earlier. She wasn't usually a fan of fragrant flavourings but they'd looked and smelled delicious.

She flicked the switch on the kettle to make another cup of tea and headed out towards the front of the shop. She could hear Megan chatting happily to a customer and smiled to herself at the other girl's sing-song Cork accent. But then she heard the customer's voice and stopped dead. She pushed her ear against the door to listen. That voice. It was unmistakeable. She began to breathe heavily and felt light-headed. Oh God, her legs were like jelly and she wasn't sure if she could move them. He was still talking and she was transported back. They were sitting in a little coffee shop in Christchurch and she was listening to him tell her about his journey around the island. He was gorgeous. Those eyes were mesmerising. She'd never met anyone like him before.

She suddenly snapped back to the present. He'd actually found her. She didn't know how he'd done it, but he had. She pushed through the door that opened at the side of the counter, a smile almost splitting her face in two. 'William, I can't believe …'

'Donna?' Megan looked at her strangely. 'Who are you talking to?'

Donna stared at the customer who'd sounded so like William and her heart sank. He must have been about fifty, with a scruffy-looking beard and tiny eyes that were too close together. Nothing like her beautiful William.

'Donna?'

'Oh, sorry. I, em, thought I heard William – William Byrne. He was, em, coming in to order a cake today. Sorry about that. I'll just grab this and head back inside.'

She whipped one of the rosewater cupcakes from the display and disappeared into the back, her heart beating like crazy. She needed to get a grip. Bloody hell! She'd laugh if she didn't feel so pathetic.

Sitting back at the little table, she began nibbling at the pink icing on the cake. It was at times like this that she missed Tina. She'd have laughed at Donna making a fool of herself like she just had and she'd have had plenty of advice to offer on the situation. Tears sprang unbidden to Donna's eyes at the thought of her sister. It was more than two and a half years since that dreadful night but the pain had never left her. She'd found a way of dealing with it but she didn't think it would ever go away.

Right, she wasn't going to allow herself one more minute of wallowing. She was due her period, so maybe that's why she was so down in the dumps at the moment. What she needed to do was make some cakes. She poured the half-full cup of tea into the sink and threw the barely-eaten cake in the bin.

'Donna, are you okay?'

'Jesus, Megan. You almost frightened the life out of me!'

'Sorry. You seem very jumpy, though. What was all that about out there?'

Donna busied herself washing her hands. 'It was nothing. I'm just a bit distracted today. I have a lot on my mind.'

Megan nodded and gave her a sympathetic look. 'Well, there's a woman outside asking for you. I forgot to get her name. Tall. Well dressed. Face like a slapped arse.'

'You're very naughty,' giggled Donna. 'But I know exactly who it is. Tell her I'll be out in one minute.'

Donna dried her hands on her apron and went to take the cake out of the store room. One of the most exciting parts of her job was seeing the reaction on people's faces when they saw the finished product. And she felt this was her best work yet. She couldn't wait to see what the customer thought. She checked the receipt and double-checked inside the box to make sure she had the right cake and carefully carried it out to the shop.

'Now, Mrs Cooper-Smith. It's all ready for you.'

'Yes, well I should hope so. I've been out here ten minutes already and I have a client to see in less than half an hour.'

'Sorry about that,' said Donna, placing the box on the counter between them. 'But I was just doing a final check to make sure everything was perfect.'

'Right, I suppose I'd better have a look to make sure it's okay before I head off. I'd hate to have to come back.'

'Of course.' Donna opened the box and turned it to face Vivienne Cooper-Smith. She held her breath as the woman stared at the cake.

The seconds ticked by and Donna was beginning to feel anxious. 'Mrs Cooper-Smith? Is it okay? I mean, do you like it? I included everything you said but if there's anything you're not happy with I can always …'

'It's perfect.' She looked up and, to Donna's shock, tears were glistening in the corners of the woman's eyes. 'Perfectly beautiful.'

Donna exhaled. She'd thought for one minute that she was going to have to redo the whole thing. She really needed to work on her confidence.

'I'm glad you like it. I really hope your husband does too.'

'He'll love it. How could he not?' Her voice wobbled and Donna was startled to see tears form in her eyes.

'God, I'm really sorry. It's not like me to get all emotional. It's just seeing the cake with everything George loves on it.' She took a dainty cloth hanky from her Coach handbag and dabbed at her eyes. 'George got sick a few years ago and I could have lost him. It's just the two of us so I don't know what I'd do without him.'

Donna nodded. 'When something like that strikes, it makes you realise what's important. I'm glad he's still around.'

'Me too,' said Vivienne, her eyes glazing over a little.

'And I'm thrilled you love my cake so much. When is the party?'

'Tomorrow night. It's just a small affair with a few friends.'

'I'm sure you'll have a great time,' said Donna, glancing at the clock. Jan would be back soon and she really wanted to make a start on that birthday cake.

Vivienne must have got the message because she reached into her bag for her wallet. 'I really can't thank you enough for the cake,' she said, handing over a hundred euros cash without flinching. 'I know we agreed on eighty, but I'd like you to take the extra twenty for yourself. You did such a brilliant job.'

Donna's eyes opened wide. She'd never had a tip before, never mind such a large one. 'I can't, really …'

'I won't take no for an answer.' She rooted in her bag again and pulled out something. 'And here's my card. I have my own law business just across town so if you ever need a solicitor, I'll look after you.'

As though getting back into character, her face became stony, all trace of tears gone. With a curt nod, she turned on her heel and was gone out the door without another word. Donna stared after her. What a strange woman. But at least she loved the cake. And a twenty euro tip! She'd put it aside and maybe she'd take Bob out for a Chinese at the weekend. He was always treating her so it would be nice to return the favour for once.

Donna glanced at the card in her hand. Vivienne Cooper-Smith, Solicitor. There were a whole lot of letters after her name which looked impressive and Donna imagined she was a woman you wouldn't want to be on the wrong side of. She slipped the card into the pocket of her jeans and headed back to her work station.

She hummed to herself as she began to make tiny pieces of clothing from icing. She was making the eighteenth birthday cake to look like a messy bedroom with clothes and things strewn all over the place. She could never get over the fact that she was actually paid for doing this. It was such great fun and it made her happy.

'I'm bloody gasping for a cuppa,' said Jan, coming through the door like a hurricane. 'You'd swear we were living in the North Pole or something, with the way they have the heat blasting in that wholesaler's. I thought I was going to faint if I didn't get out of there quickly.'

Donna laughed at Jan's flushed face and her usually perfect grey bun beginning to unravel. 'Come on, I'll make you a cup of tea but I've had my break already.'

'Ah, just take a few minutes, Donna, love. I don't get to see enough of you these days.'

'You see me almost every day!'

'But it's not the same. I'm delighted you have your own place now but I miss having you around at home.'

'Well, come on then. But just a few minutes. I wouldn't want the boss to say I'm slacking off.'

'I'll have a word with her for you.' Jan winked and led the way into the kitchen.

They chatted for a while about trivial stuff until Jan's face turned serious. Donna knew there was something on her mind.

'Go on then,' said Donna, raising an eyebrow.

'Go on what?'

'I can tell you want to say something. Go on – spit it out.'

Jan laughed. 'You know me too well. I was just going to ask you about Bob …'

'What about him?' Donna shifted uncomfortably on the chair.

'Is there any chance you'll be taking him off my hands any time soon?'

The question hung in the air for a few seconds until Donna managed to speak. 'Wh— what do you mean?'

'I know I shouldn't be poking my nose in, but it's been a few months now and Bob spends half his time in your place anyway. Is there any chance you might make it a more permanent arrangement?'

Donna was taken aback. She loved Jan but she didn't want to discuss the ins and outs of her relationship. She was Bob's mother, for God's sake. It just didn't feel right. And besides, she wasn't ready for that full-time commitment yet.

'I'm sorry if I upset you by asking, love. It's just that seeing you both together makes me so happy. I couldn't wish for a better daughter-in-law.'

'Whoa! Back up there just a minute, Jan. You're jumping ten steps ahead.'

Jan took a sip of her tea and looked sheepish. 'I just mean that the two of you are great together and I pray to God every day that it's the real thing. You do love him, don't you?'

God, this conversation was getting more and more uncomfortable. 'Yes, of course I do, but it's still early days.'

'I know, love, and I'm sorry for asking. Forget I said anything.'

'It's okay, Jan. No harm done.'

Donna spent the next hour working on her cake but she was feeling unsettled. Jan was like a mother to her and she loved her to bits. She knew Jan loved her too but Bob was her son. What would happen if they ever split up? If things went bad between her and Bob, would Jan abandon her? Donna couldn't bear the thought. She'd no plans to leave him but, as she knew only too well, sometimes life took twists and turns that weren't part of the plan.

She took a step back to survey her work so far. Not too bad at all. It would be a while before it would all start to come together but it was looking good. She felt her spirits lift again. She was worrying unnecessarily. She and Bob were solid and loved each other deeply. She'd lost her family once but nothing was ever going to tear her new family apart.

Chapter 22

Donna was glad to step out of the rain and into her warm flat. She'd left the heat on before she went out so the place was lovely and toasty. She couldn't wait to get out of her wet clothes and warm up. Her nightly visits had become weekly ones and she hated herself for the fact that she didn't even look forward to that visit any more. It just made her sad, frustrated and completely emotionally drained. She was exhausted now and all she wanted to do was snuggle up on the sofa by herself and catch up on last night's *Emmerdale*.

Ten minutes later she was in her furry pyjamas and rooting in the fridge for something to eat. She decided on some cheese and crackers and poured herself a small glass of white wine. She didn't drink much but every now and then she'd indulge in a glass or two. On her way over to the sofa, she grabbed the phone to check for messages. There were none, but she was surprised to see a missed call from Lexie. It had come in at half six, which would be half one in the morning over there. It wasn't like Lexie to ring at that time. She hoped there was nothing wrong. She quickly dialled the number.

'Hiya, Donna.'

'Lexie, are you okay? I saw the missed call and had to ring straight away.'

'Yeah, sorry about that. If I'd remembered it was Wednesday night, I wouldn't have rung. Are you just in? How are things?'

'Yep, I'm just in the door. And things are just as they always are. Like they'll always be.'

'Ah, Donna. You don't know that. Things can turn around and you know you've got to have—'

'Honestly, Lexie, I'm not being rude but can we please talk about something else? I'm too drained to go over this again. So tell me, what's up with you? It's not like you to ring at this time.'

There was a silence and Donna could feel her heart beginning to quicken.

'Lexie? What's happened?'

'Oh, Donna. It's over.' There was a gulp, followed by a sob, and then she began to cry softly. 'I … hate … him.'

Donna was alarmed. 'Who? Brendan? Of course you don't hate him. Come on, tell me what's happened.'

It took a few moments for Donna to compose herself but then the story flowed out. Some woman had called to their house the other day demanding to see Brendan. Lexie had told her he was in work and asked if she could give him a message. 'Yes,' she'd said. 'You can tell him that just because the pregnancy test was negative doesn't mean he can walk away.' She'd turned and left while Lexie was left with her mouth gaping open, trying to make sense of it all.

'Wow,' said Donna, trying to take it all in. 'But maybe there's an explanation. I'm sure Brendan gets plenty of women throwing themselves at him in his line of work. Maybe he rejected her and she wasn't happy. Maybe—'

'He had an affair with her, Donna. He admitted to it.'

'Oh God, Lexie. That's awful. I can't believe Brendan did something like that. Can you talk it through? Get counselling or something?'

'But that's not all,' said Lexie, a sob catching in her throat. 'Apparently he's been sleeping with other women for the last two years.'

Donna shook her head in disbelief. 'Did that woman tell you that? Because you know what they say about a woman scorned. I wouldn't believe it.'

'No, Donna. Brendan told me himself. And he wasn't even particularly sorry about it. Sorry he was found out, maybe, but not remorseful about what he'd done.'

'I'm in shock here,' said Donna, pushing her food away. She suddenly didn't feel hungry.

'And how do you think *I* feel?'

'I'm sorry. Of course.' Donna wasn't sure what to say. She'd thought that Lexie and Brendan were the perfect couple. 'And did he say why? Or does it even matter?'

'Oh yes, he didn't hold back. He said I'm gorgeous and he loves having me on his arm when we go out. He said that I'm a great wife and he loves being married to me.'

Donna was confused. 'Well, that doesn't make sense.'

'Oh, but you haven't heard the best bit yet. I'm not exciting enough. Apparently his *needs* weren't being met in the bedroom so he decided to seek out women who'd give him what he needed.'

'Bastard! And had you no idea this was going on?'

'Of course I bloody well didn't! What do you take me for?'

Donna recoiled at the viciousness in Lexie's voice. 'I'm sorry, Lexie. I didn't mean anything by—'

'No, *I'm* sorry, Donna. I just can't believe how my whole life is falling apart. I thought we were happy. We *were* happy.'

'I know you were,' said Donna, feeling desperately sorry for her friend. 'And maybe you could get that back again. Maybe you could—'

'He's gone. There's no going back. He packed up his things and left this afternoon.'

'Oh God, I can't believe it's come to that already.' Donna was finding it hard to keep up. It seemed unbelievable that all this could have happened since she spoke to Lexie last week.

'How could he have done it to me, Donna? How could he have taken my heart and trampled it into the ground?' She was sobbing again and this time Donna felt tears running down her own cheeks.

There really were no words so Donna just waited until Lexie's sobs subsided. She wished she was there beside her so that she could give her a hug. It was heartbreaking to think she was at the other side of the world with no proper friends to comfort her. Lexie had lots of friends over there but, as she'd said on many occasions, they were just social friends – none of which she could really talk to.

'And … and …' Lexie was attempting to speak through her sobs, 'that woman could have been pregnant. He … he almost made another woman pregnant when he'd told me in no uncertain terms that he wasn't ready for a baby.'

Donna thought back to a previous conversation when Lexie had contemplated tricking him so that she could get pregnant. Thank God for small mercies.

'I just wish I hadn't listened to him,' continued Lexie. 'I could have had a child by now.'

'Lexie. You don't mean that.'

'I do, Donna. I have plenty of love to give to a child myself. I don't need him or any man to help with that.'

'But, Lexie, you're so young. You'll meet other men and have plenty of chances to have children.'

'Well, if I do, it's going to be in Ireland, where I belong. I should never have come over here.'

Much as Donna wanted to see her friend, she didn't want her making any rash decisions. 'You can't mean that, Lexie. You've had some brilliant times over there and moving to Australia was exactly what you needed back then. Give yourself some time and have a think about what you want to do.'

'I don't need time, Donna. That's one of the reasons I was ringing you tonight. I'm coming home.'

'What? When? How can you have decided that already?'

'Well, don't sound too excited about it.' Donna could hear the pout in Lexie's voice.

'I am. There's nothing I'd love better than to see you but I just want to be sure you're making the right decisions. What if Brendan comes back? What if he changes his mind?'

'Fuck him, Donna! So what if he changes his mind. I'm not changing mine. Maybe, just maybe, I could have forgiven one lone incident, but I can't get over two years of infidelity.'

'Of course you can't. And I'm sorry to have even suggested it. So what's the plan, then? Are you going to book flights soon?'

'First thing in the morning. I've already spoken to Gran and I'm going back to stay with them until I get on my feet. I don't know what my next step will be but at least I'll be home and surrounded by the people I love.'

Donna felt a lump in her throat. 'Don't worry, Lexie. We'll be here for you. I know it's going to be hard for you but it will be great to catch up. I can't wait for you to meet Bob properly. He's such a ...'

'Such a what?'

'Jesus, I'm so sorry, Lexie. Here's you just after breaking up with your husband and I'm telling you how wonderful my man is. I'll shut up now.'

'Don't be silly. I'm dying to meet Bob. I know we met briefly a couple of times but that was before you and he were a couple. I'm sure I'll love him just as much as you do.'

'I hope so.' Donna could have kicked herself for mentioning Bob. Lexie was sounding a little chirpier than she had at the start of the conversation but it couldn't be easy to hear about other people's fabulous relationships.

'Right,' said Lexie, breaking into Donna's thoughts. 'I'm falling asleep here so I'll say goodbye. I'll email you tomorrow as soon as I have the flights booked and we can make some plans.'

'Night, Lexie. I hope you sleep well. We'll chat again soon.' Donna was relieved the conversation was over. Much as she felt sorry for Lexie, she just didn't know what to say. It was difficult over the phone. It would be much better when she was sitting right in front of her.

She glanced at the time on the DVD display and saw it was only ten o'clock. Still early enough. She was usually a bit of a night owl but Lexie's news on top of her already emotional evening had her feeling exhausted. She switched off the telly and brought her glass and plate into the kitchen. An early night would do her good. She wasn't in work tomorrow but she had plenty of other stuff to do to keep her busy.

Ten minutes later, she was about to hop into bed when the shrill ring of the phone almost frightened the life out of her. She was tempted to ignore it but she knew she couldn't, just in case. Please God it wouldn't be Lexie ringing back for another chat. She needed time to absorb the whole thing before she listened to any more. She switched the light in the living room back on and grabbed the phone, which was still on the sofa.

'Hi, Donna, love. Just checking in.' Bob! She might have known. He always either called in or rang on Wednesday nights for an update. She brought the phone back into her room and snuggled down into her feather duvet. She gave him a brief summary of her visit and filled him in on the whole Lexie saga.

'Poor Lexie,' he said, after listening to it all for more than twenty minutes. 'What a horrible thing to happen.'

'I know. But at least she's coming home. It will be lovely to have her back after all this time.'

Bob continued chatting about his day. He told her about a designer he'd interviewed who had about thirty animals living in his apartment with him. Apparently his signature pieces were animal print. He described a shirt that had been sent in to him by an up-and-coming designer and it sounded horrendous. He made her laugh, which was exactly what she needed. They said goodbye and arranged to meet back at her place the next evening.

Donna smiled to herself as she switched the phone off and placed it on her locker. She felt very sorry for Lexie but it made her even more aware of how lucky she was to have a man like Bob. Compared to Brendan, he was an absolute saint.

Her room was never completely dark because of the light from the streetlamps streaming in through the curtains. She kept meaning to get blackout lining to sew onto them but it was just on a long list of things she needed to do. She lay on her back and glanced around the room. There was a dressing table strewn with odd bits of creams and make-up. An old pine locker stood at one side of the bed and a wooden chair, which could double up as a bedside table, stood at the other. The walls were painted in a dusky pink and the cream duvet cover also had soft pink flowers running along the top. The room screamed 'Donna' with not a trace of Bob in sight.

That was it. She may not be ready for a full-blown live-in with Bob yet but maybe they could 'Bob-ify' the place. They could choose a paint colour together and repaint the room. She could get him to bring over some of his things and leave them there. It would be a gesture – a nod to the future they were going to have together. He'd understand she just wasn't ready to take the next step but it would be good to show a bit of dedication.

She closed her eyes and turned on her side. She couldn't wait to talk to Bob about it tomorrow. They'd never spoken about him moving in but since Jan had brought it up, it had got her thinking. Did Bob feel she wasn't committed to the relationship? She didn't think so but if he had any doubts, she'd set him straight tomorrow. It was still early days and this would be a step in the right direction.

She hadn't been sleeping well lately but she could feel herself beginning to drift off. Life was suddenly looking up. Lexie was coming home and it felt like another piece of the jigsaw of her life was slotting into place.

Chapter 23

'I can't believe this is all the luggage you have,' said Donna, taking one of the cases from Lexie and pulling it along. 'I'd have thought you'd have masses of stuff.'

'There wasn't a lot I wanted to keep from my life over there, to be honest. Most of my stuff went to charity shops.'

Donna nodded. 'Well, it will be an excuse to go shopping. Not that we ever needed an excuse!'

'True. God, I'm so thankful to be home for Christmas. I've never really enjoyed the festive season over there and this year would have been an absolute nightmare, considering the circumstances.'

Donna put her free arm around her friend and hugged her. 'And we're glad you're here too. Come on, Bob just texted me. He's still frantically looking for parking so we can save his sanity and just hop into the car.'

Within minutes, the three of them were heading out of the airport and onto the M50 that would take them back to Lexie's grandparents' home on the north side of the city. Lexie had gone quiet in the car and Donna noted how pale and fragile she looked. Her long blonde hair was limp and dull and her make-up-free skin was blotchy and dry. It broke Donna's heart to see her usually fun-loving, chirpy friend showing the strain of the last few months. Still, she was where she needed to be now and Donna was going to give her whatever support was necessary. Lexie had been there for her during the dark times so now it was Donna's turn to repay the favour.

'You'll have to direct me from here,' said Bob, breaking the silence, and Donna noticed that they were already on the Navan Road.

Lexie suddenly perked up. 'It's right at the next lights and then immediate left and we're there. God, it feels good to be home.'

Donna could feel her heartbeat quicken as they got closer to her childhood home. She hadn't been back there since soon after the fire and she'd thought she'd never have to. Lexie seemed to sense her tension and reached out to squeeze her shoulder.

'I'm sorry if this is hard for you, Donna. Maybe you shouldn't have come.'

'No, I'm fine, honestly. My life has moved on now and if you're going to be living with your grandparents, I'll be spending a lot more time here.'

'But still. All the bad stuff that happened when we were kids, and then the fire and everything …'

Donna wished Lexie would shut up. As if she needed reminding.

'Are you okay, love?' Bob looked at her, his face full of concern. 'If you like, we can stop around the corner and I can help Lexie with her bags.'

'Will you two stop! I'm a big girl now. I'm absolutely fine. And we've made lots of good memories here too, Lexie. We got up to some mischief, didn't we?'

Lexie laughed and her whole face lit up. 'We certainly did. God, do you remember when we took a scissors to old Mr Farnham's flower beds?'

'Oh God, we made such a mess of them, didn't we?' Donna had tears running down her face. 'It served him right, grumpy old fart.'

'It sounds like you two were trouble,' said Bob, taking a left as instructed. 'I might need to hear more of those stories from the past so that I can decide if I want to stick around.'

'I think I'll have to censor them so.' Donna wiped her eyes. She'd been glad of the laugh to disguise the tears that had been threatening to fall. At least it looked as though they were tears of laughter.

Lexie shot forward in her seat. 'Just here on the left – the one that looks like Santa's Grotto. Jesus, Granddad has excelled himself this year!'

They all gasped at the house. It was like they'd taken every Christmas cliché and landed it in the garden. There was an enormous blow-up snowman, a row of lit-up dancing reindeer and a myriad of Santas, both in the garden and hanging from the roof. There were strings of various-coloured lights strewn in no particular pattern around the front of the house and on some of the bushes. Donna knew the Byrnes had always gone over the top at Christmas but she'd never seen anything quite like this.

The front door flung open as they parked the car and Lexie's grandparents stood there, huge smiles on their faces, waiting to welcome their only granddaughter home. Donna was happy to see the scene unfold but she also felt a little bit jealous. Although she had Jan and Bob, she'd never had that warm, fuzzy feeling of being part of a loving family.

Donna and Bob got out of the car to hug Lexie and say they'd catch up with her later. It was difficult for Donna to avoid looking at the house next door that she'd once called home and she really didn't want to hang around. It looked very clean, she noted as they drove away, waving to Lexie and her grandparents. There was new pebble dash on the front and the old wooden hall door had been replaced by a red PVC one. Maybe the change was a good thing because it no longer resembled the house from Donna's childhood.

'How did it feel to see your old house again?' asked Bob, putting one hand on her knee. 'It couldn't have been easy.'

Donna shifted in her seat to look at him. 'You know, I've avoided coming here over the last couple of years. I suppose I was afraid of my own feelings. And I have to admit, it was emotional seeing the house again – even being on the street – but I'm glad I came. It's part of my old life and nothing is ever going to change that.'

Bob squeezed her knee. 'You have a great attitude, Donna. I don't know many who would have come through what you did and still be so strong and positive. I love you, you know.'

'I love you too, Bob.' And she did. At that moment in time, there was nothing in her life that was more certain.

* * *

Donna pushed the posh food around on her plate and hoped nobody would notice she wasn't eating. It wasn't that she wasn't hungry. In fact she was starving. But the sucky-in knickers she was wearing under her clingy, figure-hugging dress were almost constricting her breathing. She'd made an attempt at the prawn cocktail starter but it had reached where the top of the knickers were resting and had given up. It was still lingering there – threatening to rise back up if she tried to force anything else in.

'Not a fan of the fine food, eh?' whispered Bob in her ear.

'I'm sure it's lovely,' she said, shifting uncomfortably in her chair. 'But unfortunately it doesn't have room to go down with these bloody ridiculous knickers on me.'

Bob shook his head and laughed. 'You're an idiot, you know. I told you that you didn't need special underwear. You always look amazing and that dress is to die for.'

Donna was secretly delighted to have Bob's approval for the dress. They were at a charity event in the Convention Centre and she'd gone out shopping especially to buy a dress for the night. It was jade green, which the shop assistant in Debenhams had told her went amazingly with her red hair and, although it was a simple design just hanging below her knees, it clung to her in all the right places. She'd even bought a pair of Kurt Geiger black suede heels for the occasion and she had to admit to herself that she looked pretty damn good.

'I feel bad abandoning Lexie on her first night back,' said Donna, relieved to be finally handing over her plate to the waiter. 'Do you think she's okay?'

Bob took a mouthful of his red wine before answering. 'I'm sure she's delighted to be at home catching up with her grandparents. She'd have been too exhausted to come out tonight anyway.'

'That's true. I'll have to spend some time with her over the next few days though, so I mightn't be around much.'

'That's fine by me. I'm not going anywhere. Maybe all three of us can go out for a meal or something next week. I'd love to get to know her too.'

'I'm sure she'd love that. Right, I'm heading to the loo. I might be a while trying to navigate my way around this underwear.'

'Just ditch them, love. Come back knicker-free and enjoy the dessert.'

Donna giggled to herself as she headed towards the ladies' toilets. She really wasn't into nights like this but Bob made it bearable. The magazine he worked for had sponsored a table at the event and Bob had wanted her to come along to meet his workmates. 'It's about time you met the gang,' he'd said to her a few weeks before. 'They're going to love you.' She'd been flattered that he wanted to show her off to his friends so she'd been determined to make a good impression. The lads were nice enough but most of them, being single and carefree, were feasting on the free wine and off chatting up girls at the bar.

She'd never been in the Convention Centre before but it was one of her favourite buildings in Dublin to look at. It's curved glass exterior leaning backwards and lit up at night time was a thing to behold. And the inside was no disappointment. She'd been amazed at the splendour of the function room with its beautifully laid out tables and warm Christmassy décor. Apparently there were more than a thousand people seated for the meal and Bob had told her that the price of a table for ten was an average of five thousand euros. Well, thank God she wasn't paying or she'd have forced every crumb of that meal down her, no matter what.

After a battle to get the offending underwear down, she decided to live dangerously and scrap them altogether, just as Bob had suggested. She stuck them in the sanitary bin in the cubicle and emerged with a guilty look and a wonderfully free belly. She washed her hands and checked out her face in the mirror. The reflection didn't look like her. She'd gone to Brown Thomas and had her make-up done by a girl at the Mac counter who'd obviously looked on her freckled face as a challenge. But she'd done a great job and Donna was delighted with the result.

After a quick lipstick touch-up, she headed back out into the function room. God, it felt good to be rid of those constricting knickers. She was a little conscious of her protruding stomach but she reckoned most people would have beer goggles on by now so it didn't really matter. Although she was happy with her own dress, the style worn by some of the women was out of this world. She'd heard a woman earlier say she'd paid three thousand euros to have hers made and she still hadn't been entirely happy with it. She made her way past a crowd of men at the bar, trying to suck in her tummy as much as possible.

And then she heard it. One of the men was reciting a drinks order to the barman and the voice brought her back to another place and time. Oh God, it was happening again. William's face, clear and beautiful, came into her mind and almost immediately tears sprang to her eyes. But she wasn't going to let her imagination win this time. She was stronger now. She was more settled.

She didn't look back but quickened her step until she was back beside Bob again.

'Well?' He raised an eyebrow. 'Knickers or no knickers?'

Donna laughed. 'No knickers! And do you know what? It feels so liberating.'

'Fantastic. And just in time for dessert.'

'I'll tell you what,' said Donna, bending over to nibble on his ear. 'Why don't we get ourselves out of here, grab a burger and I'll treat you to a bit of dessert back at my place.'

'Now there's an offer I can't refuse.' Bob stumbled to his feet and led her towards the door.

Donna smiled and felt proud of herself. From now on, *she* was in control. She'd never again let her imagination or her memories drag her down.

Chapter 24

Will handed a fifty euro note to the barman and told him to keep the change. He loaded the drinks onto a tray and headed back to his table. He'd only arrived back into Dublin that afternoon and his parents had dragged him along to this charity ball thing. His mother had even organised a tux for him so he really hadn't had any excuses. He'd been dreading the night but it hadn't turned out too badly after all.

'Here you go,' he said, to nobody in particular, as he placed the tray on the table. 'Help yourselves.'

'William!' His mother hissed under her breath. 'You should give the drinks out to whoever asked for them. We're not at some bikers' convention.'

William bent over to whisper in her ear. 'I've never actually been to a bikers' convention, Mum. Have you?'

Vivienne Cooper-Smith reddened and glared at him. But he just smiled back and winked at his dad. The last couple of years had taught him a lot of things, one of them being how to deal with his mother. His time away meant that he no longer felt trapped or suffocated by her and he wasn't afraid to give her as good as he got. In a funny sort of way, the distance he'd put between them had helped him understand her a little bit better and he probably loved her more now than he ever had.

'So when are we going to meet this girl of yours?' asked his dad, tucking into his dessert of chocolate torte with Chantilly cream. 'She sounds like a cracker.'

'She is, Dad. Well, you've seen the pictures. She's gorgeous.'

His mother sniffed loudly. 'Well, it's all very well and good being beautiful, but does she have a brain to go with it? You don't want to waste all those qualifications you have by hooking up with some brainless bimbo.'

'Vivienne!' George glared at his wife. 'That's no way to speak about the lad's girlfriend. Sure, you know nothing about her. I'm sorry about your mother's ignorance, son.'

'Well, I … I was only saying … You should be working at what you qualified for rather than a dead-end job. Just because she has no ambition—'

'That's enough, Vivienne. You can't make judgements like that.'

'Don't worry, Dad. I can handle her.' Will was delighted his father had stuck up for him. He was usually so mild-mannered that Vivienne could say whatever she wanted and he'd just mumble: 'Yes, dear.'

'Tell us a bit more about her, Will,' continued George, ignoring the daggers looks he was getting from his wife. 'You said she's Italian?'

'Yes. Silvia was born in Italy but her family moved to Perth when she was ten and she's been there ever since. Well, at least until she came over to London.'

'And this is the girl who was your … your *companion* while you were travelling?' Vivienne emphasised 'companion' as though it was a dirty word.

'I told you, Mum. Silvia and I hooked up for a few months in Australia but we parted ways when I headed off to New Zealand and she went back to Perth.'

'Don't say "hooked up", William. It's such a vulgar term. So how come this … this Silvia ended up in London with you?'

'What can I say,' said Will, a smile spreading across his face. 'She missed me too much to stay away. Now why don't you two go and mingle. I just noticed some of your friends over there talking to that new BBC presenter.'

Vivienne's head shot around when she heard that snippet and she was already up off her chair and straightening her skirt. 'Well, okay then. If you're sure you'll be alright here for a bit. Come on, George. Didn't you want to talk to Gerry Kilbane about the new carpet for the clubhouse?'

She didn't wait for an answer from either of them and was over like a shot to the little group that was beginning to form around the presenter. Will smiled as his dad trotted after her with a sigh. He might be learning to talk back to her, but George Smith would always be at his wife's beck and call.

Will was glad that most of his parents' friends had moved away from the table. He didn't feel like chatting to a group of strangers. The small talk over dinner had been excruciating and all he wanted to do now was go home and get some sleep. His phone beeped and he pulled it out of his pocket, expertly flipping up the cover with one hand.

'*Hi, Sweetie. I hope you're having fun with your parents. It's great to be here but missing you loads. Sil. xxx*'

He answered her text straight away, saying he missed her too. And he did. It was funny how they'd fallen into an easy relationship again and they'd got closer and closer over the last few months. They were living together in London now but Silvia had wanted to go and join her family in Italy for Christmas. Her mam, dad and brother were coming over from Perth so it was going to be a huge family affair. Will's parents, particularly his mother, had begged him to come home for the festive season and he'd given in. It hadn't been entirely unselfish of him, of course. Despite the differences he'd had with his parents over the years, there really was nowhere he'd rather be for Christmas than at home.

He downed the last of his beer and glanced over at his parents. His mother hadn't changed a bit over the last few years but his father was looking gaunt and frail. His 'brush with death', as his mother called it, had frightened him and although he liked to pretend he was unbreakable, Will knew that he worried a lot about his mortality. 'When you think you're off to face the Grim Reaper,' he'd confided in him during a long phone call earlier in the year, 'you begin to realise how fragile life can be.'

It was after eleven and he was hoping to entice his parents into heading home soon. There were only a few days left before Christmas and he was planning on an early-morning trip into town to do a bit of shopping. But he'd have one more drink first.

As he stood at the bar, a tenner in his hand, trying to catch the attention of the over-worked barman, he noticed a girl staring. He smiled at her and she looked away, embarrassed. He was used to it. His deformed left hand caused a lot of morbid curiosity but it didn't faze him. There were worse things in life. Jack's face came into his mind and he sighed. It was almost four years since he'd taken his life and that day had changed Will forever. So what if he had a gammy hand? It reminded him of how lucky he was. He could have been killed in that earthquake. So many people were. He'd been lucky to escape with cuts, bruises and even a crushed hand.

He took his drink and headed back to the table. He was glad to see it was completely deserted now so he could just sit and think. His thoughts wandered, as they so often did, to Donna. Beautiful Donna. He'd made his peace long ago with the fact that he'd never see her again and he was happy with Silvia, but it didn't stop him wondering. What had happened to her on that day? He knew she wasn't dead, according to the information given out by the Christchurch authorities. But was she injured? Was she on her way to meet him when the quake struck or was she not even going to bother? Did she ever think of him? So many questions.

He gave himself a mental shake and downed the rest of his drink in one. He'd have to stop torturing himself with questions that were never going to be answered. Right, it was time to call it a night. He'd see if his parents were ready to come home and, if not, he'd get a taxi by himself. He just wanted to be home in bed so that he could talk to Silvia. It was an hour later in Italy so if he didn't get back soon, it would be too late to ring. He stuck his scarred hand in his pocket as he headed over to where his parents were chatting. It was what he did. The hand reminded him so he always shoved it out of sight when thoughts of the past began to haunt him. Donna was just a ghost of the past and some day he'd forget about her completely.

* * *

Donna lay in bed beside Bob and, in a funny sort of way, his gentle snores were relaxing her. Or maybe it was the few glasses of wine she'd had earlier. Either way, she felt happy. It had been a good night and it was going to be a wonderful Christmas. She thought back to Christmas last year and smiled at the memory of her kiss on the beach with Leo. Then she shuddered at the thought of her indiscretion afterwards.

She'd had some fun times on her travels. It all seemed like a different lifetime ago but she was glad she'd done it. It wasn't as though she'd just fecked off on her jollies – she'd done it with a purpose in mind. Tina. Tears immediately sprung to her eyes at the thought of her sister. She felt sad about her mam too, but Tina was the one she really mourned.

She turned onto her other side and tried to clear the dark fuzz that was threatening to consume her again. She let her thoughts turn to Lexie and how wonderful it was to have her around again. Tomorrow, thanks to Jan giving her the day off, she was going to spend the entire day with Lexie and they were going to go Christmas shopping.

Donna couldn't wait. She'd never really had a good girlfriend to go shopping with since Lexie had left. Tina had never really been into shopping and then after the fire … Jesus! There she was again, letting morbid thoughts overtake her.

Christmas Day was only a few days away and she was really looking forward to it. She and Bob were going to have dinner with Jan and Chris and they'd even invited Lexie over for the evening. It was great that there were no arguments between her and Bob about where they'd have Christmas dinner – his family was her family.

The light seeping through the curtains shone on her jade-green dress, which she'd hung on the front of the wardrobe, and Donna stared at it for a moment. Ever since she was a child, she'd believed in signs. She knew that most of them were just things she made up – situations or things she manipulated in her own mind to give her hope. But looking at the dress shining in the dark room, she felt a renewed sense of hope. It was a sign that things were changing. She was moving on. At last she felt strong enough to leave the past behind and move on with what she knew was going to be a wonderful future.

* * *

'I wish you were here with me, Sil. My bed feels so empty.'

'Same here,' whispered Silvia. 'But we'll be back home in a week and we can ring in the New Year together.'

They chatted for a few more minutes but Silvia couldn't stay on any longer. She said her grandmother's house was packed full of family and no matter where she moved, someone could hear her conversation.

'It will make our quiet apartment seem all the more enticing next week,' said Will, smiling at the picture she painted of the mad Italian house. 'Night, sweetie.'

In a way, it was good to be back home. He hadn't always felt that way but he'd mellowed a lot in the last few years. Maybe it was because he knew he was just there for a visit. Maybe it would be different if he was coming home to stay. But either way, except for missing Silvia, he was happy to be spending Christmas with his family.

He made sure his alarm was set for early and pulled the duvet up tightly around him. He was going to have a busy day tomorrow. He'd shunned his mother's offer of lunch because he had other plans. He'd decided he was going to drop in and see Jack's parents in the afternoon. He hadn't seen them since the funeral and he thought it was about time he spoke to them. He hadn't been particularly nice to them around that time. He'd never actually said it but he'd blamed them in a way for Jack's suicide. If they'd only spoken about his depression instead of ignoring it. They'd brought Jack up to believe that depression was something to hide – something to be ashamed of. He'd blamed himself too – he should have seen the signs. He should have listened to his friend more rather than moaning about his own problems. But time was a great healer and Will now knew that there was no point blaming anyone. Jack's death was awful but it wasn't his or anyone else's fault.

The room was roasting hot. Much to his father's annoyance, his mother loved to put the heat on full blast. It was great during the day but it made it almost impossible to sleep at night. He kicked off the duvet and lay flat on his back in his boxers.

Before his visit to Jack's parents in the afternoon, he had something important to do in the morning. He was going shopping for a very special purchase. He wasn't usually given to rash decisions but this one felt right. He hoped it would be the key to his happiness and secure the future he'd always dreamed of. He closed his eyes and silently prayed that it would all work out as he planned.

Chapter 25

Donna had always been a northside shopper. When she was growing up, most of her Saturdays were spent on Mary Street where Penneys offered the best bargains for cash-strapped teens and the Jervis Centre was the best hangout to look for boys. She would have considered Grafton Street too posh for someone like her, with its opulent shops and high-end fashion. But things had changed. There was no longer such a big divide between the north and south side and in fact Donna now preferred the buzz and atmosphere around Grafton Street.

They'd come in early to beat the crowds but it seemed everyone else had the same idea. The streets were heaving with Christmas shoppers, all frantic to stock up on last-minute Christmas gifts, and every restaurant and coffee shop had queues out the door. But they'd decided on breakfast in a little coffee shop in the Stephen's Green Centre and, although they had to wait a few minutes for a seat, it was worth it. The food was gorgeous and the staff friendly and helpful.

'So how does it feel to be home?' asked Donna, stuffing a forkful of poached egg into her mouth. 'Are you still happy with your decision?'

Lexie nodded straight away. 'I'm very happy to be home. But it's funny – it still kind of feels like I'm on holiday. I'm not sure it's quite hit me yet that I'm here to stay.'

'That's understandable. I'm sure it will take a while.'

A toddler at a nearby table squealed his delight at the pancakes that the waitress had just put in front of him and Donna smiled at the sight of his little face. She glanced at Lexie, who was watching him too with tears in her eyes.

'Aw, Lexie. It will work out. That'll be you one day, dining with your child, and all this will be a distant memory.'

Lexie sniffed and shifted her chair slightly so that the toddler wasn't in her eye-line. 'I hope you're right. Right now it feels like my life has been torn apart and I can't ever imagine being able to put it back together again.'

'I've been there,' said Donna, grabbing Lexie's hand and squeezing it. 'Not with a man but with my family. I hit rock bottom, remember?'

'Of course. I'm sorry, I'm just being silly. My troubles can't even come close to what you went through.'

'I'm not saying that, Lexie. I'm just trying to tell you that things *will* get better.' Donna smiled then. 'But the irony of the situation isn't lost on me.'

'What irony?'

'Well, after the fire – when I was at my lowest …'

'Go on.' Lexie was sitting forward now, her earlier tears forgotten.

'I wanted to kill anyone who told me things would get better. I swear, every time I heard those words, I was filled with rage.'

Lexie laughed at that. 'Well, I haven't quite got to that stage yet but give me a bit of time. So go on then. Distract me from my morbid thoughts. Take me out of the depths of my depression. Isn't that how it's supposed to work?'

'Yep. That's how it works. But I didn't say I was very good at it.'

'Tell me about Bob.'

That took Donna by surprise. 'What do you want to know? You probably know everything about him. Actually, if he knew that you knew half the stuff, he'd be mortified.'

'You mean like his post-coital snore?' giggled Lexie. 'Or the way he likes his belly rubbed?'

Donna glanced around to make sure nobody had heard. 'Oh God, I shouldn't really share that stuff, should I? You'd better not tell him I told you. He'd die!'

'Your secrets are safe with me. You really love him, don't you?'

'I do …'

'But?'

'But what?'

Lexie shook her head. 'I know you only too well, Donna. There was definitely a "but" coming.'

Donna thought for a minute. Did she want to tell Lexie about William? Did she want to tell her that, although she loved Bob, she was still hankering after a man she'd met only briefly in New Zealand? She'd tell her some day, but now wasn't the right time.

'Donna?'

'You're right, Lexie. There was a "but". It's just that I'm afraid to let myself love Bob completely in case it all goes wrong. I've had enough heartache to last me a lifetime and I really don't need to add a broken heart to that.'

'Aw, Donna. You poor thing. But Bob adores you. I've seen the way he looks at you. I don't think you need to worry on that score.'

'Maybe,' said Donna, not wanting to look at Lexie. She felt bad for lying to her but it wasn't entirely a lie. She still found it hard to believe that she could be happy – that something bad wasn't waiting around the corner to crush her again.

'We're a right pair, aren't we?' Lexie waved at the waiter to bring the bill. 'Come on, let's cheer ourselves up with a bit of shopping. I fancy treating myself to a bottle of Jo Malone from Brown Thomas. I think I deserve a treat.'

Donna was glad to change the subject. 'Good idea. And we can have a look in the Christmas shop while we're in there. They sell the most beautiful decorations and I want to get a special one for Jan's tree.'

They walked arm in arm down Grafton Street, the sound of buskers and carol singers lifting their mood. As they passed a jeweller's shop, Donna couldn't help noticing a couple kissing passionately right in front of the window. Were they on their way in to buy an engagement ring? Or even a wedding ring? Had he just proposed? She wondered would she ever be in that situation. Lexie had obviously seen them too because she made a disapproving noise and quickened her step.

'It'll be okay, Lexie. *We'll* be okay.' And she meant it. A picture sprang to her mind of two little girls sitting on a wall outside their houses. They were wondering if they'd still be best friends when they grew up. 'Let's be best friends forever – BFF,' an eight-year-old Donna had said. 'Okay,' Lexie had replied. 'Even when we get married and are mammies.' Donna smiled at the memory, as they stepped out of the cold into Brown Thomas. Where would she be without her BFF!

* * *

'Let me know if you need any help, sir,' said the eager shop assistant, his eyes bulging at the thought of an expensive sale.

'Thanks, but I'm just browsing at the moment.' Will had been looking at engagement rings in a jeweller's on Grafton Street for the last twenty minutes and he was still none the wiser. What had started out as a great idea was now beginning to feel like a bad one. The more he looked at rings, the more he realised he really didn't know much about Silvia's taste in jewellery.

Would she like something simple on her finger or a big statement ring? Coloured stones or diamonds? White gold or red gold? New or antique? He didn't know the answers to any of those questions and, furthermore, he hadn't even got a clue what size to get. He really hadn't thought any of it out very well.

'I can take some out for you to have a closer look, if you like.' Will could almost see the shop assistant salivating. 'Sometimes it's easier to make a decision when you can hold the rings and get a better sense of them.'

'I think maybe I'll leave it for—'

'And of course we have twenty per cent off for today only. It would be madness to pass up on it if you're planning to buy anyway.'

Will sighed. 'Okay, then. Let's have a look at that tray there.'

The poor guy almost choked with excitement as he fumbled with the keys to open the cabinet. He took out the tray Will had pointed to and set it down on the glass counter.'

'Any idea what the lady would like? A solitaire, a cluster? How about this one here? It's a real beauty.' He placed a solitaire ring on a cloth and Will almost choked when he saw the price tag. Four thousand euros!

'I'm … I'm not sure about that one, to be honest. I was thinking more …' That's when he saw it. It was perfect. Like magic, it shone from the cabinet as if it was calling out to him. 'That one!'

The assistant looked confused. 'But, sir, I assume you're looking for an engagement ring? That one is more of a dress ring.'

'Well, can I see it, please? It could be just what I'm looking for.'

'Of course.'

It was a beautiful ring – white gold with the most gorgeous lime-green stone surrounded by small diamonds. All the other rings paled into insignificance as soon as he'd seen this one.

'Here, take a closer look,' said the assistant, clearly realising that he wasn't going to get a sale on the more expensive rings. 'It's quite a pretty ring, isn't it?'

Will nodded. But something just didn't feel right. No matter how perfect the ring was, he just couldn't see it on Silvia. Maybe he was over-thinking it. Maybe he should just buy it and they could have it adjusted if it didn't fit. He spent a few minutes twirling it around in his hand until, eventually, he placed it back down on the cloth.

'I'm sorry, but I'm going to leave it for today. Thanks for your help. I just need to have a think.' Will got out of there as fast as he could and breathed a sigh of relief. A loved-up couple were standing at the window of the shop snogging the face off each other and it suddenly hit him. Maybe it just didn't feel right because Silvia wasn't there with him. Surely buying an engagement ring should be something they did together. He'd been silly to think he could do it on his own.

God, he needed a drink after that. He was close to the Westbury Hotel so maybe he'd pop in for a beer. He liked it there, although he hadn't been in a while. He loved how the bar upstairs looked down on the street below and the seats were roomy and comfortable.

Ten minutes later he was sitting with a beer in his hand watching the world go by. He loved London but there was something relaxing about being back in Ireland. Although Dublin was a busy city, somehow the pace of life seemed slower.

He thought of Silvia and wondered what she was doing. He missed her. It was strange how he'd found the whole ring business so stressful. He felt sure he'd ask her to marry him at some stage, but maybe now wasn't the right time. Although that ring had been perfect. Maybe he'd bring her over in the New Year and they could look at it together. What did he know about rings? It would be much better if she chose it herself.

It was funny to think that, less than a year ago, Will had thought he'd never see Silvia again. But despite breaking up, they'd kept in touch regularly. And after the earthquake, she'd phoned him almost every day to check up on him. She'd said she missed him. She was miserable in Perth without him.

He'd stayed with his parents for a couple of months while he was having treatment for his hand but he'd always known he wouldn't settle there again. As luck would have it, one of his college friends opened a bar in London and offered him a job. By mid-May, he was living in a flat in London and working as a manager in the bar.

A few weeks later, Silvia had arrived with a whole lot of luggage and a declaration of love. She'd taken him by surprise at first but it hadn't taken him long to realise she was exactly what he needed. He'd been torturing himself looking for Donna since he'd come back to Ireland and had become more and more frustrated with the process. He'd checked out every social networking site he could think of for Donnas from Dublin but he hadn't found a match. Silvia had been a distraction and, once he'd settled into life with her, he'd tried to put Donna firmly from his mind. They'd fallen back into an easy relationship and things had blossomed from there.

He drained the last of his beer and checked his watch. Much as he'd love to stay and have another, he really needed to make a move. He left a generous tip on the table and headed back downstairs and out to join the hordes of shoppers. Just ahead of him, two girls were linking each other and laughing loudly. Suddenly one of them dropped something and when she turned back to pick it up, Will's heart almost stopped. It was Donna. He was sure of it. That hair, those freckles. He stood rooted to the spot for a few seconds until he finally found his voice.

'Donna.' The word came out as barely a whisper and he'd already lost sight of her as shoppers zig-zagged in every direction.

'Donna.' He tried again. Louder this time. But it was no use. He rushed off in the direction she'd been walking but there was no sign of her. He checked inside a few of the nearby shops in case she'd gone in to one of them. It wasn't long before he realised his search was futile. He couldn't believe that he'd actually seen her. She'd been right there in front of him. If only he'd been quicker to react. He shook his head at his own stupidity. After all this time of wondering, he'd actually found her. And lost her. Again.

Chapter 26

'Thanks for this, Donna,' said Lexie, dropping her suitcases in the hall. 'Granddad is coming in with a box of stuff and that's the last of it.'

'It's no problem. I'm delighted to have you here.' And Donna meant it. The two girls had been seeing a lot of each other in the few months Lexie had been home but Donna had been finding it difficult to visit her on their old street. When Lexie had announced she'd had enough of living at home, Donna hadn't hesitated in offering for her to come and stay at her place.

'Here you go, love.' Lexie's granddad arrived at the door carrying an enormous box filled to the brim with stuff and left it down beside the rest of the luggage. 'Do you need me for anything else or can I get off? Your gran has the dinner almost ready.'

'You head off, Granddad,' said Lexie, placing a kiss on his cheek. 'We can take it from here.'

'Okay, love.' He turned to Donna. 'And I hope you get your problem sorted out, whatever it is. My Anna is saying a prayer for you.'

'My what?' said Donna, looking from him to Lexie.

Lexie turned puce and shot her a warning look. 'She'll be fine, Granddad. I'll look after her.'

They waved him off and, as soon as he was out of sight, Donna turned to her friend. 'My problem? Do you want to enlighten me?'

'Sorry about that, Donna. It's just that I couldn't tell them I wanted to move out because they were driving me mad.'

'So you told them what exactly?'

'I wasn't specific. I just said you had a personal problem and you could do with a friend so I was moving in with you.'

'Oh, great. Now they're going to blame me for you moving out. Why could you not just have said you wanted to stand on your own two feet instead of relying on them?'

'I know, I know. It just came out. But no harm done, is there?'

Donna sighed. 'I suppose not. Now let's get this stuff into your room and we can have a cup of tea. Maybe we'll order in a pizza later. I've been feeling shitty all day and have barely eaten anything.'

Half an hour later they were sitting on the sofa, feet curled up underneath them, mugs of steaming hot tea in their hands. Donna felt quite excited for Lexie to be there. It felt like old times. When they lived next door to each other, they'd slept in each other's houses regularly. This felt like a grown-up sleepover and Donna was going to enjoy every minute of it.

'So how did Bob take it?'

'Take what?' Donna sipped her tea.

'Me moving in. I'm sure he's not thrilled about it and, I swear, as soon as I can get the deposit together, I'll be out looking for a place of my own.'

'Relax, Lexie. Bob was absolutely fine about it. Almost *too* fine, actually.'

Lexie raised her eyebrows. 'What do you mean?'

'Oh, don't mind me. I'm just being silly.'

'Come on. You can't leave it at that.'

Donna put her empty cup on the coffee table and considered how much she wanted to say to Lexie. 'There's no story, really. It's just Bob. He's … well, it's just that he seems …'

'Jesus, Donna. Please don't tell me you two are in trouble. You're the most loved-up couple I know.'

'No, no. Nothing like that. We're fine. It's just that sometimes I wonder about the type of relationship we have.'

Lexie said nothing so Donna continued.

'I mean, we definitely love each other and we have fun together but it's not wildly exciting.'

'Oh, for fuck's sake,' spat Lexie, all trace of her earlier concern gone. 'Is that all? Believe me, you can live without wild excitement in your life.'

Donna was a bit taken aback. 'I know what you're saying but sometimes it feels like we're both just settling. It's an easy relationship. We're comfortable with each other.'

'But is that the worst thing? A lot of people would kill for a relationship like that.'

'But he didn't even flinch when I suggested you move in. Don't get me wrong – I'm delighted he's happy about it, but I just wish he'd have shown some concern for the fact that we won't have the place to ourselves any more.'

'He loves you, Donna. He's just doing what any supportive boyfriend would do. I'm sure he'd prefer to have you on your own but at least you still have your own bedroom.'

'That's just it, Lexie. I'm not sure he'd prefer to have me on my own. He's nearly more excited about having you here than I am!'

Lexie laughed at that. 'I'm sure that's not the case.'

'Seriously. He started talking about what sort of food you like so we can stock up and he was thrilled to hear you like rom-coms too!'

Lexie drained her tea and left it down with a bang. 'Do you love him?'

'Yes, definitely.'

'And does he love you?'

'I'm pretty sure he does.'

'Do you have good sex?'

'Lexie!'

'I'm serious. If it's more of a friendship thing, which you seem to be suggesting, you wouldn't be enjoying the sex, would you?'

Donna thought for a moment. 'Well, yes. We have good sex – not mind-blowing, but good.'

'Right so. I can't see what the problem is. Unless one of you has been unfaithful, and I don't think that's the case.'

Donna bit her lip.

Lexie looked alarmed. 'Please tell me you haven't, Donna.'

Donna still hadn't told anyone about Will but now seemed as good a time as any. 'Well, I haven't been unfaithful exactly.'

'But?'

'But there *is* another guy. I'm not seeing him or anything but I think about him all the time. And sometimes when I'm with Bob – properly with him, if you know what I mean – I picture this other person.'

'Who is it?' Lexie was looking at her accusingly.

'You don't know him.'

'But is this serious? Does Bob know about him? How come you didn't tell me this before?'

'I'm sorry, Lexie. I just didn't think the time was right. And the thing is, I barely know this other guy and I probably never will.'

'Now you really have me intrigued,' said Lexie. 'Tell me everything.'

So Donna began. She told her about tripping her way into the tourist office that day and into the arms of the most intriguing and handsome man she'd ever met in her life. She told her about going for coffee, how they almost kissed and how she'd dreamt about him all night. And then she began to explain about that dreadful day, but it became too much for her.

'Oh, Donna, you poor thing.' Lexie moved over to hug her. 'I'm always going on about my problems and I forget how much you've had to deal with this last year.'

'It was such an awful day,' sobbed Donna, letting the tears flow freely. 'Seeing all those people trapped and injured and not knowing if I was going to get out of it alive. It was like the end of the world.'

'I can't even begin to imagine.'

They sat there in companionable silence for a few minutes, Donna lost in thought. She avoided thinking too much about that day because it was one of the scariest days of her life but telling Lexie about it had dredged up all the horror and helplessness she'd felt back then.

After some time had passed, Lexie spoke but kept her voice to a whisper. 'So you never got to see him again?'

Donna shook her head. 'When I got to the square, there was no sign of him. But there were people running everywhere, screaming and crying. Pieces were falling off buildings, alarms were going off – the whole place was in total chaos.'

'God, it must have been terrifying.'

'It was. All I could do was make my way back to where I was staying. I don't even remember walking back. I think I was in shock or something.'

'Of course you were. How could you not have been? And you didn't have his number to ring?'

'I did at first but I must have lost it in the chaos. And I hadn't given him mine so there was no way of getting to him. I know that it sounds ridiculous but I honestly think I fell in love with him that day.' She began to cry softly again.

Lexie gasped. 'That's a big statement, Donna. But do you think maybe it's down to the situation?'

'What do you mean?'

'It's just such a crazy thing to have happened. The whole thing of meeting him and then losing him because of an earthquake. It's like something you'd read about. Maybe if you'd found him, things would have been different but because you never saw him again, you're romanticising about him.'

Donna just nodded. How could she explain to anyone the depth of her feelings for William? She'd felt it from the first moment she'd laid eyes on him and she was pretty sure he'd felt it too.

'Bob is *here*, Donna. He's a reality. And he loves you so much. I can see it in his eyes. Don't throw it away for a memory.'

'You're right, of course,' said Donna, wiping her eyes. 'I should stop putting obstacles in the way.'

Lexie smiled. 'I'm glad we have that sorted. I can see you and Bob together when you're old and grey and have masses of grandchildren all around you.'

'Now let's not get ahead of—' Donna paled. It was the grandchildren comment that did it. She'd been feeling sick for days. But they'd been careful. Think, Donna, think. When had she had her last period? Oh God. It couldn't be … she couldn't be … Bile rose up in her throat and she had to make a dash for the bathroom. The last thing she remembered was putting her head against the cold tiles and sliding to the floor.

Chapter 27

The air was warm but the breeze cool as Will and Silvia walked hand in hand around Hyde Park. April was Will's favourite month. It was as though the world was suddenly coming to life after the dark winter and the bursts of colour from the newly sprouting blooms exuded happiness.

'Let's go and sit down for a bit,' said Silvia, pointing to an empty bench just beside a fountain with a beautifully sculpted figure in the centre. 'My feet are killing me.'

'I did tell you not to wear those new boots. You need sensible shoes for walking.'

'The words "sensible" and "shoes" don't go well together, as far as I'm concerned. Unless you're an old fuddy-duddy, of course.'

Will pretended to be offended. 'Are you calling me an old fuddy-duddy, then?'

'Well, if the shoe fits … excuse the pun!'

She ducked out of his way as he tried to tickle her and they landed on the bench with a thud. The tickling soon turned to kissing and Will could feel himself harden as Silvia's tongue probed inside his mouth.

'Jesus, Sil,' he said, gasping for air. 'If you don't stop now, I might just take you right here on the park bench.'

'Behave! There'll be plenty of time for that later. You know how *Match of the Day* always turns me on.'

Will laughed. But it was true. Not only was Silvia beautiful, clever and kind, she also loved football. They'd usually spend Saturday night in with a few beers, a bucket-load of nachos and football on the telly. She was every man's dream.

A woman walked past with a whole clatter of children, two in a double buggy and another few running along beside her. They all squealed with delight when they spotted the fountain and the woman doled out coins for them to throw in.

'Don't forget to make a wish,' she said, as the children ran excitedly towards the water with their precious coins.

Silvia snuggled in further to Will as they watched the scene unfold. He wondered if they were both thinking the same thing. They'd never discussed the future in any great detail but Will knew that Silvia wanted a big family. Even though she just had one brother, she was very close to her extended Italian family. She'd told him that her mother had wanted more children but sadly it hadn't happened.

He thought back to that day just before Christmas when he'd almost bought her an engagement ring. It just hadn't felt right in that moment in time but he was sure that he'd know when the time was right. He was a romantic at heart and wasn't given to spontaneity. He wanted to plan it properly. If he was going to propose, it would be with all the bells and whistles. He'd make it a moment to remember for both of them.

'Are you happy here in London?'

The question took Will by surprise. 'Why do you ask?'

'I'm just curious. You worked very hard to get your law qualifications and now you're working in a bar. Don't you want to use your degree?'

Jesus. Had she been talking to his mother? 'Where's this coming from, Silvia? It never bothered you before that I was just a lowly barman.'

'It doesn't bother me, Will. And I never said you were a lowly anything. But it bothers me to be making sandwiches in a coffee shop when I've got a degree in business and finance. I want more for myself. I have ambitions.'

'I know, Sil. I have too. Well, I'd certainly like to be making more money. But we've applied for hundreds of jobs. There's just nothing out there at the moment.'

'But what if we were to move – go somewhere else where the job situation is better.'

Will looked at her in surprise. 'Like where? Are you talking about moving back to Perth?'

'Maybe. Oh, I don't know. I'm just fed up earning a pittance and every penny we have is going on rent and bills.'

'But we get by, don't we? And we're happy.'

Silva sat up straight. 'But I don't want to just get by. I want more than that. I want us to think to the future. I want us to be able to save. To buy a place of our own.' She gazed over at the children, who were now chasing each other around the fountain.

Will's mouth went dry. 'Do you mean you want us to properly settle down?'

'Well … yes. Isn't that what you want too?'

'Of course I do. But I suppose we've just never talked about it – about the future.'

'Well, we're talking about it now.' Silvia took his hand. 'Will, I'm an Italian woman. I'm loyal and passionate but also have a huge sense of family. And that's what I want for us. I'm not in this for just the fun of it. I didn't come all the way from Perth to have a fling.'

'But you know this isn't a fling.' Will wasn't sure where this was going.

'Let me finish. I love you, Will. And I'm pretty sure you feel the same way. So why don't we take our relationship to the next level. Let's get married.'

The words hung in the air for a few moments. Will opened his mouth but no words came out.

'Will?'

'I … what exactly do you … I mean, is that a proposal?'

Silvia laughed. 'If that's what you want to call it, then yes. I think if we have something to drive us – something to focus on – we'll achieve what we want much quicker. Weddings don't come cheap so we'll need to get our act together.'

Jesus. She was talking about a wedding already.

'We should broaden our thinking,' she continued. 'Let's apply for jobs further afield and see what comes up. If you did some Italian classes and learned the language, we could even consider Italy.'

It was all moving very fast.

'So what do you say? Will?'

'Well, yes, I suppose.'

Silvia glared at him. 'Is that the best you can do? I've just asked you to marry me!'

'I'm sorry. You just took me by surprise. But yes! Absolutely yes, I'll marry you. I can't think of anything better.' He bent over and kissed her, cupping her face in his hands.

The sound of laughter made them pull apart and they realised the children were pointing at them and giggling. They laughed too and snuggled in to each other. Will's head was spinning. They were engaged – just like that. He felt happy about it. At least, he thought he did. He also felt a little cheated. He'd imagined the scenario so many times. How he'd ask her. Where they'd be. What she'd say. But Silvia had just trumped him with her casual proposal and sensible approach.

'Come on,' said Silvia, standing up suddenly and pulling him off the bench. 'We need to go home and start planning. Isn't it exciting?'

Will nodded with as much enthusiasm as he could muster. 'Very.'

'I can't wait to start telling everyone. Do you think we should get the ring before we tell them or just go ahead and tell them anyway?'

Jesus! 'Let's just wait for a while. We need time to enjoy the moment ourselves before anyone else knows.'

'You're right. But I have to tell Nonni straight away. You know I tell her everything.' Nonni was Silvia's grandmother in Italy and the two were very close. Somehow Will didn't think the news would remain a secret for long.

As they headed out through the park gates, Will thought back to that flight he'd taken from Sydney to New Zealand. It was just after he'd said goodbye to Silvia. He hadn't shed a tear. He hadn't felt devastated. The realisation had dawned on him that Silvia just wasn't the one. And now he was about to commit the rest of his life to her. So what had changed?

He glanced at her beautiful face as they headed towards home and it dawned on him. *He* had changed. The earthquake had taught him that life could be snatched away at any moment and he should grab whatever chance of happiness came his way. And Silvia made him happy. He suddenly got a spring in his step and was overcome by a surge of happiness. Silvia was going to be his wife and they were going to have a wonderful life together.

* * *

Gastroenteritis was what the doctor had concluded. The pregnancy test had come back negative and Donna hadn't even been able to celebrate because she'd puked for three days straight.

When Lexie had found her collapsed on the bathroom floor, she'd immediately called an ambulance and had stayed by her side until she was finally admitted to a ward. Bob had taken over then, arriving at the hospital in a panic after receiving a phone call from Lexie.

It was almost a week later and Donna was finally beginning to feel human again. God, she never knew gastroenteritis could be so vicious. Her stomach felt as though she'd done a thousand push-ups because it was so sore from all the heaving and her throat was stripped raw from the retching. But at least the vomiting had stopped and she felt ready to try and eat something.

'Here you go,' said Bob, placing a steaming hot bowl on the coffee table in front of her. 'Homemade vegetable soup. And it's my mam's recipe so if that doesn't make you better, I don't know what will.'

'Thanks, love. I actually think I might manage a few spoonfuls.'

'Well, just take it slowly. Your stomach needs to adjust to food again.'

Donna smiled. 'Oh, so you're a doctor now as well as a maid?'

'Well, with you being laid up, I'm your *everything* at the moment, so you'd better watch out!' He kissed her lightly on the top of the head and headed back into the kitchen.

Bob had been a godsend this last week. They'd kept her in hospital for two days, after which she'd come home and collapsed in a heap on the sofa. She'd had no energy and, furthermore, the vomiting had continued. Not as viciously or as often as it had in the first couple of days, but just as debilitating. Lexie had come down with the bug too but, luckily for her, it was a much milder dose and had only lasted twenty-four hours. She'd told Bob to stay away. She already felt guilty about Lexie and didn't want him getting sick too. But he'd been insistent. She needed looking after and he wanted to be the one to do it.

'How's that going down?' He peeped out from the kitchen and Donna laughed. He was wearing rubber gloves up to his elbows and holding his hands in the air as though he was about to perform surgery.

'Good,' she lied. She'd had a couple of spoonfuls but she was so tired of throwing up at this stage that she was too nervous to try any more.

'That's great. I'm just popping an apple tart in the oven so maybe you'll try a bit of that in a while.'

Donna was gobsmacked. 'You've made an apple tart?'

'Don't be silly, Donna. Mam baked it this morning and told me to bring it over. I'm just heating it up.'

He disappeared back into the kitchen and Donna flopped back on the sofa. She couldn't deny Bob's dedication to her. He'd held her hair as she'd puked into a bucket and cleaned up the splashes when she'd missed. It hadn't bothered him that he might get the bug too – his only concern was for her and to get her well again.

She flicked around the channels on the telly before throwing the remote down on the sofa. She'd had enough of *Toddlers & Tiaras* and day-time talk shows to last her a lifetime. What she really needed to do was get back on her feet again. She'd already missed a week of work and she hated that somebody else had to be brought in to fill the orders for cakes. She glanced at the bowl of soup and knew she'd have to make a better effort. Sitting up, she dipped her spoon in again and had another go. It was really quite nice. And once she'd had a few spoonfuls, her stomach began to settle. Thank God the worst seemed to be over.

What a week it had been. And it had started with the scary thought that maybe she was pregnant. Would it have been such a bad thing? Probably. She wasn't ready for that sort of commitment. She wondered how Bob would have felt. She didn't think he was ready for it either. Despite their closeness and despite how much they loved each other, they just didn't talk about the future. She wasn't sure what that meant. Were they afraid to burst the bubble of what they had by taking things to another level? Or did they both know in their hearts that they weren't destined to be together?

Chapter 28

'I'm not sure I want to do this now, Donna. Maybe we should leave it until after Christmas.'

Donna took Lexie's hand and squeezed it. 'You need to do it now. If you keep putting it off, nothing will ever get sorted.'

'I know,' sighed Lexie. 'The sensible part of my brain is telling me that I just need to get the ball rolling and be rid of that man once and for all.'

'But?' Much as Donna wanted to see her friend happy, she hoped she wasn't having second thoughts. She was used to having her around now and she'd be devastated if that changed.

'But the emotional side – the mushy side that I'm trying to ignore – is remembering all the good times. Because we really were happy once. I really believe he loved me ...' Big fat tears sprang to her eyes.

Donna knew at that moment that she couldn't be selfish. Much as she wanted to keep Lexie here, she needed to get behind her and respect whatever decision she wanted to make.

'I mean, you saw him,' continued Lexie, taking a tissue from Donna. 'Didn't you think he loved me? Didn't you see how well he treated me?'

'I did, Lexie. There's no doubt he loved you. And if you've changed your mind about any of this, I'll support you. If you want to go back and give it another go, if you want to try and work things out I'll be here for you. It's a big decision – a final one – so please think carefully.'

'Are you mad, Donna?' Lexie stared at her. 'I will *never* forgive him for what he's done and I'll most definitely never, *ever* go back to him.'

'I … I just thought you were having a rethink, Lexie. I really want you here but I don't want to be selfish about it.'

'You could never be selfish, Donna. You're the most loving and kind-hearted person I know. Brendan and I have both moved on but I suppose it's only natural that I think back to happier times. I want to make our split official but it's just hard to think of having to go through all the legal stuff.'

'Lexie Byrne?' The young assistant who'd greeted them earlier, dressed in grey pencil skirt and white blouse with a frilly front, interrupted their conversation. 'Mrs Cooper-Smith said she's sorry for the delay but she'll be another five minutes. Can I get you some tea or coffee?'

'Not for me, thanks,' said Lexie.

'Me neither.' Donna could have murdered a cup of tea but she didn't want to be the only one.

The assistant smiled, turned on the heel of her sensible black leather shoes and disappeared back through the large white door.

Donna felt as though they'd stepped back in time as they sat in the shabby but lavish waiting room. The ceilings were high with a large dusty chandelier hanging from an ornate plaster rose and the chairs were a mishmash of shapes and sizes – some with faded green upholstery and some with beautifully carved high backs. Even the assistant looked as though she belonged in a 1950s movie with her full red lips and powdered white face.

It was a year since Lexie had arrived home and, for Donna, it felt like she'd never been away. They'd fallen into the easy friendship of their childhood and Donna loved having her around. Lexie didn't speak much about Brendan except to assure Donna she was over him. But Donna wasn't a fool. It couldn't be that easy, especially when she'd spent years with him and thought they'd be together for life. So it had taken Donna by surprise when Lexie herself had suggested taking the first steps to a divorce.

'Are you sure that's what you want?' Donna had asked, feeling a mixture of relief and sadness.

'I'm sure,' Lexie had replied. 'There's nothing left and I might as well move on with my life as a free woman.'

That's when Donna had remembered the card that Vivienne Cooper-Smith had left when she'd picked up the cake. Donna didn't know any other solicitors so she thought they might as well give her a try.

'She'll see you now.' The assistant was back, standing at the over-sized door and smiling sweetly. 'Follow me.'

They followed her through the door, which surprisingly opened almost straight onto a flight of stairs going downwards. Donna idly thought of the possible claims from anyone rushing through the door and tumbling straight down. The irony of it wasn't lost on her and she was still smiling when they were led into a stale-smelling office with Vivienne Cooper-Smith sitting behind an enormous desk.

She stood up to shake their hands. 'Dana, nice to see you again. And this is Lexie, I presume?'

'Em, yes, this is Lexie. And it's Donna, actually.' She could have bitten her tongue off because the woman in front of her didn't look as though she liked to be corrected.

'Yes. Donna. That's what I said.' It wasn't what she'd said.

'So,' she continued, indicating for them to sit down, 'you want a divorce, Lexie.'

She was straight to the point and Donna could see Lexie felt a bit intimidated.

'We just want to find out what's involved initially,' said Donna, while Lexie gathered her thoughts. 'It's probably complicated because her husband is in Australia.'

'Ah, you must have studied law, so.' Vivienne smiled sweetly and Donna felt like shrinking under the table.

'Well, no, I just assumed—'

'That's the problem with the general public. They just *assume* things without proper knowledge. Maybe you can tell me the whole story and I'll tell you what the law says.'

Lexie piped up. 'Well, there's no need to—'

'It's okay, Lexie,' said Donna, not wanting to get on the wrong side of a woman who looked as though she could crush anyone with her stare. 'Mrs Cooper-Smith is right. We should just find out where you stand legally instead of assuming. It might all be more straightforward than we think.'

That seemed to satisfy Vivienne and she turned her attention to Lexie. 'So, do you want to start with telling me the basic facts. I assume you brought the marriage certificate with you?'

'Yes, I have it here.' Lexie pulled a brown envelope out of her bag and shoved it across the table.

'Good. Now I'm going to take some notes today and we can arrange to meet again maybe next week.' She glanced at her watch. 'I'm running a bit behind at the moment and I need to be out of here in half an hour.'

Donna resisted the urge to say something. A half an hour wasn't much to lay your whole life on the table. She just hoped she hadn't made a mistake bringing Lexie here. She sat back and listened as Lexie spoke about her marriage to Brendan and watched as Vivienne Cooper-Smith nodded and took notes. It irritated Donna to see the woman check her watch every couple of minutes but she decided to let it go since Lexie seemed oblivious to it.

'Right, I think I have enough to go on with for now,' said Vivienne, when Lexie had finished speaking. 'Just give me a few days to get some stuff together and I'll be in touch.'

'Is that it?' Lexie looked surprised. 'I mean, don't you need to hear more details?'

'Details aren't important at the moment. The bad news is that because he's in Australia, things might move a little slower.'

That's what Donna had been afraid of. She'd heard of these family law cases that went on for years and years and she didn't want Lexie to end up a snivelling mess at the end of it all.

'But the good news,' continued Vivienne, 'is that if what you're saying is correct and that your husband won't block anything, things should run relatively smoothly.'

'That's brilliant, isn't it, Lexie?' Donna looked at her friend, who looked very pale, and felt sorry for her. 'I mean, it's great that it won't be messy or anything. It would be awful if you and Brendan ended up fighting over stuff.'

'I suppose.'

Vivienne waded in again. 'And the fact that you didn't own your own house and neither of you have pensions to worry about makes things a whole lot easier.' She glanced at her watch again.

'We won't keep you any longer,' said Lexie, standing up. 'Thanks for your time.'

'No problem. Melissa, my assistant, will be in touch with another appointment.'

They shook hands with her and headed out to where Melissa was sitting at a much smaller desk. Lexie took her wallet out of her bag and handed her credit card to the girl.

Melissa looked at her blankly.

Lexie looked uncomfortable. 'I assume you take credit cards.'

'Well, yes, of course we do. But Mrs Cooper-Smith said that I wasn't to charge you for today.'

'Oh.' Lexie looked at Donna, who shrugged.

'In fact,' continued Melissa, 'she said that we wouldn't be charging you anything at all until the matter goes to court. And at that stage, we can talk about working something out.'

Donna was stunned. Even though Vivienne Cooper-Smith had left her card and said she'd look after her if she ever needed a solicitor, she hadn't expected the woman to waive her fees.

'That's very kind of her,' said Lexie, clearly delighted at not having her card laden down. 'I really appreciate it.'

'Ah, Dana, I was hoping I'd catch you.' Vivienne breezed out of her office, fixing a red silk scarf under the collar of her tweed coat. 'I'm flying but I forgot to say thanks again for the amazing cake. My George loved it and so did everyone else.'

Donna reddened. 'You're welcome. If you ever need another one, just pop down to me and I'll sort you out.'

'I'll do that. Melissa, you'll get me on my mobile if it's urgent but otherwise I'll return all calls in the morning.' She nodded her goodbyes and was gone with a whoosh of her coat, leaving a trail of White Linen perfume behind.

'It's her son,' said Melissa, leaning over as though she was telling them a state secret. 'He's coming home.'

For some reason, Donna was surprised she had a son. 'He lives abroad, then?'

'Not any more. He was living in London for a while but he and his fiancée are coming back to live in Ireland.'

Donna idly wondered if they'd be in the market for a wedding cake. She'd only just started doing tiered cakes but already she was getting a brilliant response. She'd done a wedding cake for a couple a few weeks before and they'd wanted a fun cake rather than a serious one. So she'd created a bedroom scene on the top tier, with the bride sitting up in bed and the groom passed out on the bed in his wedding suit. The couple had said it was genius and she'd even got a few orders for next year as a result.

'Donna?' Lexie was staring at her.

'Sorry, what?' She was miles away.

'I was just saying we should get going. Bob said he'd have dinner ready at six.'

They thanked Melissa again and headed outside into the cold December air. Donna shivered and pulled the zip of her parka jacket right up to her chin.

'That went well,' said Lexie, linking Donna as they headed towards the bus stop. 'I feel like there's a weight lifted off already.'

'That's brilliant, Lexie. All we need now is to find you a decent man.' She had the words out before she realised how insensitive it sounded, given the circumstances. But Lexie didn't seem to mind.

'Maybe in time. If I could only find someone like Bob, I'd be happy. He's been such a good friend to me, Donna. You both have.'

Donna squeezed her arm. That was Bob all over – the best friend a woman could have. He was definitely her best friend. But was that enough? Only time would tell.

* * *

Will glanced at Silvia as the 'fasten seat belts' sign lit up and the plane started its bumpy descent to Dublin airport.

'Any regrets?' he asked her, taking her hand.

'Not one. It's going to be a great new adventure for us and I can't wait to see what the future holds.'

He squeezed her hand but wished he shared her confidence. It was eight months since their engagement – or secret engagement, as they liked to call it. After that day in the park when Silvia had proposed, he'd managed to convince her that they should keep it to themselves for a while.

'It wouldn't be fair to tell your parents news like this over the phone,' he'd offered. 'Why don't we plan a trip to Perth next year and we can tell them face to face?'

'Next year?' she'd replied, her face falling. 'That's too long to wait.'

'But it won't stop us making plans, Sil. We can still talk about the future and by the time we tell everyone, we'll know exactly what we want.'

She'd reluctantly agreed and he'd been relieved. He wasn't sure why he was so reluctant to make their engagement public. He knew he loved her and was pretty sure they had a future, but something was holding him back. Maybe it was the thought of how his parents would react – or at least his mother. She'd already shown her disdain for their relationship so telling her they were getting married wouldn't be easy. But it wasn't just that. He was scared. Scared of committing to one woman for the rest of his life. What if she wasn't *the one*?

'Are you happy to be going home?' Silvia burst into his thoughts.

He looked at her and smiled. 'Of course. It will be great to show you around, take you to all my old haunts and introduce you to my family and friends.'

'I sense a "but" there.'

'I think I'll be much happier when we can find a place of our own. It's not going to be easy living with Mum and Dad.'

'You over-think things, Will. It'll be great. Your dad told me on the phone that he was looking forward to having a full house again. We'll be one big happy family.'

'Don't bank on it. Wait until you meet my mum!'

Silvia laughed but Will was serious. He was dreading the two women meeting. Silvia was used to big Italian families – all sitting around tables eating pasta, chatting non-stop and singing 'That's Amore'. She might not be prepared for his stern, judgemental mother and their more docile lifestyle.

Silvia had taken control of their lives as soon as he'd agreed to marry her. Before he knew it, she had an offer of a job as a financial manager in a large pharmaceutical company in Dublin and was pushing him into taking a job with his mother. It had been the last thing he wanted to do but Silvia could be very persuasive.

'We need to save money if we're going to get married,' she'd said. 'Nothing comes cheap these days and if we stay here in London, we won't be able to save a penny.'

It was true. They'd just been living from day to day over there with no thought to the coming years but the money they'd earn in Ireland would set them up for the future. So Will had agreed and, just after Christmas, he'd be back working with his mother and he was completely dreading it.

He looked out at the sea of green below and thought of Jack. How would he feel if he knew Will had come full circle and was now coming home? Would he be proud of him for all he'd done over the last number of years? He closed his eyes and tried to imagine his friend's face. It was beginning to fade from his memory and he hated that. Sometimes it took him a minute or two to form a clear picture of him. God, he wished Jack was still alive. Now that would be something worth coming home for.

There was a sudden thud and Will realised they'd landed. Home sweet home. He looked at Silvia's excited face and felt a surge of excitement too. Maybe being home wouldn't be so bad after all. And he was sure his parents would fall in love with Silvia just as he had.

Chapter 29

'Right, my two gorgeous girlies. I'll love you and leave you.'

'Where was it you said you were going?' asked Donna, watching as Bob smoothed out imaginary creases from his new Ralph Lauren quilted jacket. 'And are you coming back here later?'

Bob bent over and kissed her on the top of her head. 'I'm interviewing that designer guy, remember? The weird and wacky one.'

Donna nodded. 'Although they all seem weird and wacky to me.'

'And where's *my* kiss?' Lexie asked, puckering up her lips and closing her eyes.

'Dahhhling,' said Bob, in his best Craig Revel Horwood accent. 'If I started on you, I wouldn't stop. Best not make Donna jealous.'

Donna threw a cushion at him. 'Go on, get out of here before I turn into the Incredible Hulk. Jealousy can be a terrible thing, y'know.'

'I'm going, I'm going. And to answer your second question, I think I'll just crash at home tonight. I promised Mam I'd help her with a delivery in the morning and I've a meeting after that.'

'Fine by me,' said Donna, topping up Lexie's wine. 'We'll have a girlie night without you. See you tomorrow.'

Donna was glad to have Lexie to herself tonight. Initially she'd been worried that Lexie would feel like the odd one out in the house, but it was actually quite the opposite. She and Bob got on so well together that in fact sometimes Donna felt left out. Lexie said it was like having another girlfriend because Bob was like no man she ever knew. He was sensitive, a great listener and he loved a bit of gossip.

'Do you think you two will get married any time soon?'

The question took Donna by surprise. 'Who? Me and Bob?'

'No, you and the plumber! Of course you and Bob. Who else would I mean?'

Donna paused for a moment. It wasn't that she didn't know the answer, but more she didn't know how to tell Lexie that she could never see it happening.

'I know I'm not a great advertisement for marriage or anything,' Lexie continued, 'but I think you two are perfect together.'

'Don't be so hard on yourself, Lexie. You were unfortunate, that's all. And Bob and I are fine just the way we are.'

'But don't you ever talk about the future? About where this is going?'

'Not really.'

Lexie sighed. 'I don't understand you two. I'd only been with Brendan for a few weeks when we started to talk about moving in together. Then it was the engagement, the wedding, where we'd live. I thought that's what couples do – plan for the future.'

Donna resisted the urge to point out how that had turned out. 'I suppose we started off as friends so it's different for us. There was no big fanfare when we got together – it just happened.'

'But still.' Lexie wasn't letting it go. 'Wouldn't you like to know what's in store for you both? Wouldn't it be nice to think about the future?'

'Not really, Lexie. I'm happy as things are. We're happy.'

Lexie sniffed. 'Well, if that's the case, then I'm happy too. But I still think you're weird.'

Donna laughed and went to get another bottle of red from the kitchen. Lexie was right. The situation was a bit weird. She'd been with Bob for a year and a half now and they plodded along just fine. Neither of them ever mentioned the future. They didn't talk about getting engaged or married. They were even still living apart and, if Donna was honest, she liked it that way. Much as she loved him, she still didn't feel ready to have Bob move in full-time.

'Do you know what, Donna?' Lexie was sitting bolt upright on the sofa when Donna came back in with the wine. 'I think I'm ready now.'

'Ready for what?' Donna was confused. Had she forgotten they were supposed to be going somewhere?

'I'm ready to tackle the box. Seeing that solicitor today made me realise that it's time to move on. I definitely don't want Brendan back, despite having a few wobbles, but I don't want to forget the good times we had either.'

The box had arrived from Australia a number of weeks ago. It had been covered in a zig-zag of duct tape and stamped with all sorts of custom and postal stamps. Lexie had taken a knife to it straight away and ripped it open. But as soon as she'd realised it was full of photos and various other memorabilia from her time with Brendan, she'd closed it up immediately.

'I'm not ready for this yet,' she'd announced to Donna and Bob, who'd been hovering, dying to go through the stuff with her. 'It's too soon.'

She'd grabbed a roll of sticky tape and sealed it back up, promising that she'd deal with it some day when she felt stronger.

'So you reckon going to the solicitor today was a good thing, then?' Donna felt relieved. She'd worried that she'd pushed Lexie into it before she was ready.

'Definitely. Now top up those glasses – I'm going to get the box.'

A few minutes later, they both had their legs tucked up under them on the sofa and the box sat between them. Lexie had just taken out a pack of photographs and Donna sipped her wine while she waited.

'Look, here's some of our trip to Monkey Mia. Look how red Brendan was. The big eejit forgot to put on suncream that morning.'

Donna took the picture and laughed. 'God, he's glowing like a beacon. I bet that hurt later on.'

'Oh, he was in agony,' giggled Lexie. I had to ask the hotel for a pot of natural yoghurt to spread all over his chest and face.'

'Ooh, sexy!'

'Far from it. I couldn't even lie beside him because of the smell. I had to sleep on the sofa.' Lexie's face became serious. 'But it was a great holiday. I was so in love with him. Here, look at these ones.'

Donna looked at picture after picture of Lexie and Brendan on the beach, in the hotel, swimming, walking and generally having fun. They'd clearly been in love back then.

'Ha! Look at this.' Lexie took a wooden boomerang out of the box and ran her fingers over the smooth varnish. 'Brendan bought me this on our second date. We'd been sitting on the grass in a local park when a guy came over with a bag full of them and tried to sell us one for thirty dollars. He told us that it would always bring us back to each other, no matter where we went in the world. He said it was a symbol of everlasting love.'

'Tell me he didn't pay thirty dollars for it.' Donna was intrigued.

'He got it for five dollars in the end. Just as well that's all he paid because it obviously didn't work.'

They both laughed and Donna was delighted to see that the contents of the box weren't making Lexie too sad. In fact, she seemed to be enjoying going through the stuff.

She flicked through another bunch of photographs and stopped at one in particular. 'God, the state of my hair in this one. Remember when you came over to us, Donna? And we were going to fix you up with a guy?'

'You mean the guy who disappeared before I got there?'

'That's the one. I didn't know him that well but he was a nice guy.

We were out celebrating his birthday in this picture. It was actually the last night we saw him.'

'Hand it over then – let me see the one who got away!' Donna stared at the faces in the picture. Lexie and Brendan were laughing at something but she couldn't get a proper look at the guy because his face was blurry. Probably due to the fact he was jumping up and down. They all seemed to be having great craic. She wondered what would have happened if Lexie had managed to get them both together. Would things have turned out differently? Maybe she'd have stayed on in Perth a bit longer and not gone to New Zealand at all. She squinted to get a better look at his face. There was something vaguely familiar about him.

'Ah, here's a better one of Will,' said Lexie, breaking into her thoughts. 'Now what do you think? He's a hottie, isn't he?'

Will! His name was Will. She'd forgotten about that. Donna's wine spilled out onto the sofa as she lunged forward to snatch the picture from Lexie's hand. She stared at it for a moment. There was absolutely no doubt. She didn't know whether to laugh or cry but all she could manage was: 'Jesus!'

Chapter 30

'Your Christmas decorations are gorgeous, Mrs Cooper-Smith,' said Silvia, as they sat down at the big dining table. 'The purple and black theme is very classy.'

'You can thank the Christmas decorators she hired for that.'

'George! Can't I have any secrets? And for your information, I picked the colour scheme myself.'

Will laughed. 'Don't worry, Mum. I've already told Silvia that you hire people to do a lot of stuff.'

'Well, I … it's not that I don't …'

'Relax, Mum. She knows it's because you're such a busy and successful solicitor. You juggle things the best you can.'

This seemed to appease her. 'Well, yes. Much as I'd love to have more time for running the house, my business keeps me working practically around the clock.'

'I really admire you for that, Mrs Cooper-Smith. I'd love to build up my own business just like you did. I don't intend to work for someone else for the rest of my life.'

'Well, that's admirable, dear. And, please, it's Vivienne. So, what sort of business would you like to run?'

Will looked at his dad and winked. It hadn't taken long for Silvia to win his mother over and he sat back and listened as the two of them chatted away like old friends.

'This is gorgeous, love,' said George, tucking into his roast beef. 'If there's one thing you're a dab hand at, it's a good old roast.'

Silvia nodded. 'It really is delicious, Vivienne. I reckon I'll be putting on a few pounds while I'm staying here.'

Vivienne beamed. 'We may be busy people but we do like to eat well. And since George here retired, he does a bit of cooking himself.'

'Wow, I'm impressed. My father wouldn't even know how to boil some pasta. You'll have to teach Will a thing or two.'

'Hey, cheeky!' Will pretended to look cross but he couldn't have been more delighted with how things were working out. Maybe staying with his parents for a while wouldn't be a bad thing after all.

'We'll give it a few minutes to let that go down and then we'll have some coffee and dessert,' said Vivienne, beaming at the clean plates. 'So, how do you feel about being here in Ireland, Silvia?'

'I have a feeling I'm going to settle in really well.'

'And we're delighted to have you both here,' said George. 'Aren't we, Vivienne?'

'Yes, yes, of course we are.' And she looked as though she meant it. Will always knew his mother would be delighted to have him home but he thought she was going to resent Silvia. Nobody was ever going to be good enough for her only son but Silvia's charm had evidently worked with her.

'We'll be looking for a place of our own after Christmas, though,' said Will, watching his mother carefully. 'Once we start earning decent money, we'll find somewhere to rent and be out from under your feet.'

'Well, there's no hurry.' Will noted the panic on his mother's face and felt sorry for her. 'You can both stay here as long as you want. There's no point in throwing money away on rent as soon as you earn it. Build up some savings first and then have a think about it.'

'That's very kind of you, Mrs Coo— Vivienne.' Silvia flashed a mouth of perfect white teeth and flicked her long chestnut hair to one side. 'Actually, it would be really good to build up our savings.'

Will felt panic rise in his throat as Silvia continued.

'That's one of the main reasons we came over here – to get some money together for the future.'

'Oh?' Will could see the curiosity on his mother's face as she leaned forward on her elbows. 'And what aspect of the future might you be saving for?'

'Well,' said Silvia, shooting a glance at Will. 'We were going to tell—'

'We were going to tell you we were moving out right after Christmas but we might just take you up on your offer and stay a bit longer.' It was the best he could come up with.

Silvia glared at him but he just couldn't let her do it. He couldn't let her tell them they were engaged to be married. It was their first night home, for God's sake. Everything was running smoothly and the last thing he wanted was for his mother to start taking over his life again.

'Well, I think that's a cause for celebration,' said George, oblivious to the tension. 'Vivienne, why don't we get those profiteroles out and I'll make coffee.'

'I'll help.' Silvia hopped up, gathered the empty plates and followed George into the kitchen, leaving Will and his mother alone.

'Is there something you're not telling me, William?' His mother was no fool. 'Now I hope you're not going to make me a grandmother at my age.'

'Mum!' Will couldn't believe his ears.

'Because you both need to get your careers going before any of that nonsense.'

Any of that *nonsense*? He'd heard it all now. He'd been just about to reassure her that Silvia wasn't pregnant but now he felt like pretending she *was*.

'William. Please tell me you haven't been silly.'

'Here we go.' Silvia was back in the room with a huge centrepiece bowl of profiteroles. 'George is on his way with the coffee.'

Will stood up, his face red with fury. He wasn't going to let his mother get away with talking like that. But then he looked at Silvia. He saw how happy she looked and how well she'd already settled in with his family. He couldn't make her feel uncomfortable.

'Here, let me take that,' he said, taking the dessert and placing it on the table. He sat back down and did what he'd always done. He bit his tongue and said nothing.

He wished he could feel really happy. He knew he was very lucky and should be on top of the world right now but there was a little black cloud hanging over him and he just couldn't seem to be rid of it. He wondered for a moment if that's how Jack had felt. Maybe he was depressed, just like Jack had been. Maybe if Jack had recognised the symptoms and sought help, he wouldn't have allowed himself to get to that point of desperation.

His bad hand, as he called it, tingled and, just like it always did, it brought him back to Christchurch and to that awful day. Maybe that was it. Maybe he hadn't dealt with what had happened on that day. A picture of Donna came into his mind and he remembered what it was like to feel completely happy. It sounded weird, but that hour he'd spent with her in the coffee shop was the happiest hour of his life. It dawned on him that maybe he hadn't tried hard enough to find her. That was it! He'd try and figure out a way to trace her and, if he did, maybe it would be the missing piece of the puzzle.

'I'll have a double helping of those,' he said, as his mother dished out dessert. He was suddenly feeling much brighter. It was good to have a purpose in life. He knew that his motivation should be Silvia and the wedding, but right now the thing that excited him – the thing that made him feel alive – was the thought of finding Donna.

* * *

'Donna! What's come over you? That wine will never come out of the sofa. The landlord isn't going to be happy when he sees— Donna? Are you okay? What's wrong?'

Donna was hyperventilating. 'Th— this guy … he – he's the one you wanted me to meet?'

'Yes. Will. What about him?'

'It's him, Lexie. It's him.' Donna flopped back on the sofa, careful to avoid the area saturated by wine, and held the picture to her chest. Big fat tears dropped down her face.

'It's who? Jesus, Donna. Either I'm a complete idiot or you're not making any sense.'

'William. My William. I can't believe I've spent almost two years wondering what had happened to him and all this time you knew him.'

Lexie looked confused for a moment and then her eyes lit up. 'Noooooo! Are you serious? Are you saying Will is the guy you met in Christchurch? The earthquake guy?'

Donna nodded and looked at the picture again. 'He said his name was William. And, yes, he's the one.'

'Oh my God! What are the chances? That's completely bonkers.'

Donna shot forward, almost knocking Lexie's wine this time. 'So is he okay? You said earlier about that picture being the last time you saw him – have you spoken to him?'

'Donna, I'm sorry but both Brendan and I lost touch with Will after that night. He had to rush home to Ireland because his father was sick and he never came back.'

'But when exactly was that, Lexie?' Donna was desperate for information.

'Just before your visit. Remember? I was going to set you two up on a date but he had to leave before you came. Actually, that night was his birthday – if I remember correctly your birthdays are on the same day!'

Donna stood up and started pacing around the room. 'But he must have gone back over to Australia because when I met him in New Zealand, he said he'd been travelling around.'

'Now that I think of it,' said Lexie, dabbing at the red wine stain, 'he rang Brendan some time later and said he was travelling up the coast. I think they had words. Brendan had been keeping Will's job open for him and he never said he wouldn't be back. Quick, grab me a carton of milk.'

Donna stopped pacing and stared at her friend. 'What on earth for?'

'This stain. I heard somewhere that if you pour milk onto a red wine stain it can make it disappear.'

'Forget about the stain,' said Donna, irritably. 'Tell me what you know about Will.'

Lexie continued to blot the stain with tissues. 'Just grab me the milk, will you? I can talk and work at the same time.'

Donna grabbed a half-full litre of milk from the fridge and passed it over to Lexie. 'So Brendan might be still in touch with him, then. Will you ask him for his number for me? This is unbelievable.'

'I can ask him, but I can't guarantee anything. I wouldn't be surprised if he wiped Will's number from his phone after the last call.'

Lexie was pouring milk over the stain and Donna watched doubtfully as it dripped onto the floor. 'Isn't it likely that we'll end up with a clean sofa but a stink of milk?'

'Well, we'll deal with that if it happens.' Lexie's face was almost touching the sofa as she tried to make the pink stain disappear. 'And can you please sit down, Donna? You're making me nervous with all that pacing.'

'Sorry.' She pulled a chair from the little kitchen and sat down heavily. 'But even if Brendan doesn't have his number any more, surely someone else does. What about the people in the bar where he worked? Surely there's someone who's still in touch with him.'

'Maybe,' said Lexie, sitting back to survey her work. 'I'll give Brendan a ring tomorrow and see what I can find out.'

Donna went over and hugged her friend. 'Thanks, Lexie. I can't believe that I might actually find him after all this time.'

Lexie nodded but looked serious. 'But what next?'

'What do you mean?'

'If you find him, Donna, what happens then? Are you both going to ride off into the sunset together? And what about Bob? Where does he figure in all of this?'

Donna felt guilty. She hadn't thought about Bob for one second while her head was full of William and the chance of finding him. If she was honest, riding off into the sunset with William was exactly what she'd been thinking about. But if and when she found William and if he felt the same way about her, she'd have to have a serious chat with Bob. But would that mean not only losing her boyfriend, but losing the mother figure she'd grown to love? Would Jan abandon her if she hurt her only son? Right now it was all ifs and maybes but she'd have to brace herself – the coming weeks could be the start of a very bumpy ride!

Chapter 31

Lexie shook her head. 'I'm sorry, Donna. The only number Brendan has for him isn't in use. He was probably using a "pay as you go" phone over there and just got rid of it when he left.'

'But somebody else must have contact details for him. Surely a person can't just disappear off the planet, for God's sake!' Donna knew she sounded desperate but she couldn't help it. It was like she'd just been given the greatest gift and it had been snatched away from her before she had the chance to open it.

Lexie sighed. 'Come on over and sit down, Donna. You'll wear a hole in the carpet at this rate.'

Donna did as she was told. 'I'm sorry I'm being so crazy about all this, but I just can't believe I might be about to lose him again.'

'Lose him?' Lexie looked worried. 'Donna, sweetie, how can you say you lost him when you never really had him in the first place? You need to get perspective on this. You knew him for what, all of one hour?'

'I knew you wouldn't understand. That's why I didn't tell you about him for so long. I should have just kept my mouth shut.'

Lexie looked hurt and Donna immediately regretted her outburst. 'I'm sorry, Lexie. I'm turning into a mad woman. But can you just make a few more phone calls and see if we can get a contact number for him?'

'The only other person who might have contact details for him is Jonah. He owns the bar.'

'So?'

'Right,' sighed Lexie, picking up the phone again. 'I'll give him a try but then I need to get going. I'm in work at twelve and I haven't even washed myself yet.'

'Thanks, Lexie. You're a star.'

But it wasn't long before Donna's mood dipped again. The only contact number Jonah had for Will was the same one that Brendan had and the address on file was his Perth one.

'So that's it,' said Lexie, standing up and stretching. 'I've filled Brendan in so all we can do is hope Will contacts him again.'

Donna perked up suddenly. 'His surname. Why didn't I think of that before? What's his surname? Maybe now I can find him on Twitter or Facebook. It was impossible with just a first name.'

Lexie's face was grim. 'Unfortunately, it's "Smith". "Will Smith". Somehow I don't think your task has been made any easier.'

Donna opened her mouth to say something but instead began to cry.

'Oh, for God's sake, Donna, cop on to yourself.'

'It's just that … I thought I was going to—'

'Seriously, you need to get a grip. I know you're frustrated about not being able to trace him but you need to start looking at what you've got instead of chasing some sort of dream.'

'You just don't understand.'

'You're damn right I don't. Do you know what I'd give to have what you have? You have a gorgeous man who loves you like crazy. Have you forgotten that? And what would he think if he knew you were off chasing another man? You could end up losing everything. Start living in the real world.' Lexie spat the words out before going into the bathroom and slamming the door.

Donna had never seen Lexie so mad and she wasn't sure whether she should go after her or just let her cool down. But before she could decide, Lexie came breezing back out to the living room and still looked angry.

'Listen, I'm sorry for shouting at you like that. I was out of order.'

Donna was relieved. 'Don't worry about it. We all say things we don't mean in the heat of the moment.'

'Oh, don't get me wrong, Donna. I meant everything I said.'

'But I thought—'

'I just shouldn't have shouted, that's all. I still think you're being stupid and you're running the risk of making a mess of your life.'

'That's harsh, Lexie.'

'It's just because I care about you, Donna.' Lexie sat back down beside her and her tone was softer. She took her hand. 'Forget about Will or William or whatever he calls himself. Give all your energy to Bob. He deserves your full attention and you deserve to be happy.'

Donna thought about arguing her point but she felt defeated. 'You're right, Lexie. You're always right. I'm such an idiot.'

'Well, they do say that love is blind. Just open your eyes and see what's in front of you. Don't let him slip away.'

'I won't,' said Donna, hugging her friend. 'I'm so glad you're here, Lexie. What would I do without you?'

'It works both ways, Donna. Now I really need to go and get ready. Why don't I come along with you tonight and maybe we can grab a bite to eat after?'

'Come along where?'

'Have you forgotten today is Wednesday?'

'Oh God, yes, of course I'd love you to come along. It will be nice to have company for a change. Will I meet you in town after work?'

'Yep, outside my place at four?'

'Perfect.' Donna headed into her bedroom and threw herself on the bed. Thank God she wasn't working today. She wasn't in the mood. She needed to just lie there and think. She felt awful that she'd forgotten it was Wednesday. She used to look forward to the day but now her mind was full of other stuff. Maybe Lexie was right. Maybe she was losing touch with the real world. She suddenly felt exhausted and began to drift off into a fitful sleep.

People were running in all directions as buildings tumbled down and smoke swirled all around her. The sound of screams filled the air and it took her a moment to realise that she was screaming too. She looked down and realised she was trapped. A heavy boulder had fallen on her chest and she couldn't breathe properly. She began to feel light-headed. Was this it? Was this the end? She'd often wondered how she'd die but had never imagined it would be like this. The sound began to fade and she felt peaceful. Dying wasn't so bad after all. And then she heard his voice.

'Stay with me. Open your eyes.' His face was blurry. 'Let's just get this thing off you.'

Suddenly she could breathe again. He'd lifted the boulder off her. He'd saved her life. 'You're bleeding,' she said, looking at the blood dripping from him but she couldn't see where it was coming from.

'I'm fine. Now let's get you out of here. Those buildings overhead don't look safe.' He lifted her up and carried her to safety. His face became clear now. It was William. Her William. And she knew at that moment that she'd love him for the rest of her life.

* * *

'I don't get it, Will. You say you love me but you won't let me tell anyone we're engaged.'

'Of course I love you, Sil. And we'll tell everyone soon.'

'But when? Why wouldn't you let me tell your parents last night? It was the perfect opportunity.'

Will checked his mirrors and signalled to pull into the right lane. They were in the city centre and the traffic was chaotic. 'I told you.

As soon as we tell them they'll be trying to organise everything for us. They'll take over and they'll railroad us into decisions we don't want to make.'

'They'll only railroad us if we let them.'

'You obviously don't know my mother very well, then.'

'And is that the only reason you don't want to tell anyone?'

Will glanced at Silvia and saw the hurt and worry in her eyes. He felt like such an idiot. He'd been allowing a memory to hold him back but maybe it was time to let it go. He'd laid awake all night thinking about Donna and how he could find her. He'd gone through every possible idea in his head until he'd come to the conclusion that nothing was going to work. With just a first name to go on and no other information, it was a dead end.

'Will?' Silvia was getting annoyed.

'Sorry, what did you say?'

'I was asking you if there was another reason you didn't want to tell people about us.'

Will thought for a moment and let a picture of Donna fill his mind. He saw her beautiful face – her green eyes and the dimple on her left cheek. He saw her freckles and her perfect nose, her wild red hair and her full, pink lips. He held her face in his mind's eye for a few moments and then he let it go. That's when he saw Silvia properly. She was there. She was real. And he loved her. He suddenly pulled the car to the left and parked at the side of the road.

'What are you doing, Will? Why are you stopping?'

'Because I love you, that's why. And because I have no proper reason not to tell the world. Come on, let's go home.'

'But I thought we were going shopping.'

Will pulled back out into the traffic and swung around the next roundabout to head in the direction of home. 'Shopping can wait. We have something much more important to do.'

'You're not making sense. What have we got to do?'

They stopped at the traffic lights and he looked at her. It was like he was seeing her again for the first time. She was beautiful, like an Italian goddess, with her chestnut hair falling over her shoulders, her brown eyes like saucers in her tanned face. That was the face he loved. That was the face he wanted to spend the rest of his life with.

'We're going home to announce our engagement,' he said, accelerating as the lights turned green. 'We're going to tell Mum and Dad and your parents and then we're going to shout it out to the world.'

Silvia squealed with excitement. 'You have no idea how happy that makes me! But what changed your mind?'

'I just came to my senses, I suppose.'

'Good,' said Silvia. 'It's about time. Your mother will always be your mother but you need to stand on your own two feet and do what *you* want to do.'

And it was with those words that Will knew without a doubt that Jack was looking down on him. That was exactly what he'd say – it's what he *had* said to him just before he died.

The rain that had been spitting earlier started to fall heavily and suddenly people were running in all directions to escape a soaking. Will put the windscreen wipers on full blast and he felt thankful that his mother had lent them her car so that they wouldn't have to get the bus. He stopped to let a girl cross the road. She had no hood on her jacket and her long red hair was dripping wet. He couldn't see her face properly but she reminded him of Donna. But he wasn't going to call her name. He wasn't going to stop the car and run after her. He wasn't going to be that person any more. The only woman he'd be thinking about from now on was the beautiful woman beside him who was going to become his wife.

Chapter 32

'Engaged!' said Vivienne, the smile not quite reaching her eyes. 'And when did this happen?'

Will beamed and pulled his fiancée into him. 'A while ago in London. We just decided to keep it to ourselves for a while.'

'Well, I think that calls for a toast,' said George, standing up from his leather armchair in the living room. 'I'm delighted for you. We both are, aren't we, Vivienne?'

Vivienne sniffed. 'Well, if it's what you really want.'

'Of course it's what we want, Mum. We wouldn't be doing it otherwise. That's why we wanted to come home to Ireland and start saving money. We need to think about the future.'

'So that's what you were talking about last night, Silvia.' Will could almost see the wheels of his mother's brain turning as she put the pieces together. 'And you didn't want her to tell us, Will. Why was that?'

'I *did* want to tell you … well, I wasn't sure if—'

'We wanted to tell you, Vivienne, but Will wanted you and George to get to know me a little better first.' Silvia always knew the right thing to say. 'He said that he wanted you to love me and then he knew you'd be happy with our news. Your opinion is very important to him.'

Vivienne blushed. 'Well, we brought him up well. It's good to know he still respects what we have to say.'

'Of course I do,' said Will. 'But we couldn't keep the news to ourselves for a minute longer. So what do you think?'

They all stared at Vivienne, even George, who was just walking into the room with a tray of glasses and a bottle of sparkling wine.

'We really want you to be happy for us, Mum.'

Even though Will had learned to stand up to his mother, he knew he'd be devastated if she wasn't happy for him. He watched her for what seemed like ages until suddenly a huge smile spread across her face and her eyes lit up.

'Welcome to the family, Silvia.'

Everyone breathed a sigh of relief and Will watched as his mum kissed Silvia on both cheeks. She then kissed him and rubbed his shoulder awkwardly. It was hardly an emotional embrace but it was the best he could hope for. Vivienne Cooper-Smith wasn't a fan of displays of emotion.

They sat around the coffee table in the living room for the next hour while Silvia told them about her life. She told them about her time in Italy when she was little – how they'd lived with her grandmother in a house on the top of a hill and how her granddad grew grapes and made his own wine.

'He used to let us taste it even when we were very young. We'd feel so grown up to hold the crystal wine glasses in our hands and swirl the wine in our mouths, just like he did, before swallowing it.'

'And why did you leave to go to Perth?' Vivienne seemed intrigued by Silvia and Will was just happy that the two of them were getting along.

'My dad is an engineer. His company were expanding and wanted him to head up the new venture in Perth. He knew that if he didn't go, they'd make things awkward for him in the job and maybe push him out eventually.'

'That doesn't seem right,' said George, who'd been largely quiet during the conversation. 'How can they tell a man with a family that he has to move to the other side of the world, or else?'

'They were a powerful company,' explained Silvia, 'so they could more or less do what they wanted. But it wasn't a bad thing in the end. We all settled into Perth quickly. It's a beautiful city.'

'And now you're settled here in Ireland,' said Vivienne, clapping her hands together. 'Will your parents come over for the wedding, do you think? Or is it a bit too far?'

'Mum, we haven't decided on any of that yet.'

'I know, Will. I'm just wondering. Now you do know that venues get booked up years in advance. Have you set the date yet? Because the first thing we'd want to do is book the hotel.'

Will shot Silvia a knowing look. He knew this would happen.

'And we'll have to start thinking about the guest list because it's important to get it right. We don't want to offend anyone.'

'Well, why don't we get Christmas out of the way first and then we can talk about the wedding.' Silvia saved the day again. 'January is always a boring month so it will be nice to brighten it up with some wedding plans.'

Will nodded. 'Good idea. It will be great to get your input, Mum, but let's not worry about that until the New Year.'

'Well, there's no harm in talking about—'

'The lad is right, Vivienne. Let's concentrate on Christmas for now. There'll be plenty of time for wedding talk after that.'

Will shot his father a grateful look. George winked and Will couldn't help smiling. He was such an even-tempered man. Will didn't know how he'd put up with such a demanding and controlling wife for all those years. They were such opposites, but somehow it worked. They'd be married for thirty-five years next year and Will wondered if he and Silvia would make it to such a milestone.

'A party!' said Vivienne, startling everyone.

Will raised an eyebrow. 'Can you elaborate on that?'

'That's what we'll do. We'll have a party to celebrate your engagement.'

'Mum, I thought we were going to put this aside until after Christmas. And we certainly don't need a party.'

'Of course you do. And I mean in the New Year. It will take a while to plan, of course, because it has to be done properly. But we'll throw you a wonderful party so that everyone can meet Silvia.'

'That's very good of you, Vivienne. Isn't it, Will?'

'Yes, but I'm not sure that—'

'The ring!' Vivienne was on a roll and not listening to anyone. 'I almost forgot. Let me see your ring, Silvia.'

Silvia blushed and for once seemed lost for words.

'You do have a ring, don't you, dear?' The words were almost accusing.

'Not yet,' admitted Silvia, looking embarrassed.

'But why not? Will, I can't believe you'd ask a girl to marry you and not give her a ring.'

'Well, actually, he didn't.' Silvia was far too honest. Will tensed and willed her not to continue. 'He didn't ask me to marry him.'

Vivienne looked from one to the other. 'Now I'm really confused.'

'I didn't *ask* her, Mum, I *demanded* she marry me!' It was all he could think of saying.

Silvia gave him a puzzled look but thankfully didn't disagree. 'And how could I refuse?'

'But that still doesn't explain the lack of ring.' Will rolled his eyes and wished his mother wasn't so nosy. She needed to know everything.

'Leave the kids alone, Vivienne,' said George from behind his newspaper. He'd evidently become bored with the conversation and at some point had picked up the paper to read.

'It's okay, Dad. The reason I didn't get a ring for Silvia yet is that I saw one here in Dublin when I was home last and I thought it would be perfect for her. I'm going to bring her to see it after Christmas.'

'Really?' Silvia looked completely surprised at this nugget of information. 'You never told me that.'

Will rolled his eyes. 'God, what is it about women that they have to know everything? Can a man not surprise his girlfriend any more?'

'I'm sorry I asked now,' said Vivienne, sipping her tea and looking uncomfortable. 'Still, it's nice for Silvia to know that you've been thinking about it.'

Silvia leaned over and hugged Will. 'It's lovely to know, actually. I can't wait to see what you've picked out. I'm sure it will be wonderful.'

Will hugged her back and thought of the beautiful lime-green ring he'd almost bought for her the previous year. A peridot ring, the jeweller had called it. He wondered if they'd still have it and, even more importantly, would Silvia like it.

They continued chatting for the next hour and Will was surprised at how comfortable and relaxed he felt. His parents weren't so bad after all. It was funny how things had come full circle. He'd spent most of his childhood wanting to get away and now he was enjoying being back. But he was back because *he* wanted to be back, not because of some misplaced loyalty to his mother. He'd spread his wings and travelled and now it was time to come home. He wondered what Jack would think. He could still hear his voice that last time they'd spoken. *'Grow a pair, man, will you?'* And now he could finally say he had.

* * *

'Here you go, love,' said Bob, handing Donna a mug of tea as she wrapped her robe tightly around her. 'You still look frozen to the bone.'

'I am! I can't get the heat into me. Honestly, I should know better than to wear that flimsy jacket at this time of year. It doesn't even have a hood.'

She sipped her tea gratefully as Bob busied himself making dinner in her little kitchen. She'd been soaked earlier on her way in to meet Lexie and the cold had gotten right into her bones. Thank God for Bob having a key to her place. He'd rung her and said he'd come over while she was out and make dinner for her and Lexie. He was always mindful of how she'd feel after her Wednesday night visits and he always managed to cheer her up.

'Pasta is done – I'm just waiting for the garlic bread.' He plonked down on the sofa beside her and took a slug from his glass of Coke. 'Why do you think Lexie didn't come home?'

'I told you, Bob. She went to visit her grandparents. She said she was going to stay there tonight and come back in the morning.'

'Hmmmm.'

'What does that mean?' said Donna, glaring at him. 'And why does it matter so much to you that she's not here?'

Bob shook his head. 'It doesn't matter at all. It's just not like her to go to her grandparents during the week. Doesn't she usually visit them on Sunday?'

'Yes, but she's allowed more than one visit a week, you know.'

'Stop getting tetchy with me, Donna. I was just wondering if she's purposefully trying to give us a bit of space.'

'Maybe.' Donna hoped that's all it was. Things had been a little stilted between them when they'd met up earlier and Donna knew it was because of their earlier disagreement. And when Lexie said she wasn't coming home, Donna had thought it was because she was still angry with her.

Bob took her hand. 'I'm glad, though. Much as I like Lexie, it's nice for us to have some alone time.'

'We don't do too badly though. We get all the time we want in our room.'

'But we're usually so knackered by the time we get in there that we're asleep in minutes.'

Donna laughed. 'That's true. But we have the whole night to ourselves now so nothing is holding us back.'

'Back from what?' Bob looked at her and pretended to be puzzled.

'I'll tell you what.' Donna left down her mug on the coffee table. 'Let's get our dinner and then I'll show you how we can make use of an empty flat.'

Bob was on his feet. 'I'm loving the sound of that. Come on. I'll dish up and we can take it in here. *Downton* will be on in a while.'

Five minutes later they were tucking into bowlfuls of creamy pasta and crunching on buttery garlic bread. Donna idly wondered if the garlic would kill the passion she hoped would happen later but she was feeling so turned on tonight, she didn't think so.

She glanced across at Bob, who was laughing at an episode of *Friends* he'd seen a dozen times. He looked very handsome in grey jeans and a purple shirt. He wore his Converse without socks and, although Donna would have laughed at that look on anyone else, it suited Bob perfectly. As she watched him rub his hand subconsciously up and down his thigh, a wave of passion washed over her and she grabbed the remote control out of his hand.

'Hey, what's that all about?'

She switched off the telly.

'I was watching that. What are you playing—?'

She kissed him full on the lips, pushing him back on the sofa and tugging at his shirt.

'Jesus, Donna,' he said, coming up for breath. 'Watch the shirt. Do you know how much it cost me?'

'I'll buy you another.' She tugged at it again and two of the buttons flew off across the room.

Bob pulled away from her. 'What's got into you?' He scrambled down onto the floor to search for the missing buttons.

'Let's live dangerously, Bob. Come on. There's nobody else here. When do we ever get the chance to make love out here on the sofa?'

'It wouldn't feel right, Donna. Jesus, I'll go mad if I don't find these buttons. They're pearl-coated and I don't think I'd ever find matching ones.'

'Forget about the bloody shirt,' said Donna, getting annoyed. 'I'll help you look for them after.'

'Ah, got them.' He stood up triumphantly, examining the precious buttons. 'Have you got a needle and thread handy? I might just get them back on now in case I lose them.'

'No. I. Have. Not.'

Bob looked at her as if he was only noticing her for the first time. 'Why are you speaking to me like that?'

'Bob, I'm trying to ignite a bit of passion into our relationship here. Now are you going to leave me hanging or are you going to come over and make mad passionate love to me?'

'Well, it's probably not a good idea to do anything out here.' He glanced around as though somebody might be watching them. 'What if Lexie walked in on us?'

'I already told you, she's not coming home.'

'But she might change her mind. You know what she's like.'

Donna sighed. 'Right, let's take it into the bedroom, if that's what you're more comfortable with.'

'Actually, I might head off, if you don't mind.' He tucked his shirt back into his jeans. 'I'll just clear these away first.'

Donna watched in shock as he gathered up the bowls and plates they'd just eaten from and brought them into the kitchen. Bloody hell. That was a first. She'd never offered herself to anyone like that before but she certainly hadn't been rejected like that either. She fixed herself and followed him into the kitchen.

'Bob, what's wrong?'

'Nothing. What are you talking about?'

'Stop acting dumb!' She spat out the words. 'Have you gone off me or something? Why don't you want to be with me?'

'Don't be silly, Donna, love.' He dried his hands with the tea-towel and wrapped them around her. 'Of course I haven't gone off you. You know what I'm like with my clothes. Call it OCD or whatever but I can't rest easy until I get the shirt sorted.'

'Right, go on home then.' She thudded back into the living room and took up his jacket from the back of the armchair. 'Here you go. Go home and make love to your wardrobe.'

'Don't be like that.'

He looked genuinely alarmed. Did he really not see what was happening here? Was he so delusional as to think he was being any way reasonable? 'Just go, Bob. I want to be on my own now.'

He took the jacket and slipped his arms in. A little piece of Donna died. She'd hoped he'd throw the jacket back on the chair and say he was sorry. She'd willed him to say he'd been silly and of course he'd stay and make love to her. But he wound his purple and grey striped scarf around his neck as though to seal the fact that he was indeed leaving.

'I'll give you a buzz tomorrow. Maybe we should go out to eat tomorrow night?' He was already at the door.

'Whatever,' said Donna, not going to him to kiss him goodbye.

He hesitated for a moment and Donna held her breath. Maybe this was where he'd change his mind. Maybe he'd throw off his coat and scarf and carry her into the bedroom to make mad passionate love to her. Prickles of sweat tickled the back of her neck at the thought of it.

'Right, I'll give you a buzz in the morning,' he said. 'Night, love.' And he was gone. It hadn't even felt like a lovers' tiff. It hadn't been passionate enough for that.

Donna stood for a moment and, for the first time in a while, she felt lonely. She wondered yet again if she was with Bob for the right reasons. Was she really in love with him or was she just afraid of the alternative, which was losing him, possibly losing Jan and going back to being that teenage girl who was lost and alone and terrified of the future?

Chapter 33

'Just a little to the left ... no, to the right, now ... down a bit ...'
Will smiled as he watched his mother barking orders at the barman.
The poor guy had mistakenly asked her if she wanted anything,
meaning a drink, and she'd said, yes, the banner over the bar needed
straightening. He was now kneeling on a bar stool, which looked
as though it could fall over and take him with it, and trying to
adjust the banner until Vivienne was happy with it. It was Will and
Silvia's engagement party and she'd spent the last couple of months
organising it. There was no way she was going to allow a single thing
to go wrong.

'It's perfect, Mum. Come and get a drink.'

'Are you mad, William? It'll be much later before a drop passes my
lips. I have to check with the caterers and I want to get those loose
chairs at the wall removed.'

'I'll ask the manager about the chairs,' said George, rolling his
eyes behind his wife's back. He then lowered his voice. 'Anything for
a quiet life.'

Will noticed how pale his father looked. He never complained but
it was clear he hadn't been feeling great lately. He'd been heading off
to bed much earlier than usual and his appetite wasn't good. Only a
week ago, Will had asked him if everything was okay and he'd said it

was, but maybe it was time to get him to go for a check-up again. He had his six-monthly check-ups with the heart doctor but it wouldn't do any harm to go to his GP and make sure there was nothing else amiss.

Will glanced across the room at Silvia, who was chatting animatedly to one of her new friends from work. She'd started her new job just after Christmas and in the short time she'd been there, she'd grown to love it. She thrived when she was busy and the job was certainly that. He saw how her eyes danced when she spoke and he knew that coming to Ireland had been the right move for them.

'William, there's John and Imelda Bohan.' His mother's voice broke into his thoughts. 'Go and shake their hands before they sit down. Actually, you should probably stay over at the door and greet people as they come in.'

Will sighed and did as he was told. Mr and Mrs Bohan were old friends of his parents' whom he hadn't seen in about ten years. He'd felt a bit irked when his mother had produced the list for the party. It had mainly consisted of her and his father's friends, with just a few of his own thrown in for good measure.

'You don't really have too many friends left here,' she'd said, and he'd glared at her.

'Thanks for reminding me, Mum.'

'Don't pout, William,' she'd continued. 'It's not becoming of you. All I meant is that most of them have emigrated and we need to fill the room.'

He smiled warmly at the Bohans and shook their hands. After an adequate amount of small talk, he indicated a table for them to sit down at. He could turn on the charm when he wanted to. Then he made his way over to his fiancée and kissed her lightly on the cheek.

'Are you having fun, sweetheart? I'm sorry you don't know half of the people here.'

Silvia took his hand and squeezed it. 'But neither do you! And, yes,

I'm having a great time. Val here said that there are a few more from work coming in so I won't feel like I have no friends.'

'That's great. Can I get you a drink, Val?'

'I've just got one, thanks.'

Will saw that she'd noticed his hand but had looked away quickly. Story of his life. Sometimes he wished people would just ask, rather than pretending they hadn't seen it. He was happy to talk about it but it seemed to make others feel uncomfortable.

'I'm just going to head back over to Mum and see if she needs a *hand* with anything.' He emphasised the word 'hand' to see if it would get a reaction. He couldn't help it. Val's eyes opened wide for a second and Will had to resist the urge to punch the air and say: 'Yessss!' He loved to be silly now and then. It brought him back to his childhood. Jack would have got the joke straight away.

The room filled up quickly and, after a few pints, Will began to enjoy himself. Some of his old school friends had come and, since Silvia was happy to sit and chat with her friends from work, Will was able to have a guilt-free catch-up with the lads.

'How on earth did you get a woman like that?' asked Terry Dillon, looking over at Silvia, his eyes wide. 'Jesus, you always fall on your feet, Willie boy!'

Will laughed at his old friend. 'I ask myself that every day. She's pretty amazing.'

'So, are you going to settle here now? I'd have thought you'd be setting up home in Italy or Australia – anywhere but here.'

'Who knows what the future will bring,' said Will, taking a slug of his pint. 'But for the moment we're happy to be here.'

'I'd love to travel,' said Frank, another friend from Will's childhood. 'I got straight into the bank after school and have been stuck there ever since.'

Will shook his head. 'You're not stuck there, mate. You *choose* to stick there. That's a different thing.'

'Since when have you been so philosophical?' laughed Terry. 'I seem to remember you saying you were stuck in a job you hated at one time.'

'But I got out, didn't I? And it was thanks to a good talking to from Jack.'

They all fell silent for a moment, remembering their friend. It was Will who broke the silence.

'Let's raise our glasses to Jack, lads. I wish he was here, but I'm sure he's with us in spirit.'

'To Jack,' said Terry, raising his pint in the air.

'To Jack.' They all clinked glasses and took a long drink before Frank brought the conversation back to travel.

'So, where was your favourite out of all the places you've been?'

Will thought for a moment. 'I loved Perth because I was there for the longest time but …' A picture of Christchurch immediately came to mind, along with Donna's face. But he really didn't want to remember her. Not now. Not on his engagement night.

'But it wasn't your favourite?' Terry was interested now.

'It was *one* of my favourite places, but I'd have to say the south island of New Zealand is one of the most beautiful places on earth.'

Terry nodded knowingly but there was an awkward silence. Will's friends knew about the earthquake and how he'd been injured. They'd all been very supportive when he'd come home at first and had to have all the treatment to his hand. He hadn't been able to drive and, when his parents weren't available to bring him to appointments, his friends had mucked in to help.

'Come on, lads. It's just my hand. No need to get all morose. I expect other people to dodge the subject but not you lot!'

'Is it painful?' It was the first time Ryan had spoken since Will had arrived at the table. He'd always been the shy one growing up and Will hadn't been surprised when he'd ended up working in a library and trying to get a deal for the novel he'd written.

'Not really, Ryan. I don't have much feeling at all around the damaged area. The worst part was getting used to not having my index finger.'

'Of all the fingers to lose,' said Terry, shaking his head. 'How unlucky could you be?'

'Actually, I thought the same thing initially but, apparently, if you're going to lose a finger, the index one isn't the worst.'

They were all curious now so Will continued.

'Your hand soon adjusts to not having the index finger there and the middle finger sort of takes over. It's weird, my hand doesn't actually feel a lot different now and I can do most things with it, so it's not so bad.'

'Uh oh,' said Terry, looking over Will's shoulder. 'Here comes your mother and she doesn't look happy.'

Will rolled his eyes. He needed to try and get a few drinks into her so she'd relax.

'William. I think you've spent enough time here. There are guests you haven't greeted yet so why don't you go and mingle for a bit.'

'I'll go in a few minutes, Mum. I'm just chatting to the lads.'

Vivienne clicked her tongue disapprovingly. 'I can see that but it's rude not to say hello when people have made the effort to come and celebrate with you.'

Will was about to argue but he didn't think it would be worth it. He rolled his eyes, without letting his mother see, and got up to go and get Silvia. If he had to suffer mingling with complete strangers, then she could do it with him. After all, it was her party too.

She didn't complain and was happy to go and talk to the guests. Silvia never complained about anything. Will realised how lucky he was and, judging by the stares of most of the male guests, they all knew how lucky he was too.

* * *

'Well, I think that was a success,' said Vivienne, carefully removing her shoes as she came in the front door. 'So, who's for tea?'

Will fell down onto the sofa in the living room. 'I think I might need some strong coffee. How about you, Sil?'

'Why don't I go and make some tea and coffee?' said Silvia, bunching up her long hair and tying it in a bobbin on the top of her head. 'Vivienne, you've done enough. Go and sit down and I'll bring a tray in.'

'That's very good of you, dear. Isn't it, George?'

'Very good. But I think I might head on up to bed and read the paper. I bought it this morning but didn't even get to open it.'

'But don't you want to discuss the evening? I want to tell you what Martha O'Connor said about Jilly Dawson's granddaughter.'

'Time enough for that tomorrow, Vivienne. My back is giving me a bit of bother so I'd be better off lying down.'

'You go on up then, love. I'll bring you a cup of tea. And thanks for all your help tonight. What would I do without you?' Vivienne placed a kiss on her husband's cheek in an uncharacteristic show of affection.

George flushed happily and headed up the stairs. Will was delighted to see his mother showing her softer side, especially to his dad, who was such a gentle soul. He headed into the kitchen to give Silvia a hand. She already had all the cups on the tray and was waiting for the kettle to boil.

'Happy?' he asked, taking her hand and kissing it softly.

'Couldn't be happier.' She twisted the ring on her finger until it caught the light. 'And everyone thought the ring was spectacular.'

Will looked at the large solitaire diamond and had to admit it looked gorgeous on Silvia's long, slender fingers. He'd taken her to the jeweller's shop on Grafton Street just after Christmas to show her the ring he'd almost bought her. She'd smiled faintly and said it was nice. He'd known straight away that she didn't like it and had quickly offered her alternatives. She'd immediately pounced on the tray of solitaires – the ones that cost a fortune – and Will had told her to pick whichever one she wanted.

'It's an investment piece,' she'd said, holding her hand up to the light and admiring the ring. Will had never really understood that phrase. Surely it was only an investment if the intention was to sell it and make a profit? The jeweller had agreed wholeheartedly with Silvia. And why wouldn't he when he was just about to clock up a sale for three and a half thousand euros.

They made the hot drinks and arranged a selection of biscuits on a plate, and Will carried the tray into the living room. He was glad to see his mother looking relaxed and happy. It dawned on him that she rarely took time to just sit down and do nothing. He made a mental note to encourage her to do just that over the coming weeks.

'I'll just take some tea up to George,' she said, pouring a cup. She took a side plate and added two gingernuts – George's favourites. 'Be back in a sec.'

'Your parents are perfect together, aren't they?'

Will looked at Silvia, startled. 'Are they?'

'Of course. Don't you think so?'

'I suppose I never really thought about it,' he said, pouring coffee into two cups. 'I always thought Mum gave Dad such a hard time that I wondered how he put up with her.'

Silvia laughed. 'Well, I hope we're like that when we're their age. She might nag him but he loves it. Don't you see how his face lights up when he rolls his eyes at something she says? They love each other very much.'

Will had never really thought about it that way but Silvia was probably right. They were married such a long time so there must be something keeping them together.

Suddenly there was a crash from upstairs. Vivienne's voice could be heard calling her husband. Will jumped to his feet just before he heard his mother's wails.

'Noooooooooooo!'

Chapter 34

Donna had a spring in her step as she walked from the bus stop to the bakery. She'd stayed working late last night and finished all the cakes that were on order for the week so Jan had told her not to come in until lunch time. She'd had a very luxurious lie-in and a delicious cooked breakfast made by Bob.

Things had been better with Bob lately. They'd had a few wobbles around Christmas time but they'd finally got their act together and he'd moved in. It was the best thing that could have happened because suddenly their relationship felt different. More grown-up. Donna loved the certainty that Bob would be there every night. She never had to ask him if he was staying and he didn't have to ask her permission either. Their sex life was still slow and it worried Donna sometimes, but she felt that it was something they could work on. The most important thing was they had a good friendship – after all, that's what a good relationship should be based on. And no relationship was perfect.

Jan had been over the moon when they'd told her about their plans to live together. Bob had been a little offended.

'Well, you could at least act a bit sorry to see me go,' he'd sniffed, when she'd tangoed around the kitchen after hearing the news.

'Of course I'll miss you, love. But I couldn't be happier for you two.'

Lexie was still living with them but she'd been looking for a place of her own. They'd both told her repeatedly that she didn't have to move out but she said it was time. She'd saved enough money for a deposit and a few months' rent and her grandparents had offered to help her out too.

Donna looked at the rain clouds above and was glad to have almost reached the bakery. It was typical spring weather. She'd left her heavy coat at home because the sun had been beaming when she left but now it looked as though there was going to be a heavy downpour.

She shoved the door open and the delicious smell of baking hit her nostrils. 'Morning, Megan. It's very quiet for lunch time. Has it been like this all day?'

'It's been fairly steady but I'm expecting the lunch rush at any moment.' She indicated for Donna to come closer and she whispered, 'Jan is in the tearoom. I'm not sure what's wrong but she's crying.'

'Crying?' Donna was alarmed. 'Did she say anything?'

Megan shook her head. 'She didn't say much when I came in and seemed a bit distant, but I didn't think too much of it. Then I was going to make myself a cup of tea while it was quiet about ten minutes ago and that's when I saw her.'

'Right, I'll go and see what's wrong. Give me a shout if it gets too busy and I'll come out and give you a hand.'

Donna hung up her coat on the hook behind the door and headed towards the tearoom. Her heart was beating fast and she could feel panic rising in her throat. It wasn't like Jan to cry, especially in work, so something awful must have happened. She braced herself and opened the door.

Jan was sitting, cradling a cup in her hands. Her eyes were red and bloodshot. She looked up when Donna entered the room and started to cry again.

'God, Jan. What is it? What's happened?' Donna pulled a chair up beside her and took her hands.

'Ah, Donna, love, it's terrible. I'm a terrible person.'

'Of course you're not. Come on. Tell me what's happened.'

Jan sniffed and blew her nose in her already-saturated tissue. Donna pulled some kitchen towel off the roll and handed it to her. They sat in silence for a moment until Jan felt ready to speak.

'It's my brother, Donna. He's dead. He died suddenly last night.'

'Ah no, Jan. That's awful. Is this the brother you lost contact with?'

'He was the only one I had,' sobbed Jan. 'And I chose to turn my back on him.'

Donna didn't know what had happened between the two siblings but she was quick to reassure Jan. 'I'm sure it wasn't as simple as that. Do you want to tell me about it?'

Jan blew her nose. 'We had a falling out. I shouldn't have let it go on for all these years but the longer it went, the easier it was just to forget I had a brother altogether.'

'You said it was a long time ago?'

Jan nodded. 'Must be more than thirty years now. It was before Bob was born.'

Donna let out a low whistle. 'That *is* a long time.'

'Our parents had died one year after the other. Well, you know all that. So there were just the two of us. I still lived in the family house in Cabra but he was married at that stage and had his own house in Castleknock.'

'Married? I hadn't even thought about the fact you might have a sister-in-law too.'

'I do, but I hated her. God forgive me, but I couldn't stand the woman.' She blessed herself as an apology to God for her hatred.

'So is she the reason you fell out?'

Jan sighed. 'In the end, there were a thousand reasons, but, yes, she was one of them. From the first day I met her, I knew she thought she was better than us. She'd taken to my brother because he had a good job and was earning good money, but she didn't like me. Not one bit.'

'I find that hard to believe, Jan. How could anyone not like you? You're the warmest and most welcoming person I know.'

'You might not have said that if you knew me back then. I was a bit of a wild child. I'd been expelled from two schools and ended up getting in with the wrong people.'

'No way,' said Donna, sitting back in her chair, unable to believe that Jan was ever that child.

'I wasn't always the fluffy home-making mammy, you know, Donna. Back then things were a lot different. I got into petty crime – nothing too serious. A bit of pick-pocketing, stuff like that.'

Donna thought back to her own deviance during her teenage years and realised she had more in common with Jan than she'd thought. 'So she didn't like you because of that?'

'I suppose. But things got messy with the house too. I wanted to stay there but she thought we should sell. They had a big mortgage on the new house and were desperate to pay something off it.'

'But you stayed in the end?'

'I did, Donna, love. But that's when relationships broke down altogether. I had to get a mortgage – pay them off. She still wasn't happy. It was a mess.'

'But your brother, Jan. What did he have to say about all this?'

Jan's eyes filled with tears again. 'He was the mild-mannered one. I knew he didn't agree with half of the things that woman said or did, but he loved her. He supported her completely and I hated him for it.'

Donna shook her head. 'I suppose there's no accounting for love. It can make us all do silly things.'

'That's true. It was only after I married my Chris that I understood that deep, unwavering love. But by then it was too late. There was so much hatred there, so many awful things had been said, that it was easier to just let the relationship slide.'

'So you never saw him again?'

She bowed her head. 'There was the odd Christmas card initially. I sent them a birth announcement when Bob was born and they did the same a few years later when they had a son. But things fizzled out after that.'

'So you have a nephew too? Weren't you ever tempted to make peace? Look how much bigger your family could have been, Jan. You could have had a brother and a sister-in-law. Bob could have had a cousin.' Donna was finding it hard to believe that someone could turn their back completely on a sibling. She felt mostly sorry for Jan but part of her felt angry.

'Of course I thought about making peace, Donna. But it's hard, you know. So much time had passed that it just got easier to let things go.' She burst into tears then and Donna was quick to go to her and hug her. Maybe she was judging her too harshly. Donna knew only too well how family dynamics can be difficult and sometimes things aren't always as they seem from the outside.

'Em, sorry to interrupt,' said Megan, popping her head in the door. 'It's getting kind of busy out there. Is there any chance of getting a hand?'

Donna looked at Jan and knew she'd have to take charge. 'I'll be out in a minute, Megan. If you stick the closed sign on the door and don't let anyone else in, we'll deal with the queue and then we're going to shut up shop for a few days.'

'But what about all the cakes?' Megan was wide-eyed.

'Don't worry about them. Jan's had some bad news. We need to close.'

Megan nodded and scurried off.

Jan shook her head. 'But, Donna, we can't be—'

'No buts, Jan. We're going to deal with this. Now give Bob a ring and see if he can meet us at home in an hour. You can tell him then. Does Chris know yet?'

'Yes. He didn't want me to come in after I got the call this morning but I wanted to. I was numb. I thought I could just forget and get on with my normal day.'

Donna shook her head. 'You were in shock, Jan. It's a lot to take in. Now just give me ten minutes to help Megan and I'll order us a taxi.'

She spent the next few minutes serving customers and as soon as the shop was empty, she sent Megan home with a huge box of cakes. She could hear Jan talking on the phone and decided to give her a few minutes before going back into her. It was hard to believe that Jan had such a colourful past. And she'd had a lot of heartache too, by the sound of it. She'd always seemed so strong and happy that Donna hadn't even considered that she could have problems too. Jan had sat and listened to Donna moan about her mother. She'd wiped her tears when that awful tragedy had happened. And she'd opened her home to her not once but twice when she was at her lowest. Now it was time for Donna to repay the favour.

* * *

'So how did she sound? I can't believe you actually spoke to her after all this time.'

'Well, how do you think she sounded, Bob? She's just lost her husband.'

'I know, Mam, but how did she react to you? Did she say much?'

'She just said she thought I should know. She sounded drained – as though she'd been crying non-stop. Her voice was kind of … kind of dead.'

Both Donna and Bob simply nodded. Sometimes there just weren't words.

'She said she'd ring back later today with the funeral arrangements,' Jan continued, her voice wobbling. 'But how can I go to the funeral? How can I go and mourn his death when I wasn't there for him when he was alive?'

Donna and Bob both went to her side and put an arm around her as she cried. Donna didn't understand or know the full story about what went on but, no matter what, it was awful to see Jan so cut up. It was Bob who broke the silence.

'You *need* to go to the funeral, Mam. No matter what happened in the past, he was your brother. She wouldn't have rung you if she didn't want you there.'

'That's true,' said Donna, picking up on Bob's point. 'Why else would she have contacted you? You should definitely go. And we'll go too, won't we, Bob?'

'Of course we will. We'll be right there by your side.'

Jan blew her nose. 'Thanks. You're very good to me. I don't deserve you two.'

'And what about me?' Nobody had heard Chris arriving in from work and he was standing in the room watching them.

'Ah, Chris, love. You're the best. I definitely don't deserve *you*!' She began to cry again and Donna and Bob shifted to make room for Chris.

They slipped quietly out of the living room to allow the couple to have some privacy and Bob let out a huge breath when they went into the kitchen. 'Well, that was full on, wasn't it?'

Donna put her arms around him and laid her head on his shoulder. 'And how about you? How are you feeling about it all?'

'I'm grand.' He pulled away so he could fill the kettle. 'I'm just worried about Mam. She's taking it very badly.'

'From what your mam said, I gather you've never met him or any of his family?'

'No, never. It was never a secret but I suppose I just grew up accepting that my uncle wasn't part of our lives.'

'But weren't you curious? Did you never think about looking him up? Your mam said he had a son too.' She knew she was pushing it but it was unbelievable to her that somebody could turn their back on family for so many years.

Bob took four cups out of the cupboard and threw teabags into them. He looked at her then. 'Why do I feel you're accusing me of something, Donna?'

'I … I'm not.' She flushed. 'I'm just trying to understand.'

'Well, maybe it's something none of us will ever understand. I don't know the whole story but I think there were a lot of things that led to them eventually losing touch.'

'That's what your mam said. But to lose touch completely? To not even care if he was alive or dead?'

'Donna!' Bob glared at her and she knew she'd gone too far.

'God, I'm sorry. That was an awful thing to say.'

'Yes, it was. How do you think Mam would feel if she heard you talking like that? Do you honestly think she didn't care? Does she look like a woman who doesn't care?'

'I know, I know. And I really do feel sorry for your mam. But to think that she could have had a brother for so many years …' A sob caught in her throat.

Bob's face softened as realisation dawned. 'You're thinking about Tina.'

Donna nodded and let the tears fall.

'Come here,' said Bob, hugging her close to him. 'I can understand how you feel but you also have to understand that there's two sides to every story. They were both to blame for drifting apart.'

'Ah, I see you're organising tea here,' said Chris, poking his head into the kitchen. 'Make your mam's a strong one, Bob. Plenty of sugar.'

'We'll be right there, Chris.' Donna turned back to Bob and smiled faintly. 'I really am sorry for how I behaved earlier. I was just reminded of … well, you know.'

'Forget about it, Donna.' He squeezed her hand. 'Now let's go back in and support her. It's what families do. And you're family, Donna.'

'Am I?'

'Of course. You're practically her daughter.'

They headed in with the tray of tea and Donna felt a little unsettled. He hadn't said daughter-in-law. He should have said: 'You're practically her daughter-*in-law*.' But he'd said 'daughter'. Maybe it was a throwaway comment. Was it a slip of the tongue or could it be that Bob loved her more as a sister than a lover.

Chapter 35

Will grimaced at his reflection as he tried to fix his tie. He couldn't remember the last time he'd worn a suit or a tie and he just knew he'd feel uncomfortable in it all day. Why was it that people just couldn't be themselves at funerals? Why did people have to conform to some tradition that says everyone must wear dark, sombre clothes that they wouldn't ever wear otherwise?

He finally got the knot in place and tucked his white shirt into his trousers. It was only eight o'clock but they'd be closing the coffin at nine to head to the church. He could already hear the front door opening and closing regularly downstairs as people came to pay their respects. He couldn't face them just yet.

He flopped down on the unmade bed and rested his head on the pillow. How things can change in the blink of an eye. You'd think he'd have learned that lesson from what happened to Jack but he never thought he'd be in this position again. At least not for a very long time. His eyes became moist and he turned to rub them against the pillowcase.

It was hard to believe his dad was dead. His lovely, quiet, unassuming father was gone. Just like that. It had been the best and worst night of his life. He'd felt so lucky to be celebrating his engagement to Silvia. It had been a fun party and, despite his mother barking orders at him, he'd relaxed and fully enjoyed it. But then the night had ended in such tragedy.

He squeezed his eyes tight as the memory of that moment filled his mind. It was a picture that would be embedded in his brain forever. His dad sitting up in the bed with his vest on. A newspaper spread out in front of him on the financial pages. His face relaxed. Relaxed and dead. His mother kneeling on the tea-soaked bed screaming at him to wake up. He never did.

'Are you okay, Will?' Silvia came into the room and sat down on the bed. A lump formed in his throat when he saw her in a black silk dress. Silvia never wore black. He sat up and leaned against the headboard.

'Not really. I still can't believe it.'

Silvia took his hand. 'Me neither. He was such a gentleman and he was lovely to me.'

'He loved you, Sil. He told me so. He couldn't wait for us to get married so that he'd have you as a daughter-in-law.'

They sat in silence for a few moments, lost in thought. Everything seemed so surreal. A heart attack, the doctor in the hospital had said. It had been sudden so there was no suffering. Thank God for that at least. But he was only sixty-two. Sixty-two years old. He should have had years left.

'Do you think you should come down now?' Silvia was looking at him with concern. 'There's already a crowd down there and your mother really isn't able to deal with everyone on her own.'

Will jumped up off the bed. 'I suppose I should. How do I look?'

'Gorgeous. Sad but gorgeous.'

He kissed her lightly on the top of the head and put an arm around her as they headed downstairs. He heard the clatter of cups and for once was thankful for caterers. There'd been so much to organise these last couple of days. He never would have thought of half the things and they were very grateful for the undertakers who'd helped them organise everything. He took a deep breath before pushing the door to go into the living room, where his father was laid out.

'I'm so sorry, love.'

'God rest his soul.'

'He was a good man.'

'Taken far too young.'

'You're the man of the house now.'

The condolences came thick and fast and Will found it hard to control his emotions. It's not that he felt he shouldn't cry. He wasn't afraid to shed a few tears. But what he was afraid of was not being able to stop. His mum was talking to Tom and Gloria, the next-door neighbours, and he overheard Gloria saying: 'I know how you feel,' followed closely by, 'He's in a better place now.'

Will could never understand why people said stupid things at funerals. Firstly, Gloria Ford didn't have the first idea how his mother felt. Wasn't her husband standing there beside her? And secondly, no, he wasn't in a better place. The best place he could be was here. Right here where he had a loving family and a great life.

'You look very smart, William,' said his mother, coming over to stand by his side. She grabbed his hand. 'We'll get through this, love.'

He looked at her and saw her vulnerability. She'd just lost the great love of her life and they both knew things would never be the same for her again. Everyone faded into the background as Will squeezed his mother's hand and looked at his father in the coffin.

He hadn't gone to see Jack in his open coffin. He hadn't been able to handle it. He'd wanted to remember him for the fun-loving, lively guy he was. So today Will was seeing a dead body for the first time. It was a strange experience. His dad had always worn his age well but, like some miracle of nature, all his wrinkles seemed to have disappeared. Jack wished they hadn't. He didn't look like his dad. His skin looked transparent, despite the make-up they'd applied, and his lips seemed to have disappeared into his mouth.

'Doesn't he look gorgeous,' some woman said, as she blessed herself and bowed her head.

Will wanted to scream: 'No, he doesn't!' but he refrained.

'It's almost time,' said the man from the funeral home. He seemed to have a naturally sombre face and Will wondered idly if he got the job because of it or if he developed it after spending time on the job.

All of a sudden somebody burst into a decade of the rosary and Will was fascinated by the low mumbling of the crowd in prayer. Did they even think about what it was they were saying? Or was it just habit to recite word after word, prayer after prayer? But he couldn't condemn it because it gave his mother comfort. She'd always found comfort in prayer and she clung now to her rosary beads and joined in with the rest of them.

And then the prayers were over. People either kissed his father or made the sign of the cross over his forehead before heading outside. They were alone then. He, Silvia and his mother. Silvia gave them both a hug and kissed George, saying she'd leave them alone for a bit.

'Oh, George,' said his mother, beginning to weep. 'What am I going to do without you?'

Will was crying too. He held onto his mother's hand tight as they said their final goodbyes and watched as the coffin was closed.

'Bye, Dad,' he whispered. 'I'll miss you.'

There were dark clouds overhead as they stepped outside the house and droplets of rain began to fall.

'That's Our Lord crying,' an old man said, knowingly. 'It means George was a good man.'

'Rain is a sign that he's being taken to heaven,' said another.

Will knew people meant well but he just couldn't wait for the day to be over. He helped his mother into the black limousine before getting in himself and smiled at Silvia, who slipped in beside him. He was thankful to have her, especially today. She'd been brilliant since it happened and he knew, without a shadow of a doubt, that she was going to be a wonderful wife.

* * *

'Do you think this is okay?' asked Donna, fiddling with the belt of a black A-line skirt. 'Or does it look too officey?'

'It's fine,' said Lexie. 'I don't know why you're getting yourself all worked up about an outfit.'

'Oh God, it's awful, isn't it? I'll find something else.'

Lexie rolled her eyes but Donna was on edge this morning and couldn't seem to settle on anything to wear. They were going to Jan's brother's funeral and she really wasn't looking forward to it. Funerals had always unsettled her but ever since the fire she'd avoided them completely. But she wanted to be there for Jan today – she and Bob had promised to support her every step of the way. It was going to be difficult for her to see people she hadn't seen in such a long time.

A few minutes later she emerged wearing a black and white knee-length dress with thick black tights.

'You're not still stressing over what to wear?' said Bob, stepping out of the bathroom with a towel wrapped around his waist. 'We'll be dead late at this rate.'

'At least I'm dressed, which is more than can be said for you. What about this one?' She twirled around to show the dress off in its entirety.

Bob whistled. 'That's perfect, Donna. Great choice.'

'You think?'

'Definitely. You look gorgeous, doesn't she, Lexie?'

'Yes, but I've been telling her that with every outfit she's tried on.'

'Right, well I'll be ready in two minutes,' said Bob, disappearing into the bedroom. 'And I'm locking the door so you can't get in to change again!'

Donna sighed. 'This will have to do. It's the most comfortable one anyway. Are you sure you don't want to come with us, Lexie? There's plenty of room in the car.'

'Although it sounds like fun, I think I'll pass for today.'

'Don't let Bob hear you talking like that. He'd go mad.'

'I know. Sorry about that. But it's not as though any of you knew the guy. A few days ago, you didn't even know he existed.'

'But Jan did. She's really upset. It's horrible when all you want to do is change the past but you know it's never going to happen.'

'Story of my life,' said Lexie.

'Right, are we ready to go?' Bob stood at the bedroom door and both girls stared at him. He was wearing a tight black T-shirt teamed with skinny black jeans that fell just above his ankle. His cream canvas shoes were on sockless feet and his still-wet, messy blond hair was held back with a hairband.

'Are you going like *that*?' Lexie didn't mince her words.

'Well, yes. I was planning to. Do I not look okay?'

'You look fabulous, Bob,' said Donna. 'But it's a funeral.' He looked as though he'd just stepped off a catwalk.

'I'm well aware of that, Donna. But I want to be myself. Let's face it – I know he was my uncle but I didn't know him. I don't want to come across like a chief mourner.'

Donna stood up. 'Oh God, I'd better go and change again. This just isn't—'

'No!' Bob and Lexie shouted in unison.

Bob ushered her towards the door. 'Come on. It looks like it's about to pour rain so the traffic is going to be chaos. See you later, Lexie.'

Donna gazed out the window as Bob pulled the car out of the car park underneath the building and out onto Dorset Street. It was still morning rush hour and traffic was heavy but once they'd turned left down North Circular Road they were going against the flow.

'I told Mam we'd pick them up at half nine,' said Bob, accelerating to get through a green light. 'It should only take us ten minutes from there.'

Donna nodded.

'Are you okay, Donna? You look a bit peaky.'

'I'm fine. Just a bit tired.'

'Are you sure?' The car swerved as Bob looked at her. 'Do you want me to stop?'

Donna couldn't answer. Everything started to swim in front of her eyes and she found it hard to breathe. She could feel prickles of sweat dripping down the back of her neck and, for one awful moment, she thought she was going to throw up.

'Donna?'

'Stop!'

Bob managed to pull over into the left lane and turn down a side street, where he stopped. He jumped out and ran around to open the passenger door and helped Donna out of the car.

'What is it?' he asked, as she struggled to catch her breath. 'Jesus, Donna. Should I call an ambulance?'

She shook her head as her breathing began to even out. She leaned against the car and began to cry.

'Donna, love, what's wrong? You're really worrying me now.'

'I … I'm sorry, Bob. I'm okay now. It's just the thought of … Don't mind me. I'm just being silly.'

'The thought of what?' Bob looked worried and Donna felt like such an eejit.

She bowed her head. 'The funeral. I've been dreading it. That's why I got so anxious about everything this morning. I got to thinking about the fire and remembering the funeral after. It was the worst time of my life.'

'God, Donna. I should have thought. I'm so sorry.' He pulled her in to him and massaged the back of her neck. It felt good. She wished she was back home in the safety of her little flat watching telly as he massaged her. Anywhere but where they were going.

'Now listen,' he continued. 'We're still early so I'm going to drop you back home. No arguments.'

She pulled away. 'No way, Bob. Your mam needs me there. I told you I'm just being silly.'

'You're being anything but silly.' He opened the passenger door for her to get back in. 'There's absolutely no need for you to be there, especially if it's going to dredge up painful memories. Dad and I will be there with her and we can pop over tomorrow if you're up to it to see how she is.'

'No, Bob. Come on or we'll be late.'

'But I can just drop you back—'

'Bob! I love you for caring so much but I'm going to the funeral and that's that. Your mam has been there for me through so much and now I'm going to let her lean on me.'

'Well, if you're sure?' Bob looked uncertain.

'I'm positive,' she said, stepping back into the car. 'Now let's get going.'

She sat back in the seat and closed her eyes. Maybe it was time she allowed herself to remember. Memories were painful but they could also be healing and she'd blocked out the past for too long.

She was sitting in the funeral car with some distant relative that she'd only just met and Jan. There was nobody else. The sheer scale of the emptiness she felt overwhelmed her and she wished at that moment that she'd perished in the fire too. She looked out the window as the car drove slowly down the street. Past ordinary people going about their ordinary lives. Oblivious to the pain she was in. How was she ever going to survive?

'Here we go.' Bob's lilting voice burst into her thoughts and she saw that they were already at Jan's house. She *had* survived. It had been difficult – it still was at times – but she'd gotten through it. And now, in contrast, her life was full of people who loved her and she felt very lucky. And suddenly she knew, without a shadow of a doubt, that by helping Jan through this difficult time, she'd find healing for herself in the process.

Chapter 36

'Are you sure you'll be okay on your own, Mum?'

'I'll be fine, William. I'm just going to watch the news and go to bed. I have a lot of meetings tomorrow so I want to be awake and alert.'

'If you're sure?' He hadn't left her alone in the house since the funeral a few weeks before and he felt reluctant.

'Stop fussing. I know you mean well but I'll be glad of a bit of time to myself.'

He felt relieved as he headed up to his bedroom. He plonked down on the bed and stretched his hands behind his head. Silvia was still in the shower so he reckoned he wouldn't have to start getting ready for at least an hour.

Things had been really strange in the house without his dad. It was as though they were all walking on glass. Will was afraid to say anything that might upset his mother, she was putting on a brave face and pretending she was fine and Silvia was unsure what to do half the time. He'd made sure that his mother had company in the house at all times. He'd hated the thought of her feeling lonely. He couldn't begin to imagine the pain of being with someone for so long and then suddenly not having them there any more. It was bittersweet that he and his mother were closer now than they'd ever been and it was mainly due to his father's passing.

The funeral had been desperately sad and it had become clear to Will that his father had been very well liked. Friends and neighbours had turned up in their hordes to pay their respects and, although Will hated the formalities of a funeral, he knew his dad would have been chuffed to have such a send-off.

The other positive thing that had come out of the day was he now had a cousin. It was his only one. A cousin *and* an aunt. He'd always known of their existence but never thought he'd meet them. Of course the circumstances hadn't been ideal but he'd hit it off with his cousin straight away and they'd kept in touch.

His name was Bob and Will was fascinated by him. He'd stood out in the crowd because of how he was dressed and his hair looked as though he'd just woken up and shoved a hairband in it. But he'd been charming and gentlemanlike and Will had immediately liked him. His mum, Jan, was lovely too and Will had felt a pang of sadness that these people were only coming into his life now.

'Aren't you ready yet?' said Silvia, wafting into the room in her robe. 'We should be leaving soon.'

'You are joking, right? It will take me all of thirty seconds to throw on my jeans and shirt. You'll be drying that hair of yours and putting on make-up for the next hour at least.'

She tutted and disappeared back out the door with her make-up bag. She always said she hated the light in the bedroom and much preferred the natural light in the bathroom to apply her make-up.

Tonight they were going to meet Bob and his girlfriend. Will hadn't met her at the funeral because she hadn't been well but he was looking forward to the four of them getting together. They had a lot of years to catch up on.

He sat up on the bed and looked at the blue jeans and black shirt he'd left out to wear. Then he thought of Bob and how exotic he'd looked. He'd said he was a fashion journalist. No pressure there, then! He knew Silvia would look spectacular – she always did – so he'd better make an effort himself. He got up to root through his wardrobe and see if he could come up with anything a little more fashionable. He was a little startled to realise he was whistling. For the first time in weeks, he was feeling upbeat. His heart felt light and he had a fluttering of excitement in his stomach. He had a feeling that tonight was going to be a good night.

* * *

'Achooo!' Donna blew her nose for about the hundredth time that day.

'I think we should cancel,' said Bob, looking at her with concern. 'We can do it another time.'

Donna shook her head. 'There's no way we're cancelling. They'll think I'm some sort of hypochondriac, cancelling because of a runny nose.'

'I could always take a picture of you and send it to them.' Bob grabbed his iPhone from the locker beside the bed. 'The colour of your nose alone would convince them that you are indeed sick!'

'Don't you dare,' said Donna, making a swipe for his phone. 'But seriously, how can I not go tonight when I dodged the funeral too?'

'You didn't dodge it, Donna. It wasn't as though you just decided not to bother.'

'But I should have made a better effort.' When they'd picked up Jan to take her to the funeral, Bob had quietly filled her in on how Donna was feeling. Jan had hugged her and insisted they drive her home. 'You'll be no good to me while you're dealing with your own grief,' she'd said. 'Get yourself home and come over tonight and we can have a chat.'

'You made a huge effort, love, so you've got to stop beating yourself up about it. Now am I going to ring to cancel or what?'

Donna shook her head. 'Definitely not. Just give me ten minutes and this face will be transformed.'

'Hmmm. Go on then. You can try but I have my doubts.'

Donna couldn't help laughing at Bob's cheekiness. It was hard to be grumpy when he was around. She really wasn't in form for going out tonight but she was going to have to grin and bear it. She couldn't let Bob down again. He seemed keen to get to know his new-found cousin and he wanted Donna by his side. He'd met his cousin's fiancée at the funeral and apparently she was, in his words, spectacular. Donna knew she had a lot of work to do if she was to compete with that!

She locked the door of the bathroom and looked in the mirror. Spectacular she was *not*! Unless it was spectacularly ugly. Her eyes were red and swollen and she had burst blood vessels all around her nose from the constant blowing. Her skin was dry, her lips chapped and she had a zit the size of a melon on her chin. 'Not a pretty sight,' she said, examining the zit with her fingers to see if it was squeezable.

But despite everything, she managed to emerge from the bathroom twenty minutes later looking close to normal. She'd made up her eyes heavily to detract from the redness and she'd even managed to cover up the broken veins with Lexie's magic green stuff. Donna had often seen Lexie use it under her foundation and she'd assumed that it was just one of those things that manufacturers dream up to make money. But seeing the results today, Donna made a mental note to go straight out and buy a tube of it tomorrow.

'Well, look at you,' said Bob, whistling. 'You scrub up well.'

'It's the best I could do under the circumstances.'

'Donna, you look fabulous.'

'I'm in my ten-year-old dressing gown, Bob.'

'Jesus, why can women not take compliments? I mean your face. *Your face* looks gorgeous. Now hurry up and get dressed. I have a taxi booked for eight and it's already a quarter to.'

After rooting through her wardrobe, Donna eventually settled on a pair of ankle-length white jeans and a sleeveless jade-green blouse.

The evenings were getting brighter and there was a sniff of spring in the air so it was time to move away from the thick black tights and furry boots. She ran a brush through her long, wavy hair before standing into a pair of not-too-high heels and was ready to go.

Donna hadn't been involved in picking the venue but she was more than happy with it. Milano was an authentic Italian pizzeria with food to die for. She'd been there a number of times and adored everything about it from their garlic dough balls to the tiramisu. Her mouth began to water as the taxi drove down the quays towards the restaurant. She was actually beginning to look forward to it.

When they stepped inside, the clink of glasses and the buzz of conversation immediately lifted her spirits. The waiter checked the reservation and informed them that the other party was already seated. He led the way towards the back of the restaurant and indicated a table where a couple were deep in conversation. They both looked up and smiled and Bob's cousin stood up to greet them.

Donna froze. She couldn't move or speak. She felt as though she was in some sort of dream. In some parallel universe she'd just entered a coffee shop in Christchurch.

'I'll have a coffee and a slice of walnut cake,' he said to the waitress, who was hovering impatiently. 'Donna?'

'Just tea for me, please.' She couldn't eat a thing. Her stomach was in knots and she was still trying to figure out what had just happened. After she'd literally fallen into William's arms, there'd been an awkward moment. And then everything had just clicked into place. As though they were old friends, he'd asked her if she fancied grabbing a coffee and she'd agreed. Just like that. It was unlike her to be so reckless but it had just felt right.

And now here he was. William. Her William. Standing right in front of her. In a restaurant in Dublin. Everything began to swim in front of her eyes and her legs buckled beneath her. As she began to fall, she was aware of a pair of strong arms catching her and placing her gently on a chair. She knew instinctively they were William's arms. What were the chances? Most would say it was a coincidence. But she knew better. The hand of fate had dealt her some heavy blows throughout her life. It had been unkind in so many ways. But today it had pushed her into the arms of the man of her dreams. For the second time. And this time she wasn't going to let go.

Chapter 37

'Donna? Donna? Are you okay?'

'Give her some water. She looks very flushed.'

'I knew we shouldn't have come out. She's burning up.'

'Should we get her to a hospital?'

'Wait, she's opening her eyes. Donna, are you okay?'

Donna slowly began to focus on the faces in front of her and it took her a moment to realise what had happened. She opened her eyes fully and took the glass of water from Bob's hand. After she took a few sips, she could finally speak. The first thing that came out of her mouth was: 'William!'

Bob looked from one to the other. 'Do you two know each other?'

'You could say that,' said Will, his eyes fixed on Donna. 'This is unbelievable.'

Donna took another sip and was beginning to feel human again. 'I can't believe it's really you. And you're okay.'

'Can someone please fill me in?' said Bob, sitting on the chair beside Donna. 'I'm confused.'

Donna looked at Will. Drank in his face. She wished they were alone. There was so much she wanted to say. So much she wanted to know.

Will was first to speak. 'Donna and I have met before. Just briefly in New Zealand.'

Bob clapped his hands together. 'No way! What are the chances of that? It's gas how the Irish always find each other no matter where they are in the world.'

Donna was still quiet and Will looked concerned. 'Donna, you don't look well. Can we get you anything?'

'No, no, I'm fine. It's just this damn cold. I can't seem to shift it and when I came in here to the heat, I just felt a bit dizzy.' It was a lie. It was purely the sight of William that had sent her into a spin, but she wasn't going to be admitting that.

'Well, why don't we order some food and then you can tell us about how you two met.' Silvia stretched out her hand to Donna. 'I'm Silvia, by the way. Nice to meet you.'

'Donna. And you too.' They shook hands and Donna was jolted back to reality. He had a girlfriend. And not *just* a girlfriend – a fiancée. It wasn't supposed to be like this.

They ordered their food and Bob demanded to know the whole story. Where did they meet? When? Were they just friends? Did they not keep in touch? Donna knew Bob well enough to know that the 'friends' question was a loaded one and he'd just thrown it in there casually because he didn't want to ask them straight out if they'd been more than friends. Donna was happy to let Will take the lead in telling the story.

'It was in Christchurch,' he began. 'The day before the earthquake.'

He left that comment hanging and Bob nodded knowingly. 'So you didn't get a chance to properly get together then?'

'It wasn't like that.' Will shot Donna a glance and she nodded. They didn't even need words. 'We met in the tourist office and got talking when we realised we were both from Ireland.'

Donna continued. 'We were both travelling alone so we agreed to do a tour of the city together the next day.'

'And it never happened because of the earthquake,' said Silvia, taking Will's hand and squeezing it. 'I can't even imagine how awful that must have been.'

'No, it wasn't awful at all. We barely even knew each other.'

'I think Silvia was talking about the earthquake, Donna,' said Bob, raising an eyebrow. 'And were you two together when the earthquake happened? I thought you said you were alone.'

Donna shook her head. 'I *was* alone. I was on my way to meet William, eh, Will, when it struck.'

'I waited for you,' said Will, his brown eyes boring into hers. 'I didn't know whether you'd decided not to come or if you were just late.'

'I'd slept it out. Of all the days. I'm so sorry. I was almost there when it happened.'

'Well, no harm done, eh?' said Bob, refilling everyone's glasses with water from the jug on the table. 'You're both here now and what a story you have to tell.'

Donna ignored Bob. 'I continued on to the square but it was so chaotic, I couldn't find you. I looked all around but I was a bit dazed from a bang on the head.'

'Oh God. You were hurt?' Will looked genuinely concerned.

'Just a few bumps and cuts. Nothing too serious. How about you?'

'Same here. Nothing much.'

'Nothing much?' said Silvia, looking at Will as though he was mad. 'How can you say it was nothing much when you've been scarred for life?'

Donna sat forward in her chair. 'Scarred? What happened, Will?'

He looked embarrassed and Donna noticed the sharp look he gave Silvia. He obviously hadn't planned on offering the information himself.

'Is it your hand?' Bob joined the conversation again. 'I noticed it at the funeral but didn't like to ask.'

Will sighed and nodded. He laid his hand out on the table for them to see briefly and then pulled it back out of sight.

Donna took a sharp breath. 'Your poor hand. What happened?'

'A large boulder from a building fell on it. Unfortunately they were unable to save one of the fingers but it could have been a whole lot worse. It's not a big deal.'

'He's so modest,' said Silvia, looking at him admiringly. 'And it *is* a big deal. The boulder didn't just *fall* on him. It happened while he was saving a child from being crushed to death.'

'Don't be so dramatic, Sil.'

'But it's true. Like you, Donna, he was wandering in a bit of a daze when he heard a woman screaming her head off. He ran to her and saw that her four-year-old son was trapped under a massive boulder. It was crushing his chest and he was gasping for breath.'

'Oh Jesus!' Bob's eyes were like saucers listening to the story. 'What happened then? Was he okay?'

Donna was quiet, thinking about her dream and how similar it was to actual events.

Despite Will's obvious mortification, Silvia continued. 'Will acted on instinct. He instructed the mother to get ready to pull the child free and he used all his strength to lift the boulder. As soon as the child was out, he let it go and couldn't move his hand out quickly enough.'

'That's awful.' Donna shook her head. 'So you were in hospital over there? I knew I should have checked the hospitals. I thought about it afterwards but I was so distraught that I just wanted to get home.'

'That's understandable,' said Will. Still those eyes. 'And, yes, I was in hospital for ten days over there and then they let me out to continue my treatment at home.'

The waiter arrived with their food, giving them all a few moments to digest all the information. Donna wasn't a bit hungry. Her nose was blocked and there was a horrible trickle of something nasty dripping down the back of her throat. But even if she was in the full of her health, she didn't think she'd be able to face eating a thing. After more than two years of wondering, she'd actually found William – or Will, as he was called. But it was all wrong. Nothing about this situation felt right and Donna couldn't wait to go home, curl up in bed and think about everything.

'Are you okay, love?' Donna realised that she was staring at her pizza when everyone else was tucking into theirs.

'Actually, Bob, I don't feel great. Would you mind if we went home?'

'You do look a bit pale,' said Silvia. 'If you ask the waiter, he'll box the food up for you so you can take it home. You might feel like eating it later.'

And that's when Donna noticed the ring. The big, sparkling solitaire on Silvia's finger. The realisation was like a slap across the face. Will would *never* be hers. She couldn't get out of the place quick enough.

'Do you mind if we don't wait?' she said, standing up. 'I … I really feel like I need some air.'

Bob jumped up. 'Of course not. Come on, let's get you home.' He threw forty euros on the table to cover their food.

'It was lovely to meet you.' Silvia seemed to move in closer to Will. Was she marking her territory? Did she sense something between him and Donna?

'I'll give you a buzz tomorrow, Bob,' said Will, standing up and shaking his hand. 'And I hope you feel better soon, Donna. I'd love to catch up whenever you're feeling up to it.'

'Yes. Yes, that would be lovely.'

Outside, Bob had to steady her as he hailed a taxi. And she hadn't even had a drop of wine. Bob seemed oblivious to the tension between her and Will and chatted excitedly about him as they headed towards home.

'Imagine you and Will knowing each other. Isn't that the craziest thing?'

'Yep.'

'He's a nice guy, isn't he?'

'Yep.'

'And that story about how he hurt his hand – he's a bit of a hero really.'

It sounded as though Bob was in love with him too. In love! Was she actually *in love* with him? She tried to push the thought out of her head but it kept coming back. It was true. And she'd probably known it from the day she met him. She was in love with Will, but there wasn't a damn thing she could do about it.

* * *

Will sat at the kitchen table cradling a cup of coffee. He'd told Silvia to go on up to bed because she was exhausted and said he'd follow her up shortly. He needed some time alone just to think. Of course he hadn't said that to her. Silvia was no fool and would sense it had something to do with Donna.

She'd already questioned him endlessly as soon as Bob and Donna had left. She wanted to know if he'd had feelings for her. If anything had happened between them. If he'd tried to find her after the earthquake. What did he feel for Donna now?

It had been like the Spanish Inquisition. Or the Italian one! Silvia was honest and direct and he'd expect nothing less from her. But he hadn't been so honest with his answers. He'd told her that Donna had just been some girl he'd met and he'd been drawn to her Irishness because he was missing home. He said he'd been curious about what had happened to her, but nothing more. She'd said she believed him. But he knew also that she'd be watching for anything that would suggest otherwise. She was a hot-blooded Italian woman, fiercely loyal and protective of her loved ones. Will knew that she wouldn't stand for it if she thought he had any feelings for Donna so he needed to tread carefully.

His heart had almost burst when she'd walked into the restaurant. What was it about that girl that had captivated him so much? He knew he loved Silvia but seeing Donna had sent him into a spin. He remembered how he'd felt when he met her that day. How long strands of her fiery hair had stuck to her pink lip gloss and how the freckles on her face seemed to dance as she spoke. He remembered thinking that she was the one. The girl of his dreams. The woman he was going to spend the rest of his life with.

He rubbed his eyes and yawned. He'd been wrong about that. Donna may have made an impact on him that day but if he'd actually met her the following day, it probably would have just fizzled out. The whole earthquake scenario had heightened all his senses and because he'd never found out what happened to her, he'd romanticised about her afterwards. That's all it was.

'Are you coming up, Will? The bed is too empty without you.'

Will was jolted out of his thoughts and looked up to see Silvia standing at the door of the kitchen. She had a delicate blue silk robe on her that fell just above her knee and her hair was tousled from sleep. She was beautiful. She was everything he could ever want in a woman. He knew that she'd felt a little threatened by Donna earlier. He couldn't really blame her. It had been a tense and awkward situation. He made a mental note to make sure Silvia knew how much he loved her and that Donna had just been a passing moment in his life.

'Am I talking to myself?'

'Sorry, Sil.' He drained the coffee from his cup and stood up. 'I just needed that coffee. I'm coming up now.'

She waited until he walked up the stairs before following him. It was as though she sensed his thoughts and wanted him to focus on the present and not get caught up on the past. And she'd be right. Maybe under different circumstances, he'd have pursued Donna and maybe, just maybe, things would have worked out. But the reality was that he was engaged to Silvia and nothing was going to change that.

He slipped into bed beside her and spooned her, pulling her close and burying his face in her hair. It took him only seconds to be aroused and he gently turned her around to face him. With deft fingers, he removed her underwear. He was already naked and he could sense her excitement. Sex was always amazing between them. They knew each other intimately and each knew what the other liked. He was inside her then, moving rhythmically. He liked to take his time. Savour the moment. Then a picture of Donna came unbidden into his mind and he wondered what it would be like to make love to her. Without warning, his whole body seemed to explode into the biggest, most sensory orgasm he'd ever had.

'Oh, Donna!' The words were out of his mouth before he could stop them and he realised he may have just made the worst mistake of his life.

Chapter 38

'I'm not sure I can be with Bob any more, Lexie.'

Lexie almost spat a mouthful of vodka and Coke back into her glass. 'What? You can't be serious.'

Donna rubbed her temples. 'Unfortunately I am.'

'But why? Is this because of Will?'

'Kind of.'

'What does that mean?' Lexie's voice was getting louder.

'Well, yes, I suppose it is. But not completely.'

'God, you're talking in riddles, Donna. Either it is or it isn't.'

'Seeing Will has definitely changed things,' said Donna, draining the last of her white wine spritzer. 'But in a way, it's just made me see things more clearly.'

Lexie rolled her eyes. 'Well, that's cleared it up, then. Not! I'm heading to the loo. Do you want to get us another drink? I think I'm going to need it.'

A barman came to take the empty glasses and Donna ordered another round. Lexie had gone with her earlier for her Wednesday visit and they'd decided to stop off for some pub grub and a few drinks on the way home. Bob had already told Donna he'd be home late because of some awards thing in work, so it was the perfect opportunity for the girls to catch up.

The city centre pub was buzzing, even though it was midweek, but they'd found themselves a nook at the back where they could have a proper chat. It was almost two weeks since that night in Milano when she'd come face to face with Will again. Her emotions had been in turmoil ever since and she knew she had some big decisions to make.

She was in love with Will. She couldn't bring herself to tell even Lexie this, but it was true. She'd known for a while now that her relationship with Bob didn't feel right. It was comfortable and she loved his company but it didn't feel like the real thing. She loved him but wasn't *in* love with him. Sometimes she sensed that he felt the same way but neither of them was willing to actually say it.

The barman came back with the drinks and she paid him, telling him to keep the change. It was a generous tip and his young face lit up with gratitude. In an ideal world, she'd explain things to Bob and he'd understand, leaving her available to fall into Will's arms. But there were two problems. Firstly, she wasn't sure Bob would understand and, secondly, Will was engaged.

After that night, Donna had hoped that Will would get her number and contact her. She'd filled herself up with the thoughts of secret meetings where they'd declare their love for each other and try to figure out a way of being together without hurting anyone. But it was a dream too far, it seemed. There'd been no phone call and, according to Bob, Will was busy organising his wedding. It had broken Donna's heart to hear that.

'Right, that's my bladder emptied,' said Lexie, sitting back down and taking a slug of her drink. 'So go on, tell me what you're thinking. And I'll have to warn you – I may take Bob's side.'

'Oh, thanks for that.'

'I just don't want you to hurt him, Donna. He's fabulous and the best thing that's ever happened to you.'

Donna sighed. 'I know. And it's precisely because I don't want to hurt him that I think I have to let him go.'

Donna explained about how her feelings for Will had resurfaced when she'd seen him again. She didn't mention love but said it was enough to make her doubt her relationship with Bob.

'But you don't even know what Will thinks, do you? Or has he been in touch?'

'No, I haven't heard a thing. But that's not the point.'

'I would have thought it's *exactly* the point.'

'Look, I'm not expecting anything to happen with Will.' Donna's voice caught in her throat and she had to pause to cough. 'He's getting married so that ship has sailed. But how can I continue things with Bob if I really don't have those deep feelings for him?'

'But seeing Will has just unsettled you. Maybe if you leave things for a few weeks, you'll realise that Bob is the one you want after all.'

Donna shook her head. 'It's not just Will. It's more than that.' She spent the next few minutes explaining about her relationship with Bob. How it felt more brotherly than anything.

'But you have sex, don't you?' Lexie didn't seem to understand or accept what she was saying. 'I mean, it's hardly like a brother–sister relationship if you have sex.'

'We do, Lexie. But not often and it's just routine. And actually, it's usually me who instigates it. He probably wouldn't care if we never did it.'

'Are you serious? Brendan used to look for it non-stop. I swear, we'd have been doing it morning, noon and night if he'd had his way.'

'That's my point,' said Donna, feeling suddenly tipsy. All the talking was making her drink quicker than usual. 'If he's not looking for it, his heart mustn't be fully in it either.'

Lexie looked thoughtful. 'I've never known a man not to want sex, even if it's not …'

'Not what?' Donna looked at Lexie, who'd stopped mid-sentence and was staring at her. 'Lexie?'

'You don't think … I mean he wouldn't be …'

'Lexie, what are you talking about?' Donna was getting impatient.

Lexie spoke slowly and carefully. 'Do you think there's a possibility that Bob is gay?'

Donna laughed and then stopped when she saw Lexie's face. 'Are you being serious? Bob? Gay?'

'Forget I said anything. I'm probably completely wrong.'

Donna's mind began to process the thought. Bob was certainly in touch with his feminine side, but gay? She thought about his hairbands and his long hair. She pictured his trousers that always sat at his ankle and how he wore shoes without socks. But then she checked herself for stereotyping and shook her head.

'No way, Lexie. I've been with him for two years now. I think I'd know if he was gay.'

Then she thought about how they were with each other. How Bob kissed her more often on the top of the head rather than on the lips. How he loved to watch telly rather than make love. Then she thought of the nights when they'd make love and it would take him ages to climax. At times she'd suspected he'd faked it in the end but he'd discarded the condom before she could check. Could Bob actually be gay? Did she know him at all?

'Donna, are you okay? I'm really sorry I said that. You know me and my big mouth. I just opened it and it came out.'

'The thing is, I'm not entirely sure you're wrong.'

The words hung in the air.

Lexie eventually spoke. 'Did you ever suspect it yourself?'

Donna thought for a moment. 'If I'm honest, I used to think it before we got together. I wondered how such a gorgeous bloke could be single. And maybe it was there in the back of my mind while we were together but I didn't want to face it.'

'It might not be true.'

'Maybe not.'

'It was just a thought.'

'I know.' Donna felt exhausted all of a sudden and all she wanted to do was be in her bed. 'Can we just go home now?'

'Of course,' said Lexie, watching Donna carefully. 'I'm really sorry, you know. That I said it, I mean. I'm really sorry.'

But it couldn't be unsaid. Donna had a lot of thinking to do.

* * *

It was almost midnight and Bob had texted to say he was on his way home. Donna turned onto her other side and closed her eyes, but sleep wouldn't come. Since Lexie had mentioned the gay word earlier, Donna hadn't been able to think of anything else. The more she thought about it, the more she was convinced that maybe, just maybe, Lexie was right. It upset her for a whole lot of reasons. Firstly, it was heartbreaking to think that, at thirty years old, he hadn't embraced his sexuality. But secondly, how could he have lied to her like that? Two whole years they'd been together. Two years of living a lie. That's if it was true.

But there was a tiny part of her that embraced the whole notion of his gayness. It would make things easier for her, wouldn't it? She wouldn't have to break up with him – she could confront him and the relationship would come to a natural end. And if they remained friends, she wouldn't lose Jan in the process.

She heard the sound of keys in the door, followed by the clattering of crockery in the kitchen. Bob was always hungry when he came home late. She envied how he could eat whatever he wanted at whatever time of the day, and never put on a pound. She, on the other hand, would only have to look at a slice of bread, especially at this time of night, and her belly would expand an inch. She was quite happy with her size twelve figure but wished she could allow herself a few more treats without worrying about her waistline.

She was glad when she heard the telly go on because she really didn't feel like talking to him tonight. She loved their chats – especially the ones they had in bed – but she had a lot to get her head around before she spoke to him again. There was always the chance, of course, that Lexie was wrong. But now that the seed was planted, she didn't think so.

It was a long time since she'd been single and she wondered how she'd cope. If she was honest, she hated the thought. She liked being part of a relationship. She loved feeling secure and loved – something that had been lacking in her earlier life. She knew she'd probably find that again. At least she hoped she would. But the heartbreaking thing was that she honestly didn't know if she'd find love again like the love she felt for Will.

He was perfect. It wasn't just how he looked or how he acted; it was the whole package. The feeling she got when she was around him. The way her heart felt like a feather and her head burst with happiness. He induced a feeling of calm within her and when she looked at him she felt complete. She wondered if Silvia knew how lucky she was. Tears sprang to her eyes and she tried hard to blink them away.

Suddenly the bedroom door burst open and Bob crashed into the room. Donna could tell by how much noise he was making that he'd been drinking. He didn't drink much usually so even two pints could have him tipsy.

'Are you awake, Donna, love?'

She tried to remain as still as possible and breathed heavily so that he'd think she was asleep. She just couldn't face him tonight.

'Donna?'

She was practically snoring now. He gave up eventually and Donna opened her eyes a slit to watch as he undressed. He folded his shirt carefully before placing it in the laundry basket and smoothed out his trousers to hang them back in the wardrobe. His shoes were new and he placed them lovingly back into their box but not before wiping them with a tissue. His every movement was careful. Thorough. Effeminate. How had she never noticed that before?

He slipped into bed beside her and within seconds, was snoring soundly. Another time, she'd have giggled at that. She'd have teased him the next day about how he'd fallen asleep before hitting the pillow. She'd have exaggerated by telling him his mouth was open wide enough to catch spiders and there was a continuous stream of drool running down his chin. But now it didn't seem funny.

She elbowed him gently in the ribs to try and stop the snoring but he just grunted and started again. She pulled the covers tightly over her head to drown out the noise. She was emotionally drained. Exhausted. Would this be one of the last nights she'd share a bed with Bob? Possibly. Did she feel sad about it? Desperately. And also a tiny bit relieved!

Chapter 39

He'd gotten away with it! He could barely believe it. Silvia most definitely wasn't a fool and Will sensed a change in her demeanour since that night, but for now, he was off the hook. He felt desperately guilty about it but it really hadn't meant anything. It was just a slip of the tongue. The fact he'd said 'Oh, Donna' just at the peak of their lovemaking was unfortunate but it hadn't been his intention to hurt Silvia. She meant everything to him and he'd have to try harder to make sure she knew that.

He flicked to the next page on the file he was reading but he wasn't taking any of it in. He was bored with his job. The pay was good and it was definitely better than working in a bar for minimum wage, but he was back to where he'd started and that didn't feel good. He'd worked so hard to get away from this. From working for his mother. From feeling strangled by her constant presence. But Silvia was insisting that they get as much money together as quickly as possible. For the wedding, she'd said. For the future.

The future. Thank God they had one. They almost hadn't after he made that blunder. He gave up on the file and sat back in his leather swivel chair and, as he'd done numerous times since, he relived that dreadful moment.

Once the words were out of his mouth, he realised his mistake. He froze for a second and prayed she hadn't heard.

'What the bloody hell did you say?' *gasped Silvia, pulling away from him.*

'Wh— what do you mean? I didn't say anything.'

'You said "Donna". You called me Donna.'

Will tried to think quickly but the orgasm had turned his brain to putty. 'No, I didn't.'

'Will, I'm not stupid, nor am I deaf. Jesus!' *She swung her legs out of the bed and reached for her underwear that had been discarded on the floor.*

'You're hearing things,' *said Will, trying desperately to think of something convincing to say. A lie that would be believable.* 'Why on earth would I say that?'

'Bloody hell, Will. I don't know. Maybe you wish I was her. Maybe it's her you want to make love to and not me.'

'Now you're being silly. I did not say her name.'

Silvia grabbed her robe from the back of the bedroom door and began to pace back and forth. 'Were you lovers?'

'Of course not. I told you all this earlier.'

'Maybe you lied. Just as you're lying about saying her name.'

'Oh for God's sake, Sil. You've gone mad. I met Donna a couple of years ago and we spent precisely one hour in each other's company.'

'That's all it takes.' *She sat down on the end of the bed.* 'A lot can happen in an hour.'

'Now you're just being silly. It was good to see her tonight. Good to find out what happened to her on that day. We shared a really bad experience over there but that's it. Maybe you felt threatened by her and that's why you thought I said her name.'

'Hmmm.'

He could see she was weakening so he warmed to the theme. 'I mean, I did let out a sort of groan at the end. It's what you do to me. You heard it wrong.'

'*Maybe.*'

'*Come on, Sil. I love you. We're getting married. Why on earth would I risk that?*'

She looked at him and he could see the worry in her big brown eyes. He reached over and pulled her back beside him on the bed. He wanted to reassure her that she was the one he wanted. He needed to convince her. Because it was true. Donna meant nothing to him other than the fact she was his cousin's girlfriend. There was no need for Silvia to feel threatened in any way.

She'd relented and nothing more had been said about it. But Will knew that she was being cool with him. It wasn't anything obvious – just subtle ways she'd say things to him. She was also making a lot more demands and looking at him as though she was daring him to object. He needed to just suck it up for now.

Because no matter how he justified it, the fact remained that he *had* said Donna's name that night. He'd asked himself again and again why it had happened and he didn't have an answer. There was no doubt that he'd had strong feelings for Donna when they'd met in Christchurch. He'd even thought at one stage that he'd fallen in love with her. But now he realised that it hadn't been love. It had been loneliness. He'd been missing Silvia so his feelings had become muddled.

But the fact remained that Donna was the only person he knew that shared the experience of that earthquake. She was the only one who could understand the awfulness, the devastation. He'd love to chat to her about it. He'd been tempted to ask Bob for her number to see if they could meet up. Not for anything romantic – just to talk. And he would have done. Except for *the blunder*, as he referred to it in his own head.

So now he was going to force himself not to think about Donna at all. He wasn't going to picture how her hair waved like a twisty slide right down past her shoulders. Or how her eyes were the same colour as grass in the springtime. He wasn't going to think about her freckles or full, pink lips. Now that he knew what had happened on that day and that she was okay, he was going to put her out of his mind for good.

The phone on his desk rang and startled him.

'Hello.'

'Hi, Will.' It was Silvia. 'Are you finishing up there soon?'

He glanced at the time on his computer screen. Almost five o'clock.

'Because I was thinking,' she continued, 'I'm finished a bit early this evening so why don't we meet at your place and go to the Shelbourne for our tea.'

'The Shelbourne? Isn't that a bit extravagant for a midweek tea?'

'Maybe. But we need to start getting things moving for the wedding and I think the Shelbourne is a good place to start.'

Will almost dropped the phone. 'You want to have our wedding in *the Shelbourne*? We'll be paying for it for years.'

'Not necessarily. I heard they do great wedding packages. And it's such a gorgeous, iconic hotel. Please say we can at least check out what they have to offer?'

'I suppose. But I don't think we—'

'Great. I'm just logging off here so I'll see you in about half an hour.' And she was gone before he could object any further.

They hadn't set a date for the wedding yet but Silvia was now pushing to have it sooner rather than later. Will had thought that it wouldn't be for at least a couple of years but she was talking about having it within the year. It felt like she was rushing things. He didn't see what the hurry was. They were both in their late twenties and beginning to settle into their jobs and their lives in Ireland. But on the other hand, why wait? They were living together anyway, so what was a piece of paper? And if it made Silvia happy, he was happy too.

'Are you finished there, William?' His mother appeared at the door looking tired and pale. 'I'm going to call it a day, so if you like, I can give you a lift home.'

'Thanks, Mum, but I'm not heading home just yet.'

'Can't that wait until the morning? I was going to cook us steak and chips – your favourite.'

Will felt sorry for his mother. She was finding life difficult without his dad. Before he died, she would never have left the office this early but now it was as though her heart wasn't in her work any more.

'So what do you say, Will? We can even pick up Silvia on the way home, if she's ready.'

'She's coming into town, Mum. We're going to go to the Shelbourne for our tea and maybe to make some enquiries about the wedding.'

Her eyes lit up and she came and sat in the chair in front of him. 'The wedding? You're going to have it in the Shelbourne? Have you set the date? This is wonderful, William, just wonderful.'

'Hold on a sec.' Will laughed. 'Nothing has been decided yet. We're just going to start making a few enquiries. Silvia is keen to set a date soon so we'll see. And don't worry, we'll keep you up to date every step of the way.'

'Well, you'll love the Shelbourne. Your daddy and I used to go there for our tea when we were younger. Not so much in later years.' Her eyes glazed over and Will's heart went out to her.

'Why don't you come with us?'

'Oh, I wasn't hinting or anything. I was just—'

'I know, Mum. But it would be good to have your opinion too. And there's no point in you cooking at home for one. We can all get our tea and see what we think of the place.'

'Well, if you're sure.' She was already up off the chair. 'I'll just go and tidy myself up.'

Will laid his head down on the desk as soon as she'd left the room. Why had he gone and done that? He wouldn't stand a chance of having his say with two strong-willed, opinionated women making decisions. It was great that Silvia and his mother got on so well but sometimes he felt outnumbered. If they wanted the Shelbourne, they'd get it, whether he liked it or not.

He shut down his computer and went to get his jacket from the hook on the back of the door. Despite constant nagging from his mother, he hadn't given in to wearing suits to work. He always looked smart in a pair of trousers and an open-necked shirt, and kept a tie on hand in case he absolutely needed it, but the formal look just wasn't for him. His mother had bought him a wildly expensive herringbone blazer in the hopes he'd ditch the quilted jacket that he wore to work every day but it remained on a hanger in the office. For special wear, he'd assured her.

His stomach rumbled as he headed down the hall to see if his mother was ready and he realised he was ravenous. Maybe tea in the Shelbourne wouldn't be so bad after all. His phone beeped just as his mother appeared at the door of her office with her coat on and her hair freshly brushed.

'This will be Silvia now,' he said, pulling the phone out of his pocket. 'Perfect timing.'

They walked to the front door as he checked his message but stopped suddenly when he read what was on the screen.

'Hi, Will. It's Donna. Can we meet? x'

Even just reading the message felt like a betrayal. It had been the last thing he'd expected. He snapped the phone shut and stuck it back in his pocket.

'Well, is she here yet?' asked his mother, staring at him. 'And why has your face gone all red? Are you feeling unwell?'

'I'm not, it's not … I mean, it wasn't her.'

'Oh, right so. Will we wait outside?'

Thank God his mother had been with him rather than Silvia. Silvia would have copped straight away that the text had unsettled him and she'd have demanded to see it. God, imagine if she knew Donna was texting him. All the work he'd put in over the last couple of weeks to get her back onside would have been wasted. He wondered what Donna wanted. Part of him was excited at the prospect of seeing her but he also knew that if he did decide to meet her, he couldn't tell Silvia. And that was hardly a good basis on which to build a relationship.

He pulled up the zip of his quilted jacket as they stepped outside the building. Although it was mid-May and the weather was beginning to improve, there was still a nip in the air. His phone beeped again and he held his breath before checking the message.

'I'll be there in five. Sil. x'

He breathed a sigh of relief but allowed his fingers to click on the previous message. He read it again. He'd need to think before answering. That was if he decided to answer at all. Probably the safest thing to do would be to delete it. He couldn't have Silvia finding the message and letting her mind run away with her. He tapped the delete button, but not before saving the number to his contacts. Under a false name, of course. It would give him time to think about whether or not he was going to meet Donna. He needed to decide whether it would be worth the risk – the risk of Silvia finding out or, more importantly, the risk of him falling for Donna all over again.

* * *

'Shit, shit, shit, shit, shit!' Donna danced from foot to foot as she frantically tried to stop the text from sending. She quickly switched the phone off in the hope that would stop it. Jesus! She'd just been messing around – typing texts to see how they'd come across. She definitely hadn't meant to send it!

Bob was in the shower and she'd been waiting for him to come out to have a chat with him. She'd lain awake all night thinking about him – whether or not he was gay and whether or not she should ask him. It certainly wasn't something that she could come right out with so she'd planned on just talking to him about their relationship and see where things went from there.

But then his phone, which he'd left on the kitchen counter, had beeped with a message. She'd ignored it at first but then that blue light had winked at her. It was flashing on and off, taunting her, calling her over to have a look. She'd busied herself chopping tomatoes and cucumber to make a salad but she'd eventually given in and had a look. The message was insignificant. It was the contacts she was interested in. She scrolled down and there it was. 'Will – cousin' it said. There was even a little picture of him. It was one of Bob's favourite things about his beloved Samsung Galaxy – the fact he could snap a picture of someone and add it to their phone number. He thought it was fun to see a picture of someone flash up on the screen when they rang. Personally, Donna thought it was creepy.

Quick as a flash, she'd grabbed her own phone and copied the number down. She'd thought it might be nice to get in touch. Exciting even. But she was also nervous about it. First she'd typed:

'Hi there, Will. We need to catch up. Call me. Donna.'

Too demanding. She deleted it. Then she tried:

'Hi, Will. It's Donna here. I hope you don't mind me texting you but I was wondering if we could meet up some day for a chat. I hope you're well. Donna.' Too formal. Deleted again. Then:

'Hi, Will. It's Donna. Can we meet? x'

That's when she'd pressed Send. All she could hope for now was that she'd switched the phone off quick enough to have stopped it. It was definitely a bad idea. If Will had wanted to meet up with her, he'd have gotten in touch. She'd obviously been just a passing moment for him – probably one of many. She tentatively switched the phone back on and crossed her fingers.

She could hear Bob singing as she waited for the screen to spring to life. His singing always made her smile but not today. Come on, come on! The bloody phone was torturing her. It was taking ages. Eventually, it lit up and she anxiously opened the messages. 'Message sent'! Shit. Well, that was that. It was in Will's hands now. Either he'd ignore the message, leaving her feeling stupid and needy, or he'd agree to meet her to warn her off. To tell her that he was in love with someone else and they were getting married. Either way, it was a lose-lose situation.

Chapter 40

'Wow, Donna. You look stunning.' Lexie's mouth gaped open when Donna emerged from the bedroom in a yellow floral dress. 'Anyone would think you were trying to impress someone!'

Donna blushed. 'Well, there's no harm in trying to look my best, is there? I hardly made a good impression in Milano that night, with my nose streaming and my eyes puffy and red.'

'Well, he'd be blind if he didn't notice how gorgeous you look today.'

Will had texted back. She'd almost died when the message had come in because she'd begun to think he was ignoring her. It had taken him two days but he'd eventually replied saying:

'Sure. How about 1.15pm on Friday. Front of Stephen's Green Centre?'

She hadn't hesitated in replying. Friday was her day off so it was perfect. The text had arrived on Wednesday and she'd spent the last two days thinking of nothing else. What was she going to wear? What was she going to say? Would she be able to contain her feelings? But she knew she'd have to. Despite how she felt, she would never purposefully break up a relationship. If she knew he was happy with Silvia, then she'd have to accept it. But a small part of her – no, a huge part of her – hoped that he felt the same as she did. That he'd tell her that *she* was the one for him and not Silvia.

She did a final check in the mirror before heading off for the bus. It was only a ten-minute bus ride so she had plenty of time. She'd toyed with the idea of being a little late. Just so that she wouldn't appear too keen. But then she'd thought of that day in Christchurch. That awful day. And she knew she couldn't be late again.

The summer sun was beaming as she strolled up Grafton Street and she was thankful for the loose cotton dress she was wearing. She glanced at her watch as she got to the top of the street and saw it was only just gone one. Plenty of time for her to get herself together before he arrived. But as she approached the entrance to the centre, she saw he was already there. He hadn't changed a bit in the couple of years since they'd first met, except maybe his hair was a little neater. She'd loved how it had fallen in loose curly tufts over his forehead. Now the curls were more controlled. He was wearing pale chinos and a open-neck blue shirt and was tapping something into his phone as he leaned against the wall. She stopped for a moment just to look at him. She adored him. How could she not?

'Hi, Donna,' he said casually, as she finally approached him. 'It's good to see you.'

He didn't kiss her.

'Will we go inside for a coffee or just go and sit on a bench inside the park?'

Donna finally found her voice. 'The park sounds nice. It's a lovely day.'

They ran across the road to avoid the traffic and Donna felt disappointed he hadn't grabbed her hand. He hadn't noticed the dress either. She'd picked it because it was almost identical to the one she'd worn the day they'd met. She'd thought it would remind him of the connection they had back then. Obviously not.

'Here we go,' he said, pointing to a bench just inside the main entrance. 'This will do nicely.'

Donna could feel every sense in her body tingle as they sat down, their bodies touching ever so slightly. She had a million things to say to him and yet she couldn't think of one single thing at that moment. Luckily, Will wasn't so tongue-tied.

'I never thought I'd see you again, Donna. Isn't it crazy that you ended up going out with my cousin?'

'Yes, crazy.' She didn't want to talk about Bob.

'But I'm glad.'

She looked at him then. 'You're glad I'm going out with your cousin?'

'Well, I actually meant I'm glad it's helped us to connect again.' He looked at her with those melting eyes. 'It's really good to see you, Donna.'

'And you too.' She began to relax. 'And will I tell you something even more crazy?'

'Go on. I hope it's good crazy.'

'It is! Do you remember when you were in Perth and staying with friends?'

His forehead creased and he looked puzzled. 'Did I tell you about that? I didn't think we spoke about Perth.'

'We didn't.'

'Now I'm really confused.'

She smiled as he creased his brow, trying to remember. 'Do you remember when your friends were going to set you up with a girl who was coming over from Ireland?'

'Yes, but how did you … NO WAY! Donna. Her name was Donna. Not you?'

Donna nodded smugly. 'Yep. That's me. Lexie is my friend. She'd been telling me about this hunk of a guy she was going to set me up with but then when I got there, you'd left.'

'That is absolutely crazy! What are the chances of that? So we were destined to meet long before Christchurch?'

'It seems so,' said Donna, feeling more confident. 'I only found out because Lexie was showing me photographs of when she was in Perth. You were in one of them and I recognised you.'

'Hang on. Slow down a minute. You said *when* she was in Perth. Is she not there any more? What about Brendan?'

'That's over, Will. I know he was your friend, but Brendan turned out to be not such a nice character after all. He had a string of other women on the go.'

Will shook his head. 'Bastard. He said something to me about that when we last spoke. That's why I wasn't bothered to keep in touch. I grew very fond of Lexie while I was over there and I hated that he was being unfaithful to her.'

'Well, you'll be glad to know she's actually living with me and Bob now. She's dying to meet up with you again.'

'Ah, that's brilliant,' said Will, his eyes lighting up. 'It'll be great to catch up with her. God, isn't life funny sometimes?'

'Yes, but sometimes very cruel too.' She stared at his hand then and her face turned serious. 'It was an awful day, Will, wasn't it? I'll never forget it.'

He nodded. 'Me neither. And I did wonder about you, you know. For a very long time. Actually, I don't think I ever stopped wondering – imagining what had happened to you, where you were, what you were doing.'

'Same here.' A sob caught in Donna's throat, taking her by surprise. 'I checked the death toll every day. I became obsessed with finding out details of the dead – hoping, praying that I wouldn't hear about a young Irish man called William.'

Those words hung in the air and they both sat in silence, lost in thought. Donna so badly wanted to tell him how she felt. She wanted to talk about the connection they'd had that day. Had he felt it too? She was sure he had. But the most important question was how he felt now. Did he feel anything for her at all or was it all in the past? Had Silvia changed all that?

'Do you ever wonder what would have happened if there hadn't been an earthquake that day?' asked Will, interrupting her thoughts. 'I mean, with us.'

'All the time.' She at least had to be honest.

'Do you believe in destiny?'

The question surprised her. 'Yes, definitely.'

'Me too. My grandmother always used to say: "What's for you won't pass you." I've always liked that saying and I think there's a lot of truth in it.'

Donna's heart lifted. This was it. He'd realised that they were destined to be together. *What's for you won't pass you*. She was for him and he was going to make sure she didn't get away this time. Her eyes filled with tears as she looked at him.

'That's what I think happened in Christchurch,' he continued.

'I think so too, Will. It's destiny.'

'Yes, because if the earthquake hadn't happened, I probably never would have got together with Silvia. She was very concerned after I was hurt and we spent a lot of time chatting on the phone. I went to live in London after my treatment was finished and she decided to come and join me.' His eyes lit up when he spoke about her. 'So how did you get together with Bob?'

She didn't want to discuss it. Her world had just been shattered again. Silvia was his destiny – not her. She suddenly needed to get out of there. She'd been fooling herself. Will was in love with another woman and there wasn't a damn thing Donna could do about it.

'Donna?' She realised Will was still waiting for an answer.

'Sorry, I just realised I have to be somewhere.' She stood up and smoothed her dress down.

'Ah, that's a pity. Maybe we can meet up again soon.'

Why did he want to meet her? Did he want to torture her? She didn't want to discuss how happy he was with Silvia and how she was his destiny.

'Unless you don't want to,' he continued.

She sighed. 'I … I don't know, Will. It's complicated.'

He raised an eyebrow. 'Bob?'

'Well, yes …' She wanted to scream that Bob wasn't the problem, Silvia was. She wanted him to know that she loved him but she couldn't say it.

He nodded. 'Okay. Well, you have my number so text me if you want to meet up.'

'Okay.'

'And one more thing,' he said, as they exited the park together, 'I know it's silly, but I didn't tell Silvia we were meeting up. She's a bit possessive. I just thought it was best not to mention it.'

Donna felt a glimmer of hope. Why would he hide it if it meant nothing? 'Don't worry. I didn't tell Bob either.'

They reached the top of Grafton Street and Will turned to face her. 'Right, I'm heading this way. Back to work, I'm afraid.'

Donna's heart began to beat out of her chest. 'It was great to see you, Will.'

'You too, Donna.' He reached over to kiss her on the cheek and she shifted slightly. On purpose. She couldn't help it. He caught her on the lips. Not quite full on but their lips touched, nonetheless. He tasted of coffee and heaven. She never wanted to be away from those lips again.

He pulled away but not before he'd allowed his lips to linger briefly. 'Bye, then. Chat soon.'

She watched as his back disappeared around the corner. Such a brief kiss and yet it filled her with hope. He hadn't offered the kiss, but he hadn't tried to avoid it either. And *he* was the one who'd suggested meeting up again. But as she turned to walk down Grafton Street, her mood dipped again. The fact remained he was getting married. He'd said Silvia was his destiny. Donna was only fooling herself if she thought she could compete with a woman like that.

But one thing had become painfully clear to her. She couldn't put things off any longer. She needed to talk to Bob. She loved him dearly but not in a romantic way. It was going to be painful but, regardless of the fact that Will wasn't going to be in her life, she had to split up with Bob.

* * *

Will walked quietly back into his office so his mother wouldn't hear. He wanted to sit and think. His head was swimming with thoughts of Donna and yet he knew it was wrong. Silvia was going to be his wife. And yet he was inexplicably drawn to Donna. Maybe it was just the connection of the earthquake. Perhaps he should be more honest with Silvia and tell her that. He felt bad that he was keeping secrets from her – secrets that didn't even need to be kept. Because, after all, there was nothing romantic going on between him and Donna.

When he'd seen her coming towards him in that yellow dress, he'd been transported back to the tourist office in Christchurch, when she'd fallen into his arms. He'd remembered how he'd felt back then. It had taken all his strength to see past that and talk to her normally. They'd sat very close on the bench and he'd felt the heat coming from her body. But he'd shaken off any inappropriate feelings and reminded himself that she was his cousin's girlfriend. His new-found cousin, whom he liked a lot.

The ringtone from his phone startled him and he grabbed it out of his pocket. It was Silvia. It was as though she was reminding him. Her timing was perfect.

'Hi, Sil. What's up?'

'Will, I have some brilliant news. You'll never guess what.'

'Go on then, tell me.' He tried to sound enthusiastic but he wasn't in the mood.

'I've just had a job offer. It's a senior position in a bank. And wait for it – the salary is *twice* what I'm getting now. Isn't that amazing?'

His mood lightened. She was a hard worker and deserved it. 'That's brilliant, Silvia. I'm really delighted for you.'

'But there's just one thing.'

He suddenly felt nervous.

She continued. 'I think it's a good thing really. It'll be good for us.'

'What is it, Silvia?'

There was a pause and he held his breath.

'The job is in Perth. Starting next month. I guess you and I will be moving back to Australia. Isn't that wonderful?'

His head began to spin and he could hear Jack's voice clearly in his head: *'Spread your wings, mate. Don't stay working for your mum forever. There's a whole big world out there and it's waiting for you. Be happy.'*

Was Jack right on this occasion or would he be making the biggest mistake of his life?

Chapter 41

'I need you and Silvia home for tea,' said Vivienne, bursting into Will's office, an excited look on her face.

'We'll be home tonight, if that's what you mean.'

'Yes, tonight. I'm leaving here shortly to get organised. I've asked George's sister, Jan, and her husband over and they're going to bring their son and his girlfriend too. It's about time we all got to know each other better.'

'T— tonight? They're coming tonight?'

'Yes, William. That's what I said. Is there a problem?'

'None at all. We'll be there.'

'Good. Now you'll have to lock up because I'm heading off. I have so much to do.' She breezed out the door and Will could hear her listing off a string of orders to her assistant.

He sat back in his chair and stretched his hands behind his head. He was trying to process the overload of information that had been thrown at him today. First there'd been his meeting with Donna. It had unsettled him. Then the call from Silvia about moving to Perth. That had been a big one and he still wasn't sure how he felt about it. And now they'd be entertaining their new-found relatives at home later. And that included Donna. He wasn't sure he was ready to see her again just yet. And even more importantly, he wasn't sure Silvia was ready either.

That was it! He'd tell Silvia about the tea and maybe she'd have an excuse for them not to be at home. He really didn't want to let his mother down but it would be such an awkward situation. He grabbed his phone and tapped into his numbers. She answered in two rings.

'Hi, Will. I bet you've been thinking about Perth all afternoon. I know I have.'

'Yes, of course. But that's not why I'm ringing you. It's about tonight.'

'What about it?'

'Well, Mum has organised for Jan to come over and has included Bob and Donna in the invitation.' He waited for her to process that.

'Okay.'

'But I'm sure you don't want to be bothered with all that. Especially after … after … you know …' Jesus, why did he have to mention that?

'After what, Will?' Her voice was cold.

'You know what I mean. I just thought you'd prefer if we weren't there. Maybe I can tell Mum you've organised something else for us for tonight?'

There was silence for a moment. 'But why would I not want to be there? You told me I was hearing things that night. You told me you didn't say Donna's name.'

'I didn't. Look, I just thought you might feel uncomfortable or something. That's all.'

'I have no reason to feel uncomfortable, Will. Sure aren't we getting married? And Donna and Bob are together so where's the problem?'

'There's no problem at all.' He could see he was losing this battle. 'So are you saying you're happy about being there when they come over?'

'Of course I am. You know how I like family gatherings and I miss that about home. So it will be good to sit around the table with family tonight.'

'Great. I'll see you at home later.'

Will ended the call and reached into his desk drawer. He took out a box of paracetamol and downed two with a sip of water. His head was thumping. There was too much to think about. He was going to have to sit at a table tonight and pretend everything was normal when in fact he'd been out having a secret meeting with another woman.

Donna. What was it about her that set his heart racing? When their lips had touched earlier, he'd had to resist the urge to run his fingers through her hair, touch her face, pull her close to him. Everything in his head had screamed danger but his heart had whispered 'do it'. He'd listened to his head but had it been the right thing to do? Could he still be happy with Silvia, knowing how he felt about Donna?

All of a sudden a blanket of uncertainty came over him. He felt odd. Off-kilter. The last time he'd felt like that was when Jack died. It was as though his life was a merry-go-round, spinning around in front of him, but he was having trouble getting on. He was suddenly questioning everything but he didn't have any answers. He closed his eyes and, with his elbows on the table, he leaned his head into his hands.

'What would you do, Jack, if you were me?' he whispered.

But Jack wasn't there. God, he missed him. All Will could do now was pray for his friend to give him strength to make the right decisions and hope that he'd have no regrets.

* * *

Donna sat at the kitchen table in the flat. She'd asked Lexie to make herself scarce for a few hours so that she could talk to Bob. Seeing Will earlier had given her the push she needed. It was the right thing to do.

She flicked through the pages of a magazine she'd bought on her way home from town. It had caught her eye when she'd gone into a shop to buy a packet of mints. The cover had pictures of high-profile celebrities who'd just split up from their partners and her curiosity had seen her hand over the exorbitant price of three euros and fifty cents.

But she wasn't reading it. Her mind was elsewhere. She felt desperately sad that her relationship with Bob was coming to an end and she dearly hoped that they could remain friends. She also hoped that her bond with Jan was strong enough and that they could maintain their relationship. She'd briefly toyed with the idea of telling Bob about Will. About how she felt. But then she realised that there'd be no need because nothing was going to happen between them and she'd cause too much hurt if she said anything.

She touched the corner of her lips where Will had kissed her earlier and closed her eyes to relive it. It had been perfect. Brief but perfect. The only thing was that it was possibly more than two years too late. How would things have turned out if that kiss had happened outside the coffee shop in Christchurch? Would they have taken it further? If they had, maybe then they'd have been together the next day when the earthquake happened. Maybe, maybe, maybe!

The sound of keys in the door startled her. Bob was home. It was time. She closed the magazine and braced herself for the conversation that she didn't want to have but knew she had to.

'Donna, come on, quickly. We've had an invitation and we have to be out of here in the next half hour.' Bob came over and kissed her on the top of the head.

'Invitation? Where to? I'm not really in form for going out, Bob.'

'I was trying to ring you,' he said. 'I only got the call in the last hour but I've already told them we'd be there.'

Donna was getting frustrated now. 'Tell who? And where are we supposed to be going?'

Bob peeled off his tweed jacket and placed it on the back of one of the kitchen chairs. 'We've been invited for tea in my aunt's house. Aunty Vivienne. Will's mam.'

'Hold on. Slow down.' She could feel herself tensing up.

'Listen, I can fill you in on the way but you better get ready. I told Mam we'd pick them up so she'll be waiting.'

'Is … is it going to be just your aunt there? I mean, just her and us?'

'No. Will and Silvia will be there too so it's going to be a real family affair. I can't wait.'

Donna's heart began to beat quickly and her mouth went dry. She couldn't do it. She couldn't sit and watch Will and Silvia fawning over each other when her lips were still tingling from the kiss. It would be torture. And how could she allow Bob to introduce her as his girlfriend to his new-found family when she was waiting to tell him it was over?

'Come on, what are you waiting for?' Bob was staring at her.

'Bob, I'm not sure … I just don't think—'

'Please, Donna. You have to come. I've already said we'd be there. It'll be great.'

She looked at him and saw how eager he was. She couldn't let him down. It might be the last time she'd go anywhere with him. And after their chat, it would probably be the last time he'd want her to.

'Right,' she said, standing up and stretching. 'I'd better go and change. Half an hour you said?'

He beamed. 'Yep. You don't have to worry about dressing up. It's just a casual thing so wear something comfortable.'

She nodded and headed into the bedroom. Part of her was filled with dread but part of her was excited. It was a complex situation but at least she was going to see Will again. She wondered if he'd thought about her since the kiss. Or did he go straight home to his fiancée and kiss her properly, long and lovingly. It made her almost mad with jealousy to think of it.

But despite how she felt, she knew Will was with Silvia and she respected that. She might not like it, but that's the way it was. Her sister, Tina, had done a good job of teaching her right from wrong and she knew that if Tina was here, she'd tell her to forget about Will. And maybe she would – in time. But for now, she was going to don the sexiest outfit she had, carefully apply her make-up and generally make herself look irresistible. Just to make Bob proud. That was all. Just as a favour to Bob.

Chapter 42

'Come in, come in.' Will opened the door wide. 'It's great to see you all.'

'And you too, love.' Jan stepped inside and kissed her nephew on the cheek and Chris followed, shaking his hand. Donna and Bob came next and Will's smile remained fixed. Donna wished she knew what he was thinking. Was all this as uncomfortable for him as it was for her? He welcomed them all and didn't flinch when Donna took his hand.

They followed him down the hall and into a beautiful dining room. It was old-worldly but very chic at the same time. There was a long, oval mahogany table with ten chairs. The cushions on the seats of the chairs were red, as were the walls, and the gold-framed mirrors and picture frames completed the regal look. It sort of reminded Donna of the Olympia Theatre. She'd been there to see a play with Jan a few months before and the colours and style were very similar.

'Now what can I get you to drink?' asked Will, after he'd taken their coats and told them to sit wherever they liked. 'Mum is just putting the finishing touches to the food. She'll be in shortly.'

'I hope she didn't go to any trouble for us, love,' said Jan, looking at the very formal dinner settings. 'Can I help her with anything?'

'Not at all. Stay where you are.'

They gave their drink orders and William disappeared out the door.

'She's done well for herself, hasn't she?' said Chris. 'I mean, this house must be worth a fair penny.'

Jan elbowed him in the ribs. 'Shh! They'll hear you.'

'I'm not saying anything bad, Jan. You've got to relax.'

'It's hard, though, love.' She lowered her voice to a whisper. 'There's been a lot of bad blood between us over the years and I want an end to it. I want to honour George's memory by embracing his family.'

Bob reached across the table and patted his mother's hand. 'And you are, Mam. I'm very proud of you.'

Just then the door opened again and Silvia came in. 'Sorry I'm late. It took me ages to get home from work. Lovely to see you all again.'

'Lovely to see you too, Silvia,' said Jan. 'And you look gorgeous.'

She sat down and Donna had to acknowledge that Jan was right. Silvia *did* look gorgeous. Her long chestnut hair fell over one shoulder and her outfit of a sheer pink blouse and loose grey slacks looked effortlessly chic. Donna felt frumpy in her own purple woolly dress and thick black tights. She'd thought she looked elegant when she'd chosen it earlier. Purple suited her red hair beautifully. But comparing herself to Silvia, there was no contest.

They all chatted amicably until Will and his mother appeared in the room with plates of food.

'Here, let me help you with those,' said Bob, getting up off his chair to help. 'And Aunty Vivienne, you haven't met my girlfriend yet. This is—'

'Dana! The cake girl.'

Bob looked at her and then over at Donna. 'How do you … when did you …?'

'Do you two know each other?' asked Will, looking a little rattled.

Vivienne nodded. 'Dana made your dad's retirement cake. Remember I sent you pictures? It was fabulous.'

'It's Donna, Mum. Not Dana. And I can't believe you two met before. That was an amazing cake, by the way, Donna.'

Donna blushed. 'Thanks. I have to admit it was one of my favourites. It's actually Jan's bakery.'

'Are you serious?' Vivienne looked shocked. 'I can't believe I was in and out of there a number of times and we didn't bump into each other, Jan.'

'Well, this family is full of surprises,' said Bob, helping Will and Vivienne to dole out the food. 'You just wouldn't know what you're going to hear next.'

'Yes,' said Silvia, speaking up for the first time. 'We were shocked when we found out about Will and Donna. Can you believe they've met before too?'

Jan nodded. 'Donna was telling us about that. It's like we've all been linked in one way or another. Maybe it was the universe trying to bring us all together.'

'Well, the universe has done a good job then,' said Chris, filling his fork with mashed potato. 'This is gorgeous, Vivienne.'

'I'm glad you like it. I have to admit I'm not a great cook but I do a pretty good roast beef dinner. There's dessert too but I'm afraid it's Marks and Spencer's best.'

The chatter around the table continued and Donna noticed that Silvia had moved closer to Will. She was eating with just a fork and was stroking his arm with her left hand. Just as she'd done in Milano, she was marking her territory. Donna couldn't wait for the evening to end.

'Let's move into the living room,' said Vivienne, when they'd finished their meal. 'It's far more comfortable and I can bring in coffee and dessert when we're ready.'

The living room wasn't quite as regal as the dining room but it was comfortable, with an eclectic mix of furniture. As they spilled into the room, Bob was chatting to his aunt so Donna inadvertently sat down beside Will. He looked a little startled and she could have kicked herself. Silvia was gone to the bathroom and Donna guessed she wouldn't be too happy with the seating arrangement when she came back.

'So, Will. Are you enjoying being back in Ireland?' She couldn't think of another thing to say.

'It's good, yes. I love travelling but it's nice to come home.'

They sat for a moment in awkward silence until Will spoke again. 'How about yourself?'

'Oh, I love Ireland. I'm not really into travelling at all. I'm glad I did it but I can't see myself going anywhere again, unless it's for a holiday.'

'Did someone mention holidays?' Silvia came back into the room and straight onto Will's lap.

Will flushed. 'Donna was just saying she's not much of a traveller.'

'Really?' It sounded like a criticism. 'Will and I love to travel, don't we, hon?'

'We do enjoy visiting other places,' said Will, looking uncomfortable. 'But as I was saying to Donna, it's also nice to come home.'

'And did you tell her our news?'

News? Donna felt her insides turning to jelly and she shot a glance at Silvia's stomach. Flat as a pancake. But maybe it was early days. Oh God, she couldn't bear it if they were having a baby.

'I haven't had a chance to tell anyone yet, Sil. I've only just found out myself.'

Silvia turned to Donna. 'We're moving to Perth. I'm going home and Will is coming with me.'

'You … you're leaving Ireland?' Donna felt her chest tightening. 'Going back to Perth?'

Will shook his head. 'Nothing has been decided yet. It's just an option at the moment.'

'It's more than an option. I've had a great job offer and we'd be mad not to go over.'

'Congratulations,' said Donna, plastering a smile on her face. 'I'm delighted for you both.'

'Thanks, Donna. I've only just got the news so Will is still digesting it. But he loves Perth. Don't you, Will?'

'It's a great place alright. I just never saw myself settling down there again.'

'It'll be an adventure.'

Donna felt uncomfortable and looked around to see what Bob was doing. That's when she saw him watching them from across the room. He had a strange look on his face. She patted the arm of the sofa and indicated for him to come over. She needed to have him there. It was too much listening to Will and Silvia talk about their plans for the future. She couldn't take much more. Thankfully he obliged and arrived over to join the conversation.

'So what are you guys talking about?'

Donna felt like screaming as Silvia launched into the story about her new job and moving to Perth. Bob said he'd be sad to see them go so soon after he'd found them. And he meant it. He was such a genuinely lovely guy and Donna wished things were different.

'So what about the wedding?' he asked. 'I thought you guys were in the process of organising it.'

Silvia's eyes lit up. 'We'd been making enquiries but no date yet. We'll just see how it goes in Perth for a while and make some decisions then.'

'Will you still get married over here, do you think?' Donna could have strangled Bob for asking all those questions. 'I'd hate to miss out on a good knees-up.'

'We're not entirely sure, are we, Will? But if we get married over there, we'll still have a party here to celebrate. Don't you worry about that.'

Donna could tell by Will's face that he wasn't entirely happy. It looked like Silvia was taking charge and making decisions without him. Donna really didn't like her much. Surely being with someone should be all about compromise. Had she even asked Will if he wanted to go to Perth? Donna didn't think so.

It was half past ten by the time they finished dessert and Donna was relieved that Jan suggested it was time to go home.

'Donna and I have an early start in the morning,' she said. 'We're in for seven so we'll be falling asleep if we don't make a move now.'

They said their goodbyes and headed out to the car. Donna noticed how Silvia clung to Will as they waved them off and she forced back the tears. She had to come to terms with the fact that Will and Silvia were together and there wasn't a thing she could do about it. Maybe it would be a good thing if they went to Perth. She wouldn't have to see them again and, as they say, 'Out of sight is out of mind'.

Bob suddenly reached over and took her hand, keeping one hand on the wheel. She looked at him and he glanced at her with tears in his eyes. She knew then that they were going home to have *the talk*. It couldn't wait for a moment longer.

* * *

Donna felt exhausted when they arrived home but she knew sleep would have to wait. She threw her coat and bag on the armchair and went into the kitchen to fill the kettle. Bob followed her in and took out two cups.

'Good night, wasn't it?' he said, popping a couple of teabags into the cups. 'I'm glad Mam and Vivienne have put their differences aside. It's good to have a bigger family.'

'It must be lovely.'

'God, sorry, Donna. I wasn't thinking.'

'It's fine. I'm delighted for your mother – and for you.'

'They're nice, aren't they? Vivienne and Will.'

'Very.'

'And Silvia. She seems to have fit in well with the family.'

'Bob.'

'And what did you think about their plans?'

'*Bob!*'

He swung around to face her.

'We need to talk,' she said, her heart thumping heavily in her chest.

He nodded. 'I know, Donna. And I've been dreading it.'

'Me too.' She took his hand and led him into the living room where they sat down on the sofa. At least he seemed to know what was coming. They sat in silence for a few moments. Donna was trying to bite back the tears because she wanted to have a level-headed conversation and not let her emotions take over. Bob was the first to speak.

'It's not working any more, is it?'

Donna shook her head and looked at him. 'I wanted it to. I really did. But something just isn't right.'

'I know,' said Bob, taking her hand and squeezing it. 'In ways, we have it all. Do you realise how many of my mates are envious of me? They say that we have the perfect relationship.'

'In a lot of ways we have, Bob. But I think we both know that something is missing. I mean, can you ever see yourself having children with me, growing old with me, spending the rest of your life with me?'

He looked thoughtful. 'I'd like you to be in my life forever, but maybe not as my partner.'

The words hung there. It was exactly what Donna had been planning to say to him but, when it came from his mouth, it actually hurt a little.

'I feel really upset about it,' he continued. 'And I've really tried to make myself feel a certain way, but I just couldn't.'

Donna nodded and let out a long sigh. 'It seems we've both been feeling the same but we've been dancing around the issue for a while.

The thing is, I love you, Bob. I really, really love you. You and Jan mean so much to me that I'd be devastated if I lost either of you.'

'I love you too, Donna. And so does Mam. You'll never lose us. You're part of our family and that will never change.' He pulled her over to him and hugged her tightly.

She began to cry. 'I don't know what I'm going to do without you, Bob.'

'I told you, love. You'll never be without me. Just because we won't be sharing a bed doesn't mean we can't be friends.'

They sat there in companionable silence but the air was heavy with unsaid words. She thought about what Lexie had said about Bob and wondered if it was true. She'd like to think that if he really was gay he'd trust her enough to tell her. She looked at his gorgeous, chiselled face with blond hair falling over one eye. What was going on in that mind of his? Was he worried about what she'd think? Was he worried about telling his mother? She wanted to be there for him. To help him through it. If it was true.

Donna wasn't sure how long they'd been sitting there. She was almost dropping off to sleep, her head resting on Bob's shoulder. She knew that once she stood up from that sofa, reality would set in and she'd have to face the uncertainty of where her life was going.

'Since we're being so honest,' said Bob, sitting up suddenly and startling her, 'I think there's other stuff we need to talk about.'

There it was. Lexie was right. She was glad she already knew because she didn't want to look shocked.

'I mean, we may as well get everything out in the open, Donna. Say what's on our minds.'

'I agree. There's nothing we can't say to each other.'

Silence again.

'Go on then,' he said, watching her carefully.

'Me?' Donna was confused.

'Yes. Isn't there something you want to tell me?'

Donna's mind began to spin. What was he talking about? She'd thought he was going to tell her he was gay but now she wasn't so sure.

'Donna?'

'What do you want me to say, Bob?'

'Just tell me the truth. I'm not stupid, you know.'

'I really don't know what you're talking about.'

He looked at her then. It was a gentle look. A look that said everything was going to be alright. And then he floored her. 'You're in love with him, Donna, aren't you? You're in love with Will.'

Chapter 43

'Wh— what?' Donna couldn't believe what she was hearing. How did he know? She wasn't sure whether to deny it or come clean. She was lost for words.

'Don't look so shocked, Donna. I've probably known it for a while.'

'But I'm not … it's not like that.'

'Look, we've already got the hard part over. But I want to be your friend. Please don't lie to me.'

That's when she knew she had to be honest. Her voice was barely a whisper. 'How did you know?'

Bob smiled for the first time since the conversation had begun. 'I think I sensed it that night when we met them in Milano. You didn't fool me when you said that the fainting was due to your cold. I could see it was more than that.'

'And I thought I'd put on an Oscar-worthy performance!'

'You might have fooled Will and Silvia, but there was no way you were going to fool me. I know you too well. We've been together for quite a while, don't forget.'

'How could I forget, Bob?'

'I'm not wrong, then?'

She nodded. 'I'm so sorry. I tried to deny it. Tried to forget about him but he kept invading my brain. And then when I saw him that night …'

'So you've been in love with him since Christchurch? Since before the earthquake?'

'I guess so. I kept telling myself that it was stupid. That it was impossible to fall in love with someone in such a short space of time. But it happened. I can't explain it – it was like something lit up inside me when we met. And it was extinguished when I lost him that day.'

'And I was just someone to keep you company until you found him again?'

Donna realised how it must look. 'God, no. It wasn't like that. I honestly didn't think I'd ever see him again. And I thought I loved you – I *did* love you. I still do.'

'But not enough.'

She shook her head. 'But unless I'm wrong, you feel the same way too?'

He reached over and shoved a stray strand of her hair behind her ear and stared at her for the longest time. She held her breath, scared of what he was going to say. Maybe she'd got it wrong. And then he slowly nodded his head and she felt relief flood through her.

'I love you, Donna, but not the way a man should love a woman in a relationship.'

Ah! Back to her gay theory.

He continued. 'You were a friend, practically a sister, before we ever got together and maybe we were just never meant to be more than that.'

'You're keeping something from me too, Bob, aren't you? You know you can tell me. As you said, let's get everything out in the open.' She took his hand and squeezed it to reassure him.

He suddenly stood up and began pacing.

'Bob, please don't be afraid to tell me. I think I already know.'

He stopped and stared at her. 'You do?'

'Come and sit back down,' she said, patting the space beside her on the sofa. 'Let's talk about this. You'll feel much better when you get it out in the open.'

'I honestly don't think you know what I'm going to tell you, Donna. Because if you did, you wouldn't be so calm.' He sat back down, his face creased with worry.

'It was Lexie who guessed,' she said. 'I suppose I've been waiting for you to tell me. I knew things weren't right between us and I wanted you to say it.'

'Lexie? But I didn't … I mean, how did she …?

'She only mentioned it as a possibility but as soon as she said it, I started to see it myself.'

'Oh God, I didn't realise I'd been so obvious.'

'Listen, Bob.' She moved in closer to him. 'There's absolutely nothing to worry about. It's time to start being yourself. We'll all be here to support you and it doesn't change who you are.'

'Change who I am? I'm not sure I understand.'

Donna squeezed his hand again. 'Being gay doesn't change a thing. It's who you are and we love you no matter what.'

'GAY!' He hopped up off the sofa and stared at her. 'You think I'm *gay*?'

'Well, I thought you said—'

'Donna, I'm not gay, I'm in love with Lexie!'

* * *

'Do you love me, Will?'

Will folded the corner of the page he was reading and closed his book. 'Of course I love you, Sil. What a stupid question.'

'But do you *really* love me. Absolutely and completely?'

'What's this about? You know I do.'

'But you seem hesitant about Perth. If you really loved me, you'd support me. Didn't I come all the way over here to be with you? I think it's time you made the same grand gesture for me.'

Will was taken aback by her insistence. They'd just come to bed after the evening with his aunt and family and he'd thought it had gone really well. He hadn't even had time to digest the information about Perth and he'd thought Silvia was happy to let him think about it for a bit. It was a big thing, moving again to the other side of the world, and he wasn't sure he really wanted to.

'I mean, what's holding us back?' she continued. 'You don't want to be working for your mother forever. You said that yourself. I love my job but the one in Perth is going to be even better. There are no kids to complicate things so there's nothing to stop us taking the plunge.'

'I suppose not.'

'Well, you could show a bit more enthusiasm.'

Will sighed. 'Silvia, you only told me about this earlier today. I need time to think.'

'What is there to think about? We're supposed to be getting married. That means living happily together for the rest of our lives. It's a no-brainer – if I go, you go.' She fixed her pillow and pulled the duvet up around her before turning her back on him.

'So is that the end of the conversation, then?' It wasn't often he got annoyed with Silvia but her behaviour was making him see red. 'Is that it? You tell me what *you* want and I don't get a say in it?'

She turned back around and glared at him. 'Well, it seems to me that maybe you have another reason to want to stay here.'

'I can't believe you're being so unreasonable, Silvia. I have to think about my mother. We've only just lost my dad, you know. She'll be on her own if we leave. And then there's the job. I'd have to give her notice and see about getting a job over there myself. There's *so* much to think about.'

'And what about *Donna*?' She spat the words.

'Oh, here we go again,' said Will. 'I never said her name. Isn't it about time you forgot about that?'

'It's not just that, Will. I see the way you look at her.'

Shit! 'What are you talking about? Tonight was only the second time you've ever met her. How can you say something like that?'

'I'm not stupid, you know. I can see there's something between you both.'

'Sil, you're imagining it.' His voice softened and he pulled her in closer to him. 'It's *you* I love. *You* I want. There's nobody else.'

'Do you really mean that?'

'Of course I do, love. As you said, we're getting married, aren't we? And we're going to spend the rest of our lives together. I can't think of anything better.'

She snuggled into him and he breathed a sigh of relief.

'Well, then you'll agree to come to Perth,' she said. 'We can still come over and get married in Ireland, if that's what you want, and your mother can come over and visit any time she likes.'

He decided not to say any more for now. A few weeks ago, he probably would have jumped at the chance of going back to Perth. He'd have been happy to move away from his mother, his job, his boring life in Ireland. He would have been excited. But that was before Donna came into his life again.

If only she wasn't with Bob. And he wasn't with Silvia. Was it possible to love two people at the same time? To be *in love* with them? The whole thing was a mess and he cursed that earthquake that had split him and Donna up in the first place. Would they have ended up together if it had never happened?

The sound of soft snores filled the room and he was relieved that Silvia had dropped off to sleep. Maybe it was the wine she'd drunk earlier that had made her so unrelenting. But he'd always known she was a fiery Italian, used to getting what she wanted, so her persistence shouldn't really have come as a surprise.

They had a lot of decisions to make over the next few weeks and, whether he liked it or not, Donna was part of those decisions. He needed to know what she thought. Were things serious with Bob or was there still a chance for him? He couldn't believe he was thinking that way but there was no point in lying to himself. She said she'd text if she wanted to meet him again. That was it. He'd give it a week and if she hadn't texted by then, he'd move on. And he'd be happy with Silvia. They could go to Perth and create a new life for themselves. He'd forget Donna in time. Just like he'd done before. Just like he'd tried to do.

* * *

Donna was lost for words. That was the second time Bob had surprised her tonight. Lexie! How had she not seen that? Her mind began to spin as she thought about times when all three of them were together. Had there been secret looks behind her back? Had they stolen intimate moments together? Had they taken her for a fool?

'Donna. Speak to me. Did you hear what I said?'

She looked at him slowly. 'I heard. You and Lexie.'

'There is no me and Lexie,' he said, blushing a deep red. 'She has no idea how I feel.'

'Oh! So nothing has happened?'

'Of course nothing has happened, you big eejit. I have feelings for her but I've never once made them known.'

Donna's head was in a spin. There was so much to take in. 'And she doesn't know?'

'Not a clue. I'm really not sure I'm her type anyway.'

'Do you know what, Bob? You're *exactly* her type.' Donna was warming to the idea. 'I think you'd make a lovely couple.'

'Do you think?'

'I do. But you need to tread carefully. Lexie has had a tough few years. She doesn't need to have her heart broken again.'

'I can't believe we're even having this conversation,' said Bob, shaking his head. 'This is the weirdest split I've ever heard of.'

Donna laughed at that. 'I know, isn't it? But seriously. I want you to be happy, Bob. And I think Lexie might be the girl to do that for you.'

'Has she ever said anything about me?'

'Actually, she never stops talking about you. She adores you.'

Bob beamed. 'Well, that's a good start.'

'But let things settle down for a bit,' said Donna. 'She won't want to take over where I left off.'

'That makes it sound so seedy.' He looked hurt.

'I don't mean it to. But she's going to worry about me, about what other people will think – you know how it is.'

He nodded. 'I'm in no rush. I'm just happy you're happy. But now what are we going to do about you and Will?'

'There *is* no me and Will.'

'But there could be. Is that what you want?'

Donna sighed and fixed the cushion behind her back. 'In an ideal world, yes. But he's with Silvia and I honestly don't think he feels anything for me. He told me today that she was his destiny.'

'He told you that? At the house?'

Donna couldn't look him in the eye.

Bob persisted. 'Donna? Is there something you're not telling me?'

'I got his number from your phone,' she said, sheepishly. 'I'm sorry, but I needed to talk to him. It was just once, I swear. I met him today at lunch time.'

Bob didn't say anything.

'Honestly, Bob. It wasn't like I was going behind your back or anything. Well, not before today. And I'd been planning to tell you.'

'It doesn't matter now,' sighed Bob, and then his face lit up. 'But surely it's a good thing if he wanted to meet you. You've got to meet him again. Tell him how you feel.'

'I … I can't. I'd only make a fool of myself. He doesn't feel the same.'

'But how do you know that?' Bob was standing up now. Pacing the floor. Planning the next move.

'Haven't you heard me, Bob? He's in love with Silvia.'

'But he thinks you're in love with me.'

Donna lowered her head. 'I'm sorry.'

'Listen, Donna. There's no need to be sorry. We're both going to move on. How did you leave things?'

'He told me to text him if I wanted to meet again.'

'Right, where's your phone?'

Donna stiffened. 'Why? What are you planning to do?'

'Not me. You! You're going to text him and say you'll meet him tomorrow.'

'I'm working tomorrow.'

'Sunday, then.'

'Bob, I'm not asking him to give up his Sunday to meet me. He'll be with Silvia.'

'Well, then Monday. Stop making excuses. Right, get typing. You're going to meet him and you're going to tell him exactly how you feel. What do you have to lose? If he doesn't feel the same, he's going to Perth so you might never have to see him again. And if he does feel the same …'

Donna's heart flipped with excitement. Bob was right. She'd tell him. Maybe it would amount to nothing but she had to do it. She called up his number and typed:

'Hi, Will. Let's meet again. How about front of St Stephen's Green at 1 p.m. Monday? Donna x'

She checked it and deleted the kiss. There'd be plenty of time for that later if things worked out. She suddenly felt exhausted. Emotionally drained.

'I need my bed,' she said, after she showed Bob that she'd sent the text.

'Me too.' He hesitated. 'Can we still share the bed for the moment? As friends? I promise there won't be any funny business, even though I'm not gay!'

'Oh God, I'm sorry about that, Bob. I just thought … it was just …'

'Don't worry about it. Don't you think I've heard it a million times before? I'm just confident – in touch with my feminine side.'

'And I love you for it. Come on, let's go to bed.'

Donna felt more content than she had in ages. She and Bob were meant to be friends. Nothing more. It just felt right. As she snuggled in under the covers, she thought about Will and wondered were they the same – destined to be friends. Or did destiny have something else in store for them?

Chapter 44

Donna was early. She'd finished work at twelve and had immediately gone into the little bakery toilets to change. On Bob's suggestion, she'd gone to River Island the previous day and bought a gorgeous knee-length, jade-green dress. 'It's your colour,' Bob had assured her. 'You want to blow his mind.'

Jan had commented on the outfit but Donna had been vague. She and Bob had decided to keep the split quiet for the moment. Just until things settled down. Jan had seemed miffed when Donna hadn't told her where she was going and Donna had felt bad for keeping secrets from her. But it wouldn't be for long.

She watched nervously as crowds of lunchtime shoppers poured through the doors of the shopping centre. What if he didn't come? He'd replied quickly to say he'd be there but maybe he'd had second thoughts. She shifted her weight onto one foot. Her new nude Next sandals were killing her but she had to admit they looked gorgeous with the dress. She checked her watch again. Bang on one o'clock.

She'd told Lexie about her split with Bob. There was no way she could keep it a secret from her friend – especially since she lived with them. But they weren't telling her about how Bob felt yet. 'One thing at a time,' Donna had said to Bob, and he'd agreed. Lexie was very sorry they'd broken up but she was thrilled that Donna was going to talk to Will. 'Imagine if you two got together after all this time,' she'd said. 'It would be like a fairy tale.' Donna was doubtful it would ever happen but there was still a little flicker of hope that she was holding on to. Almost ten past one now and no sign. Her hope was fading fast.

'Hello, Donna.'

Donna almost jumped out of her skin. She'd been looking down Grafton Street, expecting to see Will coming from that direction, when her shoulder was tapped from behind. She swung around and her mouth gaped open.

'Silvia! What are you doing here?' She felt panic rise up inside her. What if Will arrived at the same time? It would be difficult to explain that one away.

'I'm here to see you.' She looked professional in a navy pencil skirt falling just below the knee and a crisp white blouse with ruffles up at the neck. 'Sorry I'm late.'

'Me? I'm not sure what you—'

'Let's not waste time pretending, Donna. You asked Will to meet you here but he sent me instead.'

Donna's heart dropped to the floor. She was glued to the spot. He sent his fiancée. How could he? If he didn't want to see her, he could have just said. She felt humiliated. Devastated. She wished she could be Dorothy – click her heels and be back home.

'Shall we walk?' said Silvia, making a sweeping gesture with her hand towards Grafton Street. 'I'm just on my lunch break so I don't have long.'

Donna nodded and fell into step beside her. She opened her mouth several times to say something but nothing came out. It wasn't an easy conversation to start. They walked slowly and in silence for a few moments until Silvia spoke again.

'He likes you, Donna. But he doesn't want to see you again. He doesn't want to be reminded.'

'Reminded? What do you mean?'

'Didn't you see his hand? Do you know what he went through on that day? It was the most awful day of his life. He said that seeing you is a constant reminder of the disaster in Christchurch.'

'Oh.' She'd hoped that meeting her might have been the one bright thing about that awful time. Obviously not.

'I think it's a bit of PTSD, to be honest.'

'It's what?' Donna could feel blisters popping up on her heels as they walked and had to resist the temptation to take off the sandals and walk in her bare feet.

'Post-traumatic stress disorder. He has nightmares, you know. And seeing you just adds to that.'

'God, I'm sorry. I didn't know.'

'How could you? You barely know him at all.'

Donna looked at her and saw the steel in her eyes. They were loaded words – she barely knew him at all. And she was right. Silvia was warning her off and she had good reason to.

'I didn't want to cause any trouble, you know,' said Donna, close to tears. 'It's just he's the only one who understands the horror of that day. I just wanted to talk to him about it.'

Silvia took her elbow and guided her expertly through a crowd of shoppers. 'I know. And I understand. Really I do. But you can't put him through the trauma any more.'

'But that was never my intention. Why didn't he tell me about this when we …' Shit. She probably shouldn't mention their last meeting. God, she wished she knew what Will had said to Silvia.

'When you last met?' Silvia stopped suddenly outside the main door of Brown Thomas. 'Don't worry. He's told me everything. He didn't say anything to you because he could tell that you were, let's say, *needy*. He didn't want to upset you.'

Needy? How could Will have said that about her? She felt a mixture of fury and devastation. She'd loved him – really loved him. And she'd been sure he felt something too.

'Don't worry about it, Donna. Will understands that you went through a lot over there too. Maybe you should talk to your own boyfriend about it. I'm sure Bob is a great listener.'

What could she say to that? 'So what did Will say? Did he just tell you to come here and warn me off? It doesn't seem like something he'd do.'

'Not warn you off, Donna. Just let you know that he can't see you again. He was going to text you but I told him it would be easier if I told you face to face.'

'I'm sure you did.' She couldn't resist the jibe. Silvia was horrible. And if what she was saying was true, Will wasn't much better either.

'Anyway,' Silvia continued, 'Will and I will be heading off in just over two weeks so we'll be out of your life for good then.'

'Heading off?'

'Yes, to Perth. Remember we told you the other night?'

'I … I didn't think Will was sure. I thought maybe he didn't want to go.'

'Of course he wants to go. Our flights are booked and we're going to start our new lives over there. We're both really excited. It's going to be wonderful.'

'Well, then I'm happy for him – for you both.' Her feet were now screaming with the pain of the blisters and she couldn't take talking to the woman for a moment longer. 'I'd better fly, though. Thanks for coming all the way in to let me know.'

'No problem.' Silvia pushed open the Brown Thomas door. 'And I was coming into town anyway. I've got to pick up some new luggage for us in here. They do a gorgeous range of Samsonite.'

'Right, good luck with it.'

'It was nice to meet you, Donna. Say hello to Bob for me.' And she was gone, taking with her all of Donna's hopes and dreams.

So that was that. It was probably only confirming what she'd suspected anyway. Will was in love with Silvia and Donna had just been an inconvenience to him. She started walking to the end of Grafton Street where she'd hop in a taxi and go home. She couldn't face the buses. Not today.

She allowed tears to flow freely down her face as she got into a taxi. She gave her address to the driver and sat back in the seat. God, she wished Bob hadn't convinced her to send that text. In a way, it was better to know but, on the other hand, sometimes oblivion was a good option.

Suddenly her phone beeped in her bag and her heart lifted slightly. Would it be Will, apologising for sending Silvia and telling her he was having second thoughts? Maybe he'd been afraid of his own feelings? She whipped it out quickly and checked the screen. It was from Bob:

'Hope the date is going well, Donna. Dying to hear all. x'

She threw the phone back in her bag and looked out the window. O'Connell Street was a hive of activity and everyone looked happy in the glow of the sun. Everyone except her. She wished things had worked out with her and Bob. Life would have been so much simpler. But she couldn't live a lie and that's what she would have been doing.

Life had been unkind to her many times but she'd never let it knock her down. She was a fighter. She'd get through this just as she'd got through everything else – with a steely determination and the love of good friends. Suddenly she didn't want to go home any more.

'Actually, I've changed my mind,' she said to the taxi driver, who watched her suspiciously through his mirror. 'Can you go here instead?'

She opened her bag and took out a card. He nodded when he checked the address and she sat back feeling a lot better. It wasn't Wednesday but to hell with it. She felt like being spontaneous today and there was no point in being all dressed up with nowhere to go. She wasn't brimming with positivity but she didn't feel too bad, and that was good enough.

She closed her eyes and felt herself drift off. The emotion of the last hour had exhausted her and she couldn't fight the sleep. Pictures of Will filled her head as she slipped into a fitful dream.

People were running in all directions as buildings tumbled down and smoke swirled all around her. The sound of screams filled the air and it took her a moment to realise that she was screaming too. She looked down and realised she was trapped. A heavy boulder had fallen on her chest and she couldn't breathe properly. She began to feel light-headed. Was this it? Was this the end? She'd often wondered how she'd die but had never imagined it would be like this. The sound began to fade and she felt peaceful. Dying wasn't so bad after all. And then she heard a voice.

'Stay with me. Open your eyes.' The face was blurry. 'Let's just get this thing off you.'

It was Will. He'd come to save her. She opened her eyes, ready to see the love of her life. But it wasn't him. It was Silvia. She lifted the boulder up and then looked at Donna with steel in her eyes.

'He's mine!' she screamed, before dropping the boulder back down on top of her, crushing her. Drifting away ... slowly ... peacefully ... gone!

Chapter 45

Will sat on his bed and examined Cookie, the one-eyed teddy he'd had since he was a baby. It was threadbare and scruffy but Will was strangely attached to it. Silvia hated it and had begged Will to get rid of it on numerous occasions.

'It's filthy,' she'd said, holding her nose for effect. 'I'll buy you a new one – one that isn't half-blind.'

He'd smiled but had firmly warned her that if she ever tried to kidnap, harm or extinguish his beloved teddy, she'd pay dearly for it. They'd laughed about it but there was just something about that teddy. It had got him through a lot in his childhood. It had been his confidant when he hadn't had any friends and it had given him comfort when he'd needed it most.

He looked at the suitcases, packed and ready, and a deep sadness overwhelmed him. Was he doing the right thing? He'd spent most of his life trying to get away from this place but in the last few months it had really started to feel like home. Silvia constantly reminded him that home was where the heart was and deep down he knew she was right. He loved her and they'd be happy wherever they lived once they were together.

'William, come on down and get this before it goes cold.' His mother's voice echoed up the stairs and he felt guilty about the fact that he was going to be abandoning her. She was being really good about everything. She'd even bought him a new iPod because his old one had broken. 'For the journey,' she'd said, without a trace of accusation in her voice. She'd certainly changed from the mother he'd known in the past.

'Come on, Will,' said Silvia, sticking her head in the bedroom door. 'Your mother has made lasagne and, to be honest, we really don't have time.'

'But the flight isn't leaving until twenty past ten tonight. We've got heaps of time.'

'Not if we've to get this lot checked in and have time to look around the duty free. We'd better head off as soon as we eat.'

Will sighed. 'Right, you go on down and I'll be there in a minute.'

It was all happening so fast. Just days after Silvia had broken the news about Perth, she'd insisted on them making a decision. 'I have to either accept or decline the job,' she'd said. 'They're not going to wait for me to decide.' And so they'd booked the flights, giving them just two weeks to wrap up their life in Ireland.

Will lay back on his bed and stretched his hands behind his head. He closed his eyes and immediately saw Donna's face. He saw it all the time. It was like Christchurch all over again. He didn't get to say goodbye.

She'd told him she'd text about meeting up again and he'd been hoping she would. But, despite checking his phone a million times, the text had never come. He'd looked on it as a sign. She just didn't feel the same way about him as he felt about her. He'd tried to deny how he felt. He'd tried to push his feelings for her aside. But he hadn't been able to get her out of his mind. Now, two weeks later, he'd resigned himself to the fact that he was never going to see her again. It was time to get on with his life.

'Will!' Silvia was at the door again. 'I swear, if you don't come down, I'm taking those cases and heading to the airport myself!'

A small part of him thought that mightn't be a bad thing. 'Sorry, Sil. I'm just tired. I'm coming now.'

'You'd better be,' she said crossly, thundering back down the stairs.

He stood up and glanced at his watch. It was only five o'clock. If it was up to him, he wouldn't go to the airport until the last minute so there'd be no hanging around. But what Silvia wanted, Silvia got and it looked like they'd be there with hours to spare.

He looked at the teddy in his hands and it suddenly occurred to him how strange it must look to Silvia. He was a grown man and still kept a cuddly toy. Maybe she was right. Maybe it was time to move on.

'Right, Cookie,' he whispered. 'It's about time I stood on my own two feet.' He took a final look at his beloved toy before tossing him into the wastepaper basket in the corner of the room. He smiled to himself. This was the start of a brand-new life and he was going to fully embrace it.

* * *

'I still can't believe it,' said Jan, as she looked from Bob to Donna. 'I honestly thought you two would be together for life.'

Donna patted her hand. 'I'm sorry, Jan. But not much has changed. We still have a really strong friendship and we'll probably see just as much of each other as we did before.'

'But you're hardly going to live together, are you?' She looked upset by it all. 'I mean, wouldn't that be awkward?'

Bob joined in. 'Funnily enough, there's nothing awkward between us at all. We're friends. We always have been. A little bit of sex got in the way but we've sorted that now.'

'Bob!' Donna was mortified.

'What?' he asked, innocently. 'Mam doesn't mind, do you, Mam?'

'I'm used to you at this stage, love. So tell me. What happens now?'

'Well,' said Bob, 'I was thinking that maybe I could move back in here? Donna said I could stay on at the flat if I wanted to but I think it would be better if I moved out.'

'Oh, I think we could manage to squeeze you in, love. But you have to promise to cook at least once a week.' Jan beamed, clearly delighted that her only son was coming home.

'Deal. Now can we please have some of those scones that I can smell? I'm really looking forward to living with a baker again.'

Donna gave him a friendly slap. 'Hey! You *have* been living with a baker.'

'But I mean one who actually bakes at home. You have to admit, your work stays firmly in the bakery.'

'That's true.' Donna laughed. 'I'm always too tired when I'm home or there's so much else to do.'

'Anyway,' said Jan, 'let's go on into the kitchen and I'll make us a brew. I've just whipped up a bowl of cream and there's a jar of strawberry jam in the fridge.'

Bob licked his lips. 'Sounds fantastic.'

They chatted happily, sitting around the kitchen table and tucking into the hot scones. But Donna could feel her mood dip as she checked her watch. Bob noticed and squeezed her hand.

'They'll be on their way soon,' he said, giving her an understanding look. 'I'm sorry, Donna.'

Jan looked from one to the other. 'What's this? Are you talking about our Will and Silvia?'

Bob nodded. 'Yes. Donna was very fond of Will. It was good for her to be able to talk to him about what happened in Christchurch.'

'Of course,' said Jan, nodding. 'I'm sad to see them go too.'

Donna gave Bob a grateful look. They hadn't told Jan the whole story. It was enough to tell her about their split for now and they could fill her in on everything else bit by bit. They all sat lost in thought for a few moments until Donna's phone rang and broke the silence. She grabbed it quickly, not checking the number before she answered it.

She listened for a few seconds before letting out a gasp. 'When?' she asked, her whole body beginning to shake. 'Okay. I understand. I can't believe it. I'll come right away.'

She dropped the phone and looked at Bob and Jan.

'What's wrong, love?' Jan took her hand. 'It's not bad news, is it?'

She shook her head. 'No, Jan. It's the best news ever. You won't believe what's happened! Bob, can you drive me? I need to go now.'

Chapter 46

Bob drove right up to the door of the hospital to drop Donna off. He told her that he'd go and get parking and follow her in. He kissed her on the cheek before she hopped out of the car.

'Good luck,' he shouted through the window but she was in too much of a hurry to reply.

She could find the room in her sleep, she'd been there so often. She nodded to the girl on reception and dashed down the corridor and through the double doors. Left then and up a flight of stairs. Another corridor and a final set of double doors. Joanna was at the desk and stood up when she saw Donna coming.

'Come on. Doctor Hamilton is in with her now.'

Donna nodded but couldn't speak. Her mouth was dry and she could actually hear her own heart beating. She held her breath and stopped outside the door that she'd gone through so many times these last few years.

'Are you okay?' asked Joanna, looking at her with concern. 'It's been a shock for you. Do you want to take a moment before we go in?'

'No. I'm ready.' She knocked briefly before pushing the door open. And then she saw her. Sitting in her big armchair, her cheeks rosy and her eyes bright. She hadn't seen her like that in a long, long time.

And she looked at her. She looked at Donna right in the eyes and Donna's heart sang. And then the most wonderful thing happened.

'Hello, Donna,' she said, tears streaming down her face.

They were the first words Tina had uttered since the night their lives had gone up in flames.

* * *

Donna sat in the family room and felt as though she was the luckiest girl in the world. Tina, her gorgeous, funny, wonderful sister was back. They'd said this could happen. They'd assured her that there was nothing physically wrong with Tina and she could revert to her normal self at any time. But more than four years on from the fire Donna had lost all hope of that ever happening. Until today.

'Are you okay there?' said Joanna, peeping into the room. 'Can I get you some tea or coffee? Doctor Hamilton just needs another little while with her and then you can go back in.'

'I'm fine thanks, Joanna. I'm just trying to take it all in. Isn't it wonderful?'

'It's fantastic.' But her face turned serious. 'It's early days, though. It will still be a long road for her so don't expect miracles at this stage.'

Donna nodded. 'What just happened is miracle enough for me.'

Joanna disappeared again, leaving Donna with her thoughts. She closed her eyes and allowed herself to think back to that night. She usually blotted the memory from her mind. It was far too painful to think about. But today she could allow the story to have a happier ending – not a happy one, but happier.

Donna couldn't see for the tears as she sat in the car on the way to the scene of the fire. Chris had offered to drive her and she'd sat in the back so that Jan could sit with her and comfort her. One fatality, Detective Joseph Simpson had said. And she'd heard nothing after that.

They stopped at a red light and Donna wanted to scream at Chris to go through it. If ever there was a reason to break the law, it was now. They continued up the Navan Road and turned at the next junction. Donna could see the flashing lights and felt bile rise in her throat.

'It'll be okay, love,' Jan said, over and over again.

It wouldn't be okay. One fatality. Things would never be okay again.

The road was blocked off and it was like something from a movie. Three fire engines were at the scene, as well as two ambulances and a number of police cars. There were people in uniform dotted everywhere – some at the house, some questioning people and others trying to stop the rubberneckers from getting too close.

Chris rolled down the window to explain who they were to a garda who'd approached them, but Donna wasn't going to wait. She opened the door and bolted out, screaming for her mother and sister.

'You can't go past here, love,' said the garda, grabbing a hold of her coat and pulling her back. 'It's not safe.'

There was no way he was going to stop her so she used all her strength to pull away. 'Tina, TINA,' she shouted, weaving her way between the emergency services cars and trucks. 'Mam, Tina, TINAAAA …'

The fire seemed to be out so Donna ran towards the door. She needed to get inside. She needed to see her mother and Tina. Maybe the detective had got it wrong. Despite the blackness of the front of the house, it didn't look too bad.

'Sorry, love, you've got to stay back.' Another garda blocked her way and, with a second one beside him, she wasn't getting any further. 'Do you know the residents of the house?'

'Yes,' she wailed. 'I live here. My mam and sister were in the house. Where are they? I need to see them.'

The garda took off his hat all of a sudden and bowed his head. And that's when she saw it. There was a body on a stretcher. All covered up, of course, but there was no doubt what it was.

'Nooooooo,' she screamed, and pushed her way over. 'Let me see. I'm family. Who is it?'

A plain-clothes detective stepped in front of her then, holding out his badge. 'Detective Joseph Simpson. Are you Donna?'

'Y— yes. Nobody will tell me anything. What's happening?'

He pulled her aside and spoke in a soft voice. 'As I said on the phone, we have one fatality. The body hasn't been identified because it's badly burned.'

He was using words like 'the body' and 'it'. It all seemed so cold. So impersonal. Donna's head was spinning and she felt as though she was in some sort of awful nightmare.

'So if you'd like to come over here with me,' he continued. Donna followed him in a trance until they reached an ambulance. 'Is this someone you know?'

She looked inside and there was Tina, a blanket wrapped around her, her face black and eyes glistening.

'Tina, oh, Tina. Thank God you're okay. Are you hurt?'

'She's not responding, miss. We're going to take her in shortly and get her checked out. Trauma can do funny things to people.'

'But she's not hurt?' She took her sister's hand and squeezed it.

'As I say, she'll have to be properly checked out but there's no noticeable injury at the moment.'

'I'm coming with her.' There was nothing she could do for her mam. She was gone. But she could be there for Tina. Tears sprang to her eyes and she let them fall. She'd probably lost her mother a long time ago but death was different. It was so cruel – so final. It was just her and Tina now and she was going to make sure Tina got the best care possible until she was back on her feet again.

But Tina had never spoken since. That was until today. The doctors had confirmed that there was nothing physically wrong with her but the trauma of the fire had caused a reaction in her brain and she'd shut down. She'd withdrawn into her own world and hadn't been able to communicate with anybody. It had broken Donna's heart to see her sister this way. Donna had thought initially that she could care for her at home but it had become apparent that Tina would need more intense care. She'd spent a while in hospital before being admitted to a psychiatric unit and she'd been there ever since.

At first, Donna had been by her side almost every day. But as time had passed, her visits had whittled down to once a week – every Wednesday. It was too difficult to be there all the time. Too heartbreaking. Tina was able to do basic stuff for herself, like wash or dress, but when Donna would sit with her, she'd just look at her with glazed eyes and not a flicker of recognition.

Donna's trip to Australia had been a desperate attempt to engage Tina – to get her interested in life again. She'd sent postcards from every place she'd visited and Jan had made a promise that she'd bring them in to Tina and read them out to her. The trip had been Tina's dream so Donna had hoped that the combination of seeing the pictures and hearing all about the places would have stimulated her. It hadn't worked. Nothing had worked and Donna had resigned herself to having a sister who wasn't engaged with life.

'Sorry for disturbing you.' The booming voice of Doctor Hamilton startled her and she jumped up from the chair.

'How is she?'

'She's doing well, but she needs rest for now. She's sleeping and there's a good chance she won't wake until morning so I'd suggest you take yourself off home.'

Donna shook her head. 'There's no way I'm leaving. I want to be here when she wakes up. I've waited for too long for this.'

He looked at her over his tiny glasses. His eyes were kind. 'It's going to be a long road, Donna, so you need to look after yourself too. At least go off and get yourself something to eat. We can ring you if she wakes.'

She hesitated for a moment and then relented. 'Okay. I won't be longer than a couple of hours. And I'll have my mobile with me all the time so please let me know if there's any further news.'

As if on cue, Bob rushed in the door. 'Sorry, the parking out there is a nightmare. What's happening? How's Tina?'

'She's good,' said Donna. 'Really good. But I'll tell you all on the way out. Thanks again, Doctor Hamilton.'

'So are you telling me I've now got to squeeze back out of that parking spot that I spent twenty minutes squeezing into? I thought we'd be here for ages.'

Donna laughed. 'Come on, I've loads to tell you. Let's go and get a bite to eat – that's if you're not in a rush?'

He linked her as they walked down the corridor. 'Of course not. I'm really happy for you, Donna. This is the best news ever.'

'It is, isn't it? It makes you think anything is possible.'

Bob nodded. 'Well, it is – if you put your mind to it.'

Donna stopped walking suddenly and checked the time on her phone. Ten to seven. Her head began to spin and a ball of excitement rose in her stomach. 'Anything is possible,' she whispered to herself.

'What was that?' said Bob. 'And why have we stopped?'

'What time are Will and Silvia going to the airport?'

'I think Mam said they were going around seven. Why?'

'Right, come on.'

'What? Where are we going?'

'To the airport.' She began to run and Bob followed.

'Hang on a sec. Why do you want to go there? Are you planning a big showdown? A fight to the death for your man?'

He laughed but then he saw the serious look on her face.

'Oh my God, Donna. Are you really going to try and stop him from going?'

They burst out the front door and Donna had to stop to catch her breath. 'No, Bob. I'm not going to try and stop him, but I'm going to tell him how I feel. I never got the chance and I think I'll always regret it if I don't say something.'

'Well, what are we waiting for then?'

Donna followed him out to the car, her head awhirl with thoughts of Tina and of Will. If life had taught her one thing, it was to have no regrets. She just hoped she wouldn't regret what she was about to do!

Chapter 47

They got a spot easily enough in Dublin's Terminal 2 car park and took the lift to Departures.

'I'm not sure this is a good idea any more,' said Donna, as they stepped out of the lift into the shiny new terminal. 'Maybe we should just go.'

'Don't be crazy, Donna. We're here now. We may as well see if we can find them at least.'

She hesitated. 'I … I don't know. I think I was full of adrenaline from everything that's happened today. I wasn't thinking straight.'

'Listen,' said Bob, swinging her around to look at him. 'Do you love him?'

'Well, yes. You know I do.'

'Really love him? Completely head over heels in love with him?'

She nodded.

'Right, you'll never get this chance again. Just tell him. Tell him how you feel. If you let him fly to the other side of the world without telling him, you'll regret it. And even if you don't get the response you're looking for, at least you'll know.'

Donna hugged him, feeling her earlier buzz return. 'You're right. Now let's go and find them.'

They ran to the Qantas check-in area, hoping to find them there, but there was no sign. Her confidence was beginning to wane again and she was torn between really wanting to see Will and wanting to forget about him and go back to Tina.

'What now?' Bob was on his tippy-toes trying to see over the heads of the crowd. 'Should we see if we can get his name announced on the tannoy?'

Donna sighed. 'I'm not sure, Bob. It seems a bit extreme.'

'Departure gates, then?'

'Good idea,' said Donna, looking to see where they were. 'And that's definitely our last chance. If they're not there, we've missed them and I'll just have to accept that it's the end.'

They rushed to the gates and scanned their eyes over the people in the queue. Donna's heart sank. It looked like their journey was in vain. It just wasn't meant to be. She thought about Tina and how she used to advise her. How she used to be the one with the sensible head whereas Donna was the hot-headed one. She realised at that moment that she couldn't be sad. Her sister was way more important than all of this and she closed her eyes and gave thanks for the wonderful gift of getting her back.

'Donna? Bob? What are you doing here?'

They both swung around and Donna's jaw dropped open when she saw Will standing in front of them. She felt completely tongue-tied as she looked into those melting brown eyes. Bob nodded encouragement at her and stepped away.

'So what brings you here?' he repeated. That dimple on his cheek.

'I … I just wanted to see you,' she began. She glanced at Bob, who gave her the thumbs up. She took a deep breath.

'Will, I need to say this to you. I know you're with Silvia now and I know—'

'Donna, I—'

'Just let me finish. This isn't easy but I have to say it. I love you, okay? I'm in love with you.' Heat rose up from her neck and she could tell she was getting that red rash she got when she was nervous. 'I have been since that day we met in Christchurch. I know you're moving to the other side of the world and planning to get married, but I just had to tell you.'

Will's eyes opened wide and he began to speak but Donna shot him down again.

'I don't want to cause you any trouble and I know you and Silvia love each other but I just wanted to let you know in case there's a chance for us. Not today, obviously, because you're moving to Perth. But in the future … just so you know …' She was aware she was babbling and she wanted the earth to open up and swallow her.

'Can I speak now?' Will asked, a twinkle in his eye.

'Em, yes, of course. Sorry.'

'I love you too.'

'Wh— what?'

'I love you, Donna. Right from that day in Christchurch too. Something magical happened then and I haven't been able to get you out of my head ever since.'

'But Silvia. You sent her to warn me off.' She suddenly realised there was no sign of the other woman. 'And where is she anyway?'

'She's gone, Donna.'

'*Gone?*'

'Yes, she's gone back to Perth. I couldn't do it. I couldn't leave.'

Donna's head was in a spin. 'But she told me … she said …'

'I didn't send her, Donna. She saw your text before I did. She answered it and deleted it before I saw it. I had no idea she went to see you. And she most definitely wasn't speaking on my behalf.'

Donna gasped. She knew there was a reason she'd taken a dislike to that woman. Imagine doing something so awful.

'I thought you hadn't texted so I took it that you weren't interested,' he continued. 'And Silvia was making all these plans and I suppose I got carried away with them.'

'But when did you change your mind? How did you find out what she'd done?' Donna felt as though she was floating on air.

'I almost didn't,' he said, shaking his head. 'We were here before the check-in desk was open so we went for a coffee. Silvia was in great form but something didn't feel right to me.'

'What do you mean?'

'I think I knew in my heart I was doing the wrong thing. I suppose I was doing what I'd always done – getting carried away by somebody else's plans and not following my own heart.'

'And then?' Donna was hanging on his every word.

'Silvia was full of chat. She was saying how delighted she was about us making a new life over there. She said she'd even forgive me for going behind her back to meet you. I hadn't told her about that so it got me thinking.'

'And you asked her about it?'

He nodded. 'She admitted what she'd done eventually but she said she only did it for us. She knew we were meant to be together and she didn't want my judgement being clouded by memories of the past.'

'And was it clouded – your judgement, I mean?'

He looked at her then and smiled. It was the sweetest, most beautiful smile she'd ever seen. He took her hand and kissed it gently.

'On the contrary. I think I'm seeing clearly now for the first time ever.' Then his smile faded and it was replaced by a serious look. 'But what about Bob? He's my cousin. How is he going to feel about this?'

'Em, sorry for butting in,' said Bob, who'd obviously been listening to the whole exchange. 'But Donna and I are just friends. Nothing more.' And then he added, 'And I'm not gay.'

'Well, I'm glad you cleared that up!' Will laughed, looking from

Bob back to Donna. 'So it looks like there's no reason why we shouldn't kiss, then?'

'Well, you can pause that for just a second while I make myself scarce.' Bob hugged Donna and clapped Will on the back. 'I'll leave her in your capable hands, Will. I need to rush off. There's a certain girl I have to see.'

'Good luck with that,' said Donna, before turning back to Will. 'Now where were we …?'

Dublin Maternity Hospital

18 months later

'Look at his tiny fingers,' said Donna, as she clutched her newborn to her breast. 'I can't believe he's actually here.'

Will kissed her full on the lips. 'You're amazing, do you know that? I've never seen anything like it. How *that* came out of down there is beyond me.'

'Don't call him *that*!' Donna slapped him playfully. 'He has a name, you know.'

'How could I forget? George Cooper-Smith.' Tears sprang to his eyes as he looked at Donna. 'Thanks, love.'

'For what?'

'For everything. For my son, for the name, for it all. Thanks for persevering. I'm the happiest man alive, you know.'

'And I'm the happiest woman.' Donna gently took the sleeping baby from her breast and placed him in the cot beside her bed. She watched his little chest rise and fall and knew her life was complete. A gorgeous baby and engaged to her soul mate. She glanced at the beautiful peridot engagement ring on her finger and her heart swelled with pride. Will had chosen it himself and she adored it.

'Hellooooo! Can I come in?'

Donna smiled as Bob popped his head around the door. 'Come on in quickly, before the nurse sees you.'

'Ah, look at him,' said Bob, peering into the cot. 'He's adorable.'

'Just like his daddy,' said Will, standing up to hug his cousin. 'Where's Lexie?'

'Nappy changing. She'll be here in a sec.' And on that note, Lexie burst in the door, a baby in one arm and a baby bag the size of a suitcase on the other.

'Trust you to disappear at the sniff of a nappy, Bob. Hiya, Donna. Give me a look. God, he's gorgeous. He's the image of you except for the hair.' She dropped her bag on the floor and bent over the bed to hug her friend. 'This little one has been grizzly all day. She's driving me mad.'

Donna offered a finger to the baby and she instantly clutched it. Emma was just six weeks old and although unexpected, the news of Lexie's pregnancy had been welcomed by the newly loved-up couple. And with Donna falling pregnant just weeks later, it seemed that everything had fallen perfectly into place.

There was another knock on the door and a bunch of blue helium balloons appeared in the room. Donna squealed with delight when she saw who was behind them. 'Tina! I'm so happy you came. Come and meet your new baby nephew.'

'I wouldn't have missed it for the world.' Tina edged closer to the cot and peered in. Tears pricked her eyes. 'Beautiful. He's the most beautiful thing I've ever seen.'

Donna clutched her hand. 'We did okay, you and me, didn't we?'

Tina nodded. 'Not too bad at all.'

'Sorry for butting in,' said Lexie, looking at the baby's cot and scrunching up her nose. 'But couldn't you afford a new teddy? I mean, that one's a bit mangy, isn't it?'

'Hey, leave Cookie alone,' said Will, bending over and cupping his hands protectively over the teddy. 'He's been on a journey. It's been tough on him.'

'Here, Lexie. Stick Emma in the cot beside George and we'll get a picture of the two of them together.' Donna reached over to the locker to get her iPhone. 'We can use it as a bribe when they're wayward teens.'

'Great idea.' Lexie gently placed her little girl in the cot beside George. 'Oh my God. Look how adorable they are together!'

Will shook his head. 'I have the strangest feeling of déjà vu. It's weird.'

'It's magical, is what it is,' said Donna, beaming. 'Just magical.'

Acknowledgements

In 1996, my husband, Paddy, and I headed off on an adventure of a lifetime. We took career breaks from our safe, pensionable jobs, threw caution to the wind and booked ourselves on a trip that would see us visit some of the most wonderful places in the world. Just before we left, I bought myself a little black-covered notebook and starting with 'Day 1', I documented the whole, year-long trip. If you've already read the book before skipping to the acknowledgements (I bet most of you haven't!), you'll know that a large part is set in Australia and New Zealand. It's been nineteen years since that trip but I think I always knew I'd write about these places one day.

That brings me to the first and most important person I have to thank – my husband, Paddy. After working at various jobs in the first few months of our trip, the real adventure began when we bought a twenty-year-old car and a two-man tent in Perth and set off driving around Australia. And I'm telling you now – if you can live huddled up with someone in a ridiculously small tent while being eaten alive by insects and fending off hurricanes, then you know you've found the one! Paddy has always been the one. He's supported me in everything I've tried to do over the years – the failures, the successes – he's always been there with a comforting hug or a whoop of joy. He understands the craziness that comes from a writer when trying to meet a deadline or deal with writer's block and he'll calmly take over in the house, leaving me to write in peace. This book was by far the most enjoyable one for me to write and that's mainly because of the memories that came flooding back to me about that special time we had together before we began the next chapter of our lives.

And that brings me to the next chapter – my children. When we'd driven right around Australia and our car finally gave up and practically blew up in the middle of the road, we knew it was almost time to say goodbye to our travels. And that's when I discovered I was pregnant with my first child. It was perfect. It meant that we couldn't be sad coming home because we had something so much more special to look forward to. And so the years of rearing my children began. Eoin, Roisin, Enya and Conor are the most special people in my life. I burst with pride every day because of them and I know how unbelievably lucky I am to have them. Each one of them plays a huge part in my writing, whether it's keeping me going with tea and biscuits, reading a section for me to tell me if it works or just a plain old hug. They inspire me every day and I love them with all my heart.

Two of my biggest cheerleaders are my parents, Aileen and Paddy Chaney, and I owe them a huge thanks for all their support. On 6th July 2015 they're celebrating their 60th wedding anniversary and I just want to say I love them with all my heart and am proud to be their daughter. Thanks to my brother and friend, Gerry Chaney, for his love, support and his genius photo-taking! As a photographer, he understands my need for me to pretend I'm far younger than I am and he obliges by erasing a few wrinkles from my pictures. Thanks to his wife, Denyse Chaney, for being the sister I never had and for cheering me on endlessly, even when I hit a brick wall and the words won't come. Denyse is the one who first reads my books before even my editor sees them and her advice is invaluable. Thank you to my in-laws, especially my lovely mother-in-law, Mary Duffy, for all her support through the years.

I'm very lucky to have a lot of great friends and I'm always afraid I'll offend somebody by leaving them out. So I apologise if your name isn't here but to all my friends, please know that I value your friendship more than anything and next time we're out, the drinks are on me! Thanks to my very lovely friend, Niamh O'Connor, whose long phone-calls keep me sane and whose kindness makes me believe there's good in the world. Thanks to Denise Deegan, Michelle Jackson and Niamh Greene who entice me out of my writing cave to go and drink some wine and laugh like I've never laughed before. I've named Niamh Greene 'Wizard of Titles' because, as well as picking the title of my last book, *One Wish*, she also came up with the title for *A Love Like This*. Writing a hundred thousand words is easy when compared to picking titles so I owe Niamh a huge thanks for her input. Thanks to my long-time friends Lorraine Hamm, Angie Pierce and Bernie and Dermot Winston. Even when my writing takes over and I lose touch for a while, they're always there for me when I resurface, proffering a glass of wine and a friendly ear. An extra special thanks to Bernie for her amazing cakes, which are always the topic of conversation at my launches. A huge thanks, as always, to Vanessa O'Loughlin, from writing.ie and Inkwell Writers, for her insightfulness and advice. Thanks to my wonderful neighbours in Larkfield who support me so wonderfully. I've said it before but I thank my lucky stars that I live where I do. It's a rare thing in this day and age to be friends with everyone who lives on the street but that's how it is here in Larkfield. I'm already looking forward to our big trip next year, girls!

And so, to the professionals who take my words and work their magic to form them into the book you have in your hands. A million times thank you to my lovely agent in the UK, Madeleine Milburn, and her team, Cara Lee Simpson and Rachael Sharples. I'm very lucky to work with such wonderful agents so thank you Maddy, Cara and Rachael for all your hard work and dedication to my books. And please come back to Ireland soon. We need to do that literary pub crawl! This book is my fifth with Hachette Ireland and I've been very lucky to have two wonderful editors, Ciara Doorley and Alison Walsh, work on it with me. It was the first time I worked with Alison and it was a pleasure to get her take on the story and her input has definitely made it a better book. And as for Ciara, what can I say? Thank you, Ciara, for the work you put into this and all my books. I know this last year has probably been one of the most exciting of your life and I'm honoured that you were still able to spend time working with me. Thanks to Joanna Smyth in Hachette for all her patience and help and to Ruth and Siobhan who take me off each year to sign books and have to put up with my incessant chattering in the car. Thanks to the rest of the wonderful Hachette team – Breda, Jim and Bernard. I'm delighted to be working with you all. And finally thanks to Emma Dunne for her copy-editing and for spotting all the things I was too goggle-eyed to see by the end.

One of the most wonderful and, at the same time, scariest moments of writing a book, is releasing it onto the world. I think writers are largely insecure and we spend our lives biting our nails. I send it to my agent and quiver until she's read it, send it to my editor and can barely breathe until she comes back to me and when it goes out to the shops ... well, I just want to hide! And that's when you, my lovely readers, come in. I've been overwhelmed these last few years by the response from readers. I still can't believe that people go into book shops and pay with actual money to buy one of my books! It's such a thrill for me that will never grow old. I also cherish every email, tweet, Facebook message, etc because it's contact from the people who read the books that make this job worthwhile. If you want to get in touch, you can do so through my website mariaduffy.ie or on Twitter at @mduffywriter. So thank you from the bottom of my heart, my lovely readers, for investing the money and the time to read my stories and I hope I can continue to entertain you in years to come.

Maria x

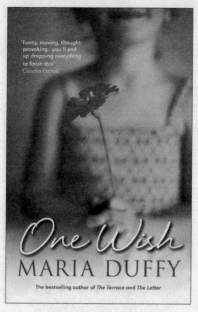

'Funny, moving, thought-provoking...you'll end up dropping everything to finish this' Claudia Carroll

One Wish

MARIA DUFFY

The bestselling author of *The Terrace* and *The Letter*

One Wish

MARIA DUFFY

Becky is used to her young daughter asking tricky questions, but lately Lilly has become fascinated by one in particular – why she doesn't have a father. And Becky realises that it's not a subject she can ignore for much longer.

What Becky remembers about Lilly's dad would fit on a Post-it: his name is Dennis, he's a successful property developer – and he doesn't know he has a daughter. And when she finally locates him, he's not at all what she expected.

Dennis might not be everyone's idea of the perfect dad. But as Becky gets to know him, she begins to wonder if she was wrong not to let him into Lilly's life before now. And she can't help but think about her own family, the people she left far behind.
Is it ever too late to change your mind, and welcome someone from your past into your present?

Also available as an ebook

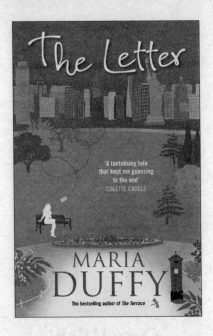

'A tantalising tale that kept me guessing to the end'
COLETTE CADDLE

MARIA DUFFY

The bestselling author of *The Terrace*

The Letter

MARIA DUFFY

Ellie Duggan is getting married in seven weeks. But just before she sets off for a fun-filled New York hen party weekend, she finds a letter addressed to her sister Caroline. Dated only weeks before Caroline died in a tragic accident, it contains some startling information which forces Ellie to face some truths about herself, Caroline's death – and even her forthcoming marriage.

Ellie has spent the three years since Caroline's death running from the truth. But as the weekend in New York comes to a close, she makes a drastic decision. As Ellie finally lays old ghosts to rest, she realises that the truth can set you free. But will she be willing to take the risk?

Also available as an ebook

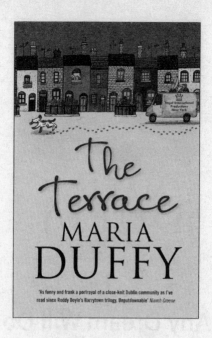

The Terrace

MARIA DUFFY

St Enda's Terrace, nestled in the heart of Dublin city, is like any other closeknit community – there's the newly-weds planning on having a baby; the single mother raising her children on her own; the upwardly mobile couple who bought in the height of the boom, and the long-timers to whom everyone goes for advice.

But behind every closed door, there are secrets. And when the street syndicate wins the national lottery, but the ticket is nowhere to be found, these neighbours are about to discover just how much has been kept hidden …

As friendships and relationships are put to the test in the search for the missing ticket, the residents of St Enda's learn that, while good times might come and go, good friends are forever.

Also available as an ebook

'... a Bridget Jones for the social networking generation' Hello! Magazine blog

Any Dream Will Do

MARIA DUFFY

It seemed harmless at the time – a few white lies here and there to make her life seem more exciting. And as far as thirty-something Jenny Breslin was concerned, it wasn't as though her online friends would ever find out the truth, right?

But then one night Jenny sends out a drunken message inviting her cyber-buddies to stay at her house in Dublin for a few days. And, as the acceptances start flooding in, Jenny starts to panic ...

Where is she going to find the gorgeous boyfriends she's boasted about? How is she going to convince her online friends that her job at the bank is as glamorous and exciting as she's led them to believe? And how is she going to get around the fact that her profile picture is years out of date, and taken in a flattering light?

When Jenny comes face-to-face with her three online friends, it turns out she's not the only one who's been stretching the truth. As true identities are exposed, friendships are put to the test. But as Jenny navigates the weekend, she learns that real friendship means accepting people as they are.

Also available as an ebook

Reading is so much more than the act of moving from page to page. It's the exploration of new worlds; the pursuit of adventure; the forging of friendships; the breaking of hearts; and the chance to begin to live through a new story each time the first sentence is devoured.

We at Hachette Ireland are very passionate about what we read, and what we publish. And we'd love to hear what you think about our books.

If you'd like to let us know, or to find out more about us and our titles, please visit www.hachette.ie or our Facebook page www.facebook.com/hachetteireland, or follow us on Twitter @HachetteIre

HACHETTE BOOKS IRELAND